vein

of

love

r. scarlett

ISBN: 978-0-9952361-1-0

VEIN OF LOVE

Cover and book design by Mae I Design & Photography
Back cover photography by Lauren Perry
Edited by Ashley Carlson and Megan Lally

Stock Photo ID: 417585937
Copyright: © glebTv

To Breanne & Megan—

For always cheering me on
& helping me blossom this story
Into what it is today.

daemon

For each and every person you rapture with your essence
Is a delicate, dark, monstrous dance
And I feel the pull,
The tenor, the touch, the strain.
I feel the urge to be yours
And you to be mine
To feel your flesh in my arms
the curvature of a body so loving
Your smile simmering into my shoulder
Golden strands of your hair slipping past my fingers
Like a celestial outflow of water
Much like blood slipping from the vein
It's too much
Or possibly not enough
Creatures like you
And me
Are aglow with our differences
More often then nought

— B T —

playlist

Beautiful Crime by Tamer
Damn Your Eyes by Alex Clare
Waiting Game by Banks
Burning Desire by Lana Del Rey
I Know I'm A Wolf by Young Heretics
Bloodsport by Raleigh Ritchie
Young God by Halsey
One Way Or The Other by Until The Ribbon Breaks
Dangerous Woman by Adriana Grande
Salt and Vinegar by Hooverphonic
Holy Water by Laurel
Heavy In Your Arms by Florence and the Machine
War of Hearts by Ruelle

chapter one

TURNING NINETEEN WAS supposed to mean ultimate freedom, but as Molly continuously glanced over her bare shoulder down Madison Avenue, she felt anything but free. The knot in her stomach coiled even tighter at the thought of the three shadows returning.

For her.

"Stop panicking," she muttered. She adjusted her sunglasses, ignoring the judgmental stares from other black-clad New Yorkers pushing past. They shouldn't have bothered themselves with why Molly was wearing her Ray-Bans at night—in fact, they should've *thanked* her. As she approached Stella's brownstone, she glanced over her bare shoulder repeatedly, the nervous drumming in her stomach refusing to subside.

Molly dug out her phone and called September.

"So did those people finally show up?" September's voice was muffled and Molly could only suspect a bag of chips was at fault.

"I left. I literally climbed out the window and ran," Molly said, breathless as she stumbled in her teetering heels on New York's uneven, gum-stained sidewalk.

"Seriously?"

"I can't waste every single birthday waiting for some figurative shadows to show up and what, *take me?* It's ridiculous." Molly huffed, the outburst releasing a bit of tension from her body.

September stuffed chips into her mouth and chewed unapologetically. "So are you heading back to the apartment then?"

"Well, I thought I'd go to Stella's birthday party for me. I won't stay long. I have to work at the museum tomorrow." Molly looked away from the shadows crawling up the wall and hoped her voice stayed calm.

September grumbled into the phone at the mention of Stella. "Well, have fun with *that.* She'll invite the entire Upper East Side. A high school reunion."

Molly's stomach twisted more as she recalled her old classmates. "No, I told her to only invite a few people." *One in particular.*

September snorted.

"You can come too, if you want. It'll be like old times," Molly said. Something that might've been a footstep echoed behind her, and she checked over her shoulder.

"You mean Stella threatening to strangle me while I fantasized about ways to gouge her perfect little eyeballs out? Yeah, that sounds tempting."

"Okay, well Tina will be there."

"She cheated off all my Spanish tests, and got pissed if I answered something wrong! Just because I'm Mexican doesn't mean I'm born knowing Spanish."

"Okay, so that's a no."

"Last time I checked, cheating off someone's schoolwork isn't exactly the strongest foundation for a lifelong friendship. And you speak *much* better Spanish than me, anyway; she should've been cheating off you. Language freak."

"I will take that as compliment instead of an insult." Molly smiled. "I'll bring milkshakes from McDonalds when I get home, okay?"

"Oh honey, *now* you're speaking my language. Can I just date you?"

Molly laughed. "I'm hanging up now." Molly's shoulders relaxed and a deep sigh parted her lips. September always made things better, lighter.

Tonight will be different. You've got this.

She'd win his heart.

Her determination died as she entered Stella's glamorous foyer. Music shook the floors and rattled her teeth as she paused in the entryway. A group of guys were dancing on a table with beers in hand, and in one dark corner just inside the foyer, a half-clothed couple was fumbling at each other in ways she was pretty sure counted as indecent exposure. When a splash of champagne soaked her Louboutins, Molly cringed.

As Molly pushed through the crowded doorway, people bobbed to the latest Lana Del Rey song and the air stank of Hermès perfume and expensive pot. Stella's parents were always out of town, and she'd have their oriental rugs professionally cleaned of any spilled Cristal and vomit before they returned. People were using antique vases as cups, a couple was making out dangerously close to a marble statuette, and every bit of Molly's inner curator wanted to scream.

Deep breaths.

She spotted her host in the middle of the living room: Stella Vanderbilt. Dark crimson hair framed her sharp, feline features, and she stood in the midst of the chaos with an exultant grin, thriving off of it. Everyone revolved around her like planets circulating the sun; they were all at her mercy, and she kept them warm and happy. But with one mood swing, Stella would scorch them to a pile of ashes under her pedicured feet.

Next to Stella was Tina Fitzgerald, the "good girl" around her parents, but a giant flirt with a voracious sexual appetite everywhere else she went.

"Molly!" Tina hollered over the booming music. Molly timidly weaved through the crowd of bodies and joined the girls in the middle. Tina threw herself onto Molly, giggling and splashing her wine.

"I said a *few* people." Molly eyed the two girls.

Stella bit her slim lower lip, the one perpetually curved into a smirk. "This is *so* much better than watching one of your stupid *avant-garde* French movies. Admit it."

Molly frowned and wiped her sweaty palms on her thighs, immediately wondering why she'd come. She wanted to have a night to relax, to forget about her stack of bills for her crappy apartment, about her internship that needed to pay those bills, and about the shadows. For once, enjoy a birthday.

Molly scanned the crowd for the reason she'd skipped her parent's dinner.

Stella raised her glass, her brown eyes sharp. "So where's the slut?"

"Her name's September, and don't call her that," Molly scolded, gritting her teeth.

"Relax," Stella whispered with a hint of a drunken smile. Molly glowered at the typical tactic used to shut her up. Everyone was always telling her to *relax*, completely unaware of the consequences if she were to ever fully let go. "You need something to drink."

Molly shook her head. "I prefer going to my internship *without* a hangover, thanks."

"You need to let loose," Stella told her, and her eyes narrowed in on Molly's sunglasses. "And take those damn things off! People won't give a damn about your eyes."

Molly waved Stella's hands away. "I need them."

Tina embraced her from behind, nearly knocking Molly over. "Come on, Mol, let go a little! Lose that pesky V-card. Sex is so fun. Great stress reliever, too, which you *need*."

Molly wanted the floor to just open up and swallow her whole. She unwound herself from the drunken girl's grasp and watched as Tina stumbled over to some guys from the lacrosse team. Somehow her tongue ended up in one of their mouths, and she soon forgot all about Stella and Molly.

"She's just wasted, Mol, don't mind her," Stella said, squeezing Molly's shoulder. "You're so sensitive. You know, guys don't like girls like that. They want fun, not work."

So I'm "work" to date? "Merci pour le conseil," Molly murmured sourly.

Stella cocked a brow. "Huh?"

"I said 'thanks for the advice.'" Molly forced a grin; it was truly what she'd said, only with a huge dose of sarcasm added.

"Okay, you're smart; don't have to flaunt it. Just drink," Stella said with a similarly fake smile, shoving a glass of champagne into Molly's hands from a passing tray.

"Um, thanks—"

"When are you gonna get a new signature ring?" Stella cried suddenly, snatching Molly's hand to glare at the discolored gold jewelry. Since the day it had been placed on her index finger fifteen years ago, neither Molly nor her family had been able to remove it, trying everything from butter to a dremmel tool. As her finger grew, the ring seemed to magically resize, never cutting off circulation, never hurting her. Over the years, Molly's confusion about the bauble had faded to complacency.

"Happy birthday, Molly," a voice echoed from behind Stella, interrupting the haughty heiress.

Molly's adrenaline spiked as the speaker walked over; he was tall and sturdy with broad shoulders and cheerful green eyes. "H-hi Michael."

Michael, the guy who had gone out of his way to sit with her at lunch on their first day of ninth grade and kept her in the friend zone ever since. They'd been texting constantly since graduation though, and his physical presence was making Molly dizzy.

Was her hair okay? She prayed to god she didn't have something stuck in her teeth.

Win his heart.

"So, how was your first year at Columbia?" he asked, folding an arm under his chest while the other held his drink.

"I-it was good." She cringed at the familiar stutter. *Keep taking those deep breaths, Molly. Try not to make a complete ass of yourself for once.*

"She had guys begging for her attention," Stella said, cutting between them. Molly thought she saw Michael's smile falter for a second, but she wasn't sure. "Working at a museum. And she's the top in her class. A guy would be a complete idiot to pass her up, wouldn't you say?"

"Yeah. Definitely," Michael said softly. Molly's eyes flickered up to see his sullen expression. Was that regret in his voice? She took a deep breath, parted her lips—

"Hey." A girl with bleached hair suddenly appeared, attaching her body to Michael's in an overt claim of property. A flush burned all the way to Molly's hairline as she shut her mouth. "Where've you been? I was looking everywherrrre," she whined, her nasally voice grating on Molly's taut nerves.

That could've been her, if she ever worked up the courage to flirt with him.

Michael smiled down at the petite, athletic girl. "Sorry, Bonnie! I was just talking to my—" He looked over at Molly and swallowed. "Friends."

"I don't remember inviting you, Bonnie," Stella said with thinly veiled contempt.

"I invited her," Michael said as Bonnie stared up at him, completely oblivious to Stella's death glare in her direction.

Molly cleared her throat.

Bonnie glanced over, narrowing her eyes as she took in Molly's sunglasses. "Oh, was I...interrupting something?"

"Huh? Oh, no, not at all. You guys remember Bonnie from high school, right? We all had gym class together," Michael said, making an effort to keep some space between Bonnie's torso and his own.

Molly simply nodded. She hadn't a clue who Bonnie was.

"Oh yeeeah, I remember you!" Bonnie said, pointing in Molly's face. "You're the girl who broke Jefferson's arm in gym class! That was crazy!"

Molly's hands grew clammy; she seemed unable to escape the memory, no matter how hard she tried. The horrible crunching noise as her hand grazed his arm. His blood-curdling, horrified scream as he curled inward on the floor, cradling his cracked limb.

Rumors had followed her into high school, and for good reason. In sixth grade she'd ripped the classroom door off with one hand, her parents explaining it away as due to faulty construction. She hadn't understood what was happening to her; the strength would come at the most random moments, and she'd never been able to control it.

Michael changed the topic fast, aware of Molly's embarrassment surrounding it. "Bonnie ended up at Notre Dame, too. We lived in the same dorm, actually."

Bonnie touched his chest. "He always walks me back at night after class. Isn't that sweet?"

They didn't wait for Molly's reply before dissolving into a laughter-filled conversation, something about "Professor Pointy-Tits" and other inside jokes. Molly glanced at Stella, whose salon-sculpted brows said, *Flirt! Show him you're interested.*

"You look good in your football equipment," Molly blurted out. "Makes you seem really...um...muscular."

Stella snorted so loud she had to wipe at her tiny nose.

"Uh, thanks Molly." A touch of color appeared on Michael's olive-toned cheeks. Beside him, Bonnie smiled sweetly.

"You do, though, Michael," Bonnie added, directing his attention back to her. "Wanna get another drink and talk about my favorite plays of yours in the last game? You *slayed* the Cardinals; it was so sexy."

That did it; Molly was toast. She searched her mind for anything she knew about football besides the fact that Tom Brady was hot—and came up empty. She'd spent too much time in books.

Michael couldn't even tear his gaze off Bonnie's at that point. "I'll talk to you later, okay, Molly?" he said, trancelike, pushing through the sea of bodies in search of an empty couch with Bonnie locked in his grasp.

"Wooow. That was brutal. Entertaining, but brutal. On that note, I need another drink," Stella said, not unkindly, touching Molly briefly on the forearm. "You might want to do the same."

Stella disappeared into the crowd as well, unabashedly pushing those unfortunate girls who happened to be standing between her and the Vanderbilts' stocked bar. Molly stared into her flute glass, ruminating on the bubbling liquid inside. Each pop was another iota of her strength breaking down; she was tired of being Ms. Perfection, Ms. Obedient, Ms. Doormat, Ms. Forgettable.

Screw it. She tossed it back in one swig, the burning sensation working its way down her throat, dulling her humiliation.

It didn't take long for her empty stomach to absorb the frothy alcohol, and Molly found herself swaying with the music. She reached for another drink, this one masquerading as a martini though it seemed to be straight vodka with the olive acting simply as a garnish. It went down with a little more difficulty, but she managed. So much for going to her internship without a hangover.

Molly grabbed another, this one a pink concoction from a gilded tray, but before she could drink it, the delicate glass shattered in her fingers. She froze as the alcohol dripped out onto the floor, several shards falling on the rug below. *Ow!* A trail of blood ran down the inside of Molly's palm where her skin had been sliced open.

Not again.

Her chest tightened and she darted through the people, head bowed, chucking the broken glass into a trashcan before stumbling up the stairs to the adjoining bathroom of an open guestroom.

She bit into her quivering lip as she washed her bloodied hand and examined it for glass. "What's *wrong* with me?"

Maybe Stella was right. It would be work to date her, because she was a freak.

Wiping away angry tears, Molly stood and went back into the large bedroom. It was spacious, framed with crown molding and decorated with old portraits of the European countryside.

A large, bronzed oval mirror hung over the fireplace, and

when she peered back at herself, she frowned. She stepped closer, her alcohol-stained heels clicking against the oak-paneled floor. When she was inches away from the mirror, Molly pushed her sunglasses up and inhaled — her eyes were a blinding, bright white, with ugly red veins streaking through them. Blindingly blue and freckled with white specks, different, but "acceptable". That was, until they glowed violently when Molly felt extreme emotions, causing those around her to become breathless at the very sight of them. Hell, even *she* could barely handle the glare in the mirror when it happened.

"I can't do this any more," she whispered, the tears spilling over. She screwed her eyes shut, crying out as the painfully icy sensation behind her lids increased to an unbearable pitch, like icepicks were chipping away at her brain.

Someone hissed and Molly spun, the sunglasses dropping to the floor. A shrouded figure lingered in the doorway, unmoving.

Her heart thudded against her ribcage and she dared not make a sound.

Another hiss echoed out, louder than the first, and Molly fell back against the fireplace. The hisses multiplied, surrounding her like an oppressive coat, causing every cell in Molly's body to shudder, to scream, *Run!*

A bellowing cry exploded from the figure then, sending Molly to the floor as she cupped her ears against the assaultive noise. The mirror above broke, glass falling in pieces onto her hair and shoulders. She couldn't speak, couldn't move. When the cry stopped, Molly shakily lifted her head.

Please don't be real.

The hood concealing the figure's face pooled around its elongated, abnormally curved neck, attached to a monstrous mouth of sharpened teeth. The dark eyes stared back at Molly, her movements stiffening. Hissing began again and Molly followed the sound upward as the woman came closer; there was something on her head, and it was writhing, scaly — *Oh god.* They were snakes, and *they were the woman's hair.*

Molly crawled back as far as she could, heart hammering, voice aching to scream out. The broken glass dug into her skin, but she ignored the ache.

The monster's gold-tinted hands glinted in the dim lighting as she waved them manically. "Daemon," she snarled.

The snakes coiled through each other and over the woman's brow. When Molly stood on wobbly legs, her attacker's mouth broke into a razor-toothed snarl. She raised a hand and swept each of the chairs out of the way, sending them one by one against walls, priceless paintings, busts of famed aristocrats.

"Please," Molly begged, the haze of alcohol making her feel powerless. "*Stop.*"

The woman sent another chair into the wall, and Molly grabbed one of the iron pokers nearest her.

"Stay back," Molly warned, arm shaky from the weight of the poker. The woman still advanced, eyes bloodshot and wild, but she froze the moment Molly's eyes aligned with hers. Her hard, sharp face looked as if it was made out of stone, while the rest of her body was covered in a ratty black cloak. As soon as Molly's eyes left hers, the woman moved again. Molly swung the poker frantically as the woman approached. "Don't. Don't come any closer--" Molly smacked the woman's arm hard enough she screeched painfully loud and Molly jolted.

Big damn mistake.

The woman lunged, swinging her hand to hit Molly's cheek. Molly fell hard, releasing the poker. When the woman sat on her back and wrenched both wrists up, Molly screamed.

"Let—go—of—me—" Molly's muffled cries were useless, her lungs crushed under the weight of the woman as she thrashed around. Pungent acidic odor stung Molly's nostrils, and she could sense the woman leaning down, lowering her mouth to the right side of Molly's exposed neck.

No!

Molly arched her back for one final fight, only to find the snakes swaying far too close to her face, snapping their fanged jaws.

A deafening roar filled the room. The woman and her snakes hissed, and the weight disappeared from Molly's back. Molly glanced up just in time to see the woman darting like a blur toward the door, only to be caught by a silhouette of a man. She held her breath, startled by the sight of him.

The man gripped the woman's throat, and within a second an ear-splitting snap resounded, followed by a thud.

Molly stared, unmoving.

He'd snapped her neck.

She swallowed her sob.

Molly's heart pulsed as she watched the woman decay before her eyes, the snakes lifeless and turning to ash.

The male figure stood above the dead woman, kicking at the dead reptiles. "Damn gorgon," he muttered in a low, somber tone, sounding more annoyed than anything.

She'd been drugged. That was the only explanation here that made any sense. Rohypnol...maybe Special K? Whatever the hell it was, it explained all of this. No snakes, no broken necks. She was just hallucinating, or maybe dreaming? Maybe she had fallen asleep in the bathroom with all the blood, and never actually made it out to the mirror.

She smiled. Somehow, that was a much better option.

"Is she dead?" asked a female voice. Several sets of heavy footsteps filled Molly's ears as she eyed the two figures coming closer, surveying the room. The girl was young, too young to be with the likes of the man that stood beside her. Molly didn't risk looking at them too long.

"What does it *look* like?" he responded roughly. Molly slowly lifted her arm and retrieved the sunglasses, putting them on.

"I wasn't talking about the fugly gorgon," the woman snapped. "I was talking about the girl."

A chilling silence filled the room and Molly searched for a weapon, zeroing in on a glinting piece of metal nearby. The man took a step toward her, but stopped when Molly grabbed the discarded fire poker.

"Don't you dare!" she said from her place on the oak floor, coughing violently as her lungs filled with oxygen once more.

"You going to kill me with that?" he laughed lazily, as if he didn't want to waste any amount of breath on her. She squinted, the shadowed room concealing his features. "Go ahead, get up. Catch your breath."

Molly stood as fast as she could, spots dancing in front of her eyes. The poker wavered as she fought waves of dizziness.

The woman folded her arms, an amused smile stretching her thin lips. "She thinks she can kick your fucking ass."

He took another confident step closer, pacing himself, *enjoying* it. "A Manhattan princess? Fight me? Tsk, tsk."

He crossed the final feet in two steps, taking hold of the poker and encircling her with his other arm. She gasped, her wide eyes taking in his bee-stung lips and lazy smirk. He placed the sharp end of the poker to his abdomen, which was ridged and defined even under his clothing. "Prove me wrong, by all means, ciccia."

chapter two

ICCIA — WHAT? IS that an insult?

Molly studied him from under her lashes, weighing the options. She could stab him, pierce through his tailored suit. She had the poker, after all.

"Drop it or I might accidentally slip and break that delicate wrist of yours." His warning tone sent dreadful chills down her spine and she stared at his hand still over hers.

Holy shit. She gripped the poker tighter.

"Tensley," the woman scolded. Now that she was only a few feet away, she could make out the girl's features — long, dull hair clipped back messily that screamed she wasn't from Molly's Upper East Side world, and thank god for that. A girl around the same age as her, but with an aged demeanor, skin dirty and tight around her delicate bones. But she was anything but delicate.

The longer Molly stared at the man, Tensley, fear soaked into her chest and made her cold. If it was him…

Molly edged back in a panic, hoping they'd let her pass. "I need to go."

Tensley went for her arm, which she swung back. "*No. We're taking you home.*"

Molly's brows lifted almost to her hairline. "No—no. No!" She couldn't stop shaking. "Are you psychotic? You just murdered someone right in front of me and you want to take me *home? Oh god*—" Molly choked on mouthfuls of air, bending over as a wave of paralyzing panic seized her.

The woman glared at Tensley's profile and shook her head. "Great job, genius. Now she's about to faint."

"I'm losing it," Molly chanted between shallow gasps. "I'm hallucinating."

"What was I supposed to say? She's being followed and we need to get her somewhere safe."

Molly's mind raced with the events of the last few minutes, how her world had flipped, dove, and plummeted in record time. "How did you know about that—the monster with the snakes—"

"It was a gorgon," the woman explained, her torn military jacket and black combat boots looking especially threatening under the dim lighting, almost pitch-black. "And it had its own agenda for you."

"What 'agenda'?"

"Not now, Lex," Tensley snapped. "I need to get her out of here. *Now.*" Molly heard him sigh and saw his boots stepping toward her. "C'mon, we're leaving before you have a fucking breakdown."

Oh hell no! Molly swung the poker at his stomach hard and he groaned.

When she raised the poker again, his hand shot out and he yanked it painfully from her hands, tossing it behind him. Molly shook as he straightened to his full towering height and eyed his stomach, where a tiny spot of blood seeped through his dress shirt. When his eyes found her widened ones, he glared. "You made me bleed, ciccia."

Molly took a large step back, but she knew he had her cornered.

"It's time to go. *Now.*" When he moved forward, she shot her hands out and shoved, her palms landing on his firm chest for a second. Her hands tingled at the power shooting up her arms from the ends of her fingertips. For once, her rare ability was coming in handy. He flew through the air like a doll, falling straight into Lex; they both went down in a pile of muscle and leather.

Oh god – it worked! Holy shit!

Molly darted past them and down the staircase, pushing through the swarm to the fire escape. She raced down several flights and into the foyer, teetering to a stop once she was outside on the deserted Manhattan street. She was definitely hallucinating; her drink had absolutely been laced.

"September," she mumbled, searching her coat pocket for her phone. She rubbed her eyes as she stumbled along, sliding a finger across the phone's screen. The heel of her shoe landed in a grate the wrong way and she pitched forward, sunglasses askew.

A strong hand wrapped around her waist and yanked her upright once more, leaving a heated trail along her stomach. A fogginess overwhelmed her. *What the – ?*

She jolted in the embrace, looked over her shoulder, and it was *him*, Tensley. His muscular build towered over her, the closeness overwhelming her senses and igniting a buried spark inside her belly. She pushed her glasses up her nose, noticing how she didn't really *mind* the way she seemed to fit against his firm frame. She shook her head, trying to escape the fogginess. She'd witnessed him nonchalantly snap that woman's neck, for god's sake— not to mention the fact that he was a *complete stranger*, and a psychopath.

"I will scream if you don't let me go right now!" Molly said, trying to shove him away. His grip only tightened, and Molly could see Lex examining them from the sidewalk.

Molly tried again, digging her elbow up under his ribcage. *Stupid random strength. Work now, huh?* "Let me go!"

He clamped a hand over her mouth and she tasted salt. "Shut *up!* You're being followed and we're trying to *help* you!"

Molly grunted against his palm, wiggling her face around.

Lex sighed behind him. "We're the least of your worries," she chimed in. "I'm Lex, by the way. You don't have to be scared, okay? We're going to keep you safe."

"Don't." Tensley hissed at his companion. "Just keep walking." His hand nudged the small of Molly's back.

Molly stood her ground, glaring at him in defiance. *Dick.* Her eyes flickered over his shoulder to the nearest alleyway. Maybe she could run.

He moved forward again, and she wanted desperately to punch him, shove him off, but her powers refused to work. She dragged her feet on the ground, heels bumping against the asphalt in a sad attempt to remain anchored.

He only yanked harder, releasing her mouth to use both hands.

"Let go of me!" she repeated, face freed, frantically searching for anyone who might still be out at that late hour. "Attack! He's attacking me! Assault! *Assault!*"

Tensley rounded on her that time, his now obsidian eyes slicing her in half as if she could feel his warning.

All the blood left Molly's face and she swore her heart thudded to a stop as his presence swarmed her.

"Tensley! Don't use that on her! Jesus Christ!" Lex chided.

Molly glanced at Lex. *Maybe she'll be more understanding…*

Molly fully faced Lex, widening her eyes. "Please, please don't let him hurt me, I have money, I can get you money—"

"I'm not going to hurt you unless you keep talking! I'm trying to take you *home!*" the man grunted, pushing Molly to walk again. "Three hundred fucking years of protection and for what? An obnoxious, bimbo blonde. Jesus fucking Christ is right."

"Is everything all right here?" All three of them turned to face an older man in a fitted business suit standing on the corner, eyeing the scene. His face darkened as he took in Molly's disheveled clothes and Tensley's grip around her waist.

Before Molly could respond, Tensley walked around her and straight up to the businessman, Lex taking his place. "Everything's fine, so back off," he said in a calm, even tone.

Molly watched as the man's face changed; he tensed, averting his eyes before suddenly scurrying away into the night. She *felt* the presence again, the presence of a warning, a threat that alerted her to stand back. *What the hell just happened?*

Molly gawked at Tensley as he returned to her side, grabbing her once more. "What did you just do to him?"

"Sent him a warning his body understood." A wolfish smile appeared on his lips. "Want to try and get away again?"

Her heart beat wildly in her chest. She broke his hold on her wrist and shoved him—hard.

He didn't move. He didn't even budge. She pushed him again and his shoulder lifted. He let out a low laugh. Embarrassment and an overwhelming dread sunk into her bones.

"Looks like your powers are unpredictable," he deadpanned, snatching her wrists again. "Wonder why."

She looked up at him in dismay. "You know about my powers?"

"I know a lot about you."

"What? How?" She glowered up at him and he simply glanced away, as if it didn't matter.

"C'mon, we'll take you home. We're not going to hurt you, I promise," Lex whispered, touching Molly's shoulder.

Tensley hissed, most likely a few curse words under his breath, shaking his head. "I have better things to do then babysit."

Molly glared at the back of his head, dark, wavy hair glistening.

As they approached people strolling down Madison Avenue, Tensley loosened his grip on her shoulder only to securely hold her against his side. She wanted to scream for help, but the couple they passed seemed so sweet, so happy…she didn't want them to come under the fire of her two captors.

When Molly saw her parents' white-paneled townhouse, her throat grew dry with renewed hope, but also terror for her family's safety.

"I'm gonna head home," Lex said, and Tensley acknowledged her with a nod.

"Wait!" Molly shouted, causing Lex to stop mid-turn. "Y-you can't leave me alone with him."

Lex's hard features softened somewhat, but she was still a fearsome sight as she stepped closer—dirt splattered across her skin, eyes as fierce as the blinding sun. "He's not going to hurt you," she whispered. "You're in good hands with him."

She turned and jogged away, the only source of comfort disappearing, weaving past the wrought iron trashcans and flourishing callery pear trees lining the sidewalk.

Tensley led Molly up the steps and leaned her up against the paneled wall, trapping her between his arms. "Key?"

Molly gaped at him. "No—*no.*"

"Fine, have it your way." He gripped her forearm and moved her out of the way, raising his leg to kick the door open with such force that it split in two, pieces falling into the entryway. Tensley fixed his collar with one swift gesture and strolled inside like he owned the place.

Molly's mouth unhinged. "How…" *Is he even human?*

Her mother was still sitting on the living room couch, another glass of merlot in hand. Molly's stomach twisted at the sight. *Is she drunk already?* Fiona gawked at Tensley, eyes low and drooping. "You—you came…"

Tensley flicked a miniature statue of Apollo on the coffee table with his fingernail, face emotionless. "Nice place."

Molly scowled.

"We called you," her mother said at Molly, as if the strange man three large strides away wouldn't hear. "Why would you leave?"

"Molly?" Her father appeared at the top of the staircase and halted, surveying the scene below. His eyes grew cold when he saw the newcomer. "Are you Tensley Knight?"

Molly's heart climbed to the top of her throat.

"In the flesh." Tensley strolled toward the staircase. "And you're Derrek Darling."

Derrek's face reddened. "Get out!"

Tensley laughed humorlessly, and Molly couldn't hide her shaking. "Where's the hospitality?"

Molly's father rolled up his sleeves and marched down the stairs. "I told your family years ago: there's no deal with us."

Tensley gave him a hard look. "Let me refresh your tiny human memory. It's a contract made in your ancestors' blood; you don't get a choice here. My family has protected yours for over three hundred years in exchange for one day producing a daemon who possessed the eyes. And what do we have here?" His eyes swung to Molly's rigid figure, his voice holding an unnerving edge. "A daemon with the blessed eyes, from your bloodline. Specifically, *your* daemon daughter, who's been promised to *me*."

Molly eyed Tensley — the grey eyes, the dark hair...the boy she had seen that *night*. It was him. He had come with the other shadows. At the memory of him holding her hand as a child, she linked her hands together tightly.

Molly's legs shook. "I'm human."

Tensley turned fast, his eyes a vibrant darkness sucking the air from her lungs. "If it wasn't for the dormant gene in your father's bloodline, he too would have the strength, the visible signs of a daemon—which you have."

Molly painfully shook now, refusing to believe what she had feared for years. "I'm—I'm human."

"You know the contract, you've read it. You know what you are—"

"You—out—now." Derrek continued down the steps, Fiona following with the wine clutched to her chest.

"I'm human!" Molly cried out, throwing her arms down.

Tensley watched her chest violently shake and then turned to her father. "You didn't show her the contract?"

Molly's father paled and fidgeted with his cuffs. "She didn't need to know."

"What don't I know? What's going on?" Molly looked back and forth between them, heart pounding. "Tell me!"

Tensley bared his teeth and stepped closer to her father, his entire face growing red. "In 1685, the Darlings had a daughter, one with glowing, blessed eyes and unnatural abilities. To protect the family from mass murder by witch hunters, they made a pact with demons for protection, and the gifted girl would be the payment. However, she was burned at the stake before they could collect her, and the Darlings were already contracted in blood—they still owed a gifted girl to my family."

Molly stared at Tensley's stone cold eyes and she swore she saw a flicker of emotion—of pity. "Is that true, Dad?"

His Adam's apple visibly bobbed. "Molly—we thought it best to not tell you."

Molly's lips quivered and her eyes burnt. "You lied to me?"

"We told you what you needed to know," her mother said.

Molly ran her hands through her messy locks and hissed. This wasn't new—anything but. She loved her parents, but their need to control what she did, what she knew, suffocated her and now, when she finally moved out and began her own life, it was handed over to the man invading her living room. "I'm not human. I'm—I'm..." Molly choked on the words and turned to face Tensley, wearing an expression of stone. "I'm a daemon...?"

"You are," Tensley said, low and soft, as if she might break if he said it too loud.

"You need to leave. Now!" Her dad jabbed his finger at the door, glaring at Tensley.

Tensley scowled. "Ungrateful *human*."

"Dad, don't!" Molly shouted.

"Where is the bedroom?" Tensley asked, turning to look at Molly. "Oh, I guess I should be more specific. Where's your room, Ms. Darling? I'd like to speak to you *privately*."

Molly's body tensed. "Why?"

Tensley shrugged. "A private matter."

A private matter? The bedroom? He couldn't mean — ?

"Stay the hell away from my daughter!" Her father raised a shaking finger and jabbed it in the air.

"Or what? You'll kill me with your bare, human hands? Try, please. It would be entertaining at the least."

Derrek stormed Tensley, and they collided. Tensley grasped him by the shoulders, quickly pinning him against the wall. He struggled to escape, gasping.

Tensley smirked and slowly bent Derrek's arm back until he gave a ragged shriek and the limb looked ready to break. *Oh god! No!*

"Don't!" Molly ran and gripped Tensley's arm. "Please, don't! I'll take you upstairs, just leave them alone!" Tensley stared down at Molly, his face blank but his eyes heated and calculating.

He gave a crisp nod, releasing her father. "Lead the way."

Derrek moaned in relief, slumping over.

"Daddy," Molly cried as Fiona raced over, both of them crouching over the white-faced man as he wiggled his shoulder around, checking its motion.

Derrek looked up, beads of sweat on his forehead.

Molly took a deep breath and pulled on Tensley's jacket, worried about another altercation. "Come on."

"Molly!" Her mother's voice broke behind them, but Molly didn't stop moving. *I need a plan. I need a plan!* Her heart thudded so loudly she swore he could hear it.

Silently, she led the way up the grand staircase and down the hallway to her old bedroom, shutting the door behind them.

Once inside, Tensley seemed to study the white comforter and ornate molding along the edges of the room. She studied him—the suit smooth across his back, straining from his broad shoulders, his thick, soft-looking hair. His suit pants were baggy, but just tight enough to tease his ass. The damn suit hugged him perfectly in all the right places. *Don't you dare find him attractive, Molly. He's a psychopath, and you do not do psychopaths!*

His finger slid across the white sheets and to the tips of the pillows. He sat down on the bed and lay back, placing his shoes on the white blanket and sending her need to keep everything tidy into overdrive.

"What's your name?" He fluffed her pillows.

"It's Molly."

One corner of his mouth quirked. "And do you know *what* I am?"

"Not exactly." She gripped the dresser behind her, hoping he'd missed the way her hands shook, her wobbly knees. If he told her what he was, there was no going back. No living in a false reality.

He stretched his arms behind his head. "I'm an incubus. A demon."

"A *demon?*" A laugh bubbled up at the back of her throat, but if she released it, she'd end up either sobbing or screaming instead, because she knew deep down in her gut, he was telling the truth. "And I 'belong' to your family?"

He nodded.

Her first instinct was to run. Her second was to push him out the window.

"You're my fiancée," he corrected, rolling up his sleeves to reveal his muscle-roped biceps. "You don't know it yet, but your eyes hold a rare power. As my wife, your power will become mine as well."

"*Your wife?*" A wave of nausea hit her fast. *This isn't happening to me.*

Tensley sat up in one swift motion and was in front of

her. She pounded against his chest and it made as much difference as punching a brick building might.

"That's all the daemon has to offer? Weak little fits?" he cajoled, chucking her under the chin like she was a toddler.

"I can't—I can't control it! The bursts of power just happen." She squirmed against him, breathless.

"Oh, you can control it. You just need the right tool," he said darkly, so close his hot breath fanned over her forehead. "Take them off."

She shoved him repeatedly. "I'm not taking anything off!"

He reached for her sunglasses and removed them without warning. When she raised her arm to hide her eyes, he gripped her wrist and lowered it with a measured gentleness. For a moment he looked breathtakingly vulnerable and Molly couldn't look away. The terrifying man was gone and she could see him—and that horrified her. In a panic, she ducked out from under his arm and moved to her doorway. His heavy breathing calmed after a bit, and he turned to face her.

"I'll bring my belongings to your house tomorrow," he declared.

Molly's eyes widened. "Your belongings?"

"I'm the head of the house," he answered coolly, gazing around her bedroom.

Her stomach of knots twisted tighter. "You aren't staying here. I don't even live here any more."

"Then where do you live?"

Oh crap. "Uh..."

He looked miffed. "You're staying here, it's safer." He

began to rummage in the first drawer of her nearby dresser, holding up a pair of white underwear with an amused expression. "How about some new lingerie?"

"Excuse me, what are you doing? No!" She ripped the panties from him and pressed them to her chest. *He threatens me one second and peeks in my underwear drawer the next? What the hell is his problem?*

"Incubi receive power, energy, and strength from physical contact. We'll get strength from each other," he said. He held up another pair of her cotton underwear. "So you're a granny panties kind of girl."

Her hand itched to slap him. "What is happening right now..."

"No one likes granny panties," he said, raising both brows. "That's *all* I'm saying."

"I am not discussing my choice of underwear with you!" She ripped the second pair out of his hands.

He laughed darkly. "Cold-hearted as I am, I have not yet reached the depths of preferring *these*."

"I really don't care what you prefer!" She stuffed all her panties in her drawer and slammed in shut, stepping back on wobbly legs. *He's such an ass!*

His eyes lowered to her knees, a flash of genuine concern racing across his grey-flecked irises. "You're bleeding."

She looked down at her cut legs and winced; they looked pretty torn up. "Didn't really notice during everything else going on. It's glass," she murmured as he went to touch a tiny cut on her kneecap. "Ow!" She scrunched up her nose and focused on her breathing. He grabbed her wrist; she yanked it back. "Don't touch me."

He scowled and narrowed his eyes at her. That damn fogginess returned. Molly's shoulder's relaxed, and when he went for her wrist again, she didn't protest.

She *wanted* him to touch her.

What the hell is wrong with me?

He guided her toward the bed without protest. She sat down on the edge, speechless as his fingertips hovered over her goose bump-covered legs.

He sucked two fingers into his mouth and Molly scrunched her nose up. *Uh, ew!*

"What are you..." she questioned as he pressed his large hand over her calf and an overwhelming sensation of warmth engulfed her. She fisted the covers and held back a gasp, focusing on her breathing and trying to ignore how his hand shot pleasant, soothing tingles down her spine. Molly gazed upon clean, fresh skin a second later, flabbergasted. *Holy – what is going on? Am I still hallucinating?* "How did you do that?"

He looked through his thick lashes at her. "I heal with my body. Demons can produce a large amount of biochemicals to heal ourselves and others by touch. Works even better with saliva." *So he sucked his fingers?*

His fingers smoothed upward over her knee, to her thigh, and she paled. She kicked her foot to his groin and he groaned, his hand retreating to cup himself.

"You're disgusting!" she seethed.

"I wasn't trying to get into your granny panties. *Trust me*," he bit back, rising gingerly to his feet.

"Get *out*," Molly said, doing her best to ignore the sensual unfurling of heat spreading its way across the places his hands had been.

He turned to the door. "Don't make this more difficult than it needs to be." Just as he opened the door, he glanced back at her with a hard, steely gaze. "And if you even *think* of hiding from me, your father won't have any limbs left to break. That's a promise."

All the anger and adrenaline racing through her veins shifted to fear, pure terror for her family's safety. Her parents weren't perfect, certainly not, but she loved them. She couldn't bear the thought of their injury, or worse…

When the door slammed shut and she waited a few minutes to make sure he was gone, she collapsed on the floor, soaking in every last detail of the night.

Molly ripped the sheets from her bed after he'd left, throwing them in a pile on the floor. Everything he'd touched, she wanted gone. Finally, she collapsed on the mattress, clutching a bare pillow to her chest. "That didn't just happen," she murmured, ignoring her parents' fervent knocks at the door. Deep down in her gut, though, she knew it had.

Tensley Knight, her demon fiancé, *existed*. And he'd most certainly arrived.

chapter three

WHEN TENSLEY'S OFFICE door opened, he hadn't expected to see his father, and certainly not at such an early hour. The older man fixed his navy suit and unbuttoned the jacket, exposing a pristine white dress shirt underneath. A dot of blood flashed crimson underneath his jaw, and he wiped it off with nonchalance.

Who did he finish off this time?

Mr. Knight's unsettling eyes focused on the mess of papers scattered across Tensley's large oak desk.

"I wasn't expecting to see you this morning," Tensley said as he leaned back in his leather chair. He needed coffee ASAP. Or some whiskey. *Fuck, definitely whiskey.*

His father looked up to meet his son's tired gaze. "Duke Abaddon's here. He wants to find more familiars, preferably blonde, to be under his control. He also wants belladonna for pleasure, in liquid and powder form."

Tensley cocked a brow. "Anything else?" He'd never worked so closely with clients like Duke Abaddon before; he usually handled the lower demons, reminding them not to screw up unless they wanted a boot up the ass. He hated getting his boots dirty.

His father's gaze hardened. "He requested to see you as well. He likes your so-called 'fuck-all' attitude."

Tensley resisted the urge to groan aloud. He knew not to piss his father off, but he always grew restless taking orders from someone else. Unlike the rest of his siblings, Mr. Knight had bred Tensley to take over the business of serving the Princes, and harshly disciplined him growing up. As much as Tensley hated the man, he still wanted to earn his approval. He wanted to be what the others couldn't, to show his father, his family, the whole damn *underworld* that he wasn't like his brother, Beau.

"Once you and the daemon are publicly together, the High Court Princes will fear us. Don't you want that again? She'll bend to your will over time," Mr. Knight scoffed, examining an invisible piece of lint on his suit.

"They should *already* fear us," Tensley muttered, shuffling papers around to find his file on Abaddon, one of the highest-ranking demons in existence. Tensley was the heir to Scorpios, the family business; after all, they'd been doing the Princes' dirty work for generations, policing all the lower demons in their New York territory with an iron fist. They were the law; as long as it benefitted them and the higher classes.

His family was depending on him to resurrect their name after Beau's scandal, and the daemon would do just that. He *really* hoped she'd become less annoying, though.

"Send him in," Tensley said when he'd located the file, fixing his posture somewhat as the large redheaded demon marched into his office.

Abaddon's flaming red hair seemed almost comically appropriate, considering his status. "Well, you bastards — got a handful of familiars to sell me?" Abaddon sent a crooked grin Tensley's way and he tensed involuntarily.

His father nodded. "Yes, Abaddon. Five blondes then? They were just disposed of to us last night." Familiars were the lowest of the low, weak, mindless, easily manipulated. Humans.

"Good, good." Abaddon made himself at home and sat down in the chair across from Tensley, knees spread far apart in a show of masculinity. A nasty white scar sliced up from his left cheek to the corner of his eye. Rumors abounded that it had been a punishment from Fallen, the High Prince of Babylon, otherwise known as the High Court. "I'm in need of some new outlets. No one seems to quell my desires any more; no one knows how to handle *it.*" Abaddon motioned to his crotch.

Tensley clenched his pen and jotted down the specifics in Abaddon's contract. The demon world was quite familiar with Abaddon's tastes; he liked pain — or more specifically, for his partner to experience it. Tensley gritted his teeth at the disgusting thought.

"A castrator might," Tensley smirked, making a show of looking utterly bored by the conversation.

Silence filled the room. Then a loud, hearty laugh rumbled in Abbadon's chest. "I love this one." He gave Tensley an approving smile, and Tensley stiffly returned it.

"And you said you needed more belladonna," his father said, steering the conversation back on track.

Abaddon leaned farther back, causing the chair to

squeak in protest. "The belladonna is the best for getting that *high*. I crave it. It makes the women looser, too."

Mr. Knight nodded at Tensley as he noted it in the document. Once he signed his initials, he passed it to his father, who pocketed it.

"I'll pass it through today. You should expect the shipment tomorrow," his father said, gesturing for Abaddon to stand up.

"I also, uh…" Abaddon scratched at the scruff along his jawline. "I need someone to cover up a maid's death. She was a low-breed bitch, but I don't want anyone snooping."

Tensley's father didn't nod this time. He simply held Abaddon's gaze. "It'll be taken care of."

Abaddon grinned and jumped to his feet, patting Mr. Knight's shoulder roughly. "I can always count on you bastards."

Silence passed between Tensley and Mr. Knight for a moment after the high-ranking demon left.

"Doesn't surprise me," Tensley finally said. "His *fifteenth* wife just mysteriously 'dies' five months ago? I don't buy it." There had been rumors of Abaddon killing his wives if they couldn't produce him an heir. The demon had been marrying women simply to kill them for many years, and Tensley hated to admit how vile he thought it all was.

Mr. Knight raised a grey eyebrow, bemused. "Whether you buy it or don't buy it doesn't matter. He's a *customer*, and a loyal one. We stay out of his way, and what he does with his concubines or wives or whomever he requests is none of our business. Understood?" Tensley glanced away, fuming, but his father went on. "So? Did you mark her?"

Tensley bristled. "No, Father. I have yet to *bed* her."

"Well get a move on. We don't want any other demons stealing her away, *especially* when she's a daemon with the blessed eyes. Mark her. Do it tonight, Tensley. I mean it."

Tensley hesitated about whether to lie or tell the truth. With heavy eyes watching him, Tensley answered flatly. "She isn't ready for that."

Mr. Knight's jaw clenched. "It doesn't matter whether she's fucking *ready* yet, Tensley. It's about protection and claiming her before some other demon sniffs her out. That damn warlock ring is useless now! His death weakened all the items he had power over, you know that. If you don't mark her soon, someone else will. Do you want to ruin three hundred years of waiting because she *isn't ready yet?*"

Tensley ground his teeth and eyed the mess of papers. He didn't bother mentioning to his father how a gorgon had been after Molly Darling already.

He'd known as soon as he met her that she wasn't ready — not for the intimacy, not for the demon world, not to bear his mark…none of it.

So he had left that night, hating himself for letting out pheromones to desire him, and decided to throw himself into his work. He hadn't slept at all, pushing his limits. All he could think about, though, was her legs wrapped around his head. He'd give her something to mewl about then.

Women never rejected him, let alone kicked him in the

balls or stabbed a fire poker into his gut, after he'd used his charming pull on them. Thinking she was a weak, prissy little girl before she swung the poker was his mistake. The daemon intrigued him, enthralled him, and he hated that. He had to remind himself that she was the enemy, the alluring siren who could destroy him like the human who'd destroyed his brother.

He wanted nothing to do with her, but he couldn't deny his immense attraction. It was *really* pissing him off. He needed a plan B and his father had just given him the idea. The ring. That would buy him time.

"I'll take care of it," Tensley responded, rolling up his shirtsleeves to reveal the scorpion tattoo on his left forearm. It was famous, and for good reason — if one was disloyal to Scorpios and got caught, the leader of the group activated the tattoo's lethal poison into their bloodstream.

"Just remember B—"

"I said I would take *care of it*," Tensley hissed, unable to refrain any more, even with his father.

"Remember what that whore did to your brother," his father said, stepping closer. An icy finger slid down Tensley's spine. "That scandal has followed us long enough."

"I'm not a weakling like him, Father. I'm not going to let her control me."

Mr. Knight stood in front of Tensley's desk, giving him one final long, dark look that said more than words ever could.

Once he'd slammed the massive door, Tensley held his head in his hands, hungrily gulping the air.

No pressure at all.

Just as he stood up to get some whiskey, his office door flew open and a dark-haired woman marched in. Her features weren't soft and carefree; they were hard and fierce, and he swore he heard a snarl leave her pinched mouth. "Who is she?"

He sighed heavily. He wasn't sure how to handle her — he didn't want to, but he couldn't figure out how to avoid it. He couldn't get her involved and he didn't have time to deal with more complications. "*Evelyn*, I told you last night: I can't say. My father wants to keep it low key until further notice."

"Bullshit!" Evelyn gripped the back of the empty leather chair and leaned forward, giving him her deadliest glare. "Is she high-born? Tell me who she is and why the fuck you ended things with me!" The leather tore under her red-lacquered nails, but she wasn't deterred.

"I told you," Tensley said through clenched teeth. "I can't. Fucking. Say. Anything."

"So your father just decided a month ago that you needed an arranged marriage?" Her face grew redder, nearly as red as her nails. "And you decided a week ago to drop the fucking bomb on me that you were getting married? Does our five years together mean *anything* to you? You said you'd propose to me! That I would be your wife!"

He groaned and moved towards her. "Evelyn," he hissed. "I have plan. I'll figure something out." His hands found her middle, tracing her curves until they settled on her wide hips. "Have I ever failed you?" His lips quirked into a cocky smile, the one he knew she loved best.

Her raw, pained expression iced over, and Evelyn was

back to her normal ferocity. "Just get *out* of this mess." With that, she flicked his hands off and marched out of the room like a soldier after a battle — whether it had been won or lost in her mind, however, Tensley couldn't tell.

She knew what he liked, knew how far to push him, and how everything was business between them. He knew she hungered after his potential power as the future Dux of Scorpios.

When she was out of sight, he rubbed his jaw. He *would* find a way to get the daemon under control.

He just needed to get the plan to work, and then he could continue on with his life as if Molly Darling didn't even exist.

chapter four

MOLLY HAD ALMOST convinced herself by the next morning that Tensley wasn't coming back. *He doesn't exist.*

She combed her curly hair out of her face with her same yellow brush, viciously stroking it until she heard a crack and stopped herself from breaking the brush in half.

Calm. Down.

Stupid brush.

Stupid emotions.

She dressed in a baby blue dress shirt and paired it with a pleated black skirt for work, completing the outfit with her massive sunglasses. She eyed her expansive collection of vintage designer shoes from years before that she had ended up leaving at her parents' house instead of taking to the apartment, and picked a pair she knew wouldn't let her down that day.

Everything's fine.

"What did he do?"

Molly spun, terrified—but it was only her dad in the

doorway, dark bags hanging underneath his usually happy blue eyes. When she stared back at him, Tensley's words chanted in her head.

He'd rip her life apart, beginning with the people she held close.

She relaxed her features and shook her head. "He didn't do anything, dad. We talked." The last thing she wanted was for her dad to pick another fight with Tensley, in case the demon really meant what he'd said about removing her dad's limbs. "Look, I need to get to the museum." Avoiding eye contact, she walked by him and downstairs.

"Did he say anything?" Fiona called from the kitchen.

"He said he's my fiancé."

"*Fiancé?* The contract never said anything about that." Derrek curled his hands into fists.

Her mother wrung her smooth hands, now blocking Molly's way out the front door. "There must be a way out. Can't we do something?"

"I don't know..."

Molly had heard the tale so many times, but as she'd aged and the shadows had never returned, she'd fooled herself into believing it wasn't true. Of course, it was fed to her in pieces her parents thought she should know, without the pieces they thought she shouldn't know.

"We'll figure something out," Fiona said, her eyes wide and unfocused. Then her features warped into a forced smile. "How about you skip the museum today and we can have a spa day, okay?"

Molly sighed. "You know I can't miss work. I worked too hard to get in."

"We could easily find you a new internship. Something

well known and accomplished," her dad added.

"I earned it on my own. I don't want to have to rely on you and Mom any more," Molly said, the cool sensation stirring behind her eyes. She took a deep breath; she needed to stay sane and maintain a sense of normalcy. "I need to go."

Molly brushed past her and onto Madison Avenue, making sure her sunglasses were securely on her face.

The street was crowded and loud, and Molly's stomach grumbled for gooey chocolate donuts as she eyed a bakery's store window. She refrained diligently, instead picking up the daily coffees and teas for her coworkers, and a whole-wheat bagel with cream cheese. If she wanted to get into the line of work she'd dreamed of, she needed to start from the bottom, even if it meant picking up coffees and dry cleaning to move up. Along with those things, she got to research, and that quenched her desires.

When she made it to the Museum of Muses, she passed out the coffees and teas to each manager, manager's assistant, and manager assistant's assistant, and was just sitting down at her tiny desk of organized colored folders when someone spoke.

"Ms. Crawford?"

Molly jumped in her seat at her mother's maiden name; it was how she'd gotten her internship the *real* way, without her parents' inadvertent help. She turned around to see her boss, Mrs. Everett standing nearby. "Yes?"

"Do you have a moment?"

Molly's heart raced. *Oh shit, I'm fired. Did I mess up?* She nodded, following Mrs. Everett's tall frame down the sleek white hallway, focused on the beat of her heels. When they entered a large office that overlooked Central Park, she took a deep breath and sat down in front of the other curators for the museum waiting there, Mr. Cho and Ms. Albinson.

"Your sunglasses, Ms. Crawford?" Ms. Albinson questioned. Molly touched underneath her glasses, heart stuttering. *What the hell is going on?*

"She's very sensitive to light. She's been approved to wear them," Mrs. Everett answered.

"Ms. Crawford, this is your second summer working with us." Molly nodded at Ms. Albinson's cool, detached tone, her large forehead wrinkled. "And you're going back to Columbia in the fall?"

"Yes," Molly's voice croaked. "To study Arts and Humanities, preferably Museum Studies."

"I see. You had the highest mark in your class, you ran the International School Exchange Program at Columbia, and you're fluent in French, English, and Spanish; quite the list of achievements for someone your age," Ms. Albinson mused, reading off the resume she held.

Molly played with the hem of her skirt. "I love language, so I wanted to focus on that."

Ms. Albinson leaned back in her chair, fixing her bold black glasses. "And what have you been working on recently?"

"I've been researching an exhibit focused on India's Deccan Courts during the sixteenth century with Mr. White. The art itself from that time period is" — she took a deep breath, seeing it in her mind — "otherworldly; it's poetic lyricism in paintings, if you will." Molly blinked a few times behind her glasses and caught faint smiles on their faces.

Mr. Cho placed his pen on the table and threaded his fingers in front of him. "You certainly seem to have a passion for working here. What we're proposing is for you to work here next school year as a *paid* intern. We only take on so many during the year, and we choose those we feel have promise." He paused. "But for us to choose you as one of our few paid interns, we must know if you can handle it. Exemplary work over the next months will secure you the position."

Molly sat there slack-jawed, staring at them for longer than necessary. *This can't be happening.*

"We know this museum is not as well-known compared to others in the city and we do not have their kind of funding, but we are interested in you becoming part of our intern team. What do you say?" Ms. Everett prompted.

"Yes, *yes*, of course!" Molly clasped her hands together and grinned widely at them. "Thank you so much."

Molly happily bounced out of the room. If she got the paid internship, she wouldn't have to worry about moving back into her parent's house or looking for a lower-paying part-time job. She rushed back to her desk to devour her paperwork and as she picked up a pen, her racing heart stalled—the ring was a reminder of the darkness looming ahead, the stupid ring she couldn't remove. She needed a plan; she needed an escape strategy.

By the time she glanced up from her research, she saw it was ten after three. *Shit!* She dug through her purse for her phone and saw September's multiple messages and several missed calls filled the screen. The latest few read:

SEPTEMBER
3:01 P.M.
Hey I'm here

SEPTEMBER
3:05 P.M.
I'm hungry and I never got my McDonald's last night. Lies.

SEPTEMBER
3:09 P.M.
Seriously where the hell are you?

SEPTEMBER
3:11 P.M.
MOLLY DARLING DO I NEED TO COME IN THERE AND KICK YOUR RICH GIRL ASS

Molly gathered her things and said goodbye to the security guards. She rushed out into the sunshine and sighed at the warmth, away from the frigid AC.

September lounged on the steps nearby, balancing a pencil on the back of her hand. Molly approached her carefully, hugging her books to her chest. "Hey September, sorry I'm late — and about last night, too. I got tired and just stayed at my parents' place."

"My stomach forgives you." September dusted off her ripped, worn-out boyfriend jeans as she stood. Her dark brown hair was braided, with random strands dyed vibrant blues, yellows, and pinks. "So? What are you all smiley about?"

Molly giggled. *I can't hold it in!* "Well, I just got offered a chance at a paid internship during the school year…"

"No way!" September clapped her hands. They hugged and a bit of September's hair got in Molly's mouth. "Sooo…" September pulled back, rocking on her feet. "How *was* last night?"

Molly chewed the inside of her mouth. "Can I go eat the equivalent of my body weight in baked goods first?"

"Ohhh, no. Spill." September folded her arms.

"It's nothing," Molly insisted, attempting a weak smile.

That earned her a raised brow. "Mol, you can tell me."

Molly shuffled her black Kate Spades against the concrete. "Do you know anything about…um…demons?"

"If you count a certain redhead who hosted your birthday party last night, then yes. I know a shit-ton about them," September joked.

This is stupid – she's not going to believe me. "Forget it," Molly sighed, starting down the steps.

September raced after her and blocked her path. "I was kidding. Well, partially." She paused. "But really, I've watched *The Exorcist* if that helps. I, however, cannot do a crabwalk down the stairs. No one is that skilled."

Molly forced a thin smile. "I'm just under a lot of pressure. The internship, my parents, school, being an 'adult', Ten—" Molly stopped. She couldn't tell September about *him*; what if it was dangerous? She wanted to go back to the time when they'd giggled about the idea of the shadows coming back, back to when it didn't seem real.

"Mol, if it's Stella and Tina, they're bitches," September said. "Do you want me to do something? 'Cause my fists would love to meet both of their plastic faces."

Molly narrowed her eyes. "*September.*"

September smirked. "What can I say? Being rough is in my blood. Brooklyn born."

"Hey ladies." Both of them turned to see Stella and Tina marching closer.

Molly's shoulders stiffened. She didn't know why the two of them were in front of the museum, since they'd seemingly made it their lives' missions to never go to a museum.

"What are you doing here?" Molly eyed the two girls.

Stella raised a brow and glanced at Tina. "The Doctors Without Borders meeting is at the Plaza at four."

"No—that's not until tomorrow," Molly insisted, pulling her planner out when the heiresses exchanged skeptical looks. Skimming the ink-laden pages, Molly's finger stilled on the bold black letters.

Damn it.

It wasn't like her to forget plans, but with the arrival of Tensley, her mind had been otherwise occupied.

"Are you too busy at the museum to keep track?" Tina folded her bone-thin arms. "We'd understand—your mom might have a fit, but it doesn't matter to us."

"No, no, I just..." Molly paused. "I didn't sleep well last night, and it slipped my mind."

Stella gave her a long, calculating look. "So where the hell did you *go*, Darling? After bolting out of my living room, that is. I planned that party *just* for you, and you ditched us. I wanted you to let loose for one night." Molly could hear the hurt in Stella's voice.

"I had to leave to see my parents," Molly said, glancing at September for support.

"You're nineteen now. Screw them," Tina huffed. Her New York accent was thicker than the rest of them, and it only made her seem more exotic. "A lot of rich hotties were there after you left, too. Michael asked where you went."

September gave Molly a wide-eyed look. "Michael was there?"

"Yup, he got back last night. He waited for you Molly," Stella interjected, all traces of her previous pain replaced with arrogance. "He only came because you promised me you'd go, and then you ditch? Thanks."

Molly's patience was waning thin. "I *needed* to go."

"Can we please go eat? I'm literally starving here! You coming?" Tina said, interrupting them. She was always skilled at diffusing the tension, though she seemed oblivious to that fact.

Molly's stomach grumbled and she glanced over at September, smiling weakly.

September rolled her eyes. "Fine. I'll be the hobo stealing tea sandwiches. It'll be like the good old days at Dalton High, except we're all mature, savvy women now – *almost* all of us, at least. Right Stella?" September grinned widely as Stella scoffed.

September and Molly trailed behind the others up Fifth Avenue, listening to them discussing the politics of their Upper East Side world.

"She dumped him, and then she slept with him a week later," Stella said, regaling the tale of Helen St. Jude's latest blunder.

"Well, I heard she slept with him and then slept with

his cousin and then dumped them both," Tina argued, gesturing back and forth.

"Are you two describing each other?" September said as she squeezed between them, hands thrust into the jeans that barely hung on to her jutting hips.

"Don't you have some old junkie car to fix?" Stella hissed. September was obsessed with old vehicles; her dad was a mechanic and she'd spent a good amount of her spare time during their school years helping him.

September sneered. "Now ladies, my affairs are quite different from your whoring ones."

"They won't let her in the hotel dressed like that," Stella muttered over her shoulder to Molly, eyes widening to stress her disapproval.

"She's fine," Molly argued, walking toward the curb. She wanted to step out in front of traffic; September and Stella had been fighting like that since they were kids.

She looked down the street to see *him*, standing at the edge of a fountain, hands in pockets. She gasped, catching the attention of her small group. Her body shut down, a deep chill settling into her bones. The urge grew to step out in traffic then.

A smirk tugged at the corner of his full lips, and Molly's heart stopped. Molly had a distinct sense this demon fiancé wasn't going anywhere soon.

Not without her.

chapter five

ALL THE BLOOD rushed to Molly's head. "Why is he here?" she muttered to herself.

"Do you know him, Mol?" September asked, squinting to get a better look. When Tensley simply stood in place and lifted his hand to wave, Tina squealed.

"Who is that, Molly?" Tina yanked at Molly's arm. "Is he your secret boy-toy? Are you shagging him?"

"You aren't British so stop with the *bloody* and the *shagging!*" Stella scolded, shaking her head.

Molly took a deep breath to compose herself. "He's a friend staying with my family."

"And you didn't tell us?" Tina was on the edge of hysteria.

"Introduce me to him!" Stella ordered, nudging Molly's side. "I can show him around the city."

"You mean your bedroom." September snorted. Stella glared.

The idea of him spending time with any of them made Molly's chest constrict painfully. He'd snap their necks. "I gotta go," she mumbled.

"You better get a good lay for ditching us! Details!" Tina hollered.

Molly ignored the blatant stares from strangers who'd heard Tina's proclamation and approached Tensley with calculated steps.

"*Leave*," she hissed. Even fully clothed, she could see his muscles straining within his clothes. They were a warning; he was not to be messed with.

Tensley half-grinned. "Hello *Darling*. Am I supposed to give you a good lay now?"

Ooooh, you jackass. She so badly wished she had carried her baseball bat with her to work that day. Oh how effectively it would have smashed his pretty white teeth out.

Tensley continued closer, his hot breath on her face causing a weird pull of desire from her navel downward. *What was that?* Her hands shot out upon contact, pressing firmly against his chest and shoving him away.

"*Get off of me*," Molly growled, relishing how surprised he looked. He didn't think she'd make a scene in broad daylight? He was dead wrong.

More people stared around them, and September's brow furrowed to the point that she looked in dire pain.

Tensley gripped her hand, bringing her small fingers to his pillowy lips for a kiss. Startling heat scorched through her, and she held her breath. Molly's whole body pulsed with embarrassment and anger...and a sensation she refused to acknowledge. Her mind grew foggy and she tried to shake it off.

Attraction.

"Don't tempt me," he said against her skin.

Molly pulled her hand back and dodged a group of businessmen. "Don't touch me."

Tensley followed with a scoff. "We're helping each other, isn't that what I told you? You're benefitting from my powers, too. You can absorb my strength." His hand caught her wrist again and easily engulfed it.

"Can I?" She hated how eager she sounded and sucked in her bottom lip. She didn't give him a chance to respond though.

When Molly glanced back, her friends were still gawking, so she waved to try and ease September's obvious concern. "Don't ever do that again," she warned through her teeth once they were out of sight.

"Do what? Kiss your hand like a gentleman? No problem." He snickered. "You should be flattered you *get* me."

Arrogant bastard.

"I'm anything but flattered," she spat, coming to a full stop on the sidewalk.

He smiled menacingly, and she swore she detected a hint of annoyance. "You don't get it." He bowed his head and stepped closer. "But since you don't understand *who* I am, I'll let it slide this once."

"*Pico*," she muttered under her breath.

He lifted her chin then, glaring down at her with those stone-colored eyes. "You do know I'm Italian, *si?* And that Italian is very close to Spanish?" He bared his teeth like a true demon of her nightmares might. "You just called me a dick in Spanish, *si?*"

Oh shit. She recollected herself and raised a brow. "Okay, fine. I'll just stick to calling you things in French then."

"Go ahead, don't follow through with my orders. See what happens to your family," he hissed.

Molly returned his gaze, burning with hatred. Why couldn't she just *smite* him with her blessed eyes, huh? Take her sunglasses off and turn him to *dust* for threatening her family?

He yanked up his suit sleeve to sneak a look at his watch before seizing her arm again. "We're late."

"Late? For what?"

He pulled her along with him, clenching her wrist tight. "A meeting that'll hopefully keep you hidden longer."

She blinked. *Hidden?* "Meeting with who?"

"People who can help us," he stated vaguely.

"Very vivid." She tugged her hand back. "I'm not going anywhere with you —"

He pulled her with him. *Ugh!* "Do you want another gorgon after you like last night?"

"*No.*"

"Then move!"

"Then let go!" Tensley did as she asked and Molly wrapped her arms around her middle. She pictured him threatening her parents, hitting them, and cringed. She couldn't stomach it and started walking beside him in livid silence. She had to protect them. When Tensley turned toward a white brick townhouse guarded by a large gate, Molly inhaled. He or whoever owned this had money — lots of money, and power. It was massive and elegant, dark green vines cascading down the stone, trimmed neatly.

"Wait," Molly called out as Tensley moved forward.

Tensley paused before entering the beautiful house and glanced over his shoulder at her. "What?"

She shook her head and stepped back. "I'm not going inside there with you. For all I know, you could have a torture room in there!"

Tensley's head lifted heavenward as his hands dragged down his face, groaning. "You gotta be fucking kidding me..." His head lowered, eyes sharp. "It's in your best interest to get inside before I make you."

Molly's arms clinched around her waist. Even as the fear tightened around her throat, she feared what was beyond those gold-trimmed doors more. "There's no way I'm going inside there."

"For fuc—" Tensley sucked in sharply, cutting himself off. He pointed to her hand. "What do you know about that?"

Molly furrowed her brow. "I've had it since your family visited us when I was four, and I haven't been able to remove it — *at all.*"

"Us meeting last night wasn't because I suddenly felt the urge to take on a pet," he said, gesturing to her.

I am not a pet, you mutt!

"I had to step in to stop the gorgon that had found you because — that ring failed to hide you, which it has done since the night we put it on your finger."

Molly frowned. "Hide me?"

"From demons."

Well, shit. She glared down at the discolored ring.

"You have two options: either follow me inside to the people who might be able to turn the protection back on, or stand out here and have your organs ripped out by the first demon who tracks you down. Either way, I don't care. Suit yourself." Without another word, he turned and marched up the smooth white steps.

Molly's chest tightened at the memory of the gorgon's teeth scraping against her throat, and the idea of a chance to get rid of Tensley if the ring worked made her feet move after him.

Molly reached the door just as he opened it and he gripped her wrist, pulling her close. "Just stay close when we go inside. Don't say a word, don't look up, got it?"

"Am I in danger?" She hated how her voice hinted at her hidden emotions — her fear, and that she was on the brink of tears.

She couldn't muster the courage to look him in the eye, but she saw his jaw relax and his Adam's apple bob nervously. He placed a tender hand on her shoulder. "Just listen to me and let me do the talking, okay? You'll be safe next to me."

Molly nodded; all traces of jest were gone from his voice, and she took that seriously.

Once they stepped inside, a flurry of faces and activity in an art deco-designed hallway, whispers about the "strange girl with Tensley" overwhelmed her.

"Who are these people?" Molly asked, trying to keep up with Tensley's strides and eyeing the men who stood at every doorway, impassive like statues.

"Employees."

"Of what? Who?"

He huffed and proceeded to ignore her, continuing down another hallway to a set of polished wooden French doors. He threw them open, not bothering to hold either open for her before entering.

Tensley mumbled under his breath as soon as they walked into the dark, immaculate office decorated in hues of black, grey, and dark blue. Molly paused by the doorway, unsure if she was supposed to follow. *I mean, he didn't slam the door in my face. That's a plus.* She inched in closer. She eyed the built-in bookcases filled with thick hardcover books. She ached to run her finger along their spines and see what books he had. She tiptoed closer to the chairs and watched as Tensley flipped through papers and filed them away.

Do I sit? Stand?

"*Where are they?*" he hissed under his breath.

Molly stiffened. "Uh..."

Someone chuckled behind her, and she spun to see the same girl from the night before. "Nice to see you both too," Lex said, shaking her head. Tensley shot her a glare in response. "They've been waiting for an hour."

Tensley sat down at the large oak desk—presumably his—and shuffled through his neatly arranged papers. "Well, *someone* wasn't where they were supposed to be."

Molly glowered. "I was working. Am I not allowed to do that now?"

His eyes flickered briefly to her, and after a long stare, he turned to Lex. "Bring them in."

Lex smiled at Molly and vanished behind the doors.

"Sit." The simple, clipped order startled Molly. She badly wanted to defy him, but trapped within his walls meant he'd have the upper hand in a fight. She plopped herself down and eyed the items on his desk, avoiding his stare.

When she *did* look up, he was studying her intently, lips slightly parted, and she found herself imagining them between her teeth—

A knock came at the door. She shook her head out of the familiar fogginess. *Thank god.*

"Come in," Tensley said gruffly.

Lex did, with two other men, one older with a shaggy salt and pepper beard that hid his features, and the other with dull brown hair and a hooked nose.

So they can help us with the ring...please, please help me!

Lex shut the door behind her, leaving the four of them staring back at each other.

"Names." Tensley stood up, buttoning the front of his suit jacket.

"Albert," the older one said in a wheezy voice, phlegmy from years of smoking.

"Jackson, sir," the other said, his eyes trained on Molly.

"Can you fix it?" Tensley asked.

Molly looked back and forth between them, trying to figure it out on her own. All their eyes focused on her and she stilled.

Tensley rounded the desk and yanked Molly up by her shoulder, holding her left hand out to them. "Fix it. Now."

Molly tried to shrug out of his grip. "Easy!"

The two men stared at Tensley, startled by his vehemence, before Albert's focus moved down to Molly's forefinger. He slid his thumb over the discolored ring there.

"What — what are you going to do?" Molly tried to take her hand back, but Tensley held it tightly in his iron grip.

Albert closed his eyes and began to chant, over and over, his two fingers pressed against the ring. His words became louder and quicker, and soon he was out of breath.

Albert's features fell, and he eyed Tensley cautiously. "It didn't work. The charm used before is too complex, and…her essence is too strong to hide."

Essence? What does that even mean?

Tensley's grasp tightened. "You. You do it now," Tensley ordered Jackson, holding Molly's hand in his direction.

Molly hissed lowly. "Seriously, stop manhandling me, just let them fix the ring—"

"No." Jackson smirked mockingly at him. The entire room grew silent at Jackson's words.

Tensley grew rigid beside her. *Oh shit.* "No?"

"Let's make a deal. You give me a hundred nyxes, and I won't discuss your new toy with other high-borns," Jackson said, leaning against the closed door to examine his nails.

"*Jackson,*" Albert warned.

Jackson waved him off. "If she was human, the cloaking charm would be easy, Al. Dark magic's encrypted, and since our chants didn't work to hide her, I'm figuring she's not human. You can make the deal, give me the money, or I'll make my own deal with a high-born who I'm sure would be very intrigued."

Tensley dropped Molly's wrist and stood to his full height. "Tell me, are you—a pathetic excuse of a warlock—threatening *me?*"

Molly cringed at his tone, wavering on the edge of losing his temper. This wasn't going to be good.

Jackson attempted to keep his calm façade from breaking, but a hint of anger flashed in his eyes. "The Knight family isn't what they used to be. You're weak, and if we don't help you, what are you going to do to us, huh? You're soft, just like your brother," Jackson said, his bravado unwavering while Albert watched in horror. Molly felt like she was stepping on glass as she watched the two men standoff.

Tensley's figure blurred, making Molly dizzy, and the next second Jackson's throat was clenched in his white-knuckled fist. *Oh god!*

Tensley leaned closer. "I don't like warlocks—hell, I hate them. But I could have ripped your beating heart out awhile back. I don't need you; I can survive without you. Don't disrespect me. Don't confuse cunning with being *soft*, because I will tear out your intestines and shove them down your throat without a second thought. We clear?"

Molly's clutched her chest, backing away. *Don't do it, Tensley. Don't do it.*

Jackson wheezed, his toes skimming the floor. When Tensley released his collar, a part of the panic lifted from Molly's chest. Jackson landed heavily on the ground, adjusted his clothing, and spat—directly onto Tensley's polished dress shoes.

No!

"You pathetic, weak demonic bastard," Jackson hissed, shoving Tensley.

It was like trying to push a freight train, and Molly watched as Tensley's jaw clenched and his nostrils flared. *Oh no.*

Tensley grabbed Jackson by the neck and slammed his other hand into the warlock's chest. A wet, sickening sound echoed in the office, and Tensley released Jackson a moment later, dropping something else on the floor. The body hit the floor and something tumbled across the floor next to Molly's shoes.

Molly stared down at the red, wet shape, for a few moments unable to process what it was.

A heart.

Her eyes travelled to the lifeless body by Tensley's polished shoes, a bloody hole in the chest.

He yanked out his heart.

Molly staggered, fighting a gag as she collided with Albert. The other warlock steadied her, cupping her clammy hand in his own. He pushed a crumpled piece of paper into her palm.

"Get away from her," Tensley said, glaring at Albert as he stepped back. Tensley walked over to his desk, opened his drawer, and used a white handkerchief to wipe his hand down. She gawked at the red smudges on the pure white fabric and tried to breathe through her nose, untrusting of opening her mouth. After a chilling silence he spoke again, voice strained. "So we can't hide her. The ring can't be fixed."

"Not by me — or him." Albert nodded at Jackson's lifeless body and paled. "Not when she's that strong."

Molly's heart ached at the loss of the ability to escape Tensley and his world.

"Leave then." Tensley's voice was emotionless, detached, and when Albert didn't move, clearly in a state of shock, he continued more firmly. *He's a heartless bastard.* "If you'd like to keep your head intact, I recommend you follow our contract and *get the hell out.*"

As Albert stumbled through the doors and slammed them closed, Molly shakily squirreled the paper he'd given her into her skirt pocket. She couldn't understand how he was so calm, so collected and *fucking fine* after killing a man. *How can he just do that? He was someone's son!* She stood in the middle of the office, averting her eyes from the *human heart* on the rug nearby. "You killed him." It came out as a whimper, and she wondered if she might really vomit.

Tensley's frame shook as his palms, one bloody, rested against the leather chair nearest him. "Don't come any closer."

"He was someone's son! He had a life, he was a breathing, living person who deserved a life and you took it from him—"

Tensley's head ticked as if he slightly was affected by her words, and he stretched his body out.

"And now, he's a body…" Molly bit into her lip to stop from crying out, but the warmth flooded her eyes and rolled down her cheeks. "You killed him, you monster! You sick basta—"

"He was going to hurt you! Fuck!" His crimson hand slammed into the chair, knocking it over. "It didn't work!"

Molly frowned, stepping back at his shaking figure. "What didn't work?"

He spun, his face contorted in anger. "That damn ring! It's been protecting you since you were four, hiding you from other demons. The warlock who made the ring is dead, along with that *ring*. That's how the gorgon found you; that's how others will be able to find you!"

Molly held her hands out like she might to a rabid beast, all sense of horror dissipating. She needed to survive this, and he was clearly losing it. "Tensley…calm down…"

"Do you know what this means? It means I can't hide you—demons will begin to notice you and will do anything to get you!" He moved forward, jabbing his finger in the air. "You don't understand this, so let me explain. I'm at your house because of *this*, because you don't even understand your abilities or how to use them, and I do. I don't choose to live in your fucking Brady Bunch home. I do this for *you!*"

He moved too close for her comfort as he yelled, veins like ropes in his neck. His eyes transformed from grey to a foreboding darkness.

"*Tensley!* Stop!" Molly shouted, stumbling back, scanning the room for a weapon, for an escape — anything!

He growled monstrously, bending his torso as he screwed his eyes shut and dug his fingers into his thighs, like he was battling himself.

The doors burst open, silencing both of them. A tall man stood at the doorway, examining Tensley and Molly.

"Calm down. Get your beast under control," the newcomer said, rushing over to the shaking Tensley.

"The damn warlocks provoked it, Illya," Tensley hissed. She saw the glint of sweat on his forehead, like he was physically restraining himself. Illya stared down at the dead warlock and frowned.

Illya's eyes found Molly's widened, damp ones, and he cautiously stepped closer. Her shoulders lifted, still on edge. *Can I trust him? Or is he going to snap my neck too...*

His yellow hair was swept to one side with a distinct widow's peak, and his bright blue eyes seemed genuine. "I'm Illya. Don't be afraid; we won't hurt you." He wore simple clothes: a jean T-shirt and dark green slacks, not like Tensley in his suit. "You must be Tensley's fiancée?"

"Just *Molly.*"

"And you're a daemon?"

Molly balked. "No! I mean…I don't think…"

That caught Tensley's attention. "You *are* a daemon."

She yanked her shaking hands through her tangled curls. "Stop calling me that! I'm not, okay? I'm just Molly, and I don't want any part of this! None of it!"

"You're a daemon," Tensley said, seemingly recovered from his inner turmoil. "Your eyes are what demons refer to as *blessed*. The Greeks called daemons the Golden Race, guardians for humans, to protect against our kind."

She wrung her hands, too stubborn to listen to him. "That's — that's crazy." *He's crazy.*

Tensley snickered once, wiped his large hands on his slacks, and cleared his throat. "It makes perfect sense. Your eyes stop demons in their tracks. You're powerful; you just don't know it yet."

"Just stop." She turned away from him, waving him off. She needed air, fresh air.

"If we have a child, they will inherit both our genes. Do you know what that could mean? A demon that could stop others with one look — and with your strength, this child would be more powerful than either of us."

Molly froze, gawking at Tensley's blood-splattered dress shoes. *No, no, I heard that wrong. He did not just say a baby…* His distant, muffled voice vibrated in her head, but she wasn't listening. She felt too hot and fanned at her face, soon clawing at her constricting throat. As she spun, she saw the body and stumbled back.

"A baby? Are you — a baby, oh god, that's not happening — ever! Stop talking, just shut up!" She sucked air through her lips in little drags, white dots dancing across her vision.

The room was silent and she didn't bother looking up, choosing to focus on her trembling hands.

"Take her home," Tensley said from somewhere on her left; she couldn't even focus any more.

Illya gently took her elbow, leading Molly away, and she couldn't fight him. When they passed a potted plant, she pulled away, eyeing the bookcase twisting in on itself, and then focused on the large pot, reaching, darting clumsily forward. "Sorry, I'm — sick — "

Molly puked, apologizing through each heave.

Illya rubbed her back until it was over. "Don't even worry; Tensley will take care of it. It's what he deserves."

Molly's knees buckled and Illya wrapped an arm around her shoulders, guiding her through some sort of back entrance with a lot less people. They stopped in the backyard, and the hazy scent of gardenias calmed Molly's stomach.

"He killed him," she said slowly, rubbing her temples.

"They provoked his demon side. Please, stop for a moment. You don't look well." Illya led Molly to a wrought iron bench near a small fountain of a winged angel levitating over the water. *Ironic.*

Molly sat heavily. "His demon side?"

Illya nodded, placing an ice-cold palm on her sweaty forehead. She flinched back. "We were cursed with two sides — some indulge more in the demon side."

"*Demon side,*" she repeated, shaking her head. Illya had a faint, lilting accent, but from where, she couldn't tell. "Wow. I just saw someone die. Like…dead. On the floor. Heart yanked out. And *he* did it." Molly looked over at Illya, stomach muscles aching from her violent retching. "He's a monster." She vigorously shook her head. "I'm not—I'm not marrying him. I'm not doing anything with him!"

Illya shook his head. "He's not—you just caught him at a bad time."

A bad time? Was there a good time? Maybe he only killed people on Tuesdays.

"I need—I need to go." She pushed out of his grip, walking past blooming violet and fuchsia rhododendrons toward the gate. *So much beauty…to mask the death.* Illya's soft footsteps followed, and Molly looked back when she felt steady enough. "Illya, please. Don't follow me. I'm fine."

His brows lifted, but after a second, he stopped moving. As she walked away, she double-checked to find him standing where she'd left him and sighed unevenly. She speed-walked away from the townhouse, hitting several shoulders and murmuring distracted apologies.

Molly slipped her hand into her skirt pocket for her cell but paused when she felt the crumpled piece of paper first. She yanked it out, unrolling it to read the scribbled writing.

One side: *Shoot the Freak*

The other side: *Athena*

Molly furrowed her brow, flipping the paper back and forth, straining to put the pieces together. Nothing added up, nothing made sense, and she pulled at the paper to straighten it out—as if that would help.

Shoot the freak?

What does it mean?

chapter six

WHEN MOLLY ENTERED her tiny apartment, she rushed into the closet she used as a bedroom and shoved the bit of clothing and toiletries she kept there into a bag. She couldn't stay there, not when Tensley was going around snapping people's necks. If she was quick enough, September wouldn't find her and ask questions.

She snatched a few loose papers from her research for the museum and for her parent's house. When she was done packing, Molly stopped, eyeing the tiny room with its exposed red bricks and squeaky floorboards.

She'd only been there a few months, but it was a place she felt safe, a solitude.

And now it was gone.

The curtain — aka the door to her room — swished, and she twisted to see September dressed in her Danny's diner striped shirt, arms crossed. Shit.

"Who was that guy, Mol?"

"He, uh, was a friend," Molly muttered, turning back to stuffing her bag.

September frowned. "He kissed your hand."

Her stomach dropped. "Uh, yeah, he's foreign. I think." *You have no idea how foreign.*

"So...what's going on?"

"What do you mean? Aren't you supposed to go to work right now?" Molly did one more quick sweep of her room, keeping her eyes down.

"Oh no — don't switch topics. Where do I start? The fact that you've been avoiding me, or that you didn't even seem to care that Michael, your lifelong crush, was at that party, because now you apparently have a foreign boyfriend?"

"He's *not* my boyfriend," Molly countered a bit too forcefully.

September wrinkled her brow, appearing taken aback. "Okay..."

Molly let her weight fall down onto her cheap mattress and the burden on her chest sharpened. "September, I..." She breathed, studying her hands: thin and dainty, one single finger still carrying the burden of her entrapment. "It's happened." Taking deep breaths of their humid, sticky apartment air, she tried to calm herself, the sensation of her glowing eyes reminding her of *why* he wanted her.

September sat down beside her and rubbed her back. "What happened?"

"Everything we joked about, everything that seemed crazy." Molly blew out a harsh breath. "They came back."

September shook her head. "Who came back?"

"The shadows — the people from thirteen years ago. They came back, September. For me." After a pregnant pause, September stood up and paced in the bit of empty space Molly's closet-bedroom offered. "I know it's crazy, and you won't believe me—"

"I believe you," September interrupted, threading her fingers through her frizzy mane. "Your eyes freakin' glow—it's not that farfetched." She stopped mid-step. "So the guy at the museum…?"

"A demon," Molly whispered.

September's eyes darted to Molly. "He's a *demon*? Like, what are demons? Like demons-*demons*? Satan-demons? Does he transform into a red creepy thing?" Then a string of Spanish words spat out of her mouth as she clenched her fists.

Molly's stomach twisted. "No! I mean…I don't think so. I don't know! Stop saying stuff like that." The thought of Tensley being something even more physically inhumane freaked her out. He wasn't human. His strength, his allure, terrified her. He could rip her own heart out if she pissed him off.

September's eyes pleaded with Molly. "Why the hell didn't you tell me before—at the museum?"

"I didn't want you involved. I was scared." Molly rubbed at her shoulder. "Scared of him. I wanted to protect you." She cradled her head in her hands. "He says I'm his fiancée."

"What? Are you serious?" When Molly simply looked up at September with red, puffy eyes, September's jaw locked and she grinded her teeth. "Carajo! Oh, he's going to get a mouthful from me."

Molly's heart stalled. She thought back to Tensley ripping out Jackson's heart for disrespecting him, and then to September's unfiltered mouth. Molly couldn't let her get hurt. She had to keep September as far from this as possible

"I need to go," Molly said, swinging her bag over the uninjured shoulder.

September followed. "Where are you going?"

Molly's throat grew dry and tight. "It's not safe to be around me, September. I love you so much, and I can't have you involved in my family's problems. Please, don't make me have to worry about you, too. I can't risk him hurting you."

"Just stay here. We'll figure something out."

"My parents have a plan," she lied through her teeth.

"Molly —"

Molly spun around. "He threatened my family! He threatened to rip my dad limb from limb if I didn't do what he said. And — and I just saw him rip out a man's heart for spitting on his shoes. I can't — I cannot risk him hurting you too, okay?"

September stood there silently, eyes wide. "He did *what?*"

"Just stay away from me, okay? Until I can figure this out."

As Molly turned, her hand on the doorknob of the crappy apartment she'd grown to love, September spoke. "Molly, you're my sister. I'm not going to abandon you."

"You should," Molly said, voice as cruel as she could make it. "You really fucking should."

Molly bit the inside of her mouth to stop from crying out as she ran down the stairs. She needed to focus, needed to keep those around her as safe as possible, and that meant sacrifice.

AS SOON AS the front door of her parents' townhouse closed, Molly heard their heated argument, and her already battered emotions stretched further. When she stepped into the living room, all of the air escaped her lungs.

Her father's usually pristine suit was torn, his bottom lip swollen and bleeding. He sniffed, rubbing the back of his hand underneath his crooked nose to wipe the smeared blood away as he limped to the couch.

"What happened?" Molly couldn't hide the wobble in her broken voice. Her father hadn't deserved this, any of this, and her heart burnt and crumbled with the knowledge that she had caused this. Her hands ached to reach out, to hold him, but she froze at the fear of crushing him with how heightened her emotions were — which meant her strength was uncontrollable. "Who did this?"

He fell down onto the sofa, lowered his eyes, and held his damaged face in his palms. "I tried to bargain with them. I told them to take me instead; I carry the gene. *My* family is the damn thing that caused this."

"Derrek, why would you just do that without discussing it with me?" Fiona went to grab his hand, but he batted it away. "What did they say?"

"They said it wasn't good enough. They said 'the daemon' is the only thing that can satisfy the contract. Apparently daemons have gone nearly extinct; Molly's the only known one left. They'll never give this up." *I'm the only one left?* Somehow, even over the years of being an outcast, she felt the loneliness engulf her. Derrek licked his bloodied lip and looked at Molly sadly. "Please go upstairs honey; I need some time to think."

Her heart caved and she turned to leave, stopping in the kitchen on the way for a huge butcher knife from the block on the counter. She gripped the knife and marched upstairs, but paused.

You want to hurt my family? Fine. Then I'll hurt you.

Molly moved to the guest room, curious if he had moved his things in.

She tapped the door twice and when she heard nothing, she peeked inside to see the neat royal blue bedroom. Her eyes automatically zoomed into the suitcase on the floor.

She threw the top open, but it was just full of books. Old books. She sat back on her heels and pushed through them. A lot of them were old sonnets and Shakespearean works. At the very top of the pile was a hardcover tome, worn and frayed from years of use. A crest of a scorpion, poised for attack, was imprinted on the reddish-brown cover. Sprawled above the crest was the title: *The Rosier.*

Flipping through the thick pages, she couldn't stop reading. The book stated that demons were heartless–that didn't shock her. They were angels of the High Court and had fallen when humans seduced them. It went on to say that the demon's partner, usually another demon, had to be a strong mate to give one another power. If a demon's mate was powerful, that demon was too.

SIX LAWS OF BABYLON

1. Thou shall not express pure affection or adoration to the extent of danger of producing a full heart.
2. If one shall produce a full heart, the Crown Prince will take appropriate action of removal of said threat.
3. Thou shall not interact equally with a demon not of their class.
4. Thou shall support the High Court.
5. Thou shall hold vigil on any suspicious activity and interference between other demons and the human populace.
6. Any threat or opposition to the High Court will be terminated through trial and execution of the Crown Prince's choosing.

"Demons who have relationships with humans must be warned that if they make love continuously to the human, they will be at risk of developing a full heart."

Molly paused, rolling her bottom lip between her teeth. "So he *can* develop a heart?" She flipped to the next page.

"If that occurs, the Crown Prince Fallen will destroy the heart and thus, the demon will be reborn…"

Why does growing a heart matter so much? Why is love such a terrible thing to them? It doesn't make sense.

Her eyes focused on the image beside the text: a sketch of a terrifying man with an unkempt mane of hair, rippled muscles, and talons, ripping out another man's heart.

Dear lord…

The door slammed and she jolted, shoving the book

back into his suitcase. She tiptoed out of the bedroom; knife clenched in hand, and glanced over the banister as she tried to move silently down the stairs.

Tensley stood in front of her father in the living room with a scowl on his face. His eyes flickered over to Molly's, but Derrek was still unaware of her presence.

"Thank you," her father said.

What?

Tensley's face stayed the same, radiating irritation. "Don't be so fucking stupid next time as to think my father would bargain with you."

After a long silence, her dad lifted a tumbler glass to Tensley. "I'd like to put everything behind us, and start fresh...as family?"

Molly balked and tightened her grip on the knife.

Her father took a seat in his leather chair, leaning back to get comfortable. Tensley grasped the drink and took a gulp, staring at Molly through the bottom of the glass. He joined Derrek on the nearby sofa.

"You know, it's funny," Tensley said, his finger tapping a constant beat on the glass. "Demons have excellent senses — we're faster, and our reflexes are definitely above yours." He paused, taking another drink as Molly gulped at the anxiety building in her throat. He sighed and licked his lips. "Scent is a well-known strength for us — we could *smell* it if someone has poisoned the food...or in your case, the alcohol."

Tensley crushed the glass with his bare hand, flinging it across the room. He stood, his chin held high as he moved closer to her father. Molly took a step forward, and Tensley's eyes sliced through hers.

"Poison — *your* kind of poison — doesn't work on demons," Tensley seethed. Molly couldn't look away from the blood dripping down Tensley's lacerated hand. "Stop trying to intervene, old man."

"She's my daughter!" Derrek jumped up, grasping at Tensley's forearm. "She doesn't deserve this! You're just using her for your family's own gain!"

Molly moved to the bottom of the staircase, preparing to attack. She hoped her strength might actually appear when she *needed* it this time.

"Stay out of my *way*," Tensley said, shoving Derrek aside and leaving the way he'd come.

Molly's shoulders relaxed and she pressed a shaky hand to her forehead.

"Derrek? What happened? Did it work?" Fiona's footsteps pounded down the staircase.

"Dad," Molly said softly, alerting him to her presence.

He hung his head and ran his hands through his thinning hair. "I want him out! He's dangerous! I'm your father and I can't protect you!"

"Dad, you have to stop. You're going to get yourself killed!"

"I'll go after him. I'll give them anything. I'm not letting him hurt you!" He moved to the front door and Molly ran after him, reaching for his arm.

"Ow!" he yelped, and Molly jumped back, trembling.

"Molly!" Her mother's shriek filled the house. "Control yourself."

A bright red handprint stood out on his skin. *Oh god! What's wrong with me?* "Dad," she said, voice shaky.

"Honey, please." His eyes glistened with tears, bruises coloring his cheekbones.

"I'm sorry, Dad; I didn't mean to..." Molly croaked. "Just stay away from him and let me deal with him."

Her dad's grimace transformed to one of panic. "Molly—"

"He can't hurt me, not like you two. He..." It was then that it settled in *so* painfully slow that her breath hitched. "You're weapons. You're weapons he uses against me and I can't let him do that. Not any more. Just *please* don't interfere. You have to leave." She fought the burn growing behind her eyes and glared at both of them. "If you love me, you'll leave the house now, go to the Hamptons until *I* get this under control. I can deal with him—he won't hurt me." She steeled her expression and hoped they didn't hear the hesitation in her voice. She wasn't completely sure he wouldn't hurt her...

Her father wrinkled his forehead, pain sketched onto his features. "Molly, what kind of parents would we be if we just left you here alone with him?"

Molly smiled softly. "Please, trust me. I can handle him."

Fiona broke out into a sob and clutched her chest.

Molly brushed past her mother on the stairs, ignoring their eyes burning holes into her back. When she reached the top floor, she ripped *The Rosier* from Tensley's suitcase and went into her bedroom. She gripped the knife and leaned against the headboard, waiting, waiting for him to return.

Her phone buzzed, and when she saw Michael's face lighting up the screen, her heart ached. *There's no way I can see him or he'll be a weapon, too.*

"Hello?" Her voice was soft.

"Molly? You okay?"

She closed her eyes and clenched the knife. "Yeah, just tired."

"Oh, okay. Well, I was wondering if, uh, you were free. You know, since we talked about going out during the year..." He was speaking rapidly; he sounded nervous.

Is he...is he asking me out? "Oh."

"It's not a date—I mean, it could be...if you wanted it to be." He laughed softly to himself. "I got Yankee tickets, front row. Since you love the Yankees as much as me, I'd thought you'd be the best person to go with. We could go for supper after...or not?"

He's asking me out? To the Yankees? Why does he have to do this now? When all this is happening? Why not a month ago? Or a week, even.

"Molly?"

But she couldn't. Not when it would endanger Michael.

She blinked back tears. "Michael, I—I'm seeing someone."

"Oh, uh, yeah, that's cool," he said, his pep sounding forced. "Guess I waited too long to make a move, huh?" She covered her mouth so he wouldn't hear her sob. "Okay, well, I'll see you later then?"

She nodded, then realized he couldn't see it. "Y-yes. Later."

When they hung up, she cried openly, hand tightening around the knife.

Tensley had just taken everything away—September, Michael, her parents, her freedom. She wasn't going to let him take anything else. Over her dead body.

"I'll destroy you." Her body shook. "And everyone around you."

chapter seven

THE GIRL LOCKED eyes with Tensley through the sultry, thick air, and he knew he had her. She licked at her dark purple lipstick, posture straightening fast as his desirable pheromones took over her senses, igniting her sex drive. When she approached him, he noted her dilated pupils, a huge indication that his power was working. He tilted his chin upward and simply smiled. That was all it took.

The redhead was mercilessly savage as she groped his chest, but Tensley couldn't argue. He needed physical contact; even someone hanging off his arm, stroking his chest, nibbling on his earlobe was doable for a period of time. The downside to being an incubus: the constant need for intimacy for health. The upside? He had no problems attracting suitors. He simply locked eyes, tipped his chin, and sent off pheromones of heightened sexual attraction, and they were swinging their hips toward him, giddy from his heated gaze. He sent off the pheromones, they chose to approach him and he charmed them with his relaxed, polished words.

When he had done the same to Molly, she'd struggled against the pull, but he had caught moments where she would heed his abilities and be drawn to him.

He moved Redhead to a crowded corner of the club and placed himself in front of her as she continued to kiss his neck. He concentrated on the industrial brick wall, feeling his energy strengthen a tiny bit. It wasn't the same as sex or if he was actually participating in the act, but he couldn't bring himself to do that. Evelyn's dark eyes flashed in his head, and his hands curled against the wall. He promised to stay loyal to her as did she. If he didn't keep up at least a bit of strength, his health would decline, and with his role, he couldn't risk being weak.

Fingers grasped his jaw, and her chapped lips scratched against his. He shoved her hand away, stepping back.

"What's your name, handsome?" she continued, her thick makeup making her look clownish in the club's strobe lighting.

He gripped her throat and shoved her back against the wall. Leaning in close, he bared his teeth. "No kissing on the mouth, understood?"

She blinked several times before she nodded. His hand spread down her throat to her collarbone and lingered, feeling her heart beating wildly. The girl wanted him. Badly.

"Good." He threw her head back and nipped at her jaw, making his way up to her ear. When she tried to touch his face, he glared and roughly removed her hands again.

He couldn't do this. He couldn't be the damn predator his kind was known as for centuries. He'd amassed enough energy tonight; he wasn't going to waste his time avoiding the Darling household.

"Come home with me," Redhead giggled, gripping at his bicep. She was lightheaded off his touch, off his incubus seduction.

He glowered down at her hand, manicured with long, red nails. "I'm not your type."

She swung her head back to the beat of the fast-paced music, then lost her footing and balanced against him, laughing loudly. "You're exactly what I'm looking for, babe."

He sneered, fed up — then transformed his pheromones from seductive to pure aggression. She took an unsteady step back. "I'm *not* your type," he repeated, yanking at the lapels on his suit jacket. He patted his breast pocket to feel the sharpened blade tucked away there, a nervous habit, and headed out the back door, exhaling when the breezy summer night air graced his hot flesh.

Just as his shoulders relaxed, his phone buzzed and all the tension returned. "What?" he answered in a clipped tone.

"Bad timing?" said Lex, too chipper for him.

"I'm busy." Cradling the phone between his shoulder and cheek, he reached into his pocket and pulled out his lighter and a cigarette laced with belladonna. He needed nicotine. *Now.*

"I hope you apologized to her," Lex said anyway, and he rolled his eyes at her stubborn desire to fix everyone's problems. "She was puking in the hallway. Did you really have to kill the guy?"

Gross. Now he'd have to replace that plant.

"He was out of line. He threatened to expose her, and then mocked me about Scorpios and my family. He wanted a hundred nyxes—what the hell does he need with that much money?" Tensley walked down a dark alley, smoke billowing behind him in a heavy stream.

Lex hummed. "Well, you terrified her."

"*Good.*"

"You don't mean that," she said.

He stopped walking, closing his eyes and registering the softness in her voice. He reminded himself Lex was just an eighteen-year-old, one who'd spent two-thirds of her life living in fear, and took a breath, moving forward.

"It's a lot easier if she sees me like everyone else in our world does: a cold, heartless bastard," he said, an ache blooming in his chest.

She laughed humorlessly. "You mean the heartless bastard who saved me when he could have just moved along to different scraps?"

"You caught me on a good day."

She laughed, the familiar sound calming his nerves.

He rubbed the back of his sweaty neck. "Where are you?"

"Calm down, *Dad.* I'm at my apartment painting my nails. Oh and I just ate the strangest, most delicious memory ever. He was on the subway, and I just leaned in a bit and touched his hand and oh my god, so good. First sour, and then so sweet." She sighed dreamily, as if she could still taste it.

"Soul eaters…" Tensley tsked.

"Is this where I'm supposed to pity you? It's not like incubi are on the top of the food chain or anything. I wouldn't mind being an incubus. All the sexy times and power," she said, snorting.

"Trust me, it's not all great, not when you don't want randoms. I don't want to be a damn predator."

"Oh my god, please don't tell me you've still got a thing with Evelyn. Isn't that *over* yet?"

"No it's not *over* yet. She'd be the perfect wife for me as the future Dux of Scorpios; she understands what's between us is just business, nothing more. We're just taking some space for the time being. I'll figure out a way to keep the daemon safe."

Lex was silent.

"I know you don't like her —"

"She hates me because she thinks I'm into you. I see you as my damn brother. She needs to calm down, possessive bitch," Lex huffed. "I'm heading out to a house party and then going undercover for a while, so if you don't hear from me for a few weeks, don't panic, okay?"

He would panic anyway. "Sure."

"Apologize to Molly," she warned. He rolled his eyes at her bossy tone.

"Lex?"

"Yeah?"

He swallowed. "Be safe."

"Always am."

He shoved his phone into his pocket after they'd hung up, surveying the busy avenue up ahead.

He didn't want the pressure, he didn't want to do anything with the daemon — but if he *didn't*, he was risking his entire family's recompense.

Tensley breathed in sharply, stretching his fingers as

the nicotine unfurled throughout his bloodstream, giving him that buzzy, lightheaded sensation. If only it could burn away his emotions, burn it all so he didn't care any more.

He threw the cigarette to the ground, stubbed it with the toe of his shoe, and imagined it was *her*.

chapter eight

AMBIENT LIGHT FROM the hallway assaulted Molly's eyes, and she peeled one open.

Shit, I fell asleep. Shit, shit, shit!

The rest of the room was dark, and she saw a figure by the door, framed by the light from the hallway.

Her heart stalled, then rebooted to the point of shattering her ribcage.

Tensley.

He walked through the darkness, and she couldn't help but note how he was shrugging out of his shirt, the defined muscles of his torso bunching and flexing with every movement. *Oh god.* Dark lines tattooed his sides. She wanted to—*stop it Molly! No psychopaths, remember?*

With one shallow breath, she pulled herself together. She'd been prepared, fighting sleep, the knife clenched in her shaking hand—and now, after a few minutes of dozing, she was vulnerable. Attempting to go unnoticed, she slid her hand across the silk covers, searching for the blade.

"I hope you don't snore," he said in a husky whisper, stalking to the bed. He leaned over her at the same moment she finally grasped the sharp edge of the knife, and she could smell his sweat, pungent and masculine.

She twisted the knife into her palm and spoke with as much steadiness possible. "No, I don't snore. Do you?" For once, the darkness was her friend; he wouldn't be able to see her red cheeks and pressured, stone-hard face. If anything, he would end up laughing in it.

Which he did anyway. "Do I look like someone who snores?"

She gnawed the inside of her cheek. "Maybe."

He stood up to his full, imposing height. "*Maybe?*" He looked across the bed at the books sprawled out on the comforter. *Oops.* "Did you take my books?"

"Uh—"

"*Don't* touch my things. If you want something, ask for it." With a gruff curse, he tossed the books back into his suitcase.

Her grip tightened on the blade. "I wanted answers," she whispered.

He watched her intently, hands beginning to tremble—trying to hold his anger at bay, she guessed. "Tell your father that if he steps out of line again, I won't stop the blade at his throat. What the hell was he thinking? If I hadn't talked my father down, he would have decapitated him. And the fucking poison? If he pulls that shit again, he's done. Got it?"

Molly flinched. He had admitted to saving her father's life and in the same breath threatened it once more. "Why?"

He searched through his suitcase, forehead wrinkled in fury. "Why *what?*"

"Why did you save him?"

"Because I figured you wouldn't be pleased if I brought you your father's head."

She swallowed a whimper. "But—that man you killed, he deserved it?"

"Would you rather him squeal about my *little secret?*"

She resisted her body's urge to shiver and scooted to the edge of the bed. "Just leave my family alone. Don't involve them in this, okay? That's all I ask." He paused and gazed at her through his lashes, a look that flashed approval. Molly hid her shaking hands. "*Okay?*"

Tensley scowled. "You're bargaining for your family's lives?"

"Yes," she said, breathless.

His eyes narrowed. "Fine. You care about your family? Then you need to follow these rules."

What now? "Oh?"

"One: Do not tell people who I am. To your low-bred kind, I'm your fiancé. If they find out, I'll either have to break their bones until they agree to stay quiet, or finish them off." Her chest tightened. He raised his finger, firmly shaking it at her. "Two: If I tell you to do something—be it to stay away from my fucking stuff, to listen to my orders, or whatever else I can think of—you'll do it without a damn word otherwise." He advanced, eyes sharp and tone bitter. "Three: Nothing romantic or sweet will ever happen between us. No cuddling, no sweet declarations of nonsense." Molly's breath stuttered in her lungs as she crawled away from him and farther up the bed. "And lastly, I don't kiss on the lips." He leaned down, a smirk tugging at his soft mouth. "But I *do* kiss everywhere else."

Molly slammed into the headboard. *What the hell is wrong with him?* "Ow!" She rubbed the knot already forming at the base of her skull with her free hand.

"Careful. Don't hurt yourself over me, *gattina*." His eyes gleamed, victorious.

Her body tensed at his voice, and if she was bleeding from clenching the knife beneath her pillow, she couldn't feel it. "*Gattina?*"

His smile deepened...dark and sexual. "Italian for kitten...tiny, small, inconsequential."

He's taunting me. She rolled away from him and onto her feet on the other side of the bed, unbalanced.

He gave her a flat look, eyes taking a moment to register the butcher knife clenched in her white fist. "You want to fight me?" He chortled deep in his throat. "Sweetheart, you don't want to fight me."

Be brave. Her hands didn't get the message though, continuing to shake uncontrollably. She convinced herself it was her rage.

"I bet you don't even know how to use one of those," he said, gesturing leisurely with his hand to the knife. "First, you have to move it—well, first you have to have *muscle* to move it fast enough, which, from my examination of your body earlier, you lack. Immensely. Second—"

"I can move it!" she hollered, slicing the blade up and down. He was getting under her skin, and his satisfied expression told her he knew it.

He clapped mockingly. "Bravo. Well, I'm thrilled we

solved that dilemma. Now let's solve another." He took one large stride and she panicked.

"Don't come any closer." She pointed the knife at him, and he slowed. "I swear, I'll do it."

His eyes flickered over her trembling stance, and he stifled a laugh as his thumb traced his bottom lip. He had a mouth meant for speaking sweet nothings, and he misused it terribly. "You're shaking, *ciccia*."

She scanned his toned stomach, the dark happy trail leading to the band of his slacks, which sat dangerously low, revealing the sharp V of his pelvic bone. Any lower — *Stop it.* When her eyes aligned with his again, a dark humor permeated his grey irises. "I'll stab you. I'm not afraid of you."

"I'd say you have nothing to fear." He tilted his head to the side. "But that'd be a lie." He was in front of her in a blur and she jolted backward, stumbling into her dresser and sending the picture frames full of awkward high school photos to the ground. *God, he's fast!* Now they were toe-to-toe — her barefooted and him in his laced-up Gucci dress shoes. "C'mon, *princess*. Hit me, *ciccia*." Her eyes widened at his burning gaze. *Stop calling me things in Italian, dickhead.* "A little something? Maybe a little bite, no?"

His low laughter rumbled in his chest. "All talk, are we? You can't hurt a thing. You that *soft?* Do you even have a backbone? Or is that, too, made out of Jell-O?"

She couldn't stab him, but she could make him back off.

She pressed the point of the knife to her own throat hard enough that it broke the skin, and she had to suppress a cry of pain.

His playful expression vanished.

"Step back or I'll do it," she said.

A large, strong hand encaged her wrist. "Drop it." Her eyes dug into his, challenging him. When Molly didn't obey, Tensley shoved her against the dresser, prying her fingers away from the knife's base with practiced ease. *Jesus Christ!* It thudded loudly on the wooden floor at the same.

Her heart raced — no weapons, nothing to protect her.

"You won't hurt me because you have a conscience," he said. "A delicate, weak heart. And I have — well, since you rummaged through my stuff, why don't you tell me?"

She swallowed, attempting to analyze his darkened features. Anger and annoyance laced his voice. *Piss off the beast, Molly. Good plan.*

She thought back to his books. "You're heartless."

"And you know what that means?" He lowered his mouth to her ear, hot breath hitting her chilled flesh. "It means I don't give a damn about a hair on your innocent little head."

He straightened, still trapping her with his solid figure. She couldn't look at him. She couldn't look at the monster about to devour her.

"If I could smell fear, I'd say you reeked of it," he said, tone low and smug. "And I hate fighting an unworthy opponent."

No — no! Be strong! The cool sensation stirred behind her eyes, and she knew her power was kicking in.

She peered up at him, her naked, glowing eyes stalling his movements.

"I'm valuable to you. You won't hurt me, because you *need* me," she said firmly.

His hardened features smoothed to an awestruck stare. She breathed shallowly and in a split second, shoved him back. He stumbled, catching his footing before he fell over.

Tensley advanced again, but wouldn't make eye contact.

"Don't," Molly said as sternly as possible. "*No.*"

He folded his arms and cocked a brow. "What's the matter with you? Never been touched by a man before?"

Her entire body flamed. "I-I..." She rubbed her neck where he'd choked her.

Tensley's face twisted oddly as he studied her; he looked genuinely surprised. "You *haven't* been touched by a man before."

She swallowed the large, uncomfortable lump in her throat, distressed beyond measure. *That is none of his goddamn business.*

He clenched and unclenched his fists, stepping back, unable to stop staring at her. She waited for him to mock her, to make fun of her, but it never came. Instead, he turned and threw a book into his suitcase. "Just don't threaten me with self-harm again, capiche?" His voice turned cold, dangerous, and he jerked his head up, dark stark eyes drilling her.

"More rules?" she said, thankful for the space between them. "Fine. My rule: Be scarce around here. Make me forget you exist."

"Fine by me," he drawled, reaching down for his suitcase. As he turned, the bag thrown over his shoulder, he paused. He tossed *The Rosier* back onto her bed. "Here.

I brought this for you. Educate yourself before you try to attack me again."

Molly glowered. "You're not staying here."

"Guestroom. I'd prefer not to sleep with someone who tried to gut me." He smiled smugly at her. "And *darling*, it'll be your death wish if you get rid of me. Remember that."

chapter nine

MOLLY DIDN'T SLEEP for the next two days. Her parents had gone off to their Hampton cottage after Molly again begged them. They said they wanted her to message them any chance she had, but she'd been failing at that.

She went to the museum like a zombie whose only source of living was research, and she didn't see any sign of Tensley. Where he had gone to, she didn't really care, as long as he didn't come back. One morning she'd actually forgotten about him, spending a blissful five minutes walking around until she tripped over his giant, oil-black combat boot where it sat in the middle of the foyer. Her chest had tightened at the unwelcome reminder of her fiancé's presence, and she'd had the niggling notion he'd left it there on purpose.

Molly's eyes strained to read one more page of *The Rosier*. She had a rhythm formed: two pages of demon history and culture, two pages of research on India's art from the sixteenth century for her internship. Balancing both scrambled her mind, and she soon found her hands turning page after page of *The Rosier*.

Why did love matter so much to them? Why did they get ripped out if they developed a full heart? The book didn't help; it was obviously meant for someone from Tensley's world with basic knowledge.

She needed more information, more knowledge to use against him. She needed to know how to play in his world and find a way to destroy the bastard.

Her stomach grumbled.

Maybe food would give her knowledge.

After a good minute of weighing the pros and cons of venturing out of her bedroom, she caved, grabbing *The Rosier* and padding down the stairs into the silent house. Strangely enough, she hadn't seen Tensley even sleeping there, so she wondered if he was staying somewhere else.

Turning into the kitchen, she froze.

Tensley sat on the small breakfast bench, leaned over, elbows relaxed on his thighs, hands hanging between his knees as he heatedly discussed something with Illya, who stood. They both turned, startled by Molly's sudden appearance.

Greeaat. Now my day is ruined.

"Sorry. I didn't think anyone was home," she mumbled, taking a step back.

"This is your house," Illya laughed, glancing down at the book in her hand. "You reading *The Rosier?*"

She nodded. "It's a bit overwhelming; I don't understand a lot of it."

"Well, you can ask us anything about it. We'd love to help," he offered.

Molly opened her mouth, hesitating. She peeked at Tensley's tensed figure. Now was her chance. Be the dumb blonde. Trick them into giving her something she could use against him. "Why are demons heartless?"

Illya blinked and glanced at Tensley.

Tensley sighed, none too thrilled. "I'm going to be late."

For what?

"I just want to understand you," Molly said softly, making sure her voice was pleasant and sweet.

Tensley watched her closely and his jaw clenched, unclenched until he looked away. "Demons don't have what *your kind* call hearts, as we already discussed."

After a good few seconds, Molly figured Tensley was done speaking. She frowned. Maybe she should have batted her lashes, damn it.

Illya cleared his throat. "When we're born, we have half of one. If a demon develops a full heart, Fallen, the Crown Prince of the High Court, will destroy it, and that demon will be reborn without morals or values. They will be worse than before."

Molly scowled. "But why does he do that?" She watched as Tensley grabbed a ruby red apple and tore a violent chunk out of it.

Illya stepped closer, leaning against the counter. "It probably stems from the fact Fallen was in love with a human girl and she ripped his own heart out. He was banished from the gods for interfering with lowly mortals. Hence, he started his own kingdom. Still a touchy subject for him."

Tensley swallowed his food and turned to face her. "He also established a rule that if a demon had a relationship with a human and conceived a child out of wedlock, the unborn child and the mother would be killed."

Her heart sank. "Have demons never heard of birth control or condoms before? That's barbaric."

Tensley laughed, but it was humorless. "Trust me. You don't have to worry about that. We're cursed."

Molly gawked back at him. "Come again?"

"The council of gods, now gone, feared that demons would overpopulate with humans and become unstoppable centuries ago, so they devised a plan to sterilize them from reproducing with humans. The only way to conceive is through affection, which if the demon doesn't stay inside their limits creates a heart, thus condemning the demon anyway. We aren't just going around knocking up humans—not only because it puts *us* in danger, but because it's basically impossible without affection."

"Sex is fine between demons; there are no emotions, no attachments between the two. It's for the sole purpose of either gaining power or exchanging it," Illya said.

Molly watched Tensley's masked expression. What did Tensley desire? Power?

"Fallen also has a rule that a demon male must be married by his twenty-ninth birthday or he will be killed. It's an ancient tradition of cementing the male demon into reproducing in wedlock. Again, the bastard's hung-up on traditions that people are too terrified to fight him on. So our wedding will take place on August fifteenth—not this summer, but the next," Tensley stated calmly.

"What if I don't marry you?" Molly retorted bitterly.

The front door slammed, interrupting what would've assuredly been a venomous response from Tensley. Footsteps thundered against the tile floor of the foyer, and when the kitchen door swung open, Molly's chest caved as the air left her gaping mouth.

September slid into the kitchen, her eyes widening at

the sight of the two demons. She skidded to a halt.

"September," she hissed in warning. "What are you doing here? I told you to stay away!"

"Hey..." Illya began to smile, but September only scowled. His warm smile faded into utter confusion.

"Who the hell are you?" September spat at Illya.

He opened his mouth and blinked, gazing at the vein pulsing on her forehead. "I'm Illya, Tensley's friend."

"Tensley's *friend?*" September barked. "That is *not* the right answer, buddy."

"God, you're loud," Tensley muttered, thrusting his fingers through his soft, thick dark hair. Molly fidgeted with her manicured nails, eying the two of them.

"She's nineteen, *dick,* and she's not interested in marrying a psycho demon," September shot back.

Tensley's gaze swept over to Molly. "Broke a rule *already?* I told you to not to tell anyone what I was."

Molly cringed. *This isn't good...*

September stomped forward, raising a white-knuckled, curled hand. "You really need to leave, or else. *Dick.*"

Molly widened her eyes. "September!"

Tensley unwound himself and stood, looming over September. "Are you threatening me?"

"Do you see any other *dicks* in the room?"

He laughed, lowering his dark eyes. "It's not smart to threaten me. And how did you even get in here?"

"I have a spare key." September shoved his shoulder, and a strange, enigmatic smile washed over Tensley's lips, like he was holding himself back. Molly squared her shoulders. "Actually, funny story, she's not living with you any more," September announced happily. "She's coming back to *our* apartment."

Molly wanted to curl into a ball. "*September.*"

His eyes sharpened at her friend's words, and he turned to look at Molly. "Is that so?"

Molly's head ached as the room spun. All she could see was Tensley ripping a complete stranger's heart out.

"Yeah, it is," September snarled. "So leave her the fuck alone."

His shoulders stiffened, and that was enough for Molly to know he was on the edge of tipping.

Molly tried to step in front of September, but Illya moved faster. "Don't."

Tensley's shoulders relaxed, and he smirked. "You're not worth my time, *dick*," he taunted.

September glowered, gritting her teeth together. Then she attacked, lunging forward and grasping his muscular shoulders. *Oh no.* A terrifying growl left his pursed lips, and within seconds Tensley was in control, deflecting September's hits and sending her sprawling to the tile.

"Don't! Please! Stop!" Molly gripped the back of his shirt and pulled—"Tensley!"—and he stumbled back, turning to face her. *Well, at least my powers worked.*

As soon as his eyes left Molly, she darted to the gasping September on the floor and helped her sit up.

Tensley looked down at them with a wrinkled nose. "You don't understand what's out there, do you? How many damn demons are after you, *thirsty* for you. I'm the only thing keeping them at bay."

Molly raised her chin and swallowed. *Is he serious?*

"He's right," Illya spoke, breaking the glaring contest.

"They've been waiting for another daemon for centuries. They'll be pissed when they hear you've been hidden right under their noses."

"*Dick*," September choked out. Even after wrestling with a demon, she still had the balls to retort.

"You don't want to fuck with me. I'll rip — "

Molly glared coldly, her heart pounding as she faced off with the monster. "Don't you dare speak to her like that."

All heads swung in her direction.

Tensley examined her scowl. "Like *what?*"

She struggled to control her volume. "Like a jackass! Why can't you be like him? Like Illya?" Molly pointed to the blond demon, who was looking September over for injury.

"I can't be like *him*," Tensley spat.

"You can't be nice?" She didn't understand. She didn't understand how they were both demons, but with such different personalities.

"Just fucking drop it." The veins in Tensley's neck throbbed. Hm, she'd struck a weak spot. Maybe that'd be her angle. That'd be her ticket to destroying him.

"Tensley." Illya narrowed his eyes.

Tensley returned the look, then marched out. The front door slammed a moment later.

Illya reached a hand out to September, his eyes soft. "I'm sorry about him. He's just stressed."

"I doubt that," September said, waving Illya's hands away and getting up on her own.

Molly stared in awe at him. How could he be a demon? He was so kind.

"I'll give you two some alone time," he said after a few beats of awkward silence, smiling and walking out.

September groaned when they were alone, leaning against the kitchen counter. "I hate that bastard."

Molly fixed her lopsided sunglasses and glared. "I told you to stay away! He almost hurt you!"

"I'm trying to *help!* You can't do this, Molly."

Molly tapped her fingers against the marble. "What do you suggest I do?"

"You can't deal with this alone. It's not like middle school; these aren't snobby twelve-year-olds we're dealing with. You need to fight back."

"I did! I *did* fight back, and it didn't help!"

September waved her hands. "Okay, okay. So the police obviously can't help with *demons.* Do you know of anything else? Anyone who could help us?"

"No!" Molly thought back to Albert. "Wait..." She dug the piece of paper out of her pocket; she'd kept it on her since meeting Albert three days prior, but wasn't sure why. "This warlock gave me something, but I have no idea what it means."

"Show it to me."

As Molly watched September eye it, she wondered if she could leave the state—just move really far away and change her name. But what about her family? He would attack them. *Slaughter* them.

"Shit, Molly."

"What?"

"I knew this sounded familiar," September whispered, squinting at her phone and the paper. She twisted the screen for Molly to see. "It's a bar in Coney Island. Maybe the guy was trying to help you? Maybe this bar is the answer."

Molly's heart stilled. "Maybe. Maybe they can help."

She wasn't going to run, and she wasn't done fighting. No, the battle against Tensley Knight had just begun.

chapter ten

MOLLY FROZE WHEN she saw the dilapidated building in front of them. It was dark inside, and a few people were lined up, waiting to enter at ten o'clock at night. The place definitely wasn't thriving like Manhattan's bars, but for Coney Island it was all right. Molly had read about the bar their entire trip over, hoping the research might make her feel less nervous about the place.

"C'mon, Mol," September hollered across the street, racing over to hook an arm through Molly's. Loud, heavy music boomed from the structure, and she squinted.

"Shoot the Freak," Molly muttered, reading the faded sign.

"Sounds pleasant, huh?" Molly shot her a glare. "Let's just get inside."

"Remember, if things go sour—"

"We leave, I know. You've been telling me this the last three hours."

They walked to the door, but a guy the size of two

Septembers blocked their way.

"IDs," he demanded, hand outstretched.

The two of them exchanged looks, and September smiled. She took his hand, shook it, and let go. When he gazed down at the money in his palm, he immediately handed it back.

"Hey!" September tried to shove it back into his closed fist.

"Get lost," he snapped.

Just as September huffed and turned, Molly thought over the note.

"Athena?" she whispered.

"I said to leave! Or I'll call the cops!" the doorman yelled.

"Athena?" she repeated, louder.

The man's pockmarked face relaxed. "Go on." He moved aside and opened the door for them.

The bar was busy and hazy with smoke. Molly swore she tasted whiskey in the air, and she had to work to stifle a cough.

"Now what?" September asked, scanning the room.

"I don't know." Molly glanced around, located the bartender, and marched over with September in tow. "Excuse me," she said to the bartender when she'd gotten his attention. "We're looking for someone to help us...with a situation."

"Looking for Cree?" he said, teeth flashing blue in the club's bizarre lighting — not the best look for him.

"Uh, well, if he knows how to get rid of demons..." September tried to laugh it off and Molly spun, her eyes widening.

The bartender stopped wiping down the counter and leaned forward. "How did you get in here?"

Both girls grew rigid.

"Uh…someone referred me," Molly said while wringing her hands.

The man simply stared back, working his mouth as if mulling over whether to toss them out or not. "You'll find Cree sitting over there."

"Well, he was friendly," September murmured as they walked away. "I could feel the hospitality just *oozing* off him."

Then she halted and the two of them stared at a brown-haired man reading over scattered papers. He didn't look much older than the girls but had a strong, rigid posture of a man who had seen and done things most had not. "Hi, are you Cree?"

"Yeah." His steady eyes flickered up and his brow furrowed. "Can I help you? He cracked a nut on the table — *crunch* — and popped it into his pinched mouth.

Molly went to open her mouth, but the sight of someone else stopped her.

Albert, still hidden by his wild beard, stood across the room, sipping a beer.

"Hey?" She turned to see the man had been trying to speak with her, his eyes filled with concern.

"You came." At the sound of Albert's voice, Molly turned to see he had stepped toward her, mouth agape. "I didn't think you'd have the balls."

"You know these girls, Al?" the man asked, his eyes staying trained on Molly.

Albert nodded his head at her. "She's the one the Knight boy was trying to hide."

They know his family?

"I'm sorry about Jackson," Molly said.

Albert's jaw relaxed and he lowered his head. "He was reckless. He was tired of following orders from the men who gave him his paycheck and he wanted out. I wish he had told me what he was planning; I would have talked him down, maybe told him to leave town and lay low for a bit." His fists clenched and Molly swore she saw the glint of tears in his dark eyes before he bowed his head again.

Molly bit her lip, unsure how to act after the silence fell between them.

Cree sat back, folding his thick arms as his eyes slid slowly up Molly's body. "Don't worry Al, I'll make sure those fucking bastards pay dearly." He looked up again, brows thick over his sable-brown eyes. "And your reason for waltzing into my bar would be?"

"You—you deal with..." Molly's eyes flickered to the cross hanging around his thick neck, half-hidden by his plain grey T-shirt. "...demons? With the Knights? You can stop them, right?"

He paused, pinching the bridge of his nose with two fingers. "What's the problem exactly?"

Molly took a shaky breath and sat down. "I'm engaged to him."

Cree's brows lifted, the first display of emotion from him. "Engaged to who?"

She nodded numbly. "To Tensley Knight and I want out. I want to end the contract."

All his attention was hers now, purely, solely hers. "Tensley Knight?"

"Yes. *My fiancé.*"

"The douche," September chimed in.

Cree analyzed Molly's hardened features. "Sit." They did so, Cree watching Molly carefully. "I've heard a lot about his family; they practically run New York City. They're the law. How long have you two...?"

"I was four when they showed up." Molly was afraid to say too much; she wanted to give as little information as possible before she determined if she could trust them.

Cree watched her, tapping his finger slowly against the oak table. "And why did they do that?"

Molly froze, trying to figure out what to say, if anything at all. She glanced at Albert who tilted his head in question at her silence.

Cree's sudden groan snapped her from her thoughts. "*Mierda*! I don't have time for uncertainty, kid. You have three options: trust your *fiancé*, trust me, or leave and figure out your own plan. I'm not keeping you here, I'm not forcing you to tell me anything, but I need to know what I'm getting my guys and myself involved in before I can agree to anything. It's your choice, your decision. Talk or walk."

Molly scowled; it was as if he could read her thoughts. "Why should I trust you?"

"I may be blunt, harsh—but I'm honest. It's not gonna be pretty. You're going to have to do things you won't like, but it all comes down to: what will you do to keep those you love safe?" He jerked his chin at her. "You have a family, right? People you want to protect?"

"He'll use them as weapons," she said, a bite in her tone. "I know, he already has."

He leaned forward and tapped his finger to his chest. "I'm not playing games. I'm telling you straight what's going to happen, when it's going to happen. I've been hunting demons since I was sixteen. I know what I'm doing. We're on the same side here. We have the same end goal. We want him removed from your life."

Molly glanced at September who shrugged. *No help there.*

What choice did she have? She didn't know the first thing about demons or getting out of a contract with one; she couldn't even control her own strength, and Tensley was ruining her life. She couldn't do it on her own. She needed someone with more knowledge, more experience before she faced him. She was desperate, and she'd do anything to get rid of the contract and Tensley.

September tapped her shoulder. "Molly?"

Molly's chest contracted, and she let out a heavy breath. "My ancestors made a deal three hundred years ago with his family."

Cree was silent, a tanned hand cupping his scruffy chin. His deep brown eyes narrowed. "Why?"

She paused again, took another deep breath, and said, "My family possesses...rare eyes."

He tensed his other hand against the wooden table. "Rare eyes?"

Molly slowly reached for her sunglasses, hesitating before she removed them. She blinked, attempting to only give him glimpses of the rare glow.

He gawked openly, lips parted. "You're a daemon."

Albert cursed. "It explains why he was so desperate to hide her. *Shit.*"

She didn't bother to tell them that her powers functioned poorly. If anything, she wanted them to believe she was capable of defending herself at any time.

Cree sat back, watching her intently. She wondered what was going through his head; he definitely seemed to be ruminating on something, planning, maybe. "There's little knowledge about daemons. I do know that your strength relates directly to your eyes — eyes that immobilize demons until you look away. They've often been linked to being demigods. All those myths of demigods have been daemons. I know a lot about their history, though — most of them were either murdered at birth, as their communities believed them to be witches, or they took their own lives due to the strain of being ostracized. Death was their curse and blessing."

Molly's stomach bottomed out, and she shakily put her sunglasses back on. "Right now, my only concern is getting rid of him."

He nodded once. "I'll train you to protect yourself and find a way to break the contract. There's a warlock I know named Lance who's gifted at contracts. He can help us."

Molly stared unblinkingly at him; his harsh stubble, the dark bags under his tired eyes, the scars littering his skin. "So, is this, like, a family job? How did you get into the business?"

"No. My family has nothing to do with the Order of Orion," he said, his shoulders tensing at the turn of conversation. "We hunt demons to protect others, to stop them from harming humans."

Molly knitted her brows. "Then why do you do this? Hunt demons?"

"My sister was murdered by a demon about nine years ago," he said matter-of-factly. "Ever since then, I've been making sure those savages pay."

Her chest tightened at his cool voice. *Good going, genius.* "I'm so sorry."

Cree tapped his finger impatiently, looking back at her. As if he was trying to read her. He stood up, both girls following while Albert stood back. "You live in Manhattan, right?"

"How did you know?" Molly asked, surprised.

His eyes lowered, taking her in from the tips of her cherry-red Kate Spades to the top of her blonde hair, one brow raised. "You dress like one of them. I'll pick you up at the stop on Ninth Avenue, close to Greenwood Cemetery. Nine-thirty sharp tomorrow. If you're late, well, you'll get your ass kicked by one of the others." He smirked at her.

Crap!

Molly wrinkled her forehead. "I can't. I told the museum I would help out later to make up for being late this week."

Cree shook his head. "That's your decision."

Molly bit her lip and squeezed her eyes shut. *Damn it.* "I'll call in sick."

"So there are more of you?" September probed.

Cree seemed to debate whether to answer. "Yep."

"Well, thanks for all the info," Molly quipped.

"Where should I meet you?" September asked, folding her arms.

He stared at her and laughed. "*You're* not coming. It's only her allowed — it's an elite, private order and we don't just let anyone near us. Just go home and rest. Here's my number." He wrote fast on a sheet of paper and tore it off, handing it to her.

Molly furrowed her brow at the messy numbers. "What do I do until then?"

Cree mulled over the question. "Find out what he lacks and what he wants, and make him think he can trust you."

Molly clinched her arms around her waist; it was drafty in the bar, and in her mind.

"Alrighty then," September said, tugging Molly away from Cree and his paper-strewn table.

She jogged through the lamplight outside to follow after September.

"So do you have any idea what Tensley lacks?" September asked as they strolled through the empty streets, looking for their bus stop. "Besides basic human decency, anyway."

"Affection," she muttered through gritted teeth. "He definitely lacks affection from anyone."

She would have to be tender with the demon, to convince him to trust her, and the last thing she wanted to be with Tensley Knight was tender.

chapter eleven

TENSLEY DODGED AGAIN and let out an angry sigh. *Damn it.*

Illya rolled up his sleeves and fixed his stance, smirking. "C'mon, Tensley."

Tensley threw his upper body forward and the fight began again, the sounds of flesh hitting solid flesh filling the room.

"Whoa!" Illya jumped as Tensley swung an arm out, just missing his eardrum. "Man, you need to relax."

Tensley growled, twisting to flip Illya over his shoulder, and slammed the blond demon flat onto the mat.

Tensley drew back, panting, before putting his hand out to Illya. "Sorry."

Once Illya was up, Tensley walked away, fetching his glass of water.

Illya coughed, still winded from Tensley's tackle. "You okay, man? You seem a bit...tense today."

"I'm fine." Tensley took a large gulp of water. Tugging his fingers through his wet hair, he took another gulp.

Illya eyed him. "How's Molly?"

Tensley's whole body tensed, and he thought of breaking the glass in his fist. "Fucking great." He slammed the glass onto the table. "She won't even let me near her with a ten-foot pole—how the hell am I supposed to protect her?"

"I'm sure your bitter attitude and the fact you killed that warlock in front of her aren't exactly pleading your case." Illya walked over and placed a hand on the table. "Well, she's not like the women from our society. The others knew who you were. They knew your background, your family, and your status. She isn't one of us. She's practically human, and you know you have to be gentle with her. If anything," Illya said, airing out his shirt by shaking it, "she's afraid of you."

Tensley thought back to when she had asked him why he couldn't be like Illya. He hated how much that comment stung. As a kid, he had *tried* to be like Illya. That fucking backfired with a heavy hand, resulting in a scolding from his parents for showing any form of weakness. Although Illya and he were both demons, they were in completely different situations. Tensley lifted his shirt over his drenched head and threw it to the side.

The two of them began to walk through Tensley's penthouse out onto the luxurious porch, surrounded by a plethora of sweet-smelling flowers and plants.

"If I don't mark her, the others are going to find out she exists," Tensley snapped. "The moment I take off that charmed ring for the engagement one, the invisibility will be gone completely. *Everyone* will find her. Not that it's doing much good now, anyway. But if I don't give her our family ring soon, Father will know I haven't done anything to her yet."

Illya sighed, his damp blond locks falling onto his forehead as they leaned against the iron railing, gazing at the landscape of Manhattan — the blaring cars, shining curves of steel, and dots of foliage that offered shades of green amongst the stone. "You'll just have to get her to trust you."

"So fake it?" Tensley cocked a brow.

"Or you could actually be a decent guy and build something," Illya said.

"I've seduced her or tried to," he muttered, rubbing his forehead hard. "To cooperate."

Illya frowned. "You didn't…"

"So I used my pheromones to be drawn to me, no real harm done," he spat, glaring at Central Park in the distance. "At least she's attractive."

"She definitely is. But maybe if you take her out for dinner, woo her, find out what she likes, make her like you without sending off pheromones to *sway* her, you'd have better luck?"

Tensley snarled in his throat. "A date," he huffed, rubbing his temples.

"I could even take that friend of hers out, too," Illya said, studying a scar on his left hand.

Tensley's eyes narrowed at his so-called friend. *I'll be fucking damned.* "You mean the big-mouthed broad?" Illya smiled sheepishly, and Tensley threw a hand up in frustration. "You gotta be kidding me! She's a bitch. You saw what she did. Tried to wring me by the neck!" *So much for loyalty.*

"She was protecting her friend from you," Illya said. "And no, I wasn't thinking of her that way. I was just trying to help you out."

Tensley was silent as he thought of taking his fiancée on a date. He didn't want to, but if he was able to protect her sooner, it was better than using his tactics again and being returned to his regular life. "Fine. Meet me at that Italian restaurant we both like—on Madison Avenue by that crappy sushi place. I'm going back to the daemon's house to take a shower there. Give the guys on watch duty a break."

"How many do you have watching over the house?"

"Three during the day, four at night." Foot soldiers of the Scorpios were assigned to look after the house—and Tensley would personally deal with them if they didn't keep their mouths shut.

Tensley left shortly after. Jogging shirtless through the streets of New York City, he made his way back to the dreadful townhouse.

The Darlings lived in the Upper East Side of Manhattan. They were well off—not as well off as *his* family, but still above average. The street was lined with high-class townhouses, with hers being the only one built in white brick. It still looked the same as the first time he'd seen it, fourteen years before.

The foyer was nice—if you loved floral designs and a purple-vomit color. God, Mr. Darling was whipped. It had definitely been decorated by a woman, and probably a drunken one. He had noted the last few days her parents hadn't been home and he shook his head at the lack of loyalty. His family lived by it, survived by it.

Tensley made his way up the elegant staircase and down the hallway. Light was seeping from underneath Molly's bedroom door, and he frowned. He opened the door but found no one. His eyes darted to the closed door of the bathroom, and he heard the water running. *Showering?* Her soft flesh came to mind, the few freckles that dotted her collarbone, her wavy blonde hair wet and slick down her back.

He heard a faint sob and glanced at the closed door. *She's crying?*

An ache throbbed deep in his core and he rolled his shoulders. He knew whatever she was crying about led back to him. He'd give anything to be Illya in that moment.

Slowly, he walked around the bedroom, examining her items. He fell onto the bed, but the pillow wasn't soft. He reached underneath and pulled out the knife she had threatened him with. He smirked and felt the sharp tip with his thumb.

The bathroom door opened, and Tensley glanced up, surprised to see so much exposed, creamy skin. A white towel hugged Molly's generous curves, and her skin glistened, wet and smooth. Her face went red; even her button nose turned rosy.

"What are you doing?" Molly's naked eyes widened when she saw the knife in his hands.

Tensley stuffed the knife back under the pillow and patted it for good measure. "You might want to hurry up; we're going out tonight."

Molly's mouth unhinged, then she screwed it shut as her brows furrowed. "We are?"

"September and Illya are coming, too."

"Oh god." She rubbed at her wide forehead with a dainty hand. Her long, pale locks were already waving around her heart-shaped face, and her lips were plump and bright red—Tensley looked away instantly when he recognized he was gawking far too much. Looking at her body was fine, but memorizing her features wasn't.

Too intimate.

Too personal.

"I need to shower." He pushed himself up and strolled toward the guest bathroom.

It didn't take long for him to get freshened up with a shower, a bit of cologne, and an understated outfit of black slacks and a pristine dress shirt. When he entered the bedroom again, Molly was sitting up on her bed, her trench coat tied tightly around her waist, emphasizing her hourglass shape and wrung her hands in her lap.

"Plotting against me?" he said. Molly flinched, rare daemon eyes wide. He hesitated, his body slowing from seeing her without her sunglasses. He sat down beside the defenseless thing, and she edged back. *God, she really is terrified of me.*

Her phone beeped, and before she could reach it, he grasped it from behind them. "Hey!" she shouted, perturbed.

SEPTEMBER
5:42 P.M.
You're going to have to hold me back from strangling him.

Tensley laughed and glanced up from the phone. Molly's normally flushed face grew bloodless. "What is this about?"

"She really doesn't like you," she muttered.

He put her phone down. "Why are you friends with her?"

Molly's eyes caught his, and he swore they were glistening. Then her lashes dropped, lying on her cheeks as they regained their rosiness. "September was the only one who accepted me when we were kids. She's my best friend. When everyone made fun of me, she told them to stop. She liked me for *me*."

"Then why are you friends with that Stella girl?"

She stilled and frowned at him. "How do you know Stella?"

He thumbed his lip. "I did my research."

Her mouth twisted ruefully, but she continued. "My parents thought they were protecting me — forcing us to be friends. They thought Stella would protect me."

One thing I fucking understand. His parents had forced him to be friends with so many demons he didn't care for — Illya was the only one he could truly call his friend. In their society, intermingling with humans was looked down upon, and incubi families of similar ranking were expected to socialize.

"No one wanted to play with me in preschool. All the kids were scared of me; they threw snowballs at me. Rocks. Sticks. You name it, they threw it," Molly said with an offhanded laugh.

He could hear the pain there, though, and an incredibly awkward feeling came over him. He felt *bad*.

"September saw through all of this; she saw me." Her eyes flashed up again, and there was a hardness in her gaze. He also didn't find it as immobilizing as before. *From exposure, from the little amount of intimacy they exchanged.* Once he marked her, he'd be immune from merging their energies.

Her fingers caught his tie, and he froze, startled by her brave actions as she tightened the fabric around his neck. "If anything happened to her, I don't know what I would do."

So you wanna play "who's in charge", sweetheart?

His lips quirked, and he touched both her hands. "Is that a threat, Ms. Darling?" He'd show her who was in charge; he'd throw her on the bed and devour her—pleasurably, of course. His fingertips skimmed the hollow of her wrist. "Because I expect people who make threats to follow through."

Her hands retreated. "Do I *look* like a threat?"

He half-smiled. She had no idea how much of a threat she actually was to him. How, if he let her in, she could control him, just like that Spanish seductress had controlled his brother.

"Why are you friends with Illya?" Molly asked suddenly.

He stared for a few seconds, guarding his features. "It just happened."

She narrowed her eyes. "*How*, though? He seems... different from you."

"Big Mouth is definitely your opposite."

"Thanks for opening up," she murmured, harshly.

He stiffened, feeling the awkward tension growing between them again and regretting it. "I have something to give you," he told her, reaching into his pocket.

Molly twisted around, watching him carefully as he produced a black velvet box.

She knitted her manicured brows and wrinkled her nose. "What is it?"

He snickered, opened it, and then handed it to her.

"A ring?" She gently took it and squinted.

"My family engagement ring. I thought it made sense to give it to you now," he said, trying to make his voice as emotionless as possible.

A small part of him hoped for a "thank you, Tensley," or a genuine smile of approval, but neither came as he noted how she simply gawked at it. A big, elegant black diamond caged in gold trim sat in her palm. It had been in his family for over seven hundred years, a symbol of the Scorpios. The family ring would be a symbol that she belonged to his family, to him. If any demon had a problem or desired Molly themselves, they would have to appeal to the Princes and Fallen.

Tensley looked down at the ring still on her thin finger, and when he touched her hand, she flinched.

Carefully, he removed it, sliding it over her creamy flesh and stuffing it in his pocket.

"You got it off…" She gawked at her bare finger.

"Anyone in my family can remove it. Plus, it's worthless now if no warlocks can charm it again." He sighed and held up the engagement ring. "Put it on."

"Do I have a choice?" As much as her steely voice startled him, it was more so the faint tremble that froze his limbs.

No. But neither do I.

Her hands shook as she slid the new ring on.

He didn't know why he felt hurt. *Irritated.* He expected more from her. He expected her to squeal and thank him. It was an honor to wear the Scorpios ring, and she didn't even show a hint of happiness. Evelyn would have screamed while Molly didn't say a word.

His blood boiled.

"Hurry up. We don't have all night. *Up.*" Tensley gripped Molly's elbow and lifted her to her feet, marching them through the room.

They were silent as they strolled outside, neither of them touching. He put his hands firmly in his pockets and stared straight ahead, ignoring her. He didn't understand why he was angry. He just was.

She'd put those damn sunglasses on again. He ground his teeth and pulled her to a halt. "You don't need to wear those all the time."

She jerked her arm out of his grip. "I feel more comfortable with them on."

"One night." He lifted a finger for emphasis.

"Please don't." Her voice was soft, but no less impactful. He didn't need to see her eyes to gauge her mental state— her tone was wobbly and strained.

"One night. That's it."

Slowly, her hand reached for the glasses and slipped them off. She tucked them into her coat and turned away.

He battled himself, but then remembered his game plan— *make her trust you.* No using his seduction to win her over, no using his pheromones, just him and her.

Tensley grasped her bicep gently and spun her around. "You don't hide your weakness. You show it off and pretend it's nothing. Then one day, you'll forget it ever *was* a weakness."

She shakily took a breath. "Do you have a weakness?"

"Everyone does, sweetheart."

"I think you lied to me," she mumbled as they turned up another street.

Tensley's brows wrinkled. "Oh?"

"You're pretending to be a wolf."

"And?"

Her eyes finally drilled into his, so steady and soft that the air deflated from his lungs. "But you won't bite me." She rose to her tiptoes and pressed a feather-light kiss against his scruffy jawbone, and the touch of power pulsed smoothly through his veins.

She had no idea.

I am the wolf. And I will fucking bite.

Hard.

He found himself leaning into her touch, but as she escaped his body, she grinned knowingly.

Don't trust her. Don't. Trust. Her.

He was beginning to lose confidence in his abilities to do that.

chapter twelve

TENSLEY FLEXED HIS fingers. His nerves had been hot-wired by the blonde vixen in front of him, and once he saw the Italian restaurant, Vincent's, ahead, he reined in his emotions. The front of Vincent's had a seating section outside, littered with black iron chairs and white tablecloths thrown over the small tables. Candles flickered on each table intimately.

The maître d', dressed all in black, nervously exchanged glances with Tensley and Molly at the entrance. "Mr. — Mr. Knight, welcome! Wonderful for you and your beautiful date to join us tonight."

Tensley pulled Molly's hand to rest on his forearm — she didn't resist, and the warmth from her palm shot strength up his bicep. The maître d' anxiously showed them to their table. The staff knew who he was, and that if they kept him waiting, they were in trouble.

Of course, they were seated in a secluded booth with a dozen red roses in the center.

Before Molly sat down, she rolled off her trench coat,

and he groaned when he saw her dress. The black satin hugged her curves, flaring mid-thigh, and the sweetheart neckline plunged dangerously low, exposing her supple breasts; she was a walking threat to his every fucking cell.

He painfully cleared his throat, begging himself for composure, and angrily sat down, fingers restlessly tapping against his thigh. He readjusted himself beneath his pants.

Keep your distance, daemon. You're dangerous to me.

All he had to do was remember his brother's vicious face and heavy fist from years ago, all caused by that human seductress, and he collected any softness, any kindness in him and replaced it with an icy detachment.

The male waiter made no qualms about eye-fucking Molly every time he came over, but she was oblivious, or pretended to be. Tensley cracked his neck in irritation. *Idiot must be new.* His fingers curled into his palm.

Molly looked over his shoulder at the street. "I wonder where September and Illya are…"

He had *almost* forgotten they were coming.

They sat across from each other, and Tensley watched her: head bowed, trained on the candle centered on the table. She was bewitched by the flickering swish of the flame, and he was bewitched by her. The smell of wax burning and the clatter of silverware and brassy laughter turned his heightened gifts into sensory overload.

Say something, damn it.

"Illya and I are nothing alike." His hoarse voice bled into what he'd imagined was peaceful quietness for her, not sensory overload. He leaned back as she looked up.

Her brows lifted. "What?"

He scowled, curling his hands and instantly unrolling them again. "Because his family is low in the hierarchy, unlike the Knight bloodline. Our family comes from Duke Sallos, ruling over thirty legions of demons. Illya can live like you, unwatched. Me, I have too many eyes on me at all times."

Her body stiffened. "Why though? What makes him different?"

"Illya was born from the union of a low-class and high-class demon. His mother believed she *adored* his father and betrayed her family and her bloodline to marry him. His father, however, was a low-class servant, desperate for power and money. He was not recognized in the High Court, and when there is no recognition, demons are punished with the surname Black. She married into that name. He charmed her, he seduced her meek character, and before Illya was even born, he left them." Each word dripped with bitterness, and he stared at the flame slowly devouring the candlestick, drops of wax rolling down its spine. "Illya was born as nothing. In court, he does not have a name. Only Black — exiled, forgotten Black." He transferred his stare to her.

Molly's nose scrunched adorably. "Why would they do something like that?"

"Because my world's focus is on hierarchy and power, and how pure your blood is. My father told the story as a caution tale for us as children." He blew out a harsh breath, the flame disappearing for a second. "And if anything happened to Illya..." Just the thought of someone harming Illya set his blood aflame, much hotter than the candle.

Molly's hand slid across the table and touched his

fingertips. "I know." His hand stilled, and he couldn't look away from her big, glossy eyes, a faint tremble in her thick, crimson bottom lip...as if she understood him.

"Mr. Knight."

Tensley's hand jerked back, instinctually pulling a knife with it and underneath the table. It was instinctual because he knew that voice—it was the voice of a murderer. He turned to face the red-haired beast. "Duke Abaddon."

Abaddon flashed his teeth. "I see we both discovered this delicious restaurant." His beady eyes transferred to Molly's bowed head. *Shit. Her eyes.* "And looks like you have a delicious date, as well." The duke reached out his hand to shake hers, but she didn't move. At the rejection, his hand fell, and he spoke to Tensley lowly, but his eyes didn't leave her. "I didn't know you cared for *humans.*"

Tensley's hand clenched the knife underneath the table. "I *don't.*"

Abaddon's focus was entirely on Molly, and the longer he stared, the more his demeanor changed to one of curiosity and suspicion—like he sensed what she was, like he was trying to pinpoint her rare essence in his mind.

Tensley leaned back, flicked his wine glass so it chimed, and cleared his throat. "Excuse us."

Abaddon nodded absentmindedly. "Of course. Enjoy your dinner." He gave Molly one last glance and turned to go back to his seat somewhere in the restaurant.

Tensley loosened his grip on the knife, but it tensed when another, much more *annoying* voice called out.

"Sorry we're late! Mr. I-Know-My-Way-Around-The-Subway got us a bit lost," September hollered from the road.

September's hair was up in a weird, messy bun with ribbons swirling out, and Tensley saw Illya smiling behind the girl. They continued to exchange genuine smiles at each other, and Tensley got the distinct sense that it had all been a setup on Illya's part so he could hook up with September. Illya sat down next to him, and September hugged Molly before removing her coat. Once she sat down, she gave Tensley a hard look.

He watched the way Molly ordered: with a soft voice, so the waiter — *damn him* — had to lean in close; how she talked with her hands, as if she was making the goat cheese, tomato sauce, mushrooms, and green peppers pizza herself; how her face genuinely lit up for the first time since he'd been reunited with her; the sheer joy she displayed when it came to discussing her favorite dish.

Note to self on her favorite type of pizza.

As the night went on, the conversation died out. A new violinist who had no idea who Tensley was came to their table, but he slammed money into his hand to leave them the fuck alone. He didn't want her to get the wrong idea: this was purely civil, to prove even a beast could be civilized.

He could feel eyes on him. He turned, hoping to catch Molly watching him, but it was only September, and she wasn't happy. Her nostrils flared unattractively, and Tensley wondered what Illya saw in her.

The light-haired demon loosened his collar, sweating buckets. "So…" Illya tapped his finger.

"Your accent — what is it exactly?" Molly leaned forward, cupping her chin with one hand.

Illya patted the side of his mouth with his napkin

before responding. "It's Russian. I grew up there until I was nine. My mother and I moved here together."

"Where's your father?" September asked through a mouthful of meatballs. Tensley clenched his fist.

"September," Molly whispered, her eyes conveying an unspoken message.

Illya's shoulders tensed, but his face still held that genial smile. "He was never my father. It was only my mother and I."

September abruptly stopped chewing, staring at Illya's profile as he continued to cut his steak.

"My mom left me and my dad, too. She's living somewhere on the west coast. She enjoyed the single life too much to *settle down*," September added. Illya stared thoughtfully at her. "We don't need those kinds of people." September raised her flute of red wine and turned to face Illya. "A toast to us."

Without a moment's pause, Illya's large hand wrapped around his own flute, and he clicked it to hers.

"To us," Illya murmured as he brought the flute to his lips.

September threw the drink back unceremoniously, her face twisting in disgust afterward. "Blech. I don't really like wine, but it's alcohol, so whatever."

Illya's gazed over the glass at September as he sipped his wine from the bottle Tensley had chosen.

"Do you miss it?" Molly's gentle cadence startled Tensley, and he shifted in his seat to face her. She was focused on Illya's confused expression. "Russia?"

Illya pondered the question, wetting his lips and setting down his drink. "No; I made my own family here in America. The arrogant bastard across from you is sufficient enough." Illya cocked his head toward Tensley, and they exchanged brotherly grins.

Molly studied them, then honed in on Tensley. When she smiled, dimples appeared, and his mouth grew dry. He wasn't used to her tender looks.

Too sweet. Not like the looks Evelyn gave him.

Sweeter and deadlier; addictive.

Fuck me.

"We should go dancing," September suggested, perking up, probably from the booze.

Illya nodded. Tensley groaned, shifting as he rested his cheek on his fisted hand.

Molly eyed him. "Maybe not tonight."

"Oh c'mon, it'll be fun," September said. She took Molly's hand and stood up, rushing away. "You've got the bill, right Tensley?" she yelled over her shoulder as they walked through the patio's gate.

"Yep. I sure do," Tensley grumbled, ignoring Illya's protests. The girls strolled ahead of them, giggling about something stupid, Tensley was sure. He was mesmerized by the way Molly's hips swung, the way her toned legs looked in those nude pumps, but it wasn't until she glanced briefly over her shoulder, biting that fucking blood-red lip, those doe eyes fluttering to meet his lustful gaze, that he knew she wanted to play.

He did, too.

chapter thirteen

SWEATY BODIES FILLED the dark club, and Molly fidgeted with her hair as she eyed the packed dance floor. People were grinding everywhere, and the more she walked, the stickier the floor became. They'd had no problems getting in once Tensley spoke to the bouncer, but Molly didn't really see the appeal of the place now that she was inside.

The music's vibration pounded in time with her heartbeat, and she watched as September wove her way through the crowd with Illya, leaving her alone next to Tensley.

The demon was quiet, and she could just make out his pinched mouth and the hard planes of his cheekbones through the darkness.

He suddenly hissed in pain, gripping his forearm under his shirt.

"Are you all right?" Molly asked, reaching out with a tentative hand.

He deflected her touch. "I need to make a call."

With that he left, shouldering his way through the crowd of intoxicated clubbers. Molly sighed and beelined for the bar, asking the nearest server for a glass of water. She checked her phone for any messages from her parents, but saw none, shoulders slouching. When she turned with her drink to gaze at the chaos, she saw Cree under a spotlight in the corner.

Molly's entire body froze at the sight of him. *What is he doing here?*

He motioned her over, and she weaved around the gauntlet of sweaty bodies.

"What's going on?" she said once she'd made it.

He snatched her arm and pushed her toward the bathroom. "In."

"Um, this is the girls' washroom — hey! What are you doing?" He slid both of them into the nearest stall, ignoring the shouts of several angry women waiting in line. "How did you know I was here?"

"We followed you," he said, like it was an utterly normal admission.

"What?"

"You and the other three. As a precaution."

"You stalked me?"

"Here." He handed her a small bottle and she reached for it, squinting at the gold liquid inside. "It's a special poison that affects demons, called golden fleece; the Greeks used it to poison them. They named it after the tale of Jason's quest to get the golden fleece, so that he might become rightful king. It's scentless to them. It knocks them out for about eighteen hours; sometimes it even kills them."

She fumbled with the bottle at the mention of killing. "And why do I need this?"

"You're gonna use it on Tensley."

She swallowed. She stared at the dagger he pulled from his back pocket and looked back up at him. "Stab him?" *I'm a fucking student studying history, not a trained killer!*

"The blade's laced with an herb that penetrates the demon's skin and deteriorates over many hours, days even, to kill them. Not to mention it drives them insane with hallucinations, fever, vomiting, and no control over their bowel movements. Often they'll commit suicide just to end the pain."

Molly recalled the look shared between Illya and Tensley at dinner; it had been loving, genuine. "No, I don't want to kill him," she said, voice rushed. "Just end the contract."

He frowned. "The only way you are gonna get rid of him is if you kill him. He's a demon; even if we can get him to call off the arrangement for the time being, he'll come after you again. Demons don't tolerate weakness or mistakes, and he'd have committed both by not going through with things."

She stared at the dagger. It curved, almost as if curling into itself. "Yeah," she said. "He probably would come after me." She took the dagger with her empty hand, and he roughly patted her shoulder.

He gestured with his thumb to the door. "There are more demons here, about seven." Her heart stopped. *Illya.* "The others are gonna deal with them. Just concentrate on Tensley, and I'll finish him off if you're not up to it."

Molly's brows lifted. "Others?"

"A few hunters came with me, for backup."

She analyzed his firm features and when she couldn't read him completely, she sighed. "Why are you helping me? What are you getting out of this?"

Cree lifted his chin and for the first time since she'd met him, he appeared soft. "I'd never turn down someone who needed help, especially against those bastards. You don't deserve what he's putting you through."

Relief flooded her, but a tiny pebble of guilt also itched within her chest. "I'll give you a signal when I've done it, okay? Don't rush me."

"Fine. Now, hide this." He took the dagger and shoved it into her small purse, crushing a few tampons and her lipstick. She clenched the small bottle in her hand and the two of them regarded each other. "Don't be afraid, okay? We've got your back." He left the stall and Molly closed it, standing there in the tiny square as drunken, girlish conversations from the sink area drifted on the air.

She thought of everything Tensley had said and done to her.

He's heartless. This'll be easy.

Molly marched out onto the dance floor; she wanted to warn September to get Illya out of there. He didn't deserve what Cree and his hunters had planned.

"You disappeared," a silky voice said behind her. She spun, the sweat-laden air catching in her throat.

Tensley.

"I had to go to the bathroom." She fidgeted with her purse and it fell to the ground, a few tampons tumbling out. Before she could even register what had happened,

Tensley bent down and gathered them up in one swift motion.

"Here," he said, handing it over.

If the dagger had fallen out, she would have been screwed. His eyes were soft and dark and — *no*. No. *He may be in the form of a man, but he's not a man. He's a monster, a demon, a beast.*

"Do you wanna get something to drink? Let's get something to drink," she insisted, taking his arm.

He dragged his feet at first but eventually followed with a scowl settled between his dark brows. When they got to the bar, she gripped the counter and tried to control the adrenaline traveling through her limbs, making them unstable.

She wiped her forehead with the back of her hand. "It's hot in here; don't you think it's hot in here?"

He narrowed his eyes.

Sweat gathered between her breasts, and she swiped her fingertips across the wetness. *Ew.*

"Here." Her eyes darted to Tensley holding a napkin, his lips a tight line. His hand pressed the napkin above the curve of her breasts and he stroked it, soaking up the sweat.

"What will it be?" the man behind the counter asked.

Molly jerked back, Tensley's hand falling from her skin. Her lips parted but nothing came out.

"One rum and diet coke, and give me your top-shelf whiskey, neat," Tensley said as he crumpled the napkin in his hand. His gaze held a fierce fire, the air refusing to cool between them.

She cupped her cheek, wishing the blush would

vanish. She shouldn't have let him touch her like that. *Damn it.* She was supposed to be poisoning him.

His forehead wrinkled more. "You feeling okay?"

"Yeah, just really hot."

The drinks arrived, and she stared at his, dark and oak-scented in the clear glass. She clenched hers and took a big gulp. It burned, but it numbed her panicked nerves.

"Easy," he cautioned, his two fingers skimming her wrist. A spark flooded through her and she gawked at his long fingers. *It's just two fingers. Imagine his entire hand on your – shut up!* The small bottle of poison was still clenched in her other fist.

"Can I try some of yours?" she asked, unable to make eye contact. If she did, it would play with her mind. Without a word, he handed it to her.

Tensley watched her intently, so Molly jumped at the next song that came on.

"Ooh, I love DJ Hale!" she cooed, turning full circle away from him, popping the cap open, and tipping the minuscule bottle of poison into his tumbler as she spun.

A drop sloshed over the side and onto her skin as she pretended to sway to the music, and for a moment she wondered if it might sizzle there. Her gasp was audible, and Tensley reached for her shoulder.

"Are you *sure* you're okay?"

"Um, yeah, sorry, just spilled a bit. Here." Molly handed the glass back with a fumbling hand.

"So you work at a museum?"

She glanced at him and then the untouched drink. She fidgeted with her purse. "As an intern."

He nodded. "And do you like it?"

"I love it." She smiled. "Actually, they're letting me help design an entire exhibit with one of the curators. It's not a very big exhibit, but it's still *amazing*." After a moment of silence, her giddiness faded and she chanced a look up at him. His eyes hadn't left hers.

Focus Molly!

"Why are you looking at me like that?" Molly asked, her eyes flitting from Tensley's broad forehead and grey eyes like a butterfly debating where it should land.

"Your eyes. They're just…they're incredible."

The rawness of Tensley's voice made something stir within Molly — something she'd been doing her best to keep buried for the better part of fifteen years, since he'd walked into her life as a shadow, a boy with a haunted face and those giant grey eyes.

But the Tensley who'd shown up a week ago was *not* the Tensley she remembered. No. Far from it. But this tone, this expression of his, so authentic and *vulnerable*…

No one had ever said her eyes were incredible.

He lifted the glass off the bar, condensation leaving a darkened ring on the wood. Her breathing was loud in her ears, and a voice screamed inside her brain.

She wasn't like him. She wasn't evil.

She wasn't heartless.

He brought the drink to his lips, but she smacked his wrist, spilling its entirety onto his shirt and slacks.

"*Fuck.*" He slammed the glass down and roughly wiped his drenched clothes.

She reached for a napkin and rubbed it over his chest and down to his pelvis. "Sorry — sorry, I'm so sorry."

For everything.

"Don't," he commanded, pushing her hand away with irritation.

Molly gazed up at the balcony in the distance, where Cree was watching them. *Do I wave now?* She thought back to what Cree had said: that her eyes would immobilize demons. If she could do that to Tensley...

She grabbed Tensley's hand again, and the anger spread like wildfire over his features.

"Do you not speak English, *daemon?* Are you fuc—"

Her eyes aligned with his just as she willed the cool sensation to spread, and he went rigid, gawking at her eyes. She steadied her breathing, noting that his hands went limp at his sides.

It works...

Holy shit, it works!

She yanked at him again and placed his palm on her hipbone.

His face softened.

"Dance with me," she said softly.

His fingers moved across the satin fabric of her dress, but the electricity from his touch made it feel like no clothing separated them. She waited for him to make a witty quip, a sexual innuendo, but his mouth was still slack and his eyes remained only eager. *Thank you, powers.* Turning, she led the way, sensing several sets of demon-hunter eyes watching her.

Once they were trapped in the dense, sweltering crowd, she pressed her entire frame against his strong length and wrapped her arms securely around his neck. Her eyes flickered past him, searching for Cree or any of the other hunters approaching. Fear swarmed her chest. How would she be able to tell who was a hunter or not? She needed to warn Illya and September while keeping Tensley safe at the same time. If she told Tensley about the hunters, he would react badly, powers or not. *Very* badly.

Tensley stiffened, sensing the danger, but she pressed closer and did something she knew she would regret. She could only think of one way to convince him to stay attached to her, however, and a deeper, carnal desire cemented her movements.

She wanted to taste him.

Her lips brushed his neck, and he froze. His hands raked along her sides, pulling her flush against him. A wave of heat pooled between them.

"Why the sudden change?" His husky, breathless voice startled her. She moaned a response, her breasts heaving against him.

He placed his leg between her thighs, and she gasped lightly at feeling his arousal. His muscles tensed, his fingertips digging into her hips — she could feel his energy growing. Lights flashed constantly, quick and bright, and their bodies meshed together.

She scanned the crowd.

Cree was walking, looking at her. His mouth moved, and he brushed another guy's shoulder. He handed the other man something thin and shiny. A weapon.

No, no, she couldn't kill Tensley.

"Let's go find the others and get out of here," she shouted into Tensley's ear over the booming bass. When he shifted, her lips brushed his earlobe. With a pounding chest, she evaded his touch and weaved through the crowd.

"They're over there," he told her, leaning in close so his own lips briefly skimmed her ear and blew strands of her hair around. She swallowed a moan.

September was laughing, and Illya wore a simple smile, unable to take his eyes away from her as she swayed to the music. His hands sat nicely on her sides — not too low and not too high.

Respectful.

September noticed them first. "Hey — !" Molly gripped her by the hand and dragged her and Illya toward the exit, corralling Tensley as well.

"I don't feel well!" Molly explained, and all three of them spilled out into the night without further question.

"He's here," Molly hissed to September, clumsily putting her sunglasses back on once she'd put a decent distance between them and the demons. "Cree wanted to kill him. He wanted me to do it *at that moment.*" She kept double-checking down various alleys to ensure Cree wasn't in their wake with his buddies.

September smirked. "Uh, duh."

"I wanted to get rid of... I didn't want someone's blood on my hands, or his hands, or *anyone's* hands. No more bloodshed!"

September shrugged. "The blood will have to be on someone's hands. He *is* a hunter...what did you expect? Peace meetings?"

"He gave me a dagger."

"He did what?"

"Ugh," Molly huffed, shaking her head. "How did he even find me?"

"Stalker one-oh-one?"

"Sarcasm is not wanted right now." Molly folded her arms. "He was going to kill Illya too if I didn't get him out of there."

That caught September's attention. She kept her voice low, glancing back at Tensley and Illya as they chattered. "Cree's gonna figure this out. He'll stop it; I know he will—hopefully without any more threats to innocent guys like Illya, though."

"I know," Molly nodded. "Cree's extreme. I can't deal with any more extreme people, demon fiancés included." She pushed her damn hormones to the side, renewing her focus on getting out of the contract. The desire settling in the pit of her belly scared her.

He's heartless. Just remember that.

Heartless.

chapter fourteen

TENSLEY STUDIED THE scene before him. Soft whispers were magnified by his enhanced hearing, but he couldn't make out all the words. *Something about "insane."* September wrapped her abnormally long, thin arms around Molly, engulfing the seductive blonde.

"She's pretty," Illya noted.

Tensley gave him a sour look. "Big Mouth?"

Illya laughed and hit Tensley's back. Hard. A hollow thud echoed there. "Yes, she is, but that's not who I was referring to. I meant *Molly*. Kind of sexy, actually."

Tensley eyed her silhouette, steadying his breathing and tilting his head. Her kisses still clung to his skin. His hands already felt extremely powerful as he stretched them, electrified by those small acts of intimacy. *God, they weren't fucking joking around about how powerful daemons were.*

"She kissed my neck."

Illya eyes widened. "She did?"

He nodded. "She was acting strange."

But god, it turned him on and his beast, his demon side. Then she left, drifting through the crowd of horny humans, the lust still evident in his briefs — the frustration, too. It led to one of two paths for demons: violence or sex.

September finally let go of Molly and walked toward them.

"Night, Tensley." September chuckled, and out of nowhere she embraced him like an old friend. He recoiled, so she leaned in closer. "If you do anything to *her*, I'll personally stalk your family, murder them, and then bury them in an airtight chamber so that if they come back to life, they'll have no chance of surviving the second time. I mean it."

He balled his hands into tight fists.

He wanted to snap her neck for a comment like that, but Tensley knew it would do more harm than good with two special eyes watching from a few feet away. Plus, they were in public. "I'd watch your back, September. Molly wouldn't want her best friend to get in a horrible accident, now would she?" He breathed heavily, tightening his grip on September's forearms. "Her only friend who accepted her. The only friend she has." September shivered and pushed away, and he chuckled. "Night, Big Mouth."

Illya gave him a disappointed look before jogging after September into the night.

Once their friends' forms had disappeared, Tensley strolled over to Molly. An adorable crease had formed between her light brows.

"Did you hug September?" she asked.

He gave her a simple smile, searching for the same

seductress he had witnessed—no, *experienced*—a few moments ago. "We have an understanding."

Under his watchful eyes, she crossed her dainty hands below her impressive chest in a childlike manner. "Hmm. Okay, well I'm going home now."

The seductress is long gone.

He had tried to charm her at the bar by acting like he was interested in getting to know her. It appeared to have worked, until she abruptly left. The two of them walked in silence now. The streets were empty and a storm was rolling in, the air heavy and stale with the smell of day-old garbage and Chinese food.

The click of her heels stopped.

A fierce whisper escaped her, one that carried the distance she'd put between them and seized him by the throat. "There's no way to get rid of you, is there?"

Anger boiled in his veins.

"Did you not just *feel me up* in there? Was I hallucinating all of that?"

"Yes, but it was just—the alcohol." She worried her bottom lip and then glared. "Why can't you just go away?"

Why is she playing me so hot and cold? He shook his head. He continued to walk, annoyed with her antics. He hadn't used any of his pheromones to control her, and it had appeared they'd actually been getting along for a few pleasurable moments back at the club.

"Tensley."

He growled in response.

"Answer me!"

He spun and a shudder moved through his immense,

agitated body. "Give it up." He went to turn away, but stopped, advancing on her like a wild animal. "Actually, give it all up. We're eventually going to fuck each other."

Molly's body grew rigid and he noted the tremble in her bottom lip.

Shit.

The silence that resulted after such a statement weighed like iron between them, expanding and shifting to an uncomfortable level.

"Look, I—" Tensley began, preparing to withdraw his crude statement, but Molly was too quick for him.

She marched over and slapped him across the cheek, sending his head flying to the left. Tensley stumbled back, cringing from the sting spreading across his face.

Her strength.

Hits like that from a human wouldn't do anything, but from a daemon? It sure as hell hurt.

Fuck.

He touched his skin hesitantly, more in shock than pain.

I'm a jackass. I deserved that.

He knew he'd crossed a line. He didn't want to hurt her, but the more she twisted him, played him, the more his demon side wanted to strangle her. "You good now?"

Her eyes sharpened. She was trembling, either from anger or fear; he couldn't tell. "You're such a jerk."

Tensley barked a laugh. "Most girls dig the jerk."

"You think most girls are hormonal and desperate for their own sparkly vampire, huh?"

He suppressed a smile. *Witty girl.* "Doubtful, considering *you* were the one who was all over me. You couldn't keep your hands off. Or your tongue." He paused, furrowing his brows. "Wait, did you just compare me to a sparkly vampire? 'Cause I'm not even close to one of those fucking things."

"Yes, I was, and no, I'm not 'hormonal' for that kind of guy," she said. Her eyes flickered over his figure, unimpressed.

He couldn't help the disappointment expanding in his chest. "Then you must be blind."

"I wish I was." She looked away.

His eyes narrowed, and he scowled. *Is she actually not attracted to me?* "Now you're just being *cruel.*"

"Now I'm just being *honest.*"

She was all over me at— his hands clenched. *She played me like a fucking fool.*

With newfound rage, he took a dangerous step forward, his pheromones sparking like an untamed fire lit by gasoline.

"If we're being *honest* then, you're a stuck-up brat who has no idea who they're dealing with. So if you want to stay on *good terms* with *me,* I would *think* next time," he retorted, stepping closer. She swallowed hard. "Is that clear enough for you to understand?"

"You're--you're—"

He leaned forward and for once, she didn't flinch. "I'm *what?*"

"You're a bastard." Her nostrils flared.

He groaned, turning to go back the way they'd come. "Let's just call it a night." He didn't want to sleep with her, not any time soon, not when she didn't even want him—or fucking *like* him. *She fucking played me and I fucking fell for it.*

"Wait!" She raced around to cut him off, her hands hovering over his chest.

Dear god, leave me alone woman! "What?"

She bit her lip hard, and once her mouth had opened and shut three times in a row, he lost his patience.

"Spit it out. Gonna call me a 'jackass' again? Because I already knew that, sweetheart."

"I'm scared, okay," she whispered.

His brows lifted.

He hadn't expected her to confess that. He stiffened when her red, puffy eyes met his. He didn't deal well with his own emotions; he certainly didn't want to try to deal with hers.

"This whole...situation...scares me." She rubbed her arms and he realized she'd forgotten her coat at the club. "*You* scare me."

Finally, she admits it.

"Just stop talking," he huffed, cursing underneath his breath. He didn't want to care, because if he cared, she had the power. "If we don't get back soon, you'll get sick — it's like fifty degrees out here." A storm had rolled in with heavy winds; he thought of giving her his leather jacket, but he didn't want to seem nice, weak. Constantly, his older brother's face flashed before him as a reminder whenever he thought of doing something chivalrous.

Don't get too close, or you'll end up just like him.

"Don't you feel anything?" she croaked.

He halted, back stiffening. "I don't have a heart, remember? You can't hold me to your rules. I'm a demon. We don't feel; we take." *Partially true.* She didn't need to know that though.

"Like my freedom?"

He thumbed his jaw. "I haven't taken your freedom yet."

"And you won't," she mumbled, crossing her arms again. She obviously didn't realize it brought more attention to her chest that way.

Rolling his eyes, he twisted around and continued the trek to her townhouse. As he looked ahead, however, he froze. Two wolves stood at the end of the road, panting.

Fuck. Fuck-fuck-fuck!

His eyes scanned the area and immediately found several more, along with the tall outline of a man.

He had to hide her, protect her. Fast.

Without thinking, Tensley grasped Molly by the back of her neck and shoved her head into his firm chest.

"Tensley!" She squirmed, her nails raking over his chest. "Let go—"

"Just *trust me!*"

"Tensley—" she whimpered.

"Don't look at him, don't speak—*please* trust me," he said.

She stilled, noting his tone, and then a moment later nuzzled into his frame as he clinched his arm tighter around her waist.

"Just trust me," he repeated against the top of her head.

"Mr. Knight? I thought that was you," Abaddon said, striding over. With a wave and a whistle, the wolves vanished.

"Yeah," Tensley answered dryly.

"I've heard rumors about you," Abaddon said.

"Engaged to a human girl? I thought your family had more class."

Tensley's jaw tensed.

Abaddon's eyes left his and traced over Molly's body where it was attached to Tensley's. "Well, aren't you going to introduce us?" Abaddon folded his thick arms across his hefty chest.

She pressed even harder against him at the comment, her hands clenching the fabric of his dress shirt.

"She's not feeling well." He stroked her back. "I should really get her to bed. Nice seeing you, Abaddon."

As Tensley stepped back, Abaddon gripped his shoulder with surprising quickness. "Wait," he said, all sense of congeniality gone. "Let me see her."

Tensley's mouth slacked, unsure of what to say. *You gotta be shitting me.* Abaddon was centuries older and stronger than him—his power ran as deep and strong as his lineage. Fallen would, if anything, take Abaddon's side if he knew the Knights were hiding a daemon from him.

"She's sick," he insisted, more sternly than before.

"You're lying." Abaddon's large, fat fingers rooted into Molly's curls, ripping her from Tensley. Her sunglasses fell off her face in the struggle and clattered to the pavement.

Fuck!

Tensley's balled hands shook beside him. He wanted to beat him to an ugly mess of bones and skin. His beast *loved* the thought.

A strangled cry left her throat, but her eyes were glued shut. Abaddon's finger traced her lips and she squirmed.

When his finger tried to enter her mouth, she bit it and he chuckled deeply in his throat. *She was asking to die.*

"Let her go," Tensley commanded, his chest heaving violently as his hands grew clammy.

Abaddon pulled at her hair again. "Open your eyes."

Molly refused, attempting to push him away, but his grip tightened.

"Open them!" He shook her hard, her head snapping back with such force it could dislocate something.

A cold dread washed over Tensley as Abaddon's mistresses—the many familiars he'd bought from Scorpios over the years—flickered through his memory. All the girls who'd showed up beaten within an inch of their life, or worse, hadn't survived. If she didn't obey him, he would end up hitting her against the concrete until she did.

"Open your damn eyes!" Tensley roared, voice shattering the dead silence. The last thing he wanted was for her to die.

Her glowing eyes flashed open and Abaddon's grip loosened immensely. "Your—your eyes." Tensley had never seen him vulnerable. The *daemon eyes* effect. "You're a daemon."

Molly shook out of his grip and pushed him back.

She stumbled, beginning to fall, but Tensley caught her, gripping her elbow and putting himself between them. "She's engaged to me, Abaddon, so don't even think about it."

Abaddon blinked and rolled his shoulders, fighting to gain back his strong, confident self. The pull Molly had over him was evident.

Abaddon couldn't tear his eyes away from her, even

when she clung to Tensley's back.

"So, she is," Abaddon mumbled, eyes trained on her ring finger.

"And don't tell anyone else about her. I'll let them know in time," he warned, backing up. Abaddon quickly nodded, but Tensley didn't believe him. Abaddon had a big mouth, and it was just a matter of time before Fallen found out.

Great.

Tensley went to turn, but Abaddon moved forward.

"Wait—what's her name?" Abaddon's hands shook wildly, and he was clearly lost in Molly's gaze.

Tensley hesitated, looking down to where Molly trembled in his arms. "Emily," he answered softly, grasping her elbow and leaving Abaddon on the sidewalk.

As they reached her townhouse, Tensley stopped at the bottom of the stairs. She turned, a blend of surprise and something else in her crystalline eyes. *Relief? Confusion?*

He loosened his collar, nerves knotting painfully in his stomach at the new threat.

"Who was he?" Strands of her glossy, fair hair blew across her flushed features and she didn't bother removing them, instead concentrating on Tensley's fixated gaze.

"A demon of high class, Abaddon, the Duke of Tormenting. He reigns in Babylon, where the higher class live in secrecy from this realm." He ground his teeth at the thought of Abaddon taking Molly for himself. To Abaddon, she would be the ultimate notch on his deformed bedpost.

"And what were those wolves doing?" she said as she wetted her bottom lip shakily. For a moment he thought of warming her face with his fingertips, then with his palms, and then with his hungry mouth. For a moment, he forgot whom they were discussing.

"They aren't really wolves. They're called familiars, and they're like pets to demons. They shape-shift into animals and humans," he explained. When he looked at her, he saw fear in her dim, glowing eyes, and he didn't like the soft look she was giving him — it was the same one from when he'd told her about Illya.

Disgusted, he made his eyes grow dark and his body rigid, sending off aggressive pheromones. "And when I fucking tell you to trust me, fucking do it. Don't hesitate, don't resist — fucking do as you're told or one day he will beat your head against the curb."

"Excuse me?" She glared. "You're not my master. You can't tell me what to do." She huffed and glanced away. "I don't need your help. Just leave me alone."

Tensley shook his head. "Fine. Weather demons and familiars and Duke Abaddon by yourself, then, if you're so fucking smart! Prove me wrong, *ciccia*." He didn't want to stay in that damn household any more; he'd send his men to watch the house. He didn't want to be around her, and with the engagement ring she'd hopefully remain untouched by other demons. Other than high-borns who sensed the claim, the rest would assume she'd been marked and was off limits.

Molly's eyes were bloodshot and he began to reach out to graze her hand, instantly pulling back. *Do not be kind. Do not be soft.*

"Fine," she bit out. She stared at him, eyes wet, and it did awful things to his heart. He regretted his tone as Molly nodded wordlessly and climbed the stairs, shutting the door behind her without one look back.

chapter fifteen

MOLLY WRAPPED HER arms around her middle and sat on the subway, watching the landscape zoom by. She glanced at her wristwatch. She didn't want to be late meeting Cree, and anxiety filled her body as to what he would say about the previous night. If Tensley wasn't going to help or protect her against other demons, including Abaddon, then she needed Cree to train her to protect herself and her family.

She glared at the text her mom had sent her, stating they were coming home tomorrow. She texted them over and over again to stay where they were, but they hadn't responded.

When the train stopped, she stood and stepped onto the platform. Very few people lingered, marching down the concrete stairs to the street level. Graffiti plagued the pillars, and large bubbly letters spelled out something Molly couldn't quite read in the harsh fluorescent lighting overhead.

She turned and froze at the sight of Cree in a dark

jacket and worn combat boots, walking toward her. She tried to read his expression. *Was he angry? Annoyed?*

"Hey," she said and awkwardly waved, but stopped herself when he didn't wave back.

"I'm glad you called me. I was worried when things didn't work out last night," he said, his brusque walk catching her off guard as he moved past her.

She caught up to him, breathless. "Yeah, Tensley seemed suspicious. Yanked me out of the club before I could do anything."

Cree spun so fast she stumbled back and gawked at his hard features. "Just say it. You couldn't go through with it. You couldn't kill him."

She swallowed and lifted her shoulders.

"You might not like what I do, hell, I don't care, but know this: I have your back. When he's ripping your life apart, I'm right there. You got it?"

She caught her breath at his words, at his support. She nodded, too stunned, too overwhelmed to speak.

Cree sighed and turned around, resuming his walk. "You said he needs you to have a kid, right? Well, what do you think is going to happen after you give him that? Either he'll keep you around to have *more*, or he'll get rid of you."

He was right.

"Let's go, just a little farther."

Up ahead was a gate of a cemetery and Molly eyed the tombstones through the fence. She turned her attention to the shops on the other side of the street—a laundromat and a Chinese restaurant—but nothing screamed where Cree was taking her.

To her surprise, he opened the Greenwood Cemetery gate and gestured for her to go ahead.

Really? The cemetery?

In front of them, beyond the cluster of tombs, stood gloved men and women in the night, some bearing knives while others simply cracked their knuckles menacingly.

Molly felt out of place in her yellow raincoat, blouse, and Tory Burch flats.

"Hey!" Cree called out, immediately cutting through the group's conversations. "We have a new member among us tonight. Don't go easy on her." Some laughter escaped, while others continued to frown. Cree stepped toward a girl with dyed pink hair and whispered something in her jewelry-laden ear.

"Follow me," the girl demanded as she marched over, moving nearly as fast as Cree had earlier. Molly glanced at Cree, who nodded reassuringly. Molly followed, stumbling behind the pink-haired girl up a hill into the woods.

"Name's Freya. You know how to fight?" the girl chirped, still staring ahead.

Molly peered up at her, studying the tattoo of an eye sprawling the width of Freya's neck. It was complex, with black lines delicately twisted around the eye. Molly couldn't look away.

"Uh... no?"

Freya shook her head, and the way her neck twisted, the eye seemed to follow Molly. "Cree trusts you to keep your trap shut, but I don't. Since he runs this place, I don't get a final say." Freya stopped walking and turned to face her. "Lose the glasses."

Molly's hand automatically reached to her sunglasses. "I really advise against that. For your own good."

Freya scowled, but after a moment of silence, she sighed. "Get into a fighting stance."

Molly balked. "A what?"

"A fighting stan—ugh, let me show you. Spread your legs wider apart and bend them at the knees." Molly did so. "Good. Now hold your hands in front, staggered, at an angle, yep, like that."

"Why am I doing this?" Molly felt like she resembled a ridiculously uncoordinated karate student. "Like this?"

Freya looked her up and down. "Yeah." A second later she kicked a foot out, slamming it into Molly's shin.

Molly gasped, nearly collapsing to the leaf-strewn, damp dirt. "Ow! Shit, that hurt! Why did you do th—"

"Demons don't wait for you to be ready. We're gonna train you to protect yourself," Freya interrupted, kicking Molly's other leg and knocking her completely over. Molly groaned as her small wrist connected with the hard ground. "First, never let your guard down. You're just giving them the perfect opportunity to attack. Second, hands up, fisted, like this." Freya showed Molly, towering over her as Molly cradled her aching arm. "And third, never wear that hideous yellow thing again. It's fucking blinding."

Molly glanced down at her raincoat. As she got to her feet, Freya came at her again and shoved Molly back, stumbling. She held her ground that time, though. Molly smiled, triumphant, until Freya pummeled her in the stomach.

"That all ya got?" Freya asked as Molly staggered to the ground again, gasping.

Molly glared at her through her disheveled hair and shoved herself to her feet. "*No.*"

Freya lunged again. Molly jumped out of the way and caught Freya by the bicep, twisting it behind her back.

Freya hissed sharply through clenched teeth and couldn't free herself. "Fu—"

Molly let go. She didn't want to break her arm; didn't need a repeat of high school gym class.

"Holy shit," Freya muttered, rubbing her arm where bright red handprints were tattooed. "Fucking death grip. You really *are* a daemon."

Molly frowned. *Yeah, and it's ruining my whole life.*

The sun settled beneath the large oak trees as they practiced defensive moves, turning the vibrant green forest to a dark, menacing wilderness. Freya pointed out her weaknesses—of which there were many—and taught her some kicks and dodging techniques.

Cree stood on the tiny hill path, looking down on them.

"That's enough for tonight," he said finally, stepping down from his rocky perch. "She needs to see the diviners."

Molly wiped the sweat from her forehead. "The diviners?"

"The term most common to describe them nowadays is witches."

Molly widened her eyes. *Witches?* "And I need to see them, why?"

He turned away and started walking down the path. "You have to make an oath, for your own protection and for the protection of the Order."

Molly glanced back at Freya who rolled her eyes

heavenward. "You'd be living your stereotype if you didn't fucking take the oath for your own damn good, chica."

Molly bit her tongue; she so badly wanted to retort, but she'd figured Freya was right.

Molly followed Cree through the pines, the echoes of birds like bells overhead, to a tiny chapel hidden among the foliage. Its roof was slanted, with holes in several spots. The brick itself was covered in wild vines that consumed its walls with an uncontrollable vigor.

He grabbed the large metal lock at the door and easily picked it. Cree opened it and gestured for her to walk ahead. She tiptoed in, eyes adjusting to the dark room.

A light flickered in the tiny room, with several tall white candlesticks illuminating at once to cast the room in yellowed tones.

Two figures sat on their knees in front of the grungy altar, and Molly's shoes clipped against the stone-tiled floor as she followed Cree in farther. The figures stood and removed their dark hoods to reveal a man and Albert. As they turned to face her, Albert grinned.

"Nice to see you," Albert said and his smile grew. "This is Oliver."

"Yo," the shorter man said with a weak wave. Two snakebite piercings sat below his thin, pouted bottom lip.

"Every hunter must take the oath to join," Albert said, his dark eyes bright. "Do you wish to take the oath?"

Molly looked at Cree for guidance. "So this means I'll be protected from the demons?"

Albert nodded. "It's a bond of community, of strength in numbers."

Molly hesitated, biting her lip.

Cree caught her arm and guided her a few steps away, leaning in. "What's the problem, Molly?"

"I'm already in a contract that's screwing me over. I'd like to avoid doing it again," she said, gesturing to the room.

"It's an oath of partnership and protection, Molly. It's not something evil. We, hunters, protect each other. It'll protect you," Cree said gently. "If I could have given my sister the same protection this oath provides, I would have." She looked up into his eyes. He was giving her protection. Of course she should take it.

"We could also help you engage fully with your abilities," Albert said. "Your eyes hold the power to control others, most importantly demons. To do so, your body must be relaxed in a state of withdrawing the energy from your eyes to expand across your whole body. Daemons are thought to be a warrior to defend humankind from the likes of chaos — demons."

Molly blinked. *Wow.*

Molly wrung her hands and sighed. "Can't I just be protected without the oath though?"

Albert's expression softened. "If you're in danger, we can sense it — literally feel your pulse race in our own, feel the fear, and we can come find you. It's an ancient ritual of agreement between you and the Order. The diviners deal in inherited powers from their families and can use spells on others — good or bad. It's only been in the last hundred years that hunters and diviners worked alongside each other. Hatred toward demons is the one thing we have all seem to have in common."

Molly weighed her options. If she was in danger and needed help, they would sense it. They would find her and help her. She swallowed. She wouldn't be alone in this terrifying world anymore.

Molly moved toward the diviners and took Albert's outstretched hand. "To bind you to the Order we'll have to draw blood for the oath." Albert brought forth a silver knife from his robe, cutting deep into Molly's left ring finger.

She scrunched her nose, recoiling at the sting from the knife. "Ow!

The blood pooled in Albert's palm as Molly clenched it.

Albert approached the altar where a thin piece of wrinkled paper sat. His clenched hand opened a bit so that some of Molly's blood dribbled onto the paper.

"Repeat after me," Albert said, strange words suddenly pouring from his mouth. Molly was mesmerized, pulled toward the words and the power. Her own lips began speaking the words in a deep haze. *Latin?* The three chanted, growing loud and vicious.

Then it stopped. Albert let go of her hand and she cradled it against her chest.

That was fast...

Molly exchanged glances at all three of them. "That's all? Did it work?"

Oliver winked. "Welcome to the club."

Molly tiredly looked at her bloody hand and jolted when Cree grabbed it, bandaging it with white cloth.

"We'll keep you safe," Albert promised. "Now I can tell you my grandmother's secret recipe for casseroles."

Molly furrowed her brow, but couldn't help stop smiling at his poor joke.

Cree let go of her hand and marched toward the door, Molly tagging after.

"That's enough for one night," he said once they'd walked through the cemetery and made it to a well-lit street in the direction of the subway station.

Molly gnawed at her bottom lip and held her hand, glaring at the red spots seeping through the bandages. "Thank you, Cree. For helping me, even after last night."

Cree's features fell, and he shook his head once. "Molly," he began, taking her hand. "We're on the same side here. I want to help you get away from that *beast*. This will help you. We're going to figure out a way to make sure demons can't detect you, okay?"

She nodded and they both kept moving.

He stopped before the subway entrance. "You think you can manage to get home?"

"Yes."

"Wait," he said as she turned away.

She paused, brow wrinkled.

He dug into his pocket and pulled out a golden hairpin with vines and lilies weaving their way around the piece. He placed it in her hand. "You might need this. It's laced with golden fleece, only activated when the skin breaks. Protect yourself."

She raised her head and watched Cree's eyes soften. "Thank you. For everything."

He nodded curtly without another word, and she watched him walk away.

WHEN MOLLY ENTERED her parents' house thirty minutes later it was quiet, and she missed her mother's non-stop talking session of nonsense and her father's silent calm as he read over documents from city hall.

"Molly." The deep voice startled her. She turned to the staircase and spotted Tensley at the top, face half-hidden by shadows.

Her stomach dropped. *Why is he here?* She wasn't sure how to respond to him, not after how they'd left things the night before. She wiped her hands on her pants, terrified he'd notice the dirt and grass stains and somehow realize what she was up to. *Trying to get rid of him.*

"May I speak to you privately in your bedroom?"

Molly nodded, traveling up the elegant staircase.

He knows. He totally knows what I'm up to.

"I wanted to apologize for my behavior toward you and your family," he said softly once she stood in the doorway.

Molly pinched her palm in disbelief. "What?"

He watched her with stark black eyes. "It was inappropriate and inconsiderate of your feelings."

Molly blinked fast.

Tensley shifted forward, hesitant but determined, and dug a hand into his pocket. "Here." He handed her a necklace, one with a small ruby. Her fingers moved before she could stop them and held the cool chain. "It was my grandmother's."

"Thanks," she mumbled. The coolness tickled her warm skin, and she ran her finger across the golden chain, body pulsing.

"I want to get to know you," he uttered in a vulnerable

tone. Again, her body pulsed. "And I want you to know me." His hand grazed her shoulder, and a strange shiver swept over her, spreading to her fingertips. "I want..." Her breath hitched at the top of her throat. "I want to kiss you," he continued, growing closer, his musky scent assaulting her senses. Her hand twitched to grasp his shirt and pull him closer, but she couldn't let go of the necklace.

Why – I was just agreeing to get rid of him – what am I doing?

She choked on air. He was a dangerous siren, his entire body singing to her – and she couldn't resist the call.

A faint smile appeared on his bee-stung lips and he slowly...so slowly...lowered them to hers.

A sweet peck.

She moaned greedily into his parting mouth. "*Yes.*"

This time, he pressed his lips hard, aggressively. His hands slid to her lower back, both of them easing down farther, teasing.

His tongue wandered into her mouth.

This is insane. I shouldn't be doing this.

He grunted against her lips.

Her fingers struggled to undo his shirt button, exposing a sculpted chest.

He cupped the back of her thighs and lifted her feet off the ground so that she clung to him. He brought her over to the bed and they fell down onto the silky sheets. He pressed heavy kisses on her collarbone.

She ached for him, completely.

All the other guys she had made out with were like feathers in the wind, blown away by the hurricane that was Tensley Knight's expert mouth. His kisses were searing, and Molly lost herself as he undressed her, popping open each button on her blouse and yanking down her jeans.

"Tensley." Her fingers buried themselves in his hair and pulled as his hands moved between her thighs. *"Tensley."*

"What the fuck?" said a scathing voice from behind them. Tensley stopped kissing her and glanced over his shoulder.

Molly sat up and a horrible feeling washed over her, knocking every bit of desire from her entire being. *How? How was it possible?*

chapter sixteen

TENSLEY KNIGHT STOOD in the doorway, shadowy eyes narrowed, chest heaving. He looked demonic, with his nose scrunched up and brows drawn together. *Two Tensleys?*

"Get off of her! Now!" said the Tensley in the doorway as he bared his teeth.

The Tensley on top of her darted off the bed and the other Tensley caught him, shoving him against the wall with a knife pressed to his throat. Books fell from Molly's many shelves as she scrambled to her feet.

Two Tensleys stood in the room. The one she had been kissing was shirtless, while the other one wore a three-piece suit. Other than that, they looked identical.

"Whom do you belong to?" Suit Tensley hissed. When he was met with silence, he slammed the heel of his hand upward into his nose and he cried out. "Answer the fucking question."

The shirtless one laughed. "Huh." His nose bled, redness dripping over his lips. "Isn't it funny that it took me less than five minutes to almost get your fiancée to spread her legs? And you haven't even gotten close."

Tensley scowled, eyes dark, and he slammed the guy's head into the wall again. "Answer the goddamn question."

The imposter's features melted into small eyes and a Roman nose, and he smirked. "Who do you think?"

Tensley frowned and thrust the knife into the guy's temple. The man gasped as Tensley twisted it, stepped back, and yanked it out. The man fell to the floor — dead.

"Prick," he spat.

Molly clenched her hands to her chest to hide their violent shaking and clutched the necklace. "Why — who was he?" The real Tensley marched over and grasped her arm, lifting her off the bed, and she flinched.

"He was a familiar. Remember? I explained that to you a few nights ago. Abaddon sent him here. Why did you do that with him?" Molly went to open her mouth, but she didn't have a reason. She lowered her lashes and he huffed. "What the hell did he say to make you fuck him?"

She shook her head. "But we didn't--we didn't even."

He grunted and searched through her drawers.

"I thought he was you."

She realized too late what slipped out, but she wasn't thinking straight. She was trembling, fighting to take in one piece before she shattered into pieces.

"So you'd sleep with me?" he said, peeking over a shoulder.

"No," she said quickly. His eyes stayed on her for a few moments before traveling to her chest. Without a word, he walked over, yanked the necklace out of her hands, and threw it to the ground. He stomped hard on the jewels until they shattered.

Suddenly all the confusion vanished and was replaced by panic—panic that she had let a stranger touch her, panic that he had almost *taken* her, and she hadn't batted an eyelash. Her hand hovered over her collarbone and she bit the inside of her mouth.

His eyes met hers. "He charmed you. He seduced you with his own blood in this necklace and damn warlock magic, weakened your powers to take advantage of you—not to sleep with you, no, to take you to someone more dangerous."

Molly curled her hand against her neck as she stared at the broken pieces. "I was almost," she murmured, vision blurring. "He was going to—I shouldn't have let him—"

She couldn't think straight. Her knees buckled underneath her and his arms shot out, catching her awkwardly against his chest.

"I'm s—sorry." She clutched at his white T-shirt.

"Not your fault, Molly." Tensley's silky voice cut through her thoughts and his hands cupped her wet cheeks. "He's gone, okay?"

"But the body…" Her voice cracked. Molly's head lifted from his chest and her eyes traced the dead man's slim figure. His skin had turned a grey tone, like ashes. Those grey ashes had been touching her. A hotness swelled in her eyes.

"He's a familiar. His body will decay within the next hour," Tensley said, gripping her chin to force her to look him in the eye. "He deserved it. They're nothing but lowlifes."

She choked on a sob.

I was tricked. Another demon was in my house. What if my family had been here?

"I can't stay here." She tightened her grip on his forearm and he flinched at the contact, putting distance between them to look down at her. His brow wrinkled, as if he was straining to not yell at her or was confused by her touch.

"We'll leave then."

She raised her brows and watched him stand, grab a random backpack, and begin stuffing too many clothes and undergarments inside it. He hissed when the zipper got jammed and gave up, tossing the bag over his shoulder.

His face was hard, the muscles in his arms tensed. His eyes met hers and then slid over her body, and he swallowed audibly when his gaze landed on her chest. "You might want to cover up."

She didn't need to look; Molly remembered that her blouse was undone, lacy bra showing. Heat spread up her neck to her hairline.

Oh god!

She quickly fidgeted with the buttons, giving a frustrated shout when her fingers refused to work. He moved in front of her and did each one effortlessly. "C'mon."

Molly stared at the dissolving body of the familiar, reaching absentmindedly for clean shorts and leaving the dirt-caked ones from her excursions with Cree in a pile on the floor. Tensley faced away the entire time, throwing things into her bag.

"*Molly.*" His hand latched around her wrist and she let him guide her out. "I'll get us a hotel room," Tensley announced in a gruff voice, pushing Molly toward the front door. Once inside the taxi he waved over, Molly ruminated on the fact that she'd been attacked, lured into almost sleeping with a complete stranger, and one who meant to do her harm.

She pulled at her shirt, unable to breathe properly as she felt Tensley's eyes heat the side of her profile. She ran shaking fingers across her tearstained cheeks, still feeling the fake Tensley's hands all over her. Molly's vision tunneled, her thoughts raced. "I can't—" she stuttered. "I think—"

Tensley took her flapping hands and slotted them between his own. "Just calm down, all right?" His voice was composed and soft, and it did crazy things to her mind— like trusting him. She threw herself across the cab and he tensed, arms frozen awkwardly as she fisted his shirt.

"Fuck, Darling. He's gone. He's not coming back."

She reveled in the harsh breaths that tickled tiny hairs on her forehead, because it calmed her senses, made him real, human almost. Soon her own rapid breathing battled his.

What am I doing?

She felt how stiff he was against her and drew away from him back to her side.

She wiped beneath her eyes, unable to look over or admit how much his presence comforted her.

"What if my parents just show up at the house and I'm not there," she muttered, hovering a hand over her moving lips.

"I'll have my men guard the house." His indifferent tone came out hollow.

Molly gawked back at him. *He'd do that?* "You will?"

He nodded curtly and she sighed, collapsing against the leather seat.

"Why were you in Brooklyn?"

Molly's heart froze. "Uh, September's dad lives there."

"Hmph." He looked out the window and impatiently tapped his finger on his thigh.

"How did you know that?"

"I have you followed. For protection."

Her mouth fell open. *"Followed?"*

"For *protection*," he said through gritted teeth.

She slouched down farther. "I couldn't—I couldn't stop myself." Tensley's body didn't move, but his eyes shifted and burnt crates in the side of her head. "As soon as I saw the necklace—"

"You couldn't resist." Tensley's somber voice cut her off and she turned to face him. "Their magic's different. It took away all choice, all decision process and controlled you. You couldn't stop yourself because he made sure of it."

A tensed silence filled the car.

Molly planted her forehead on the cool window and watched traffic zoom by her as the buildings blended together.

When the car stopped and she stepped out, she stared up at the Plaza Hotel. Tensley led the way and Molly could only concentrate on following his shoes, his steps.

I should have known he wasn't the real Tensley. Damn it. I should have known something wasn't right.

"Molly." His clipped tone drew her out of her thoughts and she followed him into the elevator. Neither spoke, simply standing on opposite sides of the window-walled elevator.

Once they entered the hotel room, she eyed the pristine

white covers and the gold-trimmed headboard, balanced with beige floral carpets and gold-beige velvet chairs.

"Make yourself at home," he said as he shrugged out of his suit jacket, tossing it on the back of the armchair. "I need to make a few calls."

She watched him go into the next room, a small study, and shut the door. Emotionally exhausted, she fell back onto the bed and climbed underneath the covers.

Breathe.

In, out. In, out.

MOLLY WOKE TO the sound of Tensley's deep voice rumbling in her ears. She squinted in the dimly lit room and saw Tensley sitting on the edge of the bed, nudging her limp hand.

"I got food," he told her, gesturing to the coffee table with a pizza box on it.

She didn't bother brushing down her wild flyaways and crawled out of bed, sitting down on the floor beside the coffee table. Closing her eyes, she inhaled the delicious scent of melted cheese and crusty dough. When she opened the box, she gawked at the large pizza with the toppings she loved.

"How did you know?"

Tensley took a seat opposite her, a crystal glass of what looked like whiskey in hand. Although he was reclined on the chair, his body still seemed rigid. "You mentioned it at the restaurant."

Her heart lodged in her throat and she couldn't tear her eyes away from him.

He remembered.

She took a piece of the goat cheese pizza and moaned after the first bite. "You didn't even miss an ingredient."

At the sound of his sharp intake of breath, her eyes fluttered open to find Tensley staring, his jaw clenched.

"Aren't you going to eat?"

"I hate mushrooms," he said brusquely.

"Oh c'mon, you can barely taste them. Just a try?"

He looked between the pizza and her and finally caved in, grabbing himself a slice.

She smirked at him. "Good?"

He hummed and swallowed a bit. Their chewing was the only sound for a while, and after a long, painful pause, she cleared her throat.

"So," she whispered. "What do you like to do?"

His mouth twisted. "Do?"

"Like...hobbies."

Tensley looked taken aback. "I like to read. But you already knew that, didn't you? Since you went through my things before."

Molly's face burnt and she took another bite of pizza. "So, what kind of books?"

"Warfare, military, history. Better to understand history's mistakes in warfare so I don't re-commit them," he said, one corner of his lips quirking. "And you? Do you like reading about ancient conquerors?"

She swallowed her pizza and sucked on her bottom lip; his eyes darted to the movement, darkening visibly. "I do," she answered shyly. "I love history—I love anything about it. I love...well, anyway."

He stared at her and gestured with his drink to continue. "Go on."

"Well…" She took a deep breath. "I've always loved history—reading in general, really—but when my parents took me to the library, apparently I used to check out history books instead of *Franklin* or *Goosebumps*. With my parents always being busy and my dad's love of history, I wanted his attention. So I developed this obsession with knowing everything possible about different cultures' histories. My mom didn't understand why I couldn't just read a simple fairytale. She pushed me for years to be like her—a vibrant, outgoing person—but that's not me. I wanted so badly to be what she wanted, but I couldn't. They both wanted me to be this perfect kid. They had good intentions, but I felt suffocated. It took me a while to realize I could never be what they wanted me to be and be happy at the same time. So I told them I was moving out and making my own decisions. My dad understood, but my mom is still upset—" She paused, sneaking a look from her linked hands to Tensley's focused face. *Said way too much.* "But, uh, my grandma gave me a ton of history books before she passed away."

Tensley's expression transformed to one of concern. "I'm sorry to hear that."

Her heart squeezed tightly at his sincere, calm voice and the softness in his eyes. She could only hold his tender gaze for so long before she had to glance around the opulent hotel bedroom. "And your grandparents? Are they still alive?"

Tensley swirled his drink. "Most of them are still alive—they don't live around here though. My mother's parents are in England and my father's mother is in Italy."

"Wow," she said, her eyes widening. "Do you see them often?"

"Every year or so," he answered before taking a large gulp of the drink.

"And do you have siblings?"

He huffed out a harsh laugh. "Four of them."

She giggled. "I always wished I had siblings, someone to hang out with."

He tsked. "Our relationship wasn't like that."

She shifted on her knees and took a bite of the crust. "Because of the way your society is?"

His eyes narrowed. "Exactly. When affection is the least tolerable emotion in someone's society, you don't really focus on making *fond* memories."

She frowned deeply. "So your family didn't show any kind of affection? A hug, even?"

Tensley snorted. "I was lucky to get a pat on the back. Some families give mild affection until puberty — that's when our hearts become at risk of developing. My father was one who believed that simple affections were too much for a demon at any age."

How could a parent do that? She stared at him, wondering if his rigid attitude was something grown over time due to lack of love and affection.

"Harsh," she muttered.

His mouth twisted ruefully and he glared at the floor. "Necessary."

What else was real? Did he need to eat food? What were facts and false information told to her by movies and books? "So demons..."

His forehead wrinkled after she dragged out her words. "Demons..."

"Are you immortal?"

He snorted. "No, I'm not. But for some of the highest demons, yes, they are gifted to drink from the cup of ambrosia, which makes them immortal. I was conceived just like you — along with the rest of my kind."

Okay, so I was somewhat wrong about that...

She shifted on her knees. "And do you sleep?"

He glared. "What's with all the questions?"

"I just want to know more..." She shrugged and looked down at her nude painted toes, nervous under his cool stare.

He sighed loudly, shaking his head. "We sleep, we eat, we fuck — everything humans do, but we're superior in strength and mind. For my kind of demon, our most important need is intimacy."

"Oh." *Oh shit that is.* She lowered her lashes, fidgeting with her hands at the mention of intimacy. "So intimacy gives you energy?"

He nodded and thumbed his bottom lip. "When incubi engage in intimacy, we absorb the other's energy. We can heal through someone else's energy, too."

"Incubi get energy from intimacy then — that's your main, uh, source?" She cringed at herself. *Real smooth.*

Again, he nodded.

She twisted her hair tight around her finger. So he could gain energy from her if they were intimate...

She watched him examine his drink as if it was the most interesting thing in the room and slowly, his eyes aligned with hers underneath his dark, long lashes.

The look punched the air out of her and she turned away. "I'm — I'm going to go have a shower, okay?" She didn't wait, rushing to the bathroom and closing the door behind her. Once she turned on the shower, she let out a huge sigh. "Get a grip, Molly."

She gathered her hair into a ponytail, slipped off her clothes, and stepped into the large shower. The water was warm on her chilly skin, cascading over her bruised body. *Freya really went for it.* After a good fifteen minutes of soaking in the warmth, she heard faint voices—two voices: Tensley's and another deep one. She kept the water on but dried off, then wiggled into her clothes and cracked the door open an inch.

Tensley stood with his back to her, while the new man stood off to the side.

"You can't prance around like a spoiled ass. You're lucky it was Abaddon; he's too dimwitted to think fast. The problem is him telling Fallen. He'll come; he'll want to see it for himself. Just keep her out of sight," the man said, his voice undeniably calloused. Cruel. "Have you given her the ring yet?"

Tensley stood higher, hands at his sides and head high. "Yes, I have, Father."

Molly adjusted her angle so she could view Mr. Knight. His skin was tan, a bronze shade, and his eyes were sharp. He'd hurt her dad. She gritted her teeth.

"Have you marked her yet?"

Tensley was silent.

Molly knitted her brow. *What? Mark me?*

"*Answer me.*"

"No," Tensley spat out, his hands curling into fists. "No, I haven't."

"But you gave her the ring? You must be fucking senseless, boy. No wonder Abaddon found her. All the demons can sense her existence now. Powerful demons will grab her!" Mr. Knight kicked at a chair, knocking it over.

Tensley stood his ground. "I know, Father."

"Do any other demons know of her yet?"

"No." His voice held a firmness that left no room for doubt. "No other demons have seen her yet."

Mr. Knight adjusted his designer jacket. "Good." He watched his son, mouth a straight line and nostrils flared. "But you must mark her *now*."

"She's not interested."

Mr. Knight gripped Tensley's shoulders so hard she saw him wince. "It doesn't matter what her interests are. Mark her. Grow to care for her. Convince her. Convince *yourself*." He released Tensley and checked his reflection in the mirror next to the TV. "Have sex with her soon, or some other incubus will. Perhaps Abaddon."

She held her breath.

Say no. Say no, Tensley!

Tensley didn't move, his hands still clenched. "I'll do it. *Tonight*."

chapter seventeen

MOLLY BACKED AWAY and stared at the closed door.

He agreed.

He agreed to that.

I'm a pawn in his game.

She needed to leave, immediately—to go where, she didn't know, but she couldn't stay there with him. The heavy weight of betrayal caused her to stagger and grip the sink.

Her fingers pried open drawers, searching for a weapon. *Damn it! I am so writing an awful review for this place.* In the furthest corner drawer, under a slim box of tissues, was a small pair of scissors. Molly tested their edges with a fingertip, and tensed.

Bingo.

Steam fogged the mirrors and settled over her as Molly reached for them. She breathed out shakily at the sound of the hotel room door shutting. *I need to make a run for it.*

She shook the anxiety off, opened the bathroom door, and scanned the room for her bag. She didn't see it.

Footsteps echoed in the hallway and Molly hid the scissors behind her back. Tensley opened the front door, halting at her stance. He narrowed his eyes and gently shut it.

"What are you doing?" His dark, classic suit was smoothed, ironed to perfection, and if someone had told her he was a demon, she would have laughed. He looked far too good in a suit.

"Uh, I was just waiting for you," she stammered.

He cocked a brow. "Waiting for me?"

She hummed an answer, too nervous to speak. "Are you, uh, heading out?" She eyed his three-piece suit.

His relaxed posture turned to steel. "A work matter." Grey eyes scanned her damp hair and she drew in a deep breath at the incredible heat swarming her chest. *Stop it.* "I don't have to go right away. The people there" – he visibly swallowed – "aren't as entertaining as you."

Her heart soared and quickly plummeted. *Do not allow him to suck you in – ugh, don't use the word 'suck'.* The edge of the scissors' blade dug into her palm.

With a smile, Tensley stepped closer until he was towering over her petite figure. He eyed her with curiosity. "What are you hiding?"

Molly's heart thudded, her grip loosening on the scissors from perspiration.

A corner of his lips quirked. "What are you hiding behind your back, Ms. Darling?" He reached a hand out to grasp her wrist.

She panicked and without thinking, sliced through his shirt.

Molly let out a gasp and Tensley's playful eyes grew

dark as he looked down to examine the white dress shirt, already dotting with blood. She dropped the scissors.

"Why the hell did you do that?" He glared and placed a large hand over his wound.

"I--I—" Tensley's other hand gripped her arm hard, and she winced. She shrieked, flailing against him when his entire frame pinned her to the wall. "Don't—don't touch me! Stop!"

His gripped tightened. "Calm down!"

She shoved him hard enough he stumbled back. "Please don't--please don't--"

Tensley snarled and hit his fist on the wall. "Please don't *what?*"

"Please don't force yourself on me!"

Tensley's expression went painfully blank. If anything, it was the first time she'd seen him look so shocked, even more so than the day she'd slapped him. "Who said I was going to force you?"

"I heard what your father said," she whispered between heavy breaths against his heaving chest. "You agreed to it."

Tensley hissed and closed his eyes, running a hand over his face. "I wasn't going to force you. I'm not going to force myself on you. *Period.*"

"What?" She gawked at him, examining his closed eyes, the way he massaged his temples with a free hand. His eyes opened, an ember now burning inside them, but she didn't look away from their intense heat.

"I'm not going to force you into sex," he clarified, his eyes softened but his voice still harsh.

"You aren't?"

He let go and pulled at his hair. "Contrary to your

assumptions, I only have and want sex with people who want to have sex with *me*." He groaned. "You think I want this? Do you think you're the only one trapped in this arrangement?"

Molly stiffened. "What?" She hadn't thought about him — she hadn't thought this was anything but good for him.

"You don't think I had a life before this?" he snapped.

"I — I just didn't realize." She hugged her middle.

"Of course you didn't," he retorted.

Tensley took off his navy jacket and white shirt, exposing the parts of his torso that were faintly inked with words; Molly assumed they were Italian, since she couldn't understand them. Her eyes darted to his midsection, where she'd sliced him. The wound was shallow, but blood continued to seep out and down his chiseled abdomen.

"You need to clean it." Molly stepped forward.

"*Don't*." Anger rang in his voice. She froze, letting her hand drop. Tensley walked over to the mini fridge and pulled out a small bottle of alcohol. He growled quietly in his throat as he poured some on the exposed wound. "Why the hell did you do this?"

Molly glanced at him, blood thumping in her head. "I was protecting myself! If I don't hurt you first, you'll hurt me."

"*Hurt* you?" Tensley barked, jaw squared and veins bulging in his neck. "Humans are just as dark as us demons. They murder, they steal, they lie. They're evil, wouldn't you agree? All those kids who bullied you." A throaty laugh escaped him. "Why should *I* ever trust *you*?" He pressed a hand against the wound, leaning against the wall.

Molly gulped down fear. His silence was killing her now.

"You threatened me," she said with venom. Tensley's nostrils flared. "You took my life away." The cool sensation burned her eyes, and she looked at him through her lashes. "How can I ever trust *you?*"

His body visibly tensed at her naked eyes. He swallowed thickly and aimed his gaze to the side. "Never trust a demon, Molly. Number one rule." He sounded just like his father had—calloused and cruel. She'd had enough.

"I want to leave now," Molly blurted out, rage burning all the wetness from her eyes.

"You can't," he responded quickly, raising a hand to halt any sudden movement. She froze at his firm tone. "Not tonight. There are twenty powerful demons downstairs waiting for me in the lobby, and if they see you, if they get a hold of you, Molly—it won't be pretty."

He sighed deeply as her powerful stance weakened at the potential threat downstairs. She couldn't control her powers, and she couldn't depend on her eyes to stop every single one of them.

"You know you're abusing me," she stated bluntly.

"I wasn't doing it on purpose." His voice was low, and for once, he didn't shy away from her gaze, instead studying her irises. "It's just my nature."

She choked on a lump--perhaps her heart in her throat— and batted her lashes to push back tears. "So I'm just a pawn in your game?" she said, feeling an overwhelming warmth radiating off his skin. He was so close, and she imagined touching his skin, reaching down...

"No," he argued, gently shaking his head. He was

fighting with himself; she could see it clearly on his exposed features.

Had he been dealing with an ongoing inner battle the whole time? Like her?

His expression was so raw, so bare. He wasn't wearing a mask, and she let hers fall too—to show him she was vulnerable, that she could be kind and open and sweet. "It's my nature to be…cruel…cold-hearted. In our culture, displays of affection are indecent; we're raised to be independent from that. Any affection is a sign of weakness, in us and our family. I can't—I wasn't raised to be like *you*…" He paused. "I'm incapable of it…"

The mask returned, but it was broken, disingenuous. Molly gnawed at her bottom lip, afraid to make a sound in case it would cause the real Tensley to vanish once more. "Oh." Her eyes left his and wandered across his naked torso, toward the tender looking cut.

She swallowed and looked up at him again, gesturing to the wound. "Can I help you heal it?"

I'm not quite sure how this power exchange works…

He visibly tensed and his gaze faltered, staring at her hand where it was inching closer to his stomach.

She waited for a sign, a nod of acquiescence, but he simply stared back at her. A strange, obsessive need fogged her mind, and she couldn't stop herself from running her fingers along his skin—

He jerked back, jabbing a shaking hand through his hair. The fog cleared and she stared at her fingers still in midair.

"You don't want me."

Her brow creased at his low voice, merely a mutter of

words strung together. She watched his chest heave, the cut rolling over his stomach and moved her way up to his contorted features.

"Tensley," she breathed and the way his entire body tensed at her voice sent shivers through her. "I just want to help."

He didn't budge nor did he refuse as she stepped closer again.

Carefully, her hand slid above the cut. His warm stomach muscles rippled from her touch. She looked up to find his brow knitted, a crease visible between them. His heated, dark eyes scorched her skin. The same heat gathered between her legs. Drawing in a shaky, quick breath, she tried to hide her sudden restlessness under his scrutiny.

"Is — is it working?" She nervously wet her lips. When all she could hear was his heavy breathing, she went to move her hand but he pulled her closer.

Her eyes aligned with his and all the air trapped in her lungs rushed out. That was all it took. One look, one gasp, and he yanked her into him, the strength of his arms securing her in place. She had no escape — and she couldn't have been more pleased. His bee-stung lips devoured her throat, nipping their way to her collarbone.

Desperately, her frantic hands ran across his hard, flexing back muscles. *Oh God, yes!* She must have cried out because he growled in response and secured the back of her thighs as he lifted her. She squealed at the sudden loss of ground, but it didn't last long. He sat down on the edge of the bed, his hands running up her bare legs and shoving her shorts out of the way.

"*Fuck,* Molly." He breathed against her outstretched

neck. She kissed his jawline, her thumb pressing firmly on each spot before she sucked. A heat scorched her stomach. His hard length poked into her inner thigh, demanding her attention. She rocked her hips against him, their cores meeting and thrusting against one another in a brutal rhythm, earning a satisfying moan from those full lips.

Am I doing it right? God, what if I'm awful?

Tensley noted her faltering, her hands shaking against his body, and smoothed his finger along her shoulder blade to the angel curls on her hairline. "You're fine; it's just you and me."

She hadn't expected that or how soft and serene his tone was. So soothing, so gentle, she trusted him holding her. She stared into his eyes and slowly leaned forward, never breaking eye contact.

He twisted his hands into her hair and smothered hot, open-mouthed kisses between her breasts. His fingers dug into her thighs when she bit into his neck, and she enjoyed the growl that grew in his throat. The scent of his skin was overwhelming—comforting, familiar, and masculine.

His hands grasped her hips, controlling the rhythm of her thrusts with his.

"Tensley," she gasped against his hot flesh.

"How far have you gone with a man, Molly?"

She glanced into his heated eyes, slowly releasing her bottom lip from the death grip her teeth had dug into them. "Making out, second base—I was too scared I'd hurt them."

His hands dug into her hipbones, bringing her completely

flush against him. "You don't have to worry about hurting me; you can't break me."

With her moan, he flipped her onto her back and lay between her legs, trapping her with his body. His hand found her crotch and felt her eagerness. She gasped loudly as he stroked his two fingers along the shorts separating him from her sensitive folds. "So wet, *ciccia*."

Her hand slid down his stomach and felt over his abdomen. As her gaze flickered to where the cut had been, she froze. It was gone—the skin flawless. Tensley's hand swept a few strands of wet hair off her forehead.

"It healed," she whispered, feeling over the dried blood.

Tensley hummed in response. She looked back up at him, and his eyes were tender and open. Her thumb traced over his jaw and stopped beside his mouth, where a tiny white scar was visible. She brushed against it and he watched her closely. She leaned forward and kissed the side of his mouth, pressing her swollen lips to the white scar. His hands tightened where they encircled her waist. She moved back slowly, her eyes shyly meeting his. His expression was unreadable.

Her thumb brushed gently over the scar again. "How did you get this?"

Tensley's behavior shifted, like a horrible avalanche. His hands gripped her fingers and yanked them away from his face, causing her to wince. His brows lowered as his mouth twisted into an ugly scowl, and he pushed himself off her to loom over the bed. Tensley selected a new shirt from the armoire, threw it on, and stalked to the door. He opened it and stepped out, hesitating and white-knuckled in the doorway.

He glanced over his shoulder at her, his eyes no longer soft, no longer tender, but full of rage, full of determination—and a hint of warning. "Be careful about declaring war against me, Ms. Darling. I don't think you know how much control I have over you. I could have you more than just rocking against me."

She sat motionlessly on the bed, her hand hovering over her trembling lips. The warmth left with him. She didn't like the way her heart still pounded—but not it ached.

She fisted the blankets and wrapped herself up, hoping to escape the shadow of the warmth that lingered after him.

What the hell just happened?

chapter eighteen

TENSLEY'S FINGERS BOUNCED against his thigh and he desperately craved a quick smoke of pure belladonna. The other incubi surrounding him in the hazy fog of the estate on Fifth Avenue chatted deafeningly loudly, drunk off booze and high on belladonna. His father felt it was the perfect time to introduce Tensley to some of his "loyal" business partners—the same people who had years ago transferred their funds and ties to the Boston organization, their rival, after his brother's scandal.

After years of rebuilding their power in Manhattan, Scorpios was just as powerful as it had been in the 1940s. With the Second World War and the Great Depression over, many demons and humans alike had made hefty deals to expand their own power.

Now standing in the midst of a crowd of rats and power-hungry cowards, Tensley wanted that damn nicotine. He was on edge, his thoughts continually going back to the blonde alone in that hotel room, guarded by two of his best men. He hadn't liked how his heart had clenched at her slouching shoulders and bowed head as he left an hour earlier, but the reminder of his growing tenderness had been enough to send him out.

"Tensley, where's your older brother?" a pudgy man asked, his waxed mustache concealing his thin upper lip.

Tensley aimed his eyes at his empty crystal glass. "He's out of town."

"Growing weak for another human, is he?" Pudgy jabbed Tensley's ribs and he tensed, ready to break the man's fingers one by one.

When he turned to scowl at the idiot, his eyes caught his father's sharp gaze. He halted.

No smartass remarks.

"He's doing business for us. That's all I know." Tensley hid his clenched hands under the table.

Pudgy's eyes were bloodshot. "Be careful, son. Your genes are drawn to weak things. It's a trait of your family — am I right, boys?"

A few other demons standing closest to them laughed.

Tensley ground his teeth, resisting the urge to fire back at him. "Excuse me, *boys*. I need another refreshment." He stood and marched toward the hallway. He wanted to destroy that bastard – *badly* – but if he wanted to run the family business, he had to play by the rules.

A hand gripped his shoulder and he turned to see Mr. Rose, Evelyn's father. His tan skin was very wrinkled and his white hair was gelled back. "Tensley," he said. "How's the nineteenth battalion?" Mr. Rose worked alongside Tensley's father as his right-hand man; it was how Tensley and Evelyn had met and grown closer over the years. Now he didn't know how the two families' relationships would evolve.

Fuck, Evelyn.

"Fine." Tensley rolled his shoulders, escaping from the older man's grasp and letting his suit settle back neatly — it was the same grip he'd seen strangle a low-class demon to death for speaking out of turn at a Scorpios meeting.

Mr. Rose nodded and moved closer, eyeing the empty hallway. "I've heard rumors, Tensley."

Tensley remained aloof. "About?"

"That you're engaged to another demon." The veins lining Mr. Rose's neck bulged. "Now, tell me — that rumor's incorrect, right?"

Tensley worked his jaw, watching the older man's features darken. "Yes. It's a lie." Mr. Rose's rigid shoulders relaxed.

I'm not engaged to another demon.

She's a daemon, actually. Dick.

"I'm glad to hear that, Mr. Knight. A strain in our partnership when you take over the business wouldn't fare too well for you," he said with a smile.

Tensley itched to retort, but held his tongue — his father had advised him to rein in his temper, and it was something Tensley actually agreed with. "No, it wouldn't," Tensley said, brushing past the demon and slipping into the nearest restroom.

He yanked at his tie and clawed at the shirt's top buttons, plotting. If Mr. Rose found out that Tensley *was*, in fact, engaged to Molly before he'd accessed her daemon powers, he risked becoming a target. Mr. Rose had many powerful ties and allegiances within Scorpios, and Tensley wasn't so sure that everyone in the organization was fully loyal to the Knight family.

Tensley glowered at his reflection and threw the soap into the sink, sending water splashing over the marbled surface.

He shouldn't have touched her. He shouldn't have given in to his goddamn desires — to the demon, the beast inside him. He craved her softness, her affection. It scared him how much he wanted that. It had been removed from his life and now that *it* sat back at his hotel room, teasing the chance of having that affection, it haunted him.

She was digging her claws into his heart, beginning to unravel him; he couldn't keep up his detached façade when she invoked such a desire to show her — show himself, that perhaps underneath all of that hard shell was a man. Not a beast. He rolled his upper lip, watching the scar from his brother crease.

He looked away.

All he could think about was her heat, her soft features as she gazed on him...her tender fingertips tracing his face...those warm, sweet lips. His chest ached as he thought back to her doe eyes.

She looked at him like he was a good man, a man who hadn't just been imagining several different ways to have her all to himself. He had felt the heat between her legs, throbbing against him. He wasn't good. He couldn't get close.

It was exactly why Evelyn would fit him better. She knew his limits and knew their marriage would be a business transaction. Fuck, he had to remember their deal; completely exclusive to each other.

Ugh. If his father found out about Molly's actions, he would be in trouble. Getting stabbed by his fiancée? No. Not a good thing.

In the end, Molly's random, aggressive gesture was a much-needed wakeup call. He couldn't be friends with her. *Don't forget who you are, Tensley fucking Knight: a cruel, ruthless demon.*

He glanced up at the mirror and frowned. His eyes were heavy, hooded, and dark. The large amount of energy he had exchanged with Molly was fading fast, and he figured it had to do with his intense emotions, which were a mix of anxiety, anger, and sexual frustration.

Taking a deep breath, he collected himself and left, determined to go back to the hotel.

Just as he stepped out of the bathroom, Tensley's name was called.

He turned to find his father watching him. "Have you?" Mr. Knight questioned, moving closer, eyes clouded and endless. "Have you marked her?"

Tensley squared his jaw. He didn't want to engage in any sexual act with her. He wasn't going to bother pursuing her now, and he *didn't* want to hurt her.

Only high-class demons could tell if a human wasn't marked, seeing the collar that formed around the woman's throat, so Tensley would just need to keep Molly away from them. His father, like Tensley, was high-middle-class, and he wouldn't know if Tensley lied.

"Yes, I have."

"Good." Mr. Knight, for once, seemed on the edge of a smile he didn't have to fake. "Now Abaddon won't bother."

That bastard.

An emptiness expanded painfully slow in Tensley's chest. He fought against it, but it kept resurfacing;

something was lacking in that space, and he longed to fill it.

"Tensley?"

He glanced up to see his father's arched brow.

"You have something else to say?"

He swallowed, a bit startled. He didn't know *what* to say, but something was eating him alive inside. He desired something from his father: acceptance, approval…something far more dangerous.

"No, sir." He turned to leave, tugging at his collar and fidgeting with his family ring.

"You were always stronger than your brother," his father's chilling voice halted him.

Tensley let out a harsh breath that he disguised as a laugh. He could hear the distant memory of the human girl screaming as Fallen ripped out his brother's heart. He could remember Fallen's warning.

"This is your lesson, boy. Demons don't love, they destroy."

Then Fallen had slashed the girl's throat.

Tensley threw open the door and marched into the thick summer air as it filled his lungs. He grasped for clarity in his mind, longing for the reminder that love was a disease, a demon's greatest weakness and fault.

"No." He breathed, tugging at his cuffs. "I'll never make the same mistake as *him*."

"LEAVE."

The two guards abruptly straightened and turned pale, fidgeting like scared field mice. They marched away from the hotel room door and vanished into the elevator.

Tensley stood in front of the door, readying himself. *No kindness, no softness.* With a roll of his shoulders, he unlocked the door and stepped inside.

Molly wasn't asleep; she sat with her legs bent at the chest, arms woven around them on the bed of twisted sheets. Her head jerked up, blue eyes narrowing as she recognized him.

She didn't budge, but he saw her chest begin to rapidly rise and fall. "What food did we just eat?"

He furrowed his brow. "What?"

"Just answer the question!" Her face grew bright red as she fisted the covers.

He glared, jerking his hand to the empty coffee table. "*Pizza.*"

Her muscles loosened and she shakily breathed out. "I was making sure it was you."

The strangled sound of her voice cut deep in his chest. *No, don't.* "I'm leaving. I've paid for you to stay here as long as needed until things smooth over." *Until I mark you.*

She scooted off the bed and stood up to him.

"Drop me off at my apartment," Molly stated.

He frowned. "I don't think that's a wise decision."

She filled her cheeks with air, slowing blowing it out with a whistle. "It's not your decision."

Tensley glared at her, but then immediately softened, and he hated her for it. "It's as much my decision as yours."

"You don't get to make any decisions for me. Got that?" Her harsh even tone startled him, and he scowled. "I'll ask September to stay with her dad."

Her eyes aligned with his, and they no longer terrified

him. They held strength, and an enchanting vulnerability. *Vulnerability?* He would have never seen that as endearing before. It was the way her eyes held him, though. The silvers and blues swirled together to create a hue of alluring radiance, with her large black pupils in the center.

What truly startled him was the feeling that wedged between his lungs and pounding heart. The feeling was a need for comfort, for affection that he'd never experienced.

He forced himself to turn his back on her, looking out the window that faced the park. He hoped she didn't see his chest rapidly falling and throat tightening as he gulped in air. She was having too much of an influence on him.

I'll just have my guards watch her. Distance. Distance is good.

His heart pounded violently. A pain began, a desire, a craving for something where his heart should have been. When he pressed a hand to his chest, he inhaled and fought a fullness gathering in his throat.

No, no, he couldn't be like Beau.

When Molly touched his arm, all his feelings expanded.

"Tensley?"

He swallowed. Her physical presence was just too much. If he wanted to save her, he'd stay away and make Molly keep her distance. He turned to face her, looking up at him in that innocent, questioning way.

"I *despise* you." He squared his jaw. "If you weren't an asset to me, I'd dispose of you *my way*," he continued, though he wasn't sure who he was trying to convince— Molly or himself. "Tread carefully, *Darling*, or I might give the beasts a taste."

Her lashes flickered, and the unique tinge of her eyes vanished under them. There were those fucking eyes again, tugging him toward her. He turned his head to the side to avoid looking straight at her.

Molly raised her chin. "The feeling's mutual."

He shoved his balled hands into his pockets and squared his shoulders. Disappointment flooded his chest.

Where was the relief? Instead, his shoulders tensed and he ached to retort, to get even.

She brushed past him into the bathroom and Tensley immediately left, angry that the feelings were still there — stronger than *ever*.

chapter nineteen

THE WIND PICKED up as Molly once again entered the cemetery, squinting at the shapeless figures ahead. Cree walked beside her, and unlike the first time she'd come, she wore a dark jacket with a hood concealing her blonde head. Three weeks ago, he had given her a sharp, curved dagger. She held it in her shaking right hand.

When she told Cree Tensley had people watching her, he brushed it off and told her the cemetery and surrounding area were charmed by the diviners so the demons wouldn't be able to track them. In there, she was safe.

After weeks of training with them, she felt tougher and stronger. She wasn't out of breath instantly when she ran, and she discovered she had a higher pain tolerance than humans. On the downside, she'd been slipping behind at the museum, coming in late after extensive midnight training sessions, messing up the research for the displays.

The fear of failure made her stomach twist into painful knots, but a voice told her she was focusing on the right thing: trying to protect her family's lives.

She struggled back and forth on whether to tell Cree of her change of heart for Tensley. He didn't deserve death, but they both needed to end the contract. Tonight, she would tell Cree. She wasn't killing Tensley.

A few demon hunters waved or said hello as they got closer, their cold exteriors shifting to ones of approval and acceptance. Some had even invited her to their home for supper since she'd been attending. It was better than sitting alone in that Plaza hotel room.

"Is it ready?" Cree asked Freya.

Her pink hair was tied up in a low ponytail at the nape of her neck. "He's restless."

Who?

"You wanna see a weakened demon?" A guy named Ryan, shorter than the rest, hollered directly at Molly. "How disgusting they really are? Their true, basic desires?"

A demon? She shoved the clawing fear to the back of her mind.

"Bring the cup," Cree said to no one in particular. Someone shifted and brought forth a large grey cup. Each took turns sipping from it before passing it along. When it made it to Cree's hefty hands, he took a large gulp, wiping his mouth on his leather jacket sleeve when he was finished. He passed it to Molly and she examined the dark liquid swaying inside.

"What is it?"

"The only way to keep up with them, their strength, speed. Demon blood," he said calmly. "It makes for a fair fight. Now drink up."

Her eyes widened. "Demon blood?" She glared down at the liquid, gagging at the sight.

"You don't have to drink it," Cree said.

She glanced at him, then saw the rest of the hunters watching her. "I'm good." She handed it back to Cree, who frowned, but didn't say anything more. She couldn't stomach the idea of drinking demon blood and her thoughts lingered on what she had been debating the last while.

Tensley.

"Release him," Cree said to two of the hunters, and they marched toward a tomb made from chipped grey stone, weathered by the years of harsh winters and trespassers. They toyed with the lock and a growl erupted from within the tomb. Molly braced herself.

"We starve them: no food, water, or any physical touch," another demon hunter said, standing behind her.

"Is that necessary?" Molly shut her mouth fast. The hunters who heard her stared coolly back. Her stomach twisted and knotted, a horrible dread sinking in.

"It's necessary when he slaughters three of our members in front of their families. It's fucking necessary then." Ryan's spat words drilled deep into Molly's chest and she looked away, only to catch Cree watching her.

The rusted door creaked open and she held her breath. In the dark tomb, half-bent, was a lanky male figure. He hesitated, the outside light too bright for him as he bowed his head, twisting his body into a tiny shape. His feet moved heavily onto the damp grass as he lifted his chin, eyes shining like polished onyx. A hiss seeped through his snarled mouth as he assessed the group.

"And then we *hunt them*," Cree finished in a dangerous, bloodthirsty tone.

Molly flinched as the group hollered thunderously, thrusting their weapons — knives, chains, axes — into the air.

The demon darted away and the crowd followed after, feet pounding on the hollow ground of the graveyard, over the hills and through the thick forest. Molly raced after them, her senses heightened by the chase. Stumbling through branches and stones embedded in the slopes, she collided with a tree and scraped her palms along it.

"Ow," she gasped, examining her stinging palms for scrapes. She glanced up at the distant voices far ahead. Her heart pounded too fast, too hard against her ribcage. Her senses were heightened to the extreme — every noise, every movement startled her. A high-pitched noise erupted in her eardrums and she recoiled, covering them against the harsh sounds.

Something moved beside her, and she turned to see a figure, tall and gaunt, a few feet away. His breath blew out heavy and fast.

Oh shit.

She darted in the opposite direction and his feet thundered behind her. Her lungs burned as she stretched her legs farther, willing them to put more space between her and the hungry demon.

Stupid, stupid, stupid — I'm a daemon, and according to Tensley they can sense me for miles! Why didn't I think of that?

Her grip tightened on the knife as his fingers clutched her hair, yanking down. She shrieked as they fell and rolled, sending her sunglasses flying. His hands clawed at her jacket, and he wheezed like a dying animal. As soon as he touched her flesh, however, his grip grew stronger.

His nails dug into her flesh, blood oozing from the cuts.

"Ow!" Molly screamed, "Cree! *Cree!*"

Use your eyes!

She turned, her eyes meeting his glazed stare. She willed herself to calm down, for each limb to relax, and delivered the sensation to him, summoning complete control over him. His eyes had been wild, but as soon as they met hers, they calmed. His hands loosened their grip.

His strawberry blond hair disturbed her. It was so light, so childlike she couldn't believe he was a demon — something so ugly, yet with the hair color of a child. Someone innocent. His raspy, hoarse breathing filled her eardrums. A dark tattoo stretched across his forearm — a scorpion, arched for battle, stinger posed.

She stared at the tattoo for a moment, *a single second*, and it was a moment too long. His sharp, dirty nails sliced into her hips, and his mouth latched onto her throat. She screamed when his teeth bit into her collarbone.

In pure desperation, she stabbed the Golden Fleece laced hairpin into his chest, deep — one, two, three times. His fingers clawed at her flesh and she pushed her arms out, keeping him a foot away. Soon he coughed, blood seeping from his mouth and dripping all over her face, until the darkness in his eyes vanished to leave only a beautiful moss-green color.

He's dead.

Guilt stabbed her in the chest. She'd murdered someone. Tensley's features blurred her vision and she gripped her shirt.

"Molly." She awkwardly tilted her head to see Cree and Freya, the others appearing behind them. Freya's face was hard, but Cree's mouth hung open. He stepped forward and pulled the dead demon off Molly, tossing him in some nearby bushes. Cree returned and helped her up, keeping Molly's hand secured in his even after she'd stood.

She staggered, only to vomit.

"Here," Cree said. He wrapped an arm underneath her armpits and guided her through the forest. She had to fight not to look back at the dead body some of them were removing. Her hands shook and she tried to steady them, but they wouldn't stop.

He was a demon. He wasn't good.

The stabbing pain wouldn't leave her chest.

Cree walked her all the way to the subway station, wiping the remaining blood from her cheeks with a handkerchief. "You did well tonight, Molly," he said, stopping at the platform.

She turned to face him, perplexed at his relaxed demeanor. "I killed him." She wiped her dirty hands on her cargo pants and bit back a sob. "I murdered —"

Cree gripped her wrist, shoved up her sleeve, and shook her arm. "*This* – this is why you killed him, in self-defense." She eyed the red marks and superficial cuts spanning her arm from the demon's attack. "If you hadn't stopped him, he would have done worse. He would have *murdered you* and enjoyed it."

She couldn't look away from the wounds, and seeing them only made them ache more.

She looked at the station, blindingly bright compared to the dark sky, and squeezed her eyes shut. "What will they do with his body?"

"That's where we get the blood," he explained. "We take them to the chapel and drain their blood before the body disintegrates."

"And you never think it's wrong? To just do that?" She gestured to pavement, but she couldn't stop seeing the man's crumpled body.

Cree shook his head, not looking at her. "I get that you have this fairytale like fantasy that even demons are worth saving, but not in my world. I told you when you first came to the bar you weren't going to like some of the things we do, but we do it as a means to an end. You don't have to agree with my methods, but trust me, we'll get rid of Tensley."

She nodded absently and bit her lip. The lingering thought she'd been carrying around in her head ached to get out. She needed to tell him. Now. "Cree, I want to make it clear though…" She paused, wanting to word it right. "I don't want to *kill* Tensley. He doesn't deserve to die. I just want him to end the contract."

Cree's warm appearance faded to a deep frown. "Molly, hunters are a family, a *unit*. We protect each other, we fight for each other, and we die for each other." He shifted from foot to foot, a soft summer breeze ruffling his longish hair. "After my sister's death, my own family handled the situation differently, and we grew apart. The hunters became my second chance for a family, a united front wanting the same end goal: to stop them from hurting innocent people."

Molly saw a wetness build in his brown eyes and reached out, threading his fingers through hers in a tight squeeze.

She licked her lips before speaking softly. "But Tensley's innocent, too, you know? He's tangled up in this contract like me and he wants out just as much as I do. I think if we talked to him, he might be willing to help us."

Cree's jaw clenched, but he didn't snap, not like she expected. He let out a long, shaky breath, still concentrating on her features. "We'll talk about it, okay? I can't decide without talking to the others. Don't think they'd be too happy working with a demon, let alone a Knight."

She smiled. "Thank you."

He laughed. "Don't mention it." He nodded his head behind her. "Ride's here."

She turned to see the subway train arriving and a few people boarding.

She grinned at him, still shaken about the demon's death but feeling a bit more at peace. *It was for the good of them all; that demon will never hurt another person.* Molly boarded the subway and waved at Cree as she whooshed by.

She'd break the contract and keep Tensley alive.

Perfect.

As long as he agrees, that is.

chapter twenty

TENSLEY LIT HIS cigarette and eyed the nineteenth battalion. His father had put him in charge of leading the patrols for any threats, and at the moment they were hunting some rogue demons who'd stolen belladonna from Scorpios. They'd found them in a disgusting warehouse on the outskirts of Queens, and now he stood apart from the criminal demons as they either talked shit about him or admired him.

Since his brother's scandal, the Knight family name definitely didn't hold the same clout, but he was no harmless kitten. *Oh, he'd show them fucking harmless.*

He inhaled deeply and blew out the belladonna smoke, watching it tangle with the summer breeze. The air was thick and stale, and he wrinkled his nose, scowling at the battalion escorting the demons out of the rundown warehouse and past the barbed wire fence that circled the property.

That's how he felt: encaged, a beast thrashing inside a metal cage.

"Sir?" The timid young soldier — a middle-class demon — edged cautiously closer to Tensley. "All of them have been detained."

Tensley looked at the seven demons, hands tied behind their backs as they were shoved into a van. One's bruised, swollen eyes flickered to his, mouth forming in a ghastly snarl. The thief's body shivered, either from his demon side craving an attack or just the need for more belladonna.

Tensley flicked his cigarette, sending its burning stub to the concrete. "Keep them in lockdown at the house. Quincy can deal with them tonight. Break some bones. I'll interrogate them tomorrow."

"Yes, sir," the boy stammered, and Tensley took off. He climbed into his Jaguar and sped back to Manhattan, wanting to forget his responsibilities for one night. His hands shook and he gripped the wheel tighter. He knew he was getting weaker without complete intimacy from another.

Tensley shouldn't have been surprised by Illya's presence as he passed through foyer of the Scorpios estate, his friend curled up in a fancy armchair near the fireplace, waiting for him.

Daniella, the secretary for Scorpios, sat behind the desk, eyeing Tensley's unbalanced demeanor.

Without a word, Illya followed him down the hallway and into his office. Tensley eyed himself in the wall mirror. Dark circles framed his grey eyes, and his skin looked sickeningly pale. He needed whiskey and he needed sleep.

Every night for the past three weeks had been spent

with obsessive thoughts ping-ponging between work and Molly. He was close to losing his shit.

The two of them walked farther into his office and Tensley shrugged out of his suit jacket, tossing it on the back of the couch.

"We had your father's meeting tonight. Why did you skip?" Illya asked.

Tensley didn't bother to look up, instead withdrawing another cigarette from the pack in his pocket. He opened the second set of French doors onto his balcony, staring out at the giant garden behind the estate.

Tensley huffed. "To avoid the bastards."

Illya leaned against a chair beside him. "Still avoiding her?"

Tensley stubbed his cigarette out on the balcony's railing before walking back into his office — black, sleek, and neat. It was decorated with dark hardwood floors and antiques from his family's past, paintings of his ancestors, of his family. Money would never be a problem for their family, not with their clients and the belladonna and the Princes.

"I'll take that as a yes," Illya muttered, strolling into the room.

Tensley shook his head angrily. "Don't mention her."

"It's been almost three weeks, man. You're weak." Illya sighed.

"I'm not *weak*, Illya," he argued, bending over to retie his shoelaces. His fingers shook and he struggled to grip the laces tight enough. "I do, however, miss the time before puberty hit when getting intimate didn't matter. Damn puberty."

"You look sick, and you can't even tie up your own shoes," Illya said. "Just get off your high horse and —"

Tensley glared at his friend. "I'm not going near her. I'm protecting us both."

Illya looked blankly back. "You know that's not true."

Tensley bared his teeth, nostrils flaring. "I want her for one thing—an heir. After that, she's gone." He stood up, head high, shoulders back, eyes sharp. "She's not your friend, Illya. Don't get attached."

"I'm not worried about my attachment; I'm worried about yours," Illya said, folding his arms.

"If she left, or disappeared, I'd be thrilled." Tensley grabbed a clear glass, filled it up with whiskey, and gulped it down. "*You* don't have to marry her; you don't have to deal with her for the next few decades." He slammed the glass onto his desk.

Illya kept his stance. "I thought you were going to get rid of her after she gave you an heir?"

"Leave if you're just going to bug the shit out of me."

Illya shifted, but didn't edge closer. "Tensley, I know you," he began. "The *real* you. Why can't you show her that person?"

He sighed heavily. "You know there are real reasons I can't."

"You mean because of your brother's past?" Illya said, voice low.

"It ruined my family; his selfishness and uncontrolled desires destroyed the person he was." Tensley's jaw tightened. "He became that heartless demon once Fallen ripped it out and *everyone* knew, every demon, every royal prick knew that my flesh and blood, a high-born, committed the ultimate sin." Tensley glared at his trembling hands and flattened them out on the table. "He developed a full heart for a Spanish *chica*." He blew out a harsh breath. "I could control myself with Evelyn because she understood my limits, but Molly — Molly's practically human. She doesn't understand anything about us."

"Then what are you afraid of?"

"Nothing — she doesn't fucking scare me," he insisted, furrowing his brows.

"Stop denying it!" Illya's face grew red and he threw his arms out. "You're scared that she's going to make you feel more than you want to, that you won't be able to control yourself and will end up like your brother. If you just rein yourself in and stop being a dick all the time, I bet you could manage it." When Tensley didn't respond, simply glaring at his fisted hands, Illya slammed his hand on the table. "Tell me, why is it that you refuse to kiss anyone, including Evelyn on the lips? Hm?"

Tensley squared his jaw.

"Because it's more intimate than sex, right? You're so fucking terrified of getting too close to anyone. Evelyn's security to you; Molly's a threat to everything you fear."

"What's it to you?"

"I want you to be happy. You're the closest thing I have to a brother and I don't want to see you struggling — and I can tell you've been struggling…a *lot*."

Tensley's body shook as he tried to control his temper, the waves of rage rolling like the tide of the sea. "I don't want to become like *him*. I still have scars from when he nearly broke my face in half — his own fucking brother." The scar on his upper lip burned at the mention, the ghost of a shattered relationship.

Silence filled the room, the air crackling with tension at each heavy breath Tensley took.

"Fallen hasn't made a move to approach either Molly or your family. If Abaddon told him, he would have already," Illya said carefully, changing the topic.

"*Or* Fallen's planning something bigger." Tensley slammed his hands onto the desk and snarled. "Shit."

"If Fallen knew about her, he would have made it clear. He would have come up here himself to see if it was true." Illya's features pinched as he spoke, defying his certainty.

Fallen would want her; he'd want to mark her, and then he'd be even more powerful than before.

Tensley rubbed his forehead and sat down in his leather armchair. "Keep an eye out for anything. Don't let any demons near her. I've had a few of my men follow her, but I trust you more."

"Just because we're supposed to hate things that aren't demons doesn't mean we have to," Illya murmured, sitting as well.

Tensley narrowed his eyes as he looked at Illya across his desk. "I don't have time for this shit. Have you heard from Lex?"

"Nothing. No one's seen her, but she's done this before. You know how she is," Illya said.

Tensley nodded; it'd been almost a month since he'd spoken to the funny little soul eater. "I still worry about that scrawny girl."

"I do, too." Illya sighed, got up, and walked toward the door. "Call me if you need anything. I'll watch for anything out of the ordinary." He paused mid-step. "She has been in Brooklyn, a lot."

Tensley furrowed his brow. "With who?"

"Goes by herself," Illya said. "Then they lose track of her."

Alarms went off in Tensley's head. "She's up to something. Keep the men on her." An ache festered in his chest and he attempted to shake it off without Illya noticing. *She went behind my goddamn back!*

"And just wait for her to do something?"

Tensley's shaking fists formed into tight balls. "Make her think she has the upper hand. Just tell my men to watch her – *closely.*"

After Illya left, Tensley sunk farther into his chair, plucking the buttons of his shirt open. He sweated profusely, and the shaking grew worse than when he'd survived withdrawal from belladonna two years ago. He wished food, water, and sleep could give him the energy he needed, but it was intimacy that truly nourished him.

He stood, flexing his hands.

"Damn it," he muttered, a cigarette pressed between his lips as the sweltering heat overwhelmed him in his designer suit. He leaned back against the wall and sighed, fingers shaking when he went for his lighter. He had smoked before--only sometimes, usually after sex—but now, he smoked most of the time...something to distract him from another craving.

He'd heard of demons going for months without intimacy, and in the end they all ended up as corpses. He couldn't keep living like that.

"Mr. Knight." A sensual voice hummed into his ears. Tensley gazed through his dark lashes, surprised to see the familiar, slender figure before him. His body pulsed.

He pressed his back firmly to the wall and lifted his head high.

A smirk warped her lips, and he took another long drag. He stepped away from the wall and, with as much strength and confidence as he could muster, managed to stop shaking. He took the cigarette from his mouth and stubbed it out in his ashtray.

"Ms. Rose." His eyes scanned over her long toned legs and her red mini-dress. Her dark hair was curled, and her eyes were sharp and endlessly black. Even a quick glance gave him a delicious pulse of strength.

"Oh, so now that you haven't seen me in a month, I'm *Ms. Rose?*" He waited for a laugh to release from her pursed lips, but she was good at keeping him on his toes. She strolled over, swaying her hips, and eyed him. "You don't look so hot, Tensley."

He held in a grunt and steeled his features. He couldn't keep his eyes off her. "I'm fine."

She giggled and then faked a pout. "Has your fiancée not been taking good care of you?" Tensley raised his chin, eyes narrowing as she lifted his limp hand to her chest. He tried to pull back, but she was stronger. "Oh, Tensley."

"Ms. Rose."

She brought his other hand to her lips and licked his pinkie. "Call me Evie. Don't you remember how you used to whisper in my ear when you were inside me?" She leaned in close, meeting his ear perfectly due to her height—unlike the short blonde fiancée of his. "Don't tell me you forgot all about me."

He turned his head, breathing hard into the shell of her

ear as he gripped her waist. She shivered against his body. "I remember." He moved past her, but she stepped into his path and shot him a shrewd look.

"That little girl doesn't satisfy you, not like I did," she hissed, her nose wrinkling and her chest rising with every breath. "Let me help you." She stepped forward, pressing her long fingers to his chest.

Tensley considered leading her into the nearest bedroom, lifting up her dress, and being satisfied again. *It would be so easy.*

"I miss you," Evelyn cooed. Her voice was so soft, perhaps the softest he had ever heard it. "Don't you miss me?"

He squared his jaw. He *did* miss her snarky comments whispered about the councilmen and how she knew just what he liked in bed.

She grabbed his shirt playfully, lifting it up to feel across his tensed stomach muscles. "You used to play with me any way, any time, any place, remember?" She pushed him hard against the wall. He stretched his neck, eyes half-closed. Her tongue licked across his collarbone, fingers skillfully unbuttoning his dress shirt. Now he was semi-hard.

God, it felt good. His body twitched with the small amount of new power. Evelyn kissed him roughly, leaving a trail of bites.

Fuck this. "Come on." Tensley pulled Evelyn toward him, palming her breasts and causing her to gasp. When he went to shove her to the wall, she firmly pushed him back. He stiffened, and his eyes widened as he stared down at the woman kissing his chest.

She was strong; there were no dark shadows underneath her eyes, no fatigue. If anything, her touch was a little *too* firm and tight. Her fingers undid the button and zipper on his pants, but he grasped her wrists before she could go any farther.

One hand wrapped around her throat. "Who did you fuck?" He bared his teeth, nostrils flared.

She tensed under his harsh tone and her awestruck expression transformed into a mirror image of his rage. "Oh, like you aren't fucking your fiancée?"

His grip tightened for a moment. "I haven't fucked her. I haven't fucked anyone!" Evelyn's expression faltered, and her mouth fell open. He glared. "But maybe I should have."

He let go and stepped back, trying to collect his anger with deep breaths.

In, out.

In, out.

All the women he had turned down because of the damn vixen in front of him. Because they promised each other to be fucking exclusive in their relationship. He growled, zipped up his pants, and proceeded to do up his shirt's buttons.

Evelyn gawked at him before punching the closest trashcan. It left a giant dent, evidence of her sexually enhanced strength. "*I* was supposed to be your fiancée! *I* was supposed to have your children, not some ugly, stupid twat. You just got engaged to someone else because your damn father told you to. You left me! What was I supposed to do? Wait for you?"

"I told you I would figure it out." His eyes bored into

Evelyn's, and her wrath faltered, leaving only fear and regret. "You're free to go fuck whoever you want, *Ms. Rose.* We're done."

Her eyes grew red and wet. "No, we're not." She stomped her stilettoed foot once. "Even before you went to go see your fiancée, you stayed with me, to the last second."

"So you should've believed me, but you *didn't*, so now we're done." He fixed his hair and rubbed the lipstick from his collarbone. "Goodbye, Ms. Rose."

She marched toward him. "Tensley, if you go back to that bitc — "

He swung around and she stopped in her tracks.

"I'm going home to *my fiancée*, Ms. Rose," he said coldly. He wasn't actually going to Molly's apartment; he simply wanted Evelyn to feel his anger.

"Goodbye."

Tensley watched Evelyn's lips shake and he turned away, strolling into the hallway.

He needed air, he needed strength, and his mind continued to go back to that damn siren.

chapter
twenty-one

MOLLY EYED HER text messages.

MICHAEL
12:06 P.M.
Hey! How are you?

MICHAEL
12:07 P.M.
Haven't heard from you in a while. Is everything okay?

MICHAEL
3:54 P.M.
Molly?

Her heart sat in her throat, pounding. She gripped the shot glass and downed it, savoring the burn.

"Just text him back." September ate a peanut from the bar.

Molly wanted to rest her head on the countertop, but

it was covered in sticky dried alcohol and peanut crumbs. She resorted to throwing her head back. "I can't. He thinks I'm in a relationship, and I heard from Tina he's been going out with Bonnie. I just can't be around him right now."

September chewed another peanut, smacking her lips — one habit she'd never gotten rid of, no matter how many times Molly pointed it out. "Well, like my Italian grandma always says, you can never eat too much pasta. So text him."

Molly brows shot up. "Because that definitely makes sense and applies to my situation right now." She shook her head and glared around the dive bar. "All I need is more pasta in my life."

"Grandma G knows where it's at."

"So have you talked to Illya at all?"

September choked on her peanut. "What?"

Molly shrugged. "You guys seemed to hit it off. He couldn't stop staring at you."

"Whoa." September took a deep breath and looked firmly at Molly. "Whoa, no. He's a demon and I do not do crossbreeds. I love D&D, but nooo — nooo forbidden romance for us two."

Molly drummed her fingers along the wooden bar top.

September reached out and stilled them. "Just don't think about it. Have fun tonight."

"I can't. I could lose my job. They pulled me aside and told me that if I don't get my act together, I'm out. No job, no money, no apartment."

"We'll find you a new job."

She also needed to tell September the new plan.

"And I had an idea..." Molly paused, thinking before saying it aloud. "To talk to Tensley and see if he'd be willing to destroy the contract." Now she'd just need the confidence to approach him.

"Uh, *what?*"

"I was talking to Cree, and he said he'd talk to the others, but I think it could work if Tensley and I both were on the same side of trying to get out of this."

"Okay, well, maybe? I don't know. I guess you'll just have to ask and see?"

Molly had wanted September to jump for joy at her idea, but her hesitation made her doubt herself. Molly sighed and scooted off the high bar stool. "I need to use the bathroom."

After she'd struggled to pee without sitting on the seat, Molly found a woman mopping in the corner as she went to wash her hands.

"Uh, hi," she mumbled, rubbing the soap between her fingers. She only responded with a nod.

As Molly dried her hands with a paper towel, water splashed on her shoes from the woman's mopping. She gasped, startled, and the woman in the blue jumpsuit shrugged.

"Sorry, I get carried away when I'm cleaning," she explained, a hint of laughter in her voice. She smiled, awkwardly shaking her drenched foot. "It's okay."

The woman studied her, the ghost of a grin displaying her uneven, yellowed teeth. "Here." Her feet moved fast and she bent down in front of her, wiping the water off her shoes with a rag from her back pocket.

"No, it's okay—it's okay," she told her. Her hair was greasy and uncombed.

"You allergic to the light or something?" She gestured to the sunglasses.

She nodded. "I'm very sensitive to light."

The woman's large, buggy eyes scanned her legs before moving up to her face again.

"I have to find my friend. She's probably looking for me." Molly stepped around her, walking away as calmly as possible.

She waved his hands. "Wait, *wait.*"

She turned and saw her hands shaking.

She licked her lips. "She left."

Molly furrowed her brows. "She left?"

"I told her you left, that you got fed up and left." Her head twitched and a horrible, twisting sensation began in Molly's chest. "Everyone left." She could still hear the music blaring loudly outside the door.

"W-what?" Molly's stutter came back full force as she tossed the damp paper towel in the trash. "I'm g-going to leave."

The woman grinned. "No, that's not an option, *daemon.*"

Shit times a million.

"Abaddon sent you, didn't he? You're one of his familiars." Molly edged farther away and she followed each step.

Crap! This isn't good, not good at all!

"Correct." She stretched out a hand. "Now, do I have to use force or are you going to come willingly?"

She swung at her, but she grabbed her wrist and wrestled her body against the mirror, shattering the glass on impact. The woman clasped a hand over her mouth, trapping the scream inside her dry throat. Her grip tightened, squeezing all the air out. Molly's teeth gnawed at her hand, and she only laughed. "Barely hurts."

"Hey, dick!" a voice roared from the side. A fist collided hard with familiar's cheekbone and Molly shoved her away. In front of her stood September, lips curled into a glower, eyes razor sharp as she observed the familiar. Molly coughed hard as September punched the familiar again, this time crying out in agony.

"Oh, fucking shit, that hurts!"

The familiar turned fully to face September, eyes scanning her contorted features. "You hit me."

"What the hell is your face made out of? Concrete? Jesus-fucking-Christ." She moaned as she shook her hand out.

"Humans don't attack demons," she hissed.

September froze. "A demon? Oh fuck no."

The familiar's hunched shoulders morphed and grew, features warping into defined cheekbones and black, greasy hair like a raven's.

The familiar pounced, gripping September's neck and pinning her to the wall.

"Get off of her!" Molly slammed her fists into her side, willing her superhuman strength to arise. It didn't. With a flick of her wrist she shoved Molly so hard she tripped and fell into the nearest stall, slamming into the toilet paper dispenser. September started gagging and her eyes rolled back as the familiar choked her, repeatedly beating her head against the tiled wall.

Molly stumbled to her feet, removed her sunglasses, and rushed the familiar again, swinging her entire body onto her back as she curled her fingers around her throat. The familiar choked and elbowed her in the side, but she didn't let go.

"You bitch!" She released one hand from September's neck and dug her nails into Molly's thigh, drawing blood. She cried out as the familiar swung her against the wall, now trapping both girls by their necks.

Her eyes met hers and she froze.

Yes!

Her grip weakened, and she made sure to blink as little as possible.

Molly opened her eyes wider. "Leave. Us. Alone."

The familiar released them and backed up. September fell to the ground like a sack of stones.

"Now get out—" Molly was suddenly thrown to the ground, a strong hand pressing her face to the filthy floor. Molly struggled, trying to twist her head so that her eyes would capture whoever was currently trapping her.

"Stop moving!" another woman's voice demanded, lifting Molly's head only to collide it with the floor again.

Pain shot through her temple as white spots raced across her vision, and all Molly could hear was her own shallow breathing, September's muffled cries, and the ringing in her ears.

"Kill the human. I'll take the daemon to Abaddon."

No!

"Fuck no. *I* got her," the first familiar hissed.

"I was the one who distracted everyone!" the second countered, tightening her grip on Molly's hair.

Molly closed her eyes and let her body relax. *Focus. Focus.* She could feel the female's fast heartbeat through the palm pressed to her temple, and she let her body unwind.

A jolt of strength rushed through her veins. *Yes!* Molly arched her back, elbowing the woman in the gut and twisting to see her. The woman stilled, mesmerized, and Molly yanked her up by the neck, a loud snap echoing in the tiny bathroom. Molly stared at the woman's unfocused eyes and slackened face, and released her hand.

The woman fell to the ground with her head at an unnatural angle.

September's shouts of pain snapped Molly from her thoughts, and she stumbled to her feet, reaching out toward the familiar currently clawing at September's throat. "*Stop!*"

A shadow burst through the washroom door, quick and flickering. It threw the familiar against the nearest wall.

Illya glanced over his shoulder at Molly.

Thank god!

"Illya?" Molly croaked, relief immediately radiating through her.

Illya stood on solid feet and glared darkly across the room as the familiar gathered herself, then lunged with ungodly speed at the demon. They wrestled back and forth, pinning each other and busting a stall off its hinges as they collided with it. Growls and hisses erupted from Illya like nothing she'd ever heard, and Molly couldn't believe he possessed such a side—demonic and aggressive, like Tensley.

"*Illya,*" Molly repeated as she moved closer to try and help. His eyes flickered to hers for a moment.

"Stay back," Illya snapped. He released a feral yell and used his body weight to fling the familiar up and around, flipping her onto her back on the floor. Illya pushed his foot down onto the familiar's veiny, thick neck.

"I'm not going to kill you," Illya spoke, face bloodied and eyes the darkest Molly had ever seen them. "Send a message to Abaddon." The familiar's face went blue, and she clawed feebly at Illya's ankle. "Tell him to forget about the daemon or we will go to the court and let the Princes judge him for breaking one of the Six Laws of Babylon. I'm sure they won't be too kind."

The familiar nodded and Illya released her. As quickly as she had appeared, she sped away, vanishing out the door in an instant.

Molly leaned against the wall, her hands unclenching. *We're safe.*

Illya tried to catch his breath. "You girls okay?"

Molly pulled her dress down to hide the cuts on her right thigh.

"Other than the near-broken neck, I'm great," September groaned, her voice nearly gone and eyes bloodshot.

Illya laughed and bent down, resting a few fingers on her collarbone. "Let me see," he whispered. "I can help." September bit hard into her bottom lip, struggling to hold in the pain. "Only if you want my help, of course." Their eyes never parted.

September nodded once and swallowed.

Leaning in, his fingers slid up her neck, and his eyes danced across her features. September, for once, was silent. His lips hovered over her bruises and his mouth met her sun-kissed skin. Heat came in waves over Molly's cheeks, and she folded her arms and debated whether she should look away. Illya's lips claimed the damaged skin, a soft kissing noise filling the empty room every time he removed his mouth. September grasped his shoulder, but didn't stop him. She moaned in utter delight.

Awkward.

Illya stopped and sat up, lips puckered, ears red. The bruises were already fading from September's neck and collarbone.

"Uh, thanks." September's hand fell from his back and she looked away.

Illya stood, turning to Molly. "Are you okay?"

"Just a bit stunned," she muttered, eyeing the quickly decaying female familiar. "I—I didn't mean to kill her. My strength—"

"Molly, you were protecting yourself and September," Illya said with a sigh. "I'll take you girls home." He helped them both up and the three of them walked in silence to the girls' apartment, a question eating at Molly the whole time. Once they stood outside, September excused herself with an awkward goodbye and vanished into the apartment building.

Molly hesitated, turning to face Illya. "How did you know where we were?"

Illya's hand gripped his side and a grimace flickered on and off. "He told me to look after you."

She pinched her brows together. "Tensley?"

He nodded.

To look after me? Her cheeks warmed and she hoped he wouldn't see.

Molly stared at the sidewalk and willed the assault of butterflies that had just bloomed in her chest away. "Doubt that. He hates me."

"He doesn't hate *you*; he hates the *idea* of you."

She glared at her five-year-old Dolce and Gabbana suede pumps, now covered in the familiars' blood and sink water...utterly ruined, like her life. "Please don't sugarcoat it."

"Demons are used to being in control of everything." Illya spoke with an unaccustomed scowl and continued to rub below his ribcage.

Molly touched his arm. "Are you all right?"

He shook it off. "I'm fine, just a bit sore. Getting too old for this." He laughed weakly and straightened his posture. "As I was saying, demons want control, but not every demon can control his or herself. It's a myth. Our society has created limits—we see kindness and affection as weaknesses."

She lowered her thick lashes and held her trembling body. "So affection's a weakness?"

"Just trust me, okay?" He put a hand on her arm. "I know him. He puts on a mask and pretends to be the myth we are. He just can't show it as easily as I can. He's paranoid of losing control—especially in front of humans—especially *female humans*."

"Why?"

"His family has a bad history with losing control, a recent history."

She frowned. "I can't. I can't trust him—-I can't trust you." She rubbed at her cheek, the one that was raw from being banged repeatedly against the bar's floor. "And why are you even friends with someone like him?"

He laughed into the air, gazing up at the starry night. "My mother's worked for his family since we were kids, and we've been friends ever since. We understand each other." Illya forced his lips into a grin, but it wasn't one that reached his eyes. "He's a good man. You'll see it one day."

She groaned. "Why doesn't he show me that, then?"

Illya was silent, watching her angry look. "He's scared, just like you. He's scared of feeling something he can't control." He exhaled into the night air. "Something happened that changed him."

She bit her lip. "What?"

"You'll have to ask him yourself." Illya rubbed at his torso again, his smile changing into more of a confused frown.

"Like he'll tell me anything." Molly scowled, kicking at a pebble and folding her arms.

A line of sweat rolled down Illya's forehead, and he coughed. "If you're wondering, Tensley isn't heartless. He may act like it, but he has part of one."

She blinked fast. "How, though?"

"I'm not sure. I have a theory Tensley's mother gave him some affection. His father, though...he believed no love should ever be displayed, regardless of their age. Without proper nurturing after puberty, the heart withers, becoming nonexistent over time. Tensley *does* care, I think, a lot more than most demons. It's why he's managed to maintain some semblance of a conscience, of how to be kind and just, even with a father and brother like the Knights." Illya stopped speaking for a moment, seeming out of breath.

"So he does care," she whispered.

"Yes. I think he does." Illya leaned against the small ash tree planted on the sidewalk. "He's been getting sick."

Her head whipped up so fast her neck cracked. "What?"

"He hasn't been getting enough intimacy," he continued softly. "I think if you help him, it would do a lot of good."

She fidgeted with her engagement ring. "I don't know, Illya."

"Just hold his hand and see, okay?"

She rubbed the back of her neck and nodded.

Illya groaned and bent over then, clutching his side.

"Are you sure you're okay? What's wrong?" She touched his back.

Illya's breaths were labored and shallow, and he pulled his shirt up to reveal a bloody gash along his skin, already swollen and infected.

"What is—did a familiar do that?"

A strange noise left Illya's lips before he could speak. "I—didn't—think—it—was—that—bad—" His body began to quiver more violently with each passing second. She put his arm around her neck and gripped him by the waist, careful of his festering injury.

"Take me to Tensley's place."

The last person she wanted to see.

Perfect.

chapter
twenty-two

"IT'S HERE," ILLYA rasped out, his shivers becoming spasms and his gasps like cries of pain.

"Stop!" Molly gripped the back of the taxi driver's seat, resolving to finish her text to September saying she wasn't coming back any time soon.

The taxi skidded to a halt in front of a high-rise art deco apartment building. She shoved money into the driver's hand and helped Illya out of the taxi.

As she entered the opulent lounge of Tensley's apartment on Fifth Avenue, her stomach twisted. What if Tensley wasn't there? Then what? How could she even help Illya? Could she even take him to the hospital?

She slammed the button for the elevator, and once the doors opened, they dodged the incoming traffic of fancy couples who appraised her disheveled appearance with disgust. Molly struggled to hold Illya up as the elevator climbed. His eyes glazed over and his body shook. He managed to tell her the floor and apartment number, and she dragged him to the right door, pounding wildly.

"Tensley, *please*." Her voice boomed through the empty, red-carpeted hallway. "Tensley!"

The door swung open and Molly nearly hit Tensley in the chest. He dodged and shot her a glare.

His brows furrowed at Illya. "What the hell happened?" he asked, grasping Illya's other arm. They shuffled into the grand apartment and laid Illya on the sleek leather couch nearest the hallway.

"You're gonna be okay, Illya. Don't worry," Molly cooed, combing at his drenched hair with unsteady fingers. *I shouldn't have listened to him. He wasn't all right. If he dies...* He mumbled weakly back.

Molly turned to face Tensley, watching her fiancé's face change from impatience to worry. "Tell me. *Now*." His voice was softer that time.

Molly to dissolved into sobs. "Illya, he—" She ran shaking palms over her sweaty face and through her messy curls. "You have to help him!" Molly rose from her crouch to find the kitchen and some towels, but Tensley grabbed her forearm.

"Tell me now, Molly. My patience is wearing thin, so *speak*."

"Uh, we were attacked, and—" Molly looked back at the couch, hoping to draw strength from Illya—but he wasn't there. She gawked at the empty cushions. "Illya?"

Her eyes swung to Tensley, who was frozen, strong and stern, looking behind her. A sinister chuckle made her jump, and she turned to see Illya, shoulders hunched and limbs twisted, standing behind them. Small spasms traveled through him as his face morphed, features sloping. He lunged at Molly, and she threw her hands up to protect her face. Tensley caught him by the middle and pinned him against the wall. Pictures fell, shattering, and Molly edged around them, transfixed.

"Motherfucker!" Tensley seethed, grasping Illya's long neck. Illya trapped one of Tensley's fingers in his mouth and bit down hard. Tensley growled, jaw clenched and face growing red, but he didn't scream. "Molly — get a knife."

Molly didn't waste any time and rushed to the kitchen, hands scattering for one of the expensive knifes in any one of his drawers. Once she retrieved one, she ran back and handed it to Tensley. He took it, glared at Illya, and ripped his shirt off. A hiss left Illya's chapped lips as he bucked against Tensley's frame, his wild, dark eyes zooming in on Molly.

"The golden one, the blessed one," Illya's voice was low and dark. "She is not yours to keep. She should be shared. She should be used up until she's nothing but an ugly, wilting corpse."

Tensley scowled. "Is that so?"

"Give her to me, to my master, the Duke Abaddon, and you will be granted your one and only desire." Illya's smirk faltered while Tensley remained silent. "The one you seek, the girl, she can be yours again, and you won't need to waste your seed on this one."

Molly frowned. *The girl?* He wasn't talking about her.

"Save it, you bastard." Tensley grabbed the little bit of fat on Illya's stomach and Molly could see something crawling underneath the skin, weaving fast. Illya's eyes rolled back and he began to cough viciously, his tongue lolling out and black as pitch. All the veins throughout

Illya's body pulsed and grew, about to burst. Tensley slid the sharp edge of the knife underneath the moving shape and cut deep, flinging it from Illya's innards to the ground in one swoop. Illya went limp and fell against Tensley, unconscious.

Molly looked closer and saw that it was a bug—a purple, shrieking beetle with a hard shell. It skittered toward her and Molly yelped, grabbing a large book off Tensley's side table and pounding the beetle over and over until it was flattened. She stared breathlessly at the dead bug, one of its tiny legs twitching in the air.

Molly flinched when Tensley stomped on it, twisting his foot to spread its guts across the hardwood.

"For good measure," he explained, dragging Illya to the couch once more. "Damn scarabs."

"Is he okay?" She wrung her hands, edging closer to the two.

"Illya." Tensley tapped Illya's cheek and his head lolled, eyes opening slowly.

Illya lifted a hand to his face, pinching his temples. "What happened?"

"Scarab. Got underneath your skin," Tensley murmured, taking a nearby blanket and holding it against Illya's bleeding cut.

Illya sighed, features worn down, brow knotted. "It was that damn familiar. He must have slipped it into my sleeve." Illya swore loudly in Russian. "Damn it."

Tensley shrugged and a faint smile appeared. "It happens." Molly couldn't believe what she was seeing: a nice, calm Tensley.

Illya's eyes flashed. "Did I hurt anyone?" He cocked

his head to see her, alarmed. "Did I hurt Molly?"

Tensley gazed over his shoulder at her stiff frame. "She's fine, just a bit in shock. I'll take care of her."

Take care of me?

"Did it say anything?" Illya swallowed thickly.

Tensley was silent, hesitant to answer. "He said I should 'share' her." He breathed evenly and rubbed his fingers against his palm. "He offered me a deal—for *her*."

There it was again. *Her*. Not Molly. *Who, then?*

"Her," Illya repeated. A painful shiver attacked his drenched body.

It was then Molly looked around the space.

The apartment was shadowed with a haphazard medley of classic and modern furniture; the dichotomy reminded Molly of Tensley's personality. The room was a continual space, a step down into a hardwood living room with black leather couches and a massive dark stone fireplace. The next space was the kitchen, which had a large marble island in the middle with silver appliances—definitely a bachelor pad.

"Get him some water," Tensley said. She jerked at first, startled, and ran to the kitchen to pour some water in a cup. "And a wet cloth." She did as she was told and raced back, almost tripping where the carpet met the wood.

Illya coughed and hacked incessantly, blood dripping from his wound onto the leather couch.

"His cut," Molly said, pointing to it as she handed the damp towel to Tensley.

"Illya, rest now." Tensley draped the wool blanket over him and held out the water, which Illya chugged. He closed his eyes then and leaned back, seeming to fall asleep fast.

Molly stood frozen, more in shock about Tensley's behavior than Illya's condition. He was being so gentle, so calm. Tensley grabbed the cloth, bright with Illya's blood, and dabbed it against Illya's forehead. He straightened and disappeared into what Molly guessed was the bathroom, returning with some slim white packages.

Tensley tore them open with his teeth and Molly saw that they were bandages. He placed them over the jagged, ugly wound.

"Won't he heal?"

He shook his head, and Molly closely examined how drained he looked. "He's too weak—and his rank don't heal as fast as mine. I'll have to exchange energy to heal him."

She wasn't sure what to do; she just couldn't stop gaping at him as a heat warmed her cheeks. He was only tending to his injured friend, yet Molly thought he looked both godly and the closest thing to a caring, *feeling* human she'd ever seen.

Maybe he *would* be okay with working to break the contract together…

Holy shit.

The butterflies in her stomach cartwheeled and flipped, and Molly longed for a stiff drink or a cold shower.

"Tell me what happened tonight," Tensley said, frowning at Illya's wound.

She eyed the back of Tensley's head. "Uh, well, September and I were out drinking. I went to the bathroom and this familiar showed up. I tried to fight him off, but another one showed up." She ran her fingers through her hair and sighed. "Then Illya showed up and saved us." She paused, worrying her bottom lip between her teeth. "He said you told him to look out for me."

Tensley's hands clenched. "You can sleep in my bed tonight, Molly. I'll watch over him," he said calmly. His eyes returned to his friend.

Molly didn't move. *His bedroom? Alone?* "The whole night? I mean—we could take turns."

"*Yes*, the whole night. Now go to bed."

Molly stood, unable to tear her eyes away. She was afraid she would never see this side of him again—a side she *wanted* to see, a side she understood.

Tensley swiveled his head toward her with a faint scowl. "Go."

"Okay, okay," she mumbled, taking hesitant steps as she navigated the apartment, searching for his bedroom. Just to make sure she wasn't hallucinating, Molly turned once more to study Tensley before going to bed, and he was just as thoughtful and pensive as ever...a watchful brother, a loving friend.

She wasn't sure who Tensley Knight was any more—the demonic beast who refused to release her from a terrible marriage, or the misunderstood man trapped in a messed up culture where survival meant being the most ruthless.

Now, she questioned how ruthless—how *heartless*—he really was.

He didn't seem heartless at all.

chapter
twenty-three

HEAVY **FOOTSTEPS IN** Tensley's hallway woke him, and he slowly raised his head to see a smallish figure approaching.

A girl?

Illya grumbled beside him, and the memories of the last few hours came rushing forth, breaking through his exhausted haze. Molly had stayed over, sleeping in his bed, and he'd decided to lounge on his leather chair. He hadn't meant to fall asleep, but it was difficult not to when he was nearly as weak as Illya, especially after exchanging energy. Tensley *really* needed to get laid— hell, even a kiss would be momentous at that point.

It was still dark outside, the large windows behind the couch showcasing the shadowed buildings of the Manhattan skyline. The living room sat in similar darkness, apart from the lamp beside Illya's feet that illuminated the oak floorboards.

He eyed Molly's curvy figure, pausing at the end of the hallway.

As the footsteps grew closer, he decided to pretend to be asleep and avoid the awkwardness. He rolled his head back and closed his eyes.

How someone so petite walked as loudly as a bodybuilder was beyond him.

Soon the footsteps paused, then began again in his direction. Tensley breathed through his nose, his heart beating more rapidly. *What the hell is she doing?*

A moment later, a soft material cloaked his frozen frame. Her hands were careful not to touch him, but she took the time to make sure his body was covered from his neck to his feet. He tried to breathe normally, as he knew she watched him. If she suspected he was pretending to be asleep, he wasn't sure how she would react.

Her footsteps began again and stopped shortly after. He peeled one eye open to see her sitting on the floor beside the couch, dabbing Illya's skin with the cloth. His other eye fluttered open, openly staring at her in interest.

She sniffled softly and used the heel of her hand to wipe away tears. "I'm so sorry, Illya."

Tensley's chest grew heavier at the sound of her voice breaking. "He's not dying," he muttered, hoping to ease whatever possible guilt she felt. Her head whipped around to him, mouth open.

The wetness on her cheeks glistened in the lamplight, contouring her heart-shaped face and creating more defined cheekbones. "He's okay?"

Tensley nodded sluggishly.

He watched as her body quivered, relaxing at the news. "I barely slept, thinking he was hurt because of me."

Tensley lowered his brows, surprised she would care so much about Illya. "Well, he's fine. Go back to bed," he ordered, angrily flustered at her fluttering wet lashes and wide eyes. He had grown somewhat immune to her eyes over the passing weeks, but they still had quite a hold on him. He wondered if he would be completely immune if he marked her.

His beast surfaced, growling in approval of the idea of marking her.

Fuck.

She watched him. "Are you okay?"

He stiffened at the soft concern laced in her voice, the affectionate tone. "I'm fine."

"Okay." She didn't move, turning back to face Illya.

He sighed. "Go. To. Bed. Molly."

"*Tensley*, shush."

He growled at her disobedience and stood, preparing to throw her over his shoulder and toss her in the bedroom. She twisted around as he marched toward her.

"You're hurt," she gasped, jumping to her feet. He halted when her body brushed against his, her hand pressing to his throbbing side where his shirt had ridden up. He hissed and gripped her wrist tightly.

"Fuck," he said quietly, looking down as her fingertips grazed the angry claw marks in his flesh. "Must be from fending him off." He pushed her hand away. "Yeah, let's touch the marks. That's a great idea."

"Do you have a first aid kit?"

He blinked, startled by her vehemence. "Yeah. In the kitchen, above the coffee machine." She sprang into action, racing into his kitchen. He walked in after her, examining her closely. Her need to care for him, to make sure he was fine made him chest warm, and at the same time, suspicious.

Is this a trick?

She used a nearby chair to step up onto the countertop then opened the cabinet to retrieve the tiny red box. He eyed her skirt as it lifted, the backs of her thighs exposed, giving him a brief view of the bottoms of her cheeks. His hands curled into fists as he refused to reach out and touch her.

Molly's usually glossy, smooth hair was a chaotic, untamed mess, frizzed and knotted. He liked this exposure; she wasn't a perfect Upper East Side doll.

He didn't need a first aid kit. It would heal in the next few hours — a perk of being a demon. In this case, it would be a bit slower than usual from his lack of intimacy, but it would heal nonetheless. "You know, I'm fine. We —"

"Take off your shirt." She hopped down from the chair.

Damn.

He gawked at her features, attempting to see the façade, but all he saw was her exhaustion from lack of sleep and stress. She searched through the first aid kit as he lifted his T-shirt over his head and tossed it onto the floor. Her eyes aligned with his toned torso as he moved closer, and he could tell she was reading the Italian words inked along his side.

Molly unrolled some bandages and placed them on the ugly lines of his skin, her cool fingertips sending a shiver down his spine.

"Lift your arm," she ordered, and he did so, muscles rippling and straining. Molly's little touches already sparked energy in his bones and blood, and it was intoxicating.

He glanced down at his abdomen and hiked his brows up. It didn't look pretty — the bandaging, that was. It was patchy and awkward. "You're doing a horrible job," he muttered, then stiffened as he waited for their tender moment to explode into insults and hateful banter.

Instead, she giggled.

He watched her nose scrunch up as a sweet smile formed on her pouty lips, dimples appearing on either side of her mouth. She couldn't seem to stop the sweet, high-pitched laughter as she continued her awful job of bandaging him. "I wanted to be a nurse when I was younger," she told him, attempting to straighten her work. "I wanted to help people." He still wasn't sure how to respond to her. Then she began giggling uncontrollably again. "I was awful then, too."

He couldn't fight the smile on his own lips. She was sleepy, he realized; they both were, and it made them vulnerable.

"Remind me to never let you do this again, *nurse*." He smiled at her bowed head. She simply responded with another adorable titter, the sound warming his chest. He didn't want this side of her to vanish. "And what do you want to do now?"

Her giggling stopped, but he could still see her body shaking with laughter. "I want to be a history teacher, or maybe work at a museum — the Met if I'm lucky," she told him, tilting her head up.

He collected tons of history books about wars, about ancient worlds. Evelyn told him he was wasting his time reading them.

"I'm going back to Columbia in the fall," she continued.

He hadn't expected that. *She's definitely smart then.* She certainly knew how to surprise him.

Her hand slipped between his fingers. The gesture jolted him — along with the power. Her affectionate touch brought him a rush of energy, and he squeezed her hand back. He couldn't believe he was holding it.

He cleared his throat. "What's your favorite discipline?"

"Ancient civilizations — particularly India. The history, the culture, the customs," she said and continued straightening her work with one hand. "It's so unique, so complex, but simple at the same time. I'm not making sense."

He couldn't help but smile at her giggle and he enjoyed her carefree self. "Have you ever been to India?"

She nodded. "Yeah, we went when I was younger, around my birthday." She moved a bit of hair from her eyes and gnawed on her bottom lip before she spoke again. "Why didn't your parents ever tell us when you were coming? We waited every year."

He shrugged. "My parents wanted to scare your parents into a corner so they wouldn't try anything. Your parents tried everything to hide you, to remove the ring, but my father stopped it. It was actually comical to watch them hide you, vanish to another country thinking they'd outsmart us, a demon family." He snickered.

Her fingers vanished from his hand suddenly, and he glanced at her. Molly's skin grew pale and she stared at him, unblinking. "You thought it was *comical?*" Her voice was strained and she stepped farther away, looking down. "It was just a funny joke to you that I spent every birthday waiting for something horrible to come?"

Fuck.

"*Me* being the horrible thing, I'm assuming?" He arched a brow and she scoffed.

That wasn't what he'd meant to say; didn't she realize how difficult this was for him? To be sensitive?

"I want to break the contract," she blurted out, eyes bulging.

"*What?*"

She waved her hands around. "You don't want this! You said you had a life before and I did, too! Why don't we just work together? Break it and—"

"Fuck, *no!*" There was no way to break a unique, complex blood contract from three hundred years ago. For one, it wasn't from either of their blood directly, and two, they didn't have a warlock of direct bloodline to sever it.

She frowned, her hands paused in midair. "But—?"

"End of fucking discussion." In a heated second, he ripped the messy bandages off his abdomen and left them pile on the floor. "It'll heal itself. Remember—I'm a demon."

Molly eyed him coolly, her warmth gone. "Like I could forget," she said, backing out of the cavernous kitchen. "I'm going home. You can stop your damn payments at the hotel; it's not needed. I don't need you 'protecting' me."

He didn't watch her go. He leaned, unmoving against the countertop.

He was pissed at himself.

Pissed that he found himself liking something.

Her kindheartedness. Her freedom with affection.

Fuck.

chapter twenty-four

SHOOT THE FREAK was loud when Molly entered through the rundown bar's front door. Her eardrums immediately ached from the music. She hadn't seen it so filled before, bodies everywhere, laughter and hollering permeating the space. As she pushed through the crowd, Molly recognized a few of hunters she'd practiced with. Cree had told her on the phone that morning that it was a special night: a full moon.

Molly's gaze raked over the hunters gathered in a corner of the bar, and she noted some guys and girls who were standing on a platform nearby, swaying. Their expressions were weak and drawn.

A hand landed on her shoulder, sending Molly about three feet into the air. "Holy shit!"

Cree stood behind her, grinning slyly. He laughed heartily at her expression, his face going somber as he took in her skintight outfit. "Didn't mean to scare you," he muttered, eyes still clinging to her body—most importantly, the tops of her swelling breasts.

"It's fine," Molly said, adjusting her lacy black crop top. Her faux leather leggings clung to her skin uncomfortably; it was too stuffy in there. *You wanted me to be a badass; well here you go badass. Just try not to suffocate.*

His eyes flashed up to hers and an enigmatic smile took over. "C'mon, sit with me," he said, taking her slender hand in his calloused one and guiding them through the sweaty, scantily clad bodies. A few other hunters, including Freya, sat around an oval wooden table.

"I don't think it's a half bad idea," Albert said. "Break the damn contract, get her out of it and keep from pissing off some powerful demons. One word and we'd be hunted — we'd be destroyed and what do you think would happen to her, huh? They'd torture her, skin her, they'd —" Albert's eyes had flickered over Ryan's head and landed on Molly's frozen frame.

The contract.

The breaking of it.

That's what they'd been discussing. And Albert was on her side...

Albert casted his eyes down at his whisky and fidgeted with his beard.

Molly glanced at the hunters around the table. *I can't trust them.* It sunk in deep and fast and she swallowed thickly.

Freya eyed Molly's outfit. "Trying something new?"

Molly faked a smile.

"I think it looks hot," Ryan announced, hair tied back in a greasy bun. He slid cards onto the table smoothly and sneered. "You should be up there." He nodded his head at the platform, the closest one a few feet away. A girl with muddy brown hair swayed tiredly on it, her head to the side, eyes hooded.

"Shut up, Ryan," Cree said sharply. "She's not one of them."

Molly furrowed her brow. "Who are they?"

"They're demons," he answered, sitting down roughly. "Captured, weakened, and used for our entertainment. Tonight is a celebration of our beginnings in the city. Our people came here almost two hundred years ago, launching the battle against those damn savages. Hunters from all over New York are here."

Molly gaped at the girl. She looked human—they all did, and she felt sick thinking back to Tensley and the change she'd seen in him, the ability for *humanity* there. But then he'd gone and said something she'd expect from a demon: that her family's torment had been comedy to him.

"Don't seem so disgusted by us, Molly," Cree said, voice fraught with irritation. Molly was startled by his tone, and worked to wipe the look from her face. "Demons would jump at the chance to do the same to anyone—*you* especially."

Molly cleared her throat. "I'm gonna go to the bathroom."

They waved her off and she shoved through the masses, trying to ignore the brown-haired demon girl to her right, but a hunter hauled the girl down from the platform and tossed her onto a nearby couch. Bruises lined the girl's bone-thin arms and deep, white scars ran over her cheeks. The girl's eyes were glazed, vacant—*wait.*

Molly recognized those green eyes, tiny but no longer glaring.

Lex. The kind girl who'd helped rescue her from the gorgon.

Molly's stomach turned.

Two hunters' hands spread over her exposed stomach as they sat on either side of her, and Lex's eyes met Molly's. One of them, a guy with a pierced brow and dark blue-colored hair, bit Lex's earlobe. She didn't even wince. His hands moved up her bare legs toward her crotch.

Those sick bastards.

Molly stopped in front of them, unable to move, unable to break eye contact with Lex. She fisted her hands to hide their shaking and breathed through her nose, afraid she'd vomit from how unsettled her stomach was.

"Hey," Molly snapped, and a flicker of understanding grew in Lex's face, her eyes weary and untrusting. The guys continued groping her dry skin. "*Hey.*"

One lifted his head, his mouth an angry line. "What?"

"She needs a break. Now." Molly gestured to Lex.

"Demons don't need breaks," he said, turning back to Lex. The other guy didn't look up.

Molly glanced back at the table where Cree sat. None of them were watching, so she tried another tactic. "Cree wants her," she said sternly. "Do you want to make him angry?"

The guy let his hand drop and sighed, defeated. "Shit, no."

"Good," she said, taking Lex's limp hand and lifting her off the faded orange couch. A few eyes aligned with hers as they moved in the thick crowd, mouths either dropping open or pressing hard into a frown of disgust, but they didn't stop her. Molly's chest filled with fear and nerves.

"Oooh, looks like Blondie's gonna have some fun tonight!" a guy cheered. "Care for a joiner?"

"Shut up!" another hissed as Molly and Lex passed them. "They're under Cree's watch. Don't piss him off."

A hand landed on Molly's shoulder and she jerked, twisting around to see Albert. His eyes flickered to the groggy Lex, balancing her weight against Molly. Her stomach dropped.

"This isn't right, Albert and you know it," Molly said, gaining his full attention. His mouth partly hidden behind his wild beard twisted downward and his eyes again moved to Lex. "Please. She needs help."

Did he see it? See how messed up this whole scene was? Her blood boiled and her fisted hands shook. This was wrong, so fucking wrong...

He didn't look at either of them and when he squeezed her shoulder, he gave her a long stare. "I'll distract him; get her out of here."

Molly let the breath she'd been holding in and nodded once. She pushed through the rest of the crowd, opened the back door and let Lex's hand go. "Are you okay?"

"What are you doing?" Lex stood back, legs wobbling as she found the brick wall and leaned against it. This wasn't the same girl Molly had met weeks before; she was damaged, weak.

She took a deep breath and ran a hand over her face. "I just—I just couldn't stand to watch them do that."

Lex stared, mouth wide open. "Is this some kind of twisted game?" She could barely form words, and Molly realized she hadn't been getting any energy.

Is this what would happen to Tensley without intimacy?

"Are you going to hurt me?"

Molly's brows lifted. "You don't remember me?"

Lex's eyes took their time noting her appearance. Maybe Molly *had* changed in those weeks, though. A lot had happened, and she did feel like a completely different person at times.

Realization dawned on Lex's hollowed features. "Tensley's fiancée."

Molly sighed, studying the engagement ring on her finger. "I couldn't watch them take advantage of you."

"Then why are you with them?"

When Molly looked up, Lex's eyes were misty. Tears rolled down her dirt-stained cheeks.

Demons cry? Lex sniffled and wiped a few fingers under her nose. Molly took off her jacket and wrapped it around the malnourished demon.

"C'mon," she said, "Let's get you something to eat."

Lex hesitated to follow, but she did.

chapter
twenty-five

THE DINER WAS empty except for a couple that was more interested in smothering each other in kisses than eating their late-night pancakes. It was a cheap-looking place that served deep fried hotdogs as an appetizer and had vinyl nineties-style yellow booths that stuck to Molly's thighs. She was also pretty sure there was gum on the edge of her seat.

Lex devoured her French fries in large bites, stuffing them into her small mouth. "This is so good," she moaned, rolling her head back in ecstasy. "I haven't eaten this type of food in a month."

Molly's eyes widened. "Is that how long they've had you?"

Lex took her time to answer. "Yeah. Leaving a college party in Queens."

"And then they paraded you around like a sex toy?"

She nodded. "They usually do that for a while before killing us." She licked the grease off her fingers. "So what made you want to help me if you're one of them?" Lex's eyes grew dark. Molly could see she was still suspicious of her. "You and Tensley not on good terms?"

Molly glanced at the window, looking at her reflection. Her hair had lost its curl and now sat on her shoulders in waves. "Tensley and I don't get along. At all."

"I can see why," Lex mumbled. "You're the complete opposite of him." She rolled her shoulders, a bone cracking. "He's an incubus, a seductive one." She grinned with food still in her mouth.

Molly hadn't thought of other demons. "What are you, then?"

Lex sat back and smoothed her flyaway strands of chestnut hair. "I'm a soul eater."

Oh. Shit.

Lex shook her head. "From the look on your face, I'm assuming Tensley didn't completely educate you." She ate another fry, and Molly saw how pointed Lex's teeth were — sharp and jagged, like a shark's. "Unlike incubi, I don't get energy from intimacy. I get energy from sucking emotions and thoughts."

"You can take people's thoughts?" Molly leaned forward, fascinated and a bit freaked out.

"Yup," she said quietly. "You want to forget something? I take that away. You want to stop feeling something? I take that away."

Molly furrowed her brow and noted the sadness in Lex's voice. "That doesn't sound like it would be very helpful."

Lex gently shook her head, eyes lowered to her bruised hands. "It gives me strength. I can use it to my advantage — if I want someone to forget something. Manipulate people's emotions. Scorpios finds me useful."

Scorpios?

Lex glanced up at Molly and her eyes were black, *hungry.* She raised her hands in embarrassment and covered them. "I'm sorry, *I'm sorry.* I'm just so weak right now."

Molly blinked and realized Lex had almost done something to her. She saw Lex's frustration, the shame in her desires. The girls sat in silence after that, but Lex didn't continue eating. Instead, she stared at the cold fries with tears in her eyes.

"Does Tensley know where you've been?" Molly asked.

"He doesn't have a clue," Lex answered, her Queens accent surfacing. "He found me when I was fourteen, crammed in a closet after stealing their belladonna." Molly arched a brow. "It's a drug that demons use for pleasure. He found me and instead of slitting my throat, he took care of me. There *was* a price to pay: his father wanted me to find information undercover. No one would expect a weak little girl to work for the most powerful, feared organization in America. Tensley protected me, though. He was like a brother to me." Lex pinched the bridge of her nose, her cheeks skeletal from lack of nutrients. She looked like she was dying, and her skin was ghastly pale. "Unfortunately he couldn't protect me from the hunters. When they take us, we usually vanish for good. But you helped me for some reason... I guess thanks are in order."

Molly took a sip of her water, sheepish. "Don't mention it."

"So, Tensley and you haven't been getting along?"

Molly fixed her sunglasses. "No, not really." She

thought back to the bandages, to his nurturing behavior with Illya.

"Surprising. I mean, he was definitely into you." Lex chuckled.

"What?"

"He was checking you out—a lot—when we were taking you home. You were too busy hyperventilating to notice." Lex folded her arms. "If he hadn't been so stressed to get you safely home, he probably would have flirted with you."

Molly flushed. *Flirted with me?* "I didn't think he found me attractive." She hated how her heart swelled knowing he thought she was pretty.

"Psh, are you fucking kidding me? Half the time he avoided looking at you because if he *did*, he would've stared like a damn fool. The poor man was awestruck by you, and you didn't even notice."

"Well...I was a bit distracted by how he was manhandling me," Molly replied sharply, glaring as she thought of Tensley's hands on her hips that first night, forcefully moving her down the street. Molly didn't want those warm feelings in her chest for Tensley, not when he'd threatened her family so many times.

Someone walked right up to the window of the diner and knocked against the glass. *Cree.* He tapped it three times and Lex recoiled, leaning back against the booth's cushions.

"Stay here," Molly told her, placing a hand over Lex's. "I'll talk to him."

Lex's hand shot out just as Molly passed by, her grip strong as iron. "No! He'll kill me!"

Molly gawked at Lex's trembling chin. "I'll talk —"

"You can't change his mind about what I am! He's the reason they took me. He's the reason I was in there." Her words tumbled out as she frantically tugged at Molly's wrist. "Please, *please* Molly. H-help me. Don't let them take me."

Molly's heart lodged itself painfully in her throat. She saw herself in Lex: the desperation for someone to help her, save her from a potentially life-threatening circumstance. Molly's black-and-white world crumbled; not all demons were bad. Molly eyed Cree over Lex's head, his stoic expression.

There'll be no mercy from him.

"Run," Molly muttered, her lips barely moving.

"What?"

"Run and don't stop. Find somewhere safe, okay? Somewhere they can't find you."

Lex gave her a watery smile and as soon as Molly stepped back, Lex darted through the diner out the back entrance. Molly ran to the front door, blocking the way as Cree tried to push his way inside.

"Move, now!" Cree shouted, but Molly stood her ground and pushed him so hard he stumbled back into the street.

"No! You're going to leave her alone." She approached him. "Let me explain, okay —"

"What the hell were you thinking? You let her run away!" He pounded a finger to his temple and widened his eyes at her. His voice was booming. "She's a *demon* that committed a crime, Molly! *The enemy.*"

"It was despicable! They were assaulting her, Cree! It

was unbearable to fucking watch!" she roared, her own voice rivaling his.

"She's a demon—they don't feel, they don't have emotions, they don't care about anything but getting what they want!" He stepped forward, towering over her petite frame.

"She was crying!"

"They mimic our emotions, Molly! Goddamn it!" He paced back and forth on the asphalt. *Mimic emotions?*

She'd seen Lex's tears, heard her voice break; it wasn't fake. *Is he lying to me?* Lex was innocent, sweet, and Cree wanted to hurt her.

"I want this done. I want to break the contract, and nothing else. He doesn't get hurt."

Cree's back tensed, and he looked over at her. "What?"

Her hands trembled as she wrung them. "I don't want to be engaged to him, but I can't hurt him—I just want the deal to end, or for him to change his mind. He's innocent. He actually—"

"He's a *demon!* How are you not registering this? They want to devour us, suck out our strength, manipulate us, and if we don't stop them first, they'll do it. He *is* heartless." His nostrils flared and he marched over, jabbing his pointer finger in the air. "As soon as you let your guard down, Molly, he'll devour you—in more ways than one—and I won't be able to stop him then. Don't be naïve, thinking he's your *friend*. He's using you, and if you think he deserves to breathe, then he's winning. He doesn't care. If he acted like it, it was because he wanted to make you vulnerable to him. To manipulate you."

"He was different—"

Cree frantically searched in his coat pocket and pulled out a frayed photograph. He shoved it in her face. "See this girl? This was my little sister Nina. You know what they did to Nina? They raped her and killed her like it was nothing. Do you want to be used by them? He'll hurt you and your family. He threatened them before; do you think he won't twist your father's arm off if need be?"

She gaped at the picture of the brunette girl around her age, her smile so wide it made her eyes crinkle. Molly's heart clenched as Cree stuffed the picture back into his pocket.

She threw her hands down. "No, of course not! I just want to end the engagement. That's all. I don't want to be in this world, with demons, and hunters, and monsters! I want to be normal and free. I don't want to worry about whether he'll hurt my mom or September, and I want to go to the museum and go to school without always thinking about *him* and *your world*." She raked her shaky fingers through her tangled locks, breathless. "I still want to end the contract, but I'm not going to do *anything* if it means someone else gets hurt." She tried to hide the wobble in her voice, fighting to appear fierce and determined. "Understood?"

Cree scowled. "You have three days, Molly. Three days to sedate him, bring him to us, and break the contract your way. After three days, if you haven't, we're doing it my way."

Molly hesitated; why did things still feel off with him? He'd kill Tensley without a second thought.

They kill demons for a living. They can't get rid of that

instinct. It wasn't what she wanted any more. Before, she'd simply wanted Tensley gone, dead or not, but now she knew better. She knew *Tensley* better, not as a demon, but as a man. She knew what Cree's end goal was and it didn't match hers: save both of their lives without death.

Cree was so far from the man she'd met at the bar, and her gut told her not to trust him. She couldn't trust him.

I'll break the contract on my own. Her eyes flickered past him to see Ryan and Albert a few feet back. *Albert.*

"Fine," she said with a slight edge to her voice. *Make him believe it.* "I'll bring him to you tomorrow night."

I hope I never see you ever *again.*

"Three days, Molly," he cautioned her again.

She pulled her jacket tighter around her midsection. "I know, Cree."

Cree watched her and after a long moment, he patted her shoulder. "Get some rest; you'll need it."

Molly numbly nodded, throat dry, cautious not to say too much. She walked down the quiet street, hoping her plan would work.

chapter twenty-six

TENSLEY'S FINGERS SHOOK as he withdrew the cigarette from his mouth and stubbed into the sidewalk outside of his apartment.

Someone spoke when he moved into the lobby, but his focus was solely on the elevator doors. He didn't want to speak to his nosy neighbors or Sebastian, the doorman; he needed to compose himself. Then someone touched his forearm and he jerked, ready to scowl at the low-breed creature that dared to speak to him in his irritated state. Molly stood before him, pale cheeks rosy.

He frowned. "What are you doing here?" He didn't hide the surprise in his voice very well.

The elevator dinged its arrival and he turned, running his fingers through his hair.

"Wait!" She leapt for his arm again. *What was* with *this girl?* "I need to talk to you."

He stopped, staring at the ceiling to keep from snapping at her. "Talk."

Her brows curved in worry. "In *private*."

The urgency in her voice made his shoulders tense. *She needs something…*

He rolled his eyes and gestured for her to follow him into the elevator. All the walls were mirrors, reflecting the two of them over and over again from different angles. She fidgeted with everything — her jacket, her golden hairpin, even the engagement ring, which also could not be removed unless he chose to do so.

Her anxiety stirred his impatience, and his heart ached. His fingers massaged the area, and he sighed. He eyed the mirror only for his eyes to focus on Molly's face, bottom lip worried between her teeth, and at that exact moment, she caught him looking. She didn't look away and let her teeth release her bottom lip painfully slowly.

He no longer was tied to his deal with Evelyn and now standing next to Molly in that small space, he was free to do whatever he liked. Nothing held him back now. She was completely *his.*

chapter twenty-seven

THE TWO OF them entered the foyer of his expensive penthouse. She walked toward the dining area, picking at her lace sleeve and eyeing the kitchen with its stainless steel knives properly placed along the wall. Molly bit the inside of her mouth.

Her eyes landed on the couch. "How's Illya?"

"He's fine," Tensley said with bite. "So, what did you want to talk privately about?"

She turned to face him. He stood by the doorway, one hand in his dark pants pocket, his eyes heavy and exhausted. She had to do it—she'd free them both, but he had to be subdued to cooperate. She couldn't risk him overpowering her.

"Don't waste my time, *Ms. Darling.*" His lips quivered when he spoke, and she thought of the hairpin coated in golden fleece that Cree had given her, the one currently secured in her hair.

No, no, no.

"Is it okay if I use your bathroom?" She mentally

slapped herself for how weak her voice sounded.

"You came here to use my bathroom?" His knuckles grew whiter by the second.

She blinked, avoiding eye contact. "I'll explain everything after," she lied. "I just need a moment, okay?"

He looked away after a long silence, exhaling. "It's down the hall, first door on the left."

She nodded and walked down the hallway. The bathroom was sleek, with bright white tiles on the wall and a large sauna bathtub that would definitely fit more than two people. She paced, running her fingers through her hair, and texted Lance to be there in twenty minutes.

She could do it. She had *to do it.* If she didn't, she would be trapped in his world, in his society, and what about her family and September? They were in danger—his world was dangerous to them. He may not hurt *her*, but he would definitely use those she loved as a tool to get what he wanted. He'd done it before. He was reckless. *Sedate him, make him break the contract with Albert's help, and both be free.*

And if Cree got his hands on him before she did, he'd murder Tensley.

Even if she felt a shard of attraction towards him and even with the rare moments of kindness he'd show her, she still feared him. His unpredictable, his anger, his power, and what if *he* turned on her. What if he *did* kill her after he got what he wanted from her?

He was a demon—and she didn't understand their nature, their messed up society.

She knew the consequences; of Tensley overpowering her and angering the demon even more, but she had to try to save herself before she lost her chance.

"You can do this," she whispered. "You *have* to." She undid the first few buttons of her blouse, showing the tops of her breasts and letting her hair fall over her shoulders in large, playful curls. She took a deep breath and marched out of the bathroom and down the hallway, where Tensley was leaning against the back of one of his black leather couches.

"What took you so long?" he muttered angrily, taking the cigarette from his lips. A gentle, curling tail of smoke expelled from them. His forehead wrinkled when he did a double take, scanning her exposed skin and messy hair.

She swallowed. "You smoke?"

He hiked a dark brow. "When did you start caring?"

She stared back; something seemed off with him. Agitated, upset even...

He held the cigarette between his index and middle fingers and watched her. "What do you want, Molly?" His voice was low, and a hint of irritation weaved through it.

Do it now. She reached up to her sunglasses and removed them, letting them hit the ground. When her eyes met his, he froze. "I want you," she said.

He cocked his head to the side. "You want *me?*" He sounded arrogant, but also a bit suspicious.

She moved slowly, each click of her high heels echoing in the silent apartment. She stood in front of him, running a finger along his bare arm, and jumped at the unexpected jolt of energy from the touch. Her cool expression faltered, heat rolling up her chest, leaving her skin blotchy, but she collected herself and continued gliding her finger along his muscular arm. She used her legs to spread his apart. She placed her trembling hands on his firm chest, pressing her entire length against his.

Just give him a taste, then attack.

"Don't you want me?" She fluttered her lashes at him. He eyed her.

She worried it wasn't working; he hadn't touched her back. It was like feeling up a damn statue. As stupid as it was, embarrassment took over her. As she straightened up, humiliated, Tensley touched her wrist.

His touch sent energy through her veins.

Oh, oh god.

His lips grazed her cheeks, then her throat. When he tugged her completely against him, she could feel his rigid need beneath her. An intense heat coiled between her legs.

His hands roamed her back, up to her hairline, and she began to panic. *The hairpin.*

She pushed his chest and he breathed in sharply, lips swollen and puckered. He stood to his full height and towered over her, prowling closer as she backed into the nearest wall.

She hit it and prayed he couldn't see how rapidly her chest rose and fell.

He smirked darkly and leaned down to kiss her outstretched neck, pausing to look through his lashes at her. All air slammed out of her lungs as she felt the familiar pull to him, like a siren, calling her to press her body against his and let him devour her.

Just a taste…

His lips found the same feverish skin as before. She let

out a moan, startled by how expertly his mouth nibbled against her neck. Her body couldn't help but curve into his. She could feel his length hardening as he lowered his mouth to the tops of her breasts, then lower as his hands caressed every inch of her sides. Her core tightened when his head leveled with her crotch, sitting on his knees, his hands gripping her thighs tightly.

"*Don't move*," he warned when her legs grew restless as he lifted her skirt, revealing her white panties.

She knew he could hear her pounding heart rattling against her ribcage. She rolled her bottom lip in her mouth just as he pulled her legs apart and pressed his mouth against her center. His hot breath against her most sensitive spot was enough to make her moan greedily.

His tongue swirled over the damp panties gently at first. "So fucking wet…" he murmured against her, and even his voice caused a ripple of leg-clenching pleasure. Her hands gripped his broad shoulders. The energy pulsed in her veins. He kissed her inner thigh, and his fingers pushed aside her panties. She watched him eye her exposed, wet sex, his tongue darting out to lick the corner of his lips.

"I'm going to love eating you out, *sweetheart*."

She whimpered softly, the need in her sex throbbing for him to continue.

He looked like he wanted to devour her.

And come back for seconds.

Hell, she wouldn't mind thirds.

He glanced up at her for a moment, a slow seductive smile taking over, and before she could say anything, he buried his head into her sex and plunged his tongue deeper and deeper.

Oh god, no one's ever done this.

"Tensley — *oh, Tensley,*" she moaned. Her hands found his hair and tugged.

He kissed her mound, moving his way back onto his feet to begin his assault on her outstretched neck.

No, no she had to stop.

She had to do it *now.*

She slid her hand into her hair and pulled the hairpin free. Her arm curled around his right shoulder to slice across his exposed shoulder blade. He gasped into her ear, staggering back.

"What the —" He reached for the hairpin, wrenching it from his back. The red-stained hairpin slid from his weak grasp, clanking against the floor. "What — *what did you do?*" His nostrils flared.

She breathed unevenly. "I had to," she said, her entire body flat against the wall, attempting to flatten her skirt and increase her distance from him.

Why wasn't the poison working?

His rage began in waves, emitting off him as it grew. "You just had to fucking seduce me and then stab me in the back?" He gestured at her legs and then to her face.

He paced in front of her, gripping the back of the closest couch.

Tensley tsked. "All you ever do is piss me off. Or is that your edge? Time to piss off Tensley again! Test his fucking limits. I'm getting this close" — he showed her his thumb and pointer finger almost pressed together, emphasizing his frustration — "to losing my fucking temper with you, and I don't play nice. I get even."

He shook his head at her, like she was a stupid little girl.

Oh, did I have news for him.

She straightened her posture in front of him. "It was laced with golden fleece."

The squeak of his fingers clutching the leather couch made her heart pound faster. He knew exactly what golden fleece was.

"Tensley, I don't want to fight you. I want you to *cooperate* for both of us."

That didn't seem to help. He kicked the couch with such force it went sliding across the room, sending paintings and vases shattering to the ground when it collided with the opposite wall. She stared at the shattered mess on his hardwood floor and he rushed toward her, a snarl leaving his lips.

She darted out of the way, tripping and righting herself against an armoire in the hall. His footsteps pounded after her and she turned, fist connecting so hard with his jaw that the crack sounded like a whip. A growl left his pursed lips and he charged, slamming her against the wall. More artwork fell.

The poison isn't working!

"Tensley, don't—don't."

His hands grasped both of her forearms and shook her. "What the hell is wrong with you?"

Fight him!

She tried to wiggle out of his tight grip, but that only angered him more and he pressed her against the wall, trapping her with his strong frame.

"Tensley," she said, attempting to elbow him in the side. "Don't! I don't want to hurt you! I'm doing this for both our sakes!"

"Don't?" His yelling didn't match his actions as his grip weakened immensely. She could see the emotions battling on his stony features, wanting to hurt her, but keeping himself at bay. He let go and his hands landed on either side of her head, body leaning forward. She gasped at the closeness of his chest pressing into hers; his arms shook uncontrollably.

It was working — the poison was weakening him.

"You'll regret this, Molly." He struggled to get the words out.

"I think you're wrong, Tensley. You'll be happy once I'm out of your life for good. You'll never have to see me again. I promise," she said, freezing him with her naked eyes. "You'll be free from me."

Tensley's knees gave out, hands weakly grasping at her sleeves, at her fingertips, until he collapsed in front of her. He coughed viciously, eyes struggling to stay open as he fought the golden fleece to the very end.

She watched as he went unconscious and his fingers sprawled, loose.

He didn't move. Neither did she.

She'd taken down the monster.

chapter
twenty-eight

MOLLY PACED IN front of Tensley's unconscious body, checking her phone for a text or phone call, anything from Albert saying he couldn't make it or was backing out or that he was there.

Anything.

She yanked at her hair, eyeing his body.

Should I tie him up? Or leave him there? Oh god.

She snatched a cushion from his couch and placed it underneath his head, smoothing back his soaked hair.

"I'm sorry, Tensley," she whispered. "It's for the best."

She whipped through the worn spell book beside her on the floor. She had tried to speak the spell to break the contract, but nothing worked. She needed Albert, she needed someone who knew what they were doing.

She held her head in her hairs and squeezed her eyes shut. "What am I doing?"

She peered down at Tensley's slacked mouth. She didn't want to hurt him, but how would their marriage work? Would he desert her? Would he begin to loathe her after she gave him what he wanted?

She couldn't hold off any longer, not with Cree threatening to do things his violent way.

Molly reached out for Tensley's cheek, still flushed from his anger.

""We could never be happy together, Tensley," she whispered into the silence, the words more hesitant than before. How many times had she thought those words with certainty? But now, as she gazed at his unconscious body, Molly wasn't sure she believed them as fiercely as she once did.

What if? What if she had tried to make it work? What if she tried now? Would he let her, or had she just ruined their chances at a future together?

She couldn't have second thoughts now. It was too late.

The knock at the door made Molly jolt. *Albert.*

Molly pushed herself off the ground and rushed to the door.

This is my chance, our chance of getting rid of the contract without anyone dying.

She threw open the door and all her nerves fired up at the sight of Cree. Her hand shot back to slam it shut, but just as it was about to close, Cree shoved it open. He gripped her by her shoulder and just as she went to shove him out, he aimed a gun at Tensley's motionless body.

Shit.

"Well, you completed the first step: sedate him," Cree said, glaring at Tensley. Molly shook her shoulder, but Cree's fingers dug so deep she recoiled and yelped. He yanked her closer. "You so much as try anything, lift one of your fingers, and I'll shoot him all the way up his spine."

Molly shook. She wanted to scream, wanted to shove Cree, but he had the power. "You said three days."

Cree arched a brow. "You were paper thin last night. I knew you would back out, just didn't think you'd be stupid enough to try it on your own."

Molly glared at the side of his face and wondered how this was the same guy from the bar.

"We got the bastard," Freya said as she moved behind Molly, hitting her in the process. Ryan followed after.

Cree gripped Molly's bicep and walked out the door. "Good. You blacked out the surveillance for the next five minutes?"

Ryan nodded, too busy staring at the unconscious Tensley. "So you're the big bad—"

"C'mon." Cree pushed Molly forward, the gun now jabbed into her side. "We're doing it my way. Got a demon to break."

Molly squeezed her eyes shut.

What have I done?

MOLLY FELL BACK against the dusty couch in Cree's apartment above the bar and looked over Tensley's limp body. His hands were tied around the back of the wooden chair, his feet to the two front legs.

Molly's stomach twisted painfully as she looked at the nearby fire flickering to embers.

Freya squeezed Molly's shoulder and reloaded the pistol aimed at him. "Good work sedating him; he won't be able to protect himself now."

Molly couldn't tear her eyes from Tensley's open mouth, long dark lashes, and relaxed jaw. He looked so utterly lifeless.

Her feet tapped the floor.

"So the famous Tensley Knight isn't so mighty after all," Ryan spat.

A few other hunters sat around the room, observing Tensley in his poisoned state, unconscious and weak. Molly swallowed, thinking of his last expression, of the fire erupting in those dark eyes as the poison took hold. A black hole had grown in the pit of her stomach and continued to expand the longer she stared at his vulnerable features.

I just buried him alive.

"Not awake yet?"

Molly jolted upward to see Cree in the doorway. He didn't even look at her; his eyes were glued to Tensley's crumpled body secured on the chair. Cree marched over and grasped Tensley's chin, lifting his drooping head for a second before letting it fall again.

"Don't do this, Cree," Molly said.

"Shut up."

Lightning flashed through the thin curtains across the large windows, and Molly found herself staring at her hand, the thin finger that wore Tensley's engagement ring.

Molly caught Cree's wrist and he gazed down at her. "Just hear me out, okay? It doesn't have to be like this. We can break the contract and let him go."

Her eyes flashed up at the sudden groan emanating from the middle of the room; it was Tensley. He lifted his head with audible difficulty. His dark eyes scanned the room, landing on her. He parted his dry, flaky lips, but seemed speechless.

Molly inched closer to Tensley, wanting to explain, wanting to comfort him, but Cree gripped her wrist and sent her a warning look. "Don't do anything rash, Molly."

The hunters stepped forward and Tensley flexed, attempting to break free, but the golden fleece had drained any strength for the time being. He breathed unevenly, rapidly.

"What the *fuck* is this?" Tensley's nostrils flared, and he glared at Molly.

"We're the Hunters of Orion," Cree said, approaching closer than the others and towering over Tensley. "I'm sure you've heard of us."

"Nope. Never even been a blip on the family's radar." Tensley's expression remained vacant, but Molly knew that expression well—he was a ticking time bomb, ready to explode. A hunter Molly didn't know very well kicked Tensley's ankle and he hissed back at him.

"*Don't.*" Molly pointed to the hunter and he simply smirked and did it again.

Tensley cursed in Italian.

"We hunt to protect humanity," Cree answered coolly, crouching in front of Tensley. "We hunt your kind, to be exact—your disgusting, monstrous kind." Cree reached behind him to a sheath at his side. He withdrew a long, silver-tipped dagger and held it in one hand. "And we kill every single one that crosses our path. Like you, Mr. Knight."

Molly furrowed her brow. "Don't you dare, Cree." Eyes shifted to her, all except for Tensley's and Cree's.

The sound of the gun reloading echoed as a reminder. *They'll shoot him.*

"You filthy bastard," Cree growled as he rammed the brass knuckles he wore across Tensley's cheekbone. It was a chill-inducing noise and Molly winced.

"*Cree.*" Molly stood up. "Stop it. What are you doing? I told you not to hurt him!" She reached to touch Cree and he recoiled.

"Sit down!" he shrieked, but she didn't stop. She gripped his forearm and spun him toward her. Cree reached up and slapped her across the cheek, making Molly's left eardrum ring like a set of cymbals. "I'm warning you."

Her fingers fanned over the burning sensation, other hand still searching for the weapon. "Just let us go and it's over, okay? You don't have to hurt him."

Cree regarded Molly with a tightened jaw. "He's not leaving."

"What?" Her eyes widened and her heart pounded.

"Sit *down.*"

"No." She gripped his shirt, pulling. When he went to hit her again, she snatched his wrist and pushed it back. Her begging eyes aligned with his steady ones and then his forehead swung forward, slamming her head and sending her flying backward. He went in to push her down but she dodged, raising her fists in a challenge.

Cree's bushy brows furrowed and he glowered at her. "Naïve bitch."

Freya kicked at the back of Molly's legs and Molly sidestepped, only to move closer to Cree. He gripped her forearm tightly and twisted, and a hot jab pierced her abdomen. She gasped and focused her vision down, realizing that a dagger was now lodged in her stomach.

Cree split in two, then blurred together. "Golden fleece also weakens daemons."

"W-what?" Her tongue grew too fat, too heavy to control.

"Unlike demons, it paralyzes daemons for a few hours," Cree yanked the weapon out and released her.

Molly promptly collapsed on all fours, the dagger thudding beside her as droplets of blood collected in a puddle on the floor. She looked through her lashes at the hunters, the ones who'd betrayed her, and then to Tensley. He still appeared stony, but a muscle jumping in his jaw told her he was trying to rein himself in.

What have I done?

Her nostrils flared, suppressing a sob, and her heart hammered in her shaking chest.

"This is the only way," Cree's heavy voice echoed in her throbbing head. "Break him."

Tensley spat blood and bared his stained red teeth. "You think I haven't been tortured? It's second nature to me."

Cree stayed silent and Molly wondered what he was debating as she tried to drag herself toward the dagger where it lay on the floor near Tensley's feet, covered in her blood.

When she reached for it, Cree's combat boot suddenly appeared and stomped on her hand. She cried out, but not from the pain—she *knew* it should hurt, but she felt nothing. The paralysis was kicking in.

"What about her? You don't mind if she takes your torture, right?" Cree continued, lifting his boot to clobber Molly's hand again.

Tensley's mouth twitched, but he held the mask steady. "You won't hurt her. You think I didn't know she was in Brooklyn? I planned for this. Last time *I* heard, your kind frowned upon hurting innocent people."

"Collateral damage." Cree's husky laugh vibrated above Molly's head, and he decided to kick her in the face instead. Blood gushed from her nose and ran in streams down her face, hitting her hands and the floorboards. "If you weren't interested in him, Molly, you'd have let me destroy him ages ago. You just wanted in his pants, you filthy puta."

Tensley hissed, as if he felt her pain. Molly swallowed blood and coughed.

"If you touch her again, I'll rip your spinal cord out through your mouth," Tensley said in a voice that was low and strangled.

"Did I strike a nerve?" Cree laughed bluntly and gripped her by the hair, dragging her weak limbs forward. "Does it bother you that she went looking for me, wanting to get rid of you?" Tensley didn't make eye contact with Molly, instead focusing on Cree.

Tensley narrowed his eyes. "Who are you?"

Cree tightened his grip on Molly's curls. "Alejandro Cree."

Tensley went as stiff as a board, nostrils flaring as he twisted against the ropes with renewed vigor.

Cree let out a bitter chuckle. "You know who I am. You know what your family *did*. Your brother killed my sister. *Nina*."

"No, he fucking didn't," Tensley ground out. "Fallen killed her. You know why? Because she wanted to control my brother, she wanted him to love her, and he wanted so badly to be like you *fucking* bastards, that he *let* her control him."

Cree jerked Molly's head around like she was a ragdoll, and she could only lay there. Tensley's gaze flickered to her for a brief moment, and it seemed to say *Hold on. Just hold on.*

"She made my brother grow a heart—the ultimate sin of a demon," Tensley argued, shifting in the chair. "And then she got pregnant, *out* of wedlock. She knew what she was doing to him, what the risks were, what she was doing to herself. My brother tried to protect her from Fallen."

"You're lying! You're lying!" The calmness that usually hovered in Cree's eyes was gone—they were wild and unhinged.

"Fallen killed her and the unborn child for breaking our law, preventing any chance of creating a weak offspring, and then he murdered my brother by cutting out his heart and leaving him as the *true* definition of what you fuckers call a demon."

Cree released Molly and she crashed next to Tensley's feet. She could barely keep her eyes open. Just when she thought it was over, Cree's combat boot slammed into her ribcage and she wheezed, the aching pain throbbing in her bones.

"You fucker!" Tensley strained against the ropes. "You're going to kill her!"

Cree laughed. "That's the point." Cree gave one final kick, this time to Molly's chest. Her lungs exploded, blood spraying from her nose and mouth and trickling down her hairline.

"No daemon, no marriage, no mixing of breeds. No threat against humanity."

"You wanted to kill her too," Tensley murmured at the same moment Molly thought it. "That was your plan from the moment she told you what she was."

"No. At first I *did* want to help her, but then she kept changing her mind and backing out. She had feelings for you, the ultimate sin," Cree scoffed. "I'm doing humanity a favor by destroying both of you tonight."

chapter
twenty-nine

CREE'S WORDS SENT a cool, prickling shiver through Molly. *He's going to kill us.*

Cree paused. "I can't decide who to kill first, though. Make her watch, or make you watch?" Cree stepped in front of Tensley, and she cringed when she heard the brass knuckles hit Tensley. He beat him, over and over again, senselessly.

Molly rested her hand on her stomach, wondering how long it'd be before she bled out. She wanted to kick him, beat him, but her limbs were nearly useless now. She blinked and saw him standing over her, examining his violent handiwork.

"You're *not* like my sister," Cree snapped. "The breeding of your two kinds needs to stop — and with the only daemon on earth destroyed, demon hunters will have had a momentous victory today."

W-what?

Molly vision faded in and out, and her limbs grew as heavy as wet wood.

Tensley was right—she did regret what she'd done.

Molly tried to move the hand closest to Tensley's exposed ankle, and found that one finger responded. The contact of their flesh jolted her for a moment, refreshed her limbs. The paralysis receded.

Yes!

Molly rested her wet cheek against the cool wood floor and exhaled. She needed to get out of there, and quickly. She squeezed her eyes shut, praying for an idea, a plan. If she could free Tensley in some way or distract Cree, they'd both have a better chance of escaping alive.

The sweat dribbled over the bridge of her nose and down her cheek—

A thought occurred.

She pushed herself forward, crawling weakly across the uneven floorboards of Cree's shitty apartment.

Just a little farther. If she could just get to the fire…

He laughed, taunting her. "Trying to escape?"

Molly reached into the dying fire to her left and grabbed a handful of embers, then flung them into Cree's face as he dove to stop her. Their skin sizzled and popped as the rank smell of burnt flesh filled the air. Molly didn't feel a thing, but Cree reared back, moaning deeply in agony.

The hunters rushed over but he held them back, clawing at his singed cheeks and joining Molly on the floor in a crouch.

The sound of the door slamming open rose above Cree's cries. Unfamiliar figures sped around her. Molly glanced up for a moment, and she swore she saw Illya and that distinctive yellow hair.

Good old Illya.

Smoke filled her nose and she gagged. She was losing consciousness, and she noticed that Tensley's chair was now empty, the rope coiled at its base.

She coughed viciously as warm flames licked around her, too close to her skin. Everyone was gone — including Tensley — replaced by a fire that was spreading fast.

This is it.

All her stupid decisions had brought her there.

Sweat dribbled down her forehead, mixing with the drying blood.

A dark form moved in front of her, appearing in the stairwell. *A shadow.* How fitting that it was the final thing she would see before the end.

The shadow moved closer, and as she focused, she saw a mouth moving, speaking to her.

Tensley?

He gathered her in his powerful arms and rushed down the stairs, flinging open the back door as she rested her cheek against his shoulder. Darkened buildings alight from the glow of the fire whizzed by them until Tensley turned into an alley.

Mist surrounded them from the nearby Atlantic Ocean as he placed her against the brick wall. Her knees gave out, but he caught her and used his body to hold her up. Her entire body was already drenched in sweat from the poison, and she honed in on Tensley's sculptured chest as he worked to remove her top.

"Molly," he said, lips pursed, eyes two dark grey pools filled with pure panic. "Don't struggle against me." He dipped his head down and she swayed; the numbness was leaving and immense pain was beginning to prickle all over her as the golden fleece wore off.

"Ow!" She shifted under his touch. "*Ow!* Am I dying— ow!"

Tensley gripped her shoulders to stop her from moving. The paralysis was replaced by an avalanche of torment.

He leaned in close until their red-stained chests were touching. "You won't if you sit still and let me help." She gasped at the sensation, at the quick relief that began the moment he brought his lips and hands to her stomach, sealing the stab wound with new skin. When he was done with her abdomen he moved to her collarbone, trailing kisses along every inch, healing bruises that hadn't even begun to show up yet, mending her shattered collarbone. His lips moved up to her throat, her jawline, her broken nose, each kiss removing some of the pain as it healed.

Power replaced the ache, along with an extreme energy she had never experienced before. He lifted her arm and pressed his rough lips to her burnt palm, and she watched the skin turn a fresh rosy pink as it mended before her eyes.

When he pulled back, the energy faded somewhat within her, but Tensley was also healing. The cuts on his face faded to nothing, leaving only lines of dried blood in their wake.

She trembled. "Where did he go?"

He didn't bother looking at her. "I don't know; he and the others got away."

Her eyelids fluttered, lined with big pearly tears as she let out a short cry. "I thought he was a good person."

"Darkness isn't all one shade, *sweetheart.*" He stood, towering over her. He ran his fingers through his drenched dark mane and glanced down the alleyway, on edge.

"He looked like the good guy. He acted like the good guy." Goose bumps ran up her bare arms as the sea's breeze picked up.

"But he wasn't the good guy, was he, Molly?" Tensley shot back, and she cringed.

"Neither were you! You threatened my family over and over again."

His nostrils flared. "To keep you in line — and based on our current situation, I should have fucking tried harder. Even if you all *had* managed to kill me, the contract would've continued with one of my brothers. You planning on killing my entire family? Because that's the only option you have."

Molly struggled to her feet, limbs still weak and sore. "I didn't *want* to kill you!" she hollered after him as he strode away. "I wanted out of this. What was I supposed to do?"

He spun around, his face contorted and demonic. He wasn't as weak as before, not even close, and she realized it had to do with their intimacy moments before. "You think *I* wanted this? Wanted to spend my time with a spoiled, naïve little brat? I had a life—I had..." He paused, his chest shaking with anger and unable to finish the sentence. "This was not my decision. This was a contract made by our ancestors three hundred years ago. I'm in the same position as you, Molly." He threw his hands down. "Fuck! I knew you were up to something in Brooklyn, but I didn't think you'd actually do it!"

Molly's mouth fell open and her stomach knotted. *He's in the same position as me...*

"I was desperate. I was trying to make a clean break for both of us and I asked you before and you said no! I refused to work with them after I saw what they did. They ambushed me and they threatened they were going to kill you if I even flinched a wrong way."

"I should fucking break you in half," he hissed, hands rolling into fists. "Do you even know what those hunters do?" He threw his hand back in the direction of the bar, where plumes of smoke were rising to the sky in swirls of black. Sirens blared as a fire truck raced by them, followed by an ambulance. "They hunt us, imprison us, starve us, and then kill us like it's a fucking game."

She swallowed, lowering her lashes to her feet. An awful taste began in her mouth as she thought about the demon she had murdered with the hunters; she felt disgusted. She had gone to a party where demons like Lex were used as sex objects.

Tensley took agitated steps back and forth in the alley, prowling like a beast. "I don't fucking trust you. They warned me about you low-breeds." His words stabbed hard in her chest, and she fought the urge to touch it, afraid to look fragile. Thick black hatred poured out of his eyes in menacing, palpable waves. "But you're my responsibility."

She gawked at his stark eyes, so cold, so *cold* it sent a chill through her spine, breathless.

"My burden."

Molly listened to the dark silence between them.

"Did you ever once, just once think," Tensley began, a

bite in his tone, "that maybe this engagement wouldn't be a disaster?"

Molly's eyes darted to his and all the air slammed out of her lungs.

"Tensley." A voice boomed from behind them.

Molly glanced over Tensley's shoulder. Three figures appeared: Illya and two other males. When she studied the others, she noted the same darkness and features as Tensley. *His brothers?*

"We have to keep moving."

"You went back for the bitch?" one of the men grumbled, gesturing angrily toward Molly. Her shoulders sagged and she lowered her head.

Tensley's only response was to turn and pin her with his coal-hot eyes. "I'm not letting her out of my sight. She's coming with me. *Move.*"

She limped after them, blood crusted on her cheeks and hands, wondering the whole time if perhaps *she* had been the monster.

chapter thirty

MOLLY EYED TENSLEY'S shadowed building up ahead and hugged her middle. Tensley, his brothers, and Illya walked a few steps in front of her, only sparing her a glare. Tensley hadn't looked back—not once. She'd noticed his hands flexing and fisting back and forth, as if he was trying to release his anger.

What did you expect? Open arms? A smile?

She swore she heard someone say her name and stopped, glancing over her shoulder. Everyone around her continued to move. She wiped at the blood underneath her nose and moved forward.

"You filthy bitch," a voice muttered from behind.

Molly spun, again finding everyone minding their own business. Her heart squeezed. *I'm losing it.*

Someone hit her shoulder and she turned, automatically apologizing. Her mouth went bone-dry. It was Cree, and he had a dagger, drawn and pointed at her.

She shrieked, swatting his hands away and fell flat on her back.

She jolted up and stared at the horrified businessman where Cree had just been. A few other people stopped, helping her to stand, and she frantically looked around.

The murderous demon hunter was nowhere in sight.

"Molly." Tensley marched toward her and gripped her bicep. His brow furrowed as she searched around them. "C'mon."

She yanked at his arm, stopping him from moving, and gritted her teeth. "I saw him. I just saw Cree!"

Tensley stiffened and eyed the busy Fifth Avenue. After a moment, he pulled at her arm again. "You're fine."

Molly stayed close to Tensley's side, her nerves on edge. *I swore I saw... What's going on?*

"Of course you get the crazy bitch as your fiancée," one of his brothers said, unable to contain his laughter.

"Shut up Cassius," Tensley snapped. "Both of you go home."

The brothers, shadowed in the darkness, didn't protest. "No need to thank us for saving your pussy ass."

"That doesn't even make sense," the second one said and slapped his brother on the head.

Tensley didn't wait to watch his brothers leave and walked toward the rotating doors of his building.

"Night," Illya called from the sidewalk, his mouth twisted in a frown.

Tensley waved him off.

The heavy-lidded man at the desk appraised their disheveled appearance with skepticism. "Rough night again, Mr. Knight?"

Tensley grumbled in response and jabbed his finger

into the button for the elevator. The man—Sebastian, according to his gold nametag—furrowed his heavy, grey brows, but his eyes were tender and he nodded.

Molly fidgeted with her shirt, torn and clinging to her stomach, caked in bright red. She gagged. *I bleed that much?*

A throbbing pain struck the back of her head and she squeezed her eyes shut. *Damnit.*

When the doors opened, Tensley moved them inside. He shifted to the opposite side, as far away as possible, and folded his arms.

She leaned against the mirror wall.

"You don't deserve to live," a voice called.

Molly's eyes darted around the small space.

Her lips quivered. "Did you hear that?"

Tensley frowned. "I didn't hear anything."

Molly swallowed thickly and twisted her head as another throb began.

"You stuck-up, two-faced bitch."

"Molly," Tensley's voice called to her and she snapped her head toward him.

She pressed her nails into her palms. *Breathe, breathe, you're fine.*

The doors opened and she followed after him, glancing at the doors around them. He dug into his pockets and pulled out the key.

Her eyes passed over him, and she saw a strange figure at the end of the hallway; body twisted, limbs angled inward. She could hear their bones crack as they walked, coming closer, *closer*. She pressed herself past him once he'd opened the door.

"What the—"

"Shut the door!" Molly demanded, desperate.

He did, giving her a long look afterward.

Her shoulders slouched, but the voices didn't vanish. Instead they grew in her head and she jabbed two fingers to her temple.

"What's going on, Molly?"

"There was a man out there—his limbs—" She cut herself off at Tensley's scowl.

He hadn't seen it. He hadn't heard any of it.

She didn't know how to begin. She didn't know how he would react.

"I don't have time for games, so spit it out or leave."

"I don't know!" Her eyes burned.

"Do humanity a favor and end your existence," said the same eerie voice surrounding her, and she swore she felt a breath on her earlobe.

"Stop it!" She jerked away. "Shut up! Leave me alone!"

"Molly?" Tensley moved closer and reached out a hand.

"Do it. *Do it!*"

Molly slammed into the ripped apart couch as the voice screamed inside her head. Angry laughter thundered around her and her eyes burned, literally *stung*, and she ran her fingers over her eyelids, rubbing aggressively. Her bruises returned, dark and purple and blue, and her stomach twisted painfully. She was bleeding, redness leaking from her nostrils and onto her white nightgown. "Stop it!"

"Destroy yourself!"

A hand gripped her shoulder and she spun.

"Molly, what's going on? Tell me!" Tensley shook her shoulders and towered over her.

She whimpered into the heel of her hand, and the annoyed look on his face warped to one of concern. "I keep hearing voices and they're telling me to kill myself." Her fingers stabbed through her hair and onto her scalp, as if she could relieve the constant whispering.

He studied her carefully and his scruffy jaw clenched.

"Tensley, I don't know what to do. Make it stop, please, just make it stop!" she yelled, angrily wiping the wetness from her eyes.

When she looked up, it wasn't Tensley but Cree smugly sneering at her; she backed up and screamed. It couldn't be fake — his eyes were rich and dark like coffee, and she was getting lost in them.

"You trust every single man you meet?" he taunted, his combat boots hitting the ground loudly with each step as he followed her.

"Leave me alone, Cree!" She fisted her hands. "Leave me—" She gagged on blood as her nose ran fast, the aching pain of her stab wound causing her to hunch over and wrap her arms around her middle. Cree went for her shoulder and she swung an arm up, pushing him back. He didn't stop. He continued forward, with force this time, and gripped her forearms so hard she yelped. She freed one arm and dug her nails into the side of his face, kneeing his groin with such power that he flew back several feet.

She rushed into the kitchen, reaching for a knife across the black marble counter and knocking over an empty glass that shattered on the floor. When hands gripped her sides, she flailed, kicking against the counter and trying to rip his hands off of her body. She used her body weight and threw herself backward so he'd hit the counter and loosen his grip.

"Molly!" He spun her around and didn't let go, his arms encaging her frame. "You're with *me!* It's just *you* and *me!*" One hand held her face, forcing her to see the grey irises in front of her. *Grey, not brown.*

She let out a pained breath and folded inward, knees giving out. "Tensley?"

"He wasn't here." He rubbed his thumb along her cheek to calm her. "It was in your head."

She rested her head on his chest. "I'm — I'm sorry."

"It's not your fault." He swung his arm underneath her legs and lifted her up off the ground. "There's glass all over the floor, and for some reason you thought it would be a smart decision to come over here with bare feet." He walked through it in his shoes, shattering it into tinier shards as he carried her to the bedroom. When he placed her down on the mattress, she gripped his sleeve, forcing him to hover above her.

"Don't leave me," she whispered. "Please."

He straightened, but didn't move away. He worked his jaw. "There's only one explanation I'm thinking of and I'm really fucking hoping it's not that."

Molly swallowed. "And that is?"

He squared his shoulders and glared down on her. "You made a blood oath with them."

Molly froze, panic seizing her motor skills. "And — and if I did?"

"It's an ancient oath of blood, pledging to always stay

loyal to the hunters and warlocks. If you *do* leave the group, you will be tried for treason and sentenced to death."

"Oh god." Molly caught her head with her hands. "I — I wasn't thinking. I just did it because I trusted Cree. I trusted him and he —" She crumpled farther. *So naïve, Molly.* Molly palmed her temples; she didn't want to be that way any more. "How do I make it stop?"

"It depends. You wait until they give up, or you taint your blood," he offered.

"Taint my blood?"

"It weakens the control and connection they have over you, and the only thing more powerful than their blood and your blood is..." He hesitated, squaring his jaw. "A higher class of demon blood."

Him.

"They'll try anything to get you to destroy yourself. They'll get inside your head, torment you in your dreams until you kill yourself," Tensley warned.

"No — no, I'm not going to let that happen. I need —" Her gaze sought his. "I need your blood?"

Tensley's lips parted. He reached down and grabbed her hands to study her palms, sitting on the edge of the bed. "The contract is in your bloodstream." His muscles locked. "Why would you let them have your blood?"

"I didn't know," she responded softly.

"Exchanging blood is a sacred act," he lectured.

"Well, no one told me that," she countered, and his face hardened.

Shit, Molly. You're trying to get him to help you. Don't piss him off.

"I just want this to stop." Warmth gathered behind her eyes. "*Please*, Tensley."

"There are side effects, Molly." His voice was low. "My blood might not mix well with your daemon blood; it might be too much for your body to handle. It's a lot stronger than any blood those savages gave you."

She leaned forward, moving her hands to his forearms; he stiffened. "Please Tensley." The whispering increased and she bowed her head. "Stop, *just stop*. I can handle it. I can't handle *this*," she begged, pointing to her temple.

"You could pass out...convulse." He stared at her, his eyes shadowed. "I could kill you."

She sucked in air fast. "I don't want to hurt anyone, Tensley. I can't keep what's real and what's not straight." Pearly tears ran down her cheeks, and she wiped at them.

"Why should I help you?" His face was stern, but his eyes, for once, were tender.

She stared back at him. "As a favor, please. I never wanted to hurt you. I *still* don't."

He snickered, and his body shifted away from her. "Already did, Darling. *Literally* stabbed me in the fucking back." Her eyes danced across his broad shoulders, the shirt straining across them. "I should be punishing you for disrespecting me, for betraying me. I should stab you in the back so you can see how it feels."

"Then do it," she said, lips trembling as the words shot out.

He glanced sideways at her, plump lips pressed together.

"Punish me because I deserve it, and then I won't hurt anyone. You said you'd get even, remember? Do it. Get even." The voices stirred in her head — chanting.

Do it, do it now. End yourself.

Tensley's expression didn't change; it was too neutral, too controlled, and she wasn't at all. She was heaving, could barely breathe. "I'm a liar, a coward —"

End it.

She recoiled at the loud voice in her head.

"Are you expecting pity?" His brows knitted.

She hid her face in her hands. "What was I supposed to do?" The wetness painted her cheeks and dribbled off her chin. "You came into my life, and you weren't kind. You kept threatening my family and no matter what I felt — what you *made* me feel for you, I'd choose them. *Every time.*" She shook steadily as more tears made their way onto her lap. "Did you expect me to just fall all over you? To be excited? Happy to marry a demon?"

Tensley's smirk faltered, and he swallowed. "You're walking a thin line, *Molly.*"

She could see the darkness filtering into his eyes. She could see the barrier he was forming between them, the waves of aggression he shot at her, a sign to back down, but right then, on edge, backing down was her last thought.

"Oh, are you touchy about that subject?" She glared at him.

"You should face your own *demons*," he said bitterly, his mouth warped into a tough frown.

The warmth returned behind Molly's eyes. "Cree said he was going to help."

"He didn't though, did he?" He snarled and jabbed his fingers through his thick hair. "I should have just left you in that burning building."

She stared at him. "But you didn't."

He paced, on edge. "I should have. You think you know me—from what? A few meetings, a few fumbles? You don't know me. Sure, I might be better than some of my kind, but that doesn't cancel out what I am."

She froze, terrified of his darkening features, of his words. "You saved me, though. Surely that meant... something..." she muttered, dumbstruck.

"Yeah, for my own purposes! There's no hero here, only a villain. Don't expect chivalry from me, because it's dead." He sounded like he was trying to convince them both, and his bunched hands loosened beside him.

She wanted to laugh aloud. Her emotions were fried, all used up by the last month of terror, anger, and lust, in revolving order. Now all three were stupidly combined in her; coupled with the warlocks' and diviners' voices, she could barely keep it together.

Her heart thundered in her throat. "I don't know what to say to make this better, but I'm sorry. I-I thought if I broke the contract without Cree it would work and you'd be free and happy, but he figured it out and came after us. I'm sorry." She stood up, lightheaded but determined to leave, to find her own damn way to get rid of the voices.

Tensley snatched her wrist halfway to the door.

"Where are you going?"

"Away from you," she snapped. Heat consumed her vision. "You're not going to help me, so I'll find my own way."

His features were distorted through her watery vision. She noted his clenched jaw, a muscle twitching there. "You'll die."

She shrugged and chuckled softly, hoping it would mask her fear, her sadness, her fragility in his grip. "Isn't that my fate? *Death.* Either from you, or some *gorgon,* or the demon hunters who've got it out for me — "

"It doesn't have to be," he murmured.

She glared, fighting the urge to sob. "Oh, you don't care about my *safety.* I'm just a source of energy to you. Someone to *breed* with."

"I care more than I should," he began, his voice unnervingly calm.

Molly's brows lowered. "First, you don't want me here, and then you tell me you care about me?"

His eyes softened and he sighed. "I'm pissed off, all right? My emotions are heightened — we experience things in extreme."

Molly couldn't tear her eyes from him and stayed quiet as he took a deep breath.

"I should say thanks — *you* were the one who got us out of there. You saved us." His hand gripped tighter around her wrist. "Sit." He guided her back to the bed and she did so, sitting down as she watched him pace. "Trust is important in my relationships. If I don't have it, well, consider yourself screwed."

She wanted to say something, but her ears ached, then her nose — and when she pressed her fingertip to an earlobe, she felt a warm wetness there. Red painted her forefinger. "I'm bleeding."

Tensley stopped moving, taking large steps toward her to examine her face. "Molly," he breathed, and she noted that his angry fire had tempered. "There's no blood."

The delusions were too much, and her voice cracked as

she wailed openly in front of him. He didn't say anything, only stared back with his hands on her shoulders. "Tensley, please. Please forgive me. I just want it to go away."

"You're not sorry," he murmured. "You're afraid."

The voices screeched in her head, and she jolted painfully. "I'm not sorry for trying to protect my family, but I'm sorry for hurting you." She wanted him to wrap his muscular, strong arms around her, to cradle her. She didn't want to be stubborn. "Trust me."

For a moment, they shared a tender, deep gaze that made her breath catch in the back of her throat. He stood and went to his bathroom, reentering with a tiny razor blade. He pressed the sharp edge to his thumb, a dot of dark red blood welling to the surface. "You might feel out of it for a few hours," he said, cautiously. "Might also crave me."

"Crave you?" Molly's crying stalled.

"Crave me entirely," he answered lowly. "Mentally, physically – *without* my influence." Her eyes fell to his torso, past his crotch, and down the lengths of his legs.

"Okay, fine," she said, nodding and scooting up on the bed.

He went with her, laying on her left and lifting his finger to her mouth. Her eyes aligned with his and she carefully swirled her tongue over the pad of his thumb, trembling as the coppery blood absorbed into her gums. She exhaled heavily when she pulled away.

The desire still existed in his eyes, in his touch. When his fingers grazed her thigh, she grew hot, flustered, and let out a tiny gasp.

"You're blushing," he whispered, one corner of his mouth quirking up.

"You do that to me most of the time," she said, voice velvety. Black and white dots filtered through her vision.

A dark smile appeared. "Can't say I'm sorry about it."

"But—it's not real."

A deep frown dug grooves into the planes of his face. "What?"

"My feelings for you..."

He swallowed thickly as if nervous to speak. "After the time in your bedroom, I promised myself I wouldn't do that to you again."

She felt dizzy, loose, out of control. Images of the room swirled. His hand grabbed the back of her neck, laying her down on the comfy feather pillows.

"Tensley." She breathed through weak lips. Her body jerked, shivering uncontrollably as she grasped his thick bicep. "What's happening?"

"My blood's overpowering theirs."

She trembled violently, and her eyes grew heavy. "Tensley?"

He stroked strands of blonde flyaways from her eyes. "Yes?"

"Your brother died?"

His touch grew stiff. "The person he was before did." Her droopy eyes still managed to register his pained expression before closing. "Fallen destroyed the man he was. He ripped his heart out and left him with no morals, no values. A heartless demon."

She hummed in response. "You're not heartless, right?"

"I should be."

chapter
thirty-one

WHEN MOLLY WOKE in Tensley's bed, she immediately noticed his chest rising and falling beside her. She reached out and tentatively skimmed the white scars across Tensley's lower shoulder, drawing closer to his warmth. After a minute, he stilled, and a rumble began deep in his chest.

She didn't stop, however.

"I'm sorry," she muttered against his skin.

His back muscles flexed.

"I'm sorry about what I did to you. I'm sorry about betraying your trust." Her voice was soft, and she wondered if he could even hear her. "I'm sorry about what happened to your brother."

She laid her palm flat against the white scars and shut her eyes. She felt light and safe and she didn't want to leave his side. When he shifted, her hand fell, and she fluttered her lashes open to find him giving her a stoic look, a look of uncertainty.

"How did you get these scars?" Her thumb brushed

his shoulder, edging close to his defined blade. She wanted to smile when she felt his body shiver from her simple touch.

"My brother." His hoarse voice startled her, and her thumb stopped rubbing soothing circles against his skin.

"Your brother did that to you?"

"He was heartless, truly, by that point." While her chin wobbled, his remained rigid. "I learned not to get in his way." He wet his bottom lip.

"I'm sorry you had to deal with that, Tensley," she told him softly.

After a beat of silence, he huffed. "You're staring."

She rubbed her finger around his shoulder again, and bit her bottom lip when his body responded with tremors. "Thank you."

His dark eyes swung to look at her. "For what?"

"For coming back for me. For taking care of me." She laid her head against his shoulder, gazing up at him. "Do you want me to talk to your brother? I don't want him to hurt you again." *God, it's like I'm drunk.*

"No!" he said, horrified. A crease formed between his brows. "I don't want you near him. Only if I'm around, okay?"

She lifted a hand and gently smoothed out the crease on his forehead with a fingertip, smiling when his stone-hard expression gave way to a content one. "You'll protect me?"

He stared directly into her eyes without fear, and he nodded.

"And I'll protect you," she told him.

A soft, beautiful smile spread across his face and she

couldn't help but giggle at his reaction. Her laughter quieted as her eyes skimmed his bare chest and the happy trail that disappeared underneath the covers sitting low on his hips, displaying his defined Adonis belt.

She stared at his mouth and licked her own. "Why don't you kiss on the mouth?"

Tensley's eyes grew violently dark. "Because it's more intimate than fucking."

She'd never thought of kissing like that, but she could see how it would be more meaningful than sex. "Is cuddling too intimate? Because I really want to touch you right now."

She didn't even blush at the words. *Definitely drunk off his blood.*

Tensley, however, stilled, and his eyes traveled over her body. Her clothes were now twisted around her frame, defining her curves—her breasts, her hips, and her small waist.

He sighed. "My blood's still battling theirs—that's why you feel out of it."

"Ooooh." The giggling began again.

"Come here next to me," he said softly. She laid her head on his shoulder and sighed dreamily, hooking a leg around his. When she gazed down, she saw a tent under the covers and buried her face into his shoulder.

"Am I turning you on, Tensley Knight?" she purred.

He scoffed, a slow smirk sliding over his edible lips. "You don't want to tempt me, sweetheart. I might just find a use for that smart mouth of yours." He took hold of her chin, angling her face up to meet his dark, seductive look. "A very good use."

She swallowed and bravely trailed her hand down his toned stomach, feeling him flex under her soft touch. Her hand slipped under the band of his sweats and nudged against his hard, hot member. He was huge, too thick for her dainty hand to completely hold him. She knew the basics of how to pleasure him from the stories of Stella and Tina's sexcapades, but it was still nerve-racking. He grunted when her hand gripped the rigid shaft and pumped gently.

Is this right?

She breathed against his clenched jaw and began pressing kisses down his heaving torso, down his navel to the band of the sweats, her hand still stroking. "Molly," he cautioned, his hand halting her. "Stop. You don't have to."

She stared at him, embarrassed. "Do you want me to stop?"

He swallowed thickly, staring at her. "No. Fuck no."

She gently pulled his member from his sweats, and it sprung erect. He was massive — veiny, tan, and rigid. "No wonder you're so cocky — no pun intended," she muttered, hearing his stunted laugh — the first true, genuine laugh she'd ever heard from him.

"I'm cocky in every sense of the word." He rested on his elbows, watching her small hand continuing to stroke his hot length, thumb slipping over his engorged head. When her hand slid close to the pulsing tip, he groaned and screwed his eyes shut. "Fuck, you're going to kill me, Darling, and I don't even give a fuck if I die with your hands on my cock."

She smirked at the control she had over him. *The power.*

With that thought, she leaned over, sweeping her hair to one side so he could still see as her lips pressed to his tip. He sucked in air fast and clenched his thighs. Her tongue swirled over the heated flesh, and he threw his head back, an arm stretched over his face.

"I've never done this," she muttered.

His head shot up. "Then stop, Molly. I'm fine. I'll take care of it."

Her hand stalled. She wanted to take care of him.

Badly.

Her mouth swallowed the tip, and his hand shot out, gripping her shoulders. He half-murmured, half-hissed a warning to stop, but she didn't. His hands rooted into her strands and she relaxed when she realized it wasn't to stop her, but to guide her up and down his swollen member. She felt all the lines and bumps as she moved his length down her throat, humming periodically.

"Molly." His hands gripped harder on her hair. "Look at me."

Am I doing it wrong? Oh god!

Her eyes flickered up as she took more of his length in her mouth and the gag reflex kicked in. He cursed as her eyes aligned with his, swimming with lust. She didn't stop her assault, taking as much as she could in her mouth and swirling her tongue. He groaned, a hand digging into the sheets beside him. His hips lifted, his legs clenched, and his member throbbed, pulsing on her tongue.

"Fuck, *stop,* stop or I'll come in your mouth. Molly," he said, hips moving faster. "*Molly — fuck, I'm coming!*" He tried to move back, but she gripped his thighs and hummed once more.

His warmth filled her throat, stream after stream, hips jerking relentlessly until they grew slack and he collapsed down onto the bed.

She slowly sat up after swallowing the thick, warm fluid and pressed the back of her hand to her swollen lips. Her eyes flitted to Tensley's soft, weak expression. Her cheeks warmed and her heart hammered fast. She couldn't look at him. *Oh god, I was awful, wasn't I?*

"You didn't have to do that," he said breathlessly, but she saw how his body already radiated strength, even after the release.

From the intimacy?

He sat up, cupped her cheeks, and brushed her hair out of her face. "Are you okay?"

Her eyes met his soft ones, and she gingerly nodded in his hands. "I'm just sleepy now."

He muttered softly in Italian, shaking his head as he looked over her features. "Damn it. That'd be my fault. I absorbed your energy too fast."

She couldn't even act shocked and closed her eyes. "Was I good?"

He laughed huskily and let his strong hands roam her face freely. She felt safe and warm and complete from his touch—like he was dropping all his boundaries and allowing himself to know her. "Too fucking good for a virgin. Jesus fucking Christ, Darling."

She smiled and couldn't help let her head droop into his hands.

"C'mon; sleep beside me." He scooped her body into his arms and laid them down, curling her against his sweaty torso.

"Will you speak Italian for me? I like how your voice sounds..." she muttered, absent-mindedly stroking her fingers along his hard pec.

"Mm, mi sono infatuata di te." His husky voice soothed her and she curled deeper into his body. His hot breath spanned across her cheekbone. "You want more?"

She cooed and nodded her head against his chest.

"Sei bellissima." His calloused hand spread across her cheek and brushed through her hair and he gripped it. "Just one more, ciccia, all right?" He kissed her closed eyelid. "Ho un debole per te."

She mulled over the words; foggy and sleepy, but she recognized the familiarity to Spanish. "Weak?"

He thumbed her heavy lip and shushed her. "Sleep, ciccia."

She wanted to argue, but as his soft words hummed at her, she couldn't resist. She hadn't felt so warm and safe in ages and she didn't want to waste it. Not for a moment.

THE SUN WOKE Molly up the next time. She tensed, noting Tensley's nearness with a frown. Sitting up was the worst of her ideas. Her head throbbed, and she poked her temples. Then she remembered what she'd done.

She glanced over her shoulder at Tensley, still sound asleep.

I did not give him a blowjob last night.

His dark mane was tossed wildly, and she found herself examining his thick, bee-stung lips.

Blinking through the haze, she crawled out of the sheets and stood in the beautiful, dark bedroom.

She noted the damp cloth on the side table and probed

her own damp forehead. *Did he take care of me?* He shifted in bed and she straightened, holding in air. She couldn't deny that heat filled her chest at the sight of him.

She liked him. *But I shouldn't like him, right? Are my feelings real?*

Then she realized the terrifying whispering, the violent taunting, was gone.

She laughed giddily and pressed the back of her hand to her smiling lips as she tiptoed to the bathroom. She examined her reflection in Tensley's enormous mirror; she should've looked like a complete disaster after Cree, but the bruises and pain were completely gone.

One good thing about being engaged to a demon.

She turned on the shower and let the hot water scorch her flesh, still feeling unclean after the diviners' torment.

After her toes and fingers were completely wrinkled, she tiptoed out and wrapped a towel around her body. She didn't bother redoing her ponytail and peeked through the door. Tensley was no longer in the room, so she continued out, goose bumps rippling over her skin from the cooler temperature.

"You're awake."

Molly flinched at the sound of Tensley's voice and blushed at the faint Italian accent.

I asked him to speak Italian to me. Ugh.

He stood in the doorway of his walk-in closet. "You look--" He hesitated, eyes lingering over her exposed legs. "Wet."

"I just had a shower," she said as softly as possible. She wiped her hair from her cheek and behind her ear, lowering her head.

He nodded and wandered into the room, eyes never leaving her. "You feeling better?"

"Yes. Thank you." She rubbed the engagement ring, an awful habit.

He noticed the movement and stepped closer. "Vena amoris."

"What?"

A weak smile formed on his sculpted lips, and he grabbed her hand. His finger rubbed across her engagement ring. "It's Latin for 'vein of love'. Traditionally, people thought a special, powerful vein ran from the fourth finger on the left hand"—his finger traced down her hand and up her arm—"directly to the heart." It continued up to her collarbone to halt above the towel at the top of her breast. She was boneless. "It's racing."

She pressed both her hands to his chest, but he didn't stop leaning forward. Her entire body shook in his embrace, shuddering from the feeling of him so close.

He ran the pad of his finger along her flesh. His thumb pressed to her bottom lip and gently, he opened it. She hesitated, gawking at his sexual, dark eyes.

Maybe she should have stopped, not egg the demon on more, but she couldn't resist him. Not anymore.

She wrapped her lips around his finger and sucked.

That did it.

chapter
thirty-two

TENSLEY'S TEETH DRAGGED across her neck. A whimper left her quivering lips, and her fingers dug deeper into his soft skin.

She didn't want it, though. She didn't want it.

But I do. All the things her friends would say if they knew — what September would think, if she told her how much she enjoyed him, his lips, his hands, his presence…

His tongue slid over the pulsing vein on her neck, and before she knew it, he was pulling his shirt over his head. She craved his flesh against hers. It was addictive. It felt wrong, yet her body sang his praises.

It's the blood, Molly.

"Tensley," she moaned. His kisses became rougher and his hands moved up and down her wet thighs, a heat beginning between her legs.

"Say it again." he said, breathless. *"Say my name."*

"Tensley."

His eyes darkened. "Do you want me?"

The question startled her, and instead of answering,

she stared at him.

"Do. You. Want. Me?" He wasn't playing games.

Her mind screamed a silent *no,* her body craved every inch of him, and she didn't know what to listen to.

He sighed heavily and muttered to himself in Italian, turning to the door.

Her desire won. "*Yes.*"

Tensley stalled, his back straightening at the sound of her voice. He turned to face her.

Taking a long, shaky breath, she let the towel fall. The cool air should have made her shiver, but the nerves in her body were so electrified that her flesh felt hot.

She wanted to try for him, try to make this work between them, so she had to show him her vulnerabilities. She had to be bare and exposed, that she wasn't a threat or weapon to him anymore.

She was his fiancée.

When she braved a look at Tensley, his jaw looked painfully clenched, and she could clearly see the tautness in his pants. He moved fast. His hands gripped her hips and tugged her to the bed so that they fell onto the soft surface together. He hovered over her, hands planted on either side of her head.

His eyes raked over her naked body. She wanted to hide, but the thrill of someone—*him*—seeing her completely exposed, vulnerable, thrilled her.

"God damn it." He stared over every inch of her, pushing a hand through his wild hair. "You're gorgeous."

Her cheeks warmed at his words. When she rolled her lip between her teeth, he grinned and lowered himself on top of her. She clawed at his back, causing a husky groan to escape from his lips. Tensley's mouth latched onto her neck, his tongue sliding across her quivering skin. He moved farther down, pressing gentle kisses between her breasts, a few inches from her belly button and on her hipbones.

"Tensley," she gasped, clutching the covers and squirming underneath. "*Please.*"

"Fuck, Molly," he drawled and shifted upward. He kissed the side of her cheek and traced his hand down her trembling stomach to her groin. She shivered with anticipation, one hand gripping Tensley's arm. His free hand began kneading her left breast, tweaking the tight bud, and she wanted more. She needed more.

"Are you wet, Molly?"

She groaned at his wicked voice. "Yes, yes." She tossed her head into the sheets, arching her back until her breasts brushed his naked torso. His finger lowered to her exposed sweetness, spinning tortuous circles into the flesh below her center. When the pad of his finger swept across her wet folds, she almost lost it and shattered beneath him.

"You're soaked," he hummed.

Her center ached, throbbed. Each possessive swipe of his finger made the pleasure and torture grow. She crooned in a lust-filled haze, moaning into her hand, into the sheets, into the air. She tried to calm her heart, but her breathing was out of control, punctuated by ragged gasps.

Her hips bucked shamelessly against his touch.

"Does that feel good, Molly?" Tensley's voice was so close that it startled her, and she turned her head to see him watching her expression intently. "I want to see how good I make you feel."

She didn't hide her flushed cheeks. His carnal gaze egged her on and without another thought, she found his hard-on through his briefs. His thick length caused her hand to loosen, startled by his large size. *Was it this big last night, too?* He froze, a painful groan leaving his supple lips.

"Fuck," he hissed through his clenched teeth as she palmed the head of his erection. He growled viciously, thrusting into her hand and pressing his finger into her sex.

She tensed.

Okay, ow.

"So tight." He wiggled his finger gently, attempting to gain more entrance. "So wet for me. Just me."

He found her bud of nerves and the sweet spot took control of every single muscle, of every limb, making her cry out. She muffled the cries into the top of his head as he sucked at her breast, her body greedily rocking against his plunging finger, moving slow and steady as she rode out her orgasm.

Tensley's faded voice coaxed her along, dragging out every last second, murmuring into her ear the entire time.

Her heartbeat slowed as she lay cocooned underneath his hard, muscled body. Slowly, the desire-induced haze faded and her eyes swung back to find him examining her heated face. His eyes were half-lidded, and gave him the appearance of a lion after a satisfying meal.

"Can we do that again?" She giggled into his cheek and couldn't stop.

His chest rumbled against hers, clutching her to him. "Addicted to me?"

She smiled, watching him lift his upper body to hover above her. She eyed his soft expression. "I didn't expect you to ever be like this." *And I like it far too much.*

His brow furrowed. "Like what?"

Her fingers traced his cheekbone, the skin silky but the scruff rough. "Sweet. You're not the demon you pretend to be..."

All tenderness, softness chilled to a painful degree. His jaw locked under her fingers. He straightened up, cleared his throat, and stood.

Molly sat up on the bed, watching as he gathered his clothing, pulling his shirt on. "Where are you going?"

"I need to get to work," he muttered, simply as an answer. "Food in the fridge, let yourself out."

Molly frowned. What had happened in the last few seconds to change his mood so much? Her saying he was not the demon he pretended to be? She swore under her breath.

She yanked the covers from the bed and stood up abruptly. "Are you okay?"

He zipped up his pants and started toward the door. "Fine," he bit out.

"Tensley," she gasped, shaking her head desperately. *I just let him — and he's just leaving?* Her skin reddened with anger and embarrassment.

His mouth became a grim line.

His pitch-black eyes darted to her chest, and when she looked down, she realized the sheets had shifted to expose her left breast. She frantically yanked it back up.

Her heart thudded loudly in her ears and her palms sweated.

He turned to look at her, his top lip curved in disgust. "Show yourself out."

Tensley left the bedroom, slamming the front door so hard the pictures on the wall shook.

She gazed down at her trembling hands, staring at the engagement ring. "Vein of love, my ass."

TENSLEY SAT IN his shadowed office at the estate, alone. He massaged his head, but the pressure behind his eyes, on his shoulders, and even spreading through his chest didn't dissolve. No one spoke to him the way Molly had—like she could see past his façade.

You're not the demon you pretend to be.

His muscles ached, and he stretched to rid himself of the sensation.

He couldn't be like his brother. He couldn't let himself go, let himself be weak for her—for anyone. His family needed him. *Scorpios* needed him. He remembered him and his family watching Fallen rip out his brother's heart in their living room. He remembered as a child hearing his mother sob when Beau was returned to them as an empty shell. He remembered the fear of being alone in the same room as his older brother, how the bruises remained in his mind long after they had vanished from his skin. He wasn't going to risk history repeating itself, not for the selfish reason of indulging in human emotions.

He hadn't expected to get so physical with her, but he couldn't seem to stop. Watching her orgasm from *his* hands satisfied him in a way he'd never experienced.

He caught himself feeling more for her than he should. That tender smile...

He wanted to taste her, consume her, possess her completely as his. Her sweetness, her softness cracked at his hard exterior, and he wanted so badly to be like Illya then. She wielded her emotions so perfectly, expressed them openly, and he couldn't even express a semblance of how deep his loneliness truly went. Only anger was appropriate.

His beast roared even when he thought of her. If he hadn't stopped himself, his beast would have taken control and marked her then and there. The beast wanted her and he would fight Tensley to get to her.

His phoned beeped and he reached for it on the massive oak desk.

ILLYA

12:34 P.M.

Do you want me to send some men to watch Molly at the Plaza tonight?

He glared and dropped the phone. As he leaned back in his chair, his beast stirred inside of him. He didn't like the thought of her alone, surrounded by horny males or worse, thirsty demons wanting a taste of her sweetness.

"Fuck no," he hissed and snatched his phone.

TENSLEY

12:35 p.m.

Don't worry; I have it covered.

chapter
thirty-three

MOLLY RAN HER hands along her thighs and eyed the three people who used to hold the control of her independence in their hands. If she didn't get the internship, she would be out of a job and experience, then an apartment, and would be forced to live at home where her parents would beg her to work for their friends and run social events.

That couldn't happen. She breathed shakily.

She was painfully awkward at socializing and small talk—*ugh, small talk*. She was made for behind the scenes, for research and analyzing, not Manhattan gossip and how nice the weather was outside.

"Ms. Crawford, when were you expecting to tell us that you were going by your mother's maiden name?" Mr. Cho asked.

Molly bristled. "Uh…well."

"I ran into your mother, and she stated that you have other intern opportunities," he continued.

Molly's stomach dropped. *How could she do that?* Yes,

Fiona disliked the idea of Molly pursuing her own path and wanted her daughter to follow in her charity-running footsteps, but she knew Molly hated the fake people who attended those things with every fiber of her being.

She uncurled her clenched hands. *Be calm.*

"I chose to use my mother's maiden name so you wouldn't be swayed by the 'Darling' status. I've dreamed of working in a museum since I was a little kid. I would beg anyone who would listen to go to a museum instead of the toy store. I've studied for this opportunity for years, and I *know* the last few months I've been dealing with personal issues, but I promise to work hard and be committed. What my mother says is completely different than how I feel—please don't let her sway you."

Ms. Albinson cleared her throat. "Molly, even with the absences and occasional late arrivals, the work you hand in at the end of the day is phenomenal. We're astounded by the professionalism and attention to detail you've displayed, and we applaud you in that respect. That said, the most important trait we need—over expert layouts and artist collaborations—is reliability, and you haven't exhibited it as of late."

Molly lowered her head and blinked back the ache behind her eyes. She'd screwed up, she'd missed her opportunity, and now she'd be a grocery bag lady. *Oh god.*

"Based on your portfolio as a whole, however, we are going to give you one more chance. So Molly, we extend our congratulations to you for joining our team during the school year."

Molly's head jerked up and she gawked at the three

smiling faces. "Oh—oh! Thank you so much!" They laughed as they shook her hand, and she signed the contract with her loopy, nervous scrawl. She couldn't think straight as she left to go get ready for the charity ball.

LIPS AS RED as blood, Molly thought as she stared at her reflection in her apartment's bathroom. She brushed some blush onto the apples of her cheeks, forcing herself to put on the smile her mother had taught her years ago. She smoothed down the red silk dress and secured the hairpin in her smooth, blonde waves.

Just in case.

"Hot damn, Mol!" September said, pulling the curtain out of the way to gawk. September wore a short black dress and heels so high only a runway model should've been able to walk in them. Completing her ensemble was a battered leather motorcycle jacket. "Well look at you, showing off your stuff." September laughed, gesturing to Molly's chest. "Count your blessings, one and two—*oh,* and three: you have a nice tush."

Molly scowled at her.

"Stop it. We need to leave now or we're going to be late and Stella will murder me with her Gucci shoes," Molly said, twisting the cap back on her lipstick. Once she grabbed her purse, her and September rushed downstairs and out into the humid summer night.

September stared at Molly with a sharp look. "You're not wearing your glasses?"

Molly shook her head. "No. I'm done hiding."

September smiled brightly and patted her on the shoulder. "So, where's the monster tonight? Ruining someone else's life for a change?"

Molly stiffened, her pleasurable morning with Tensley sending a flush over her face. "He isn't a monster," Molly mumbled.

September halted. "What?"

Molly shrugged; she'd been just as evil to Tensley by going behind his back to Cree, if not worse. "I mean...I haven't been a saint when it comes to him either," she murmured.

She clenched her hands. Every choice she made since her birthday a month before had led to *someone's* unhappiness, whether her parents', Cree's, or her own. For once, she wanted to be happy. She wanted to think only of her own desires.

The two strolled down the streets of Manhattan, and in no time had arrived at the Plaza Hotel. People in elegant formalwear filled the hallways and ballroom. A woman asked for their names at the front as they went inside.

"Well this certainly isn't some grunge scene party," September said, speaking over the multiple conversations around them and sipping a drink she'd grabbed from a tray.

"Molly!" Stella cried, rushing over to kiss both of her cheeks like they were in Europe. Stella wore a tight navy dress, showcasing her thin arms and swanlike neck. Her red hair was smoothed back into a sleek style that didn't look out of place with her feline features.

She looked over Molly's dress, gawking at her ample

cleavage. "Thank god! No sunglasses! You look beautiful!" Stella's narrowed eyes gazed at the person standing behind Molly. "Oh. Hey, September."

"*Stella*." September slurped her drink.

Stella turned her attention back to Molly. "Why didn't you come with Tensley?"

"He's sick," Molly said, nodding too much.

Stella furrowed her brows. "But he's here."

Panic hit her in the stomach like a punch. "Oh?" Molly's pleasant voice cracked.

"I was just talking to him over by the entrance." Stella pointed to the doorway, but Molly couldn't see him anywhere. "Well, I'll talk to you shortly. Tina was on her fourth glass of wine the last time I saw her; I need to keep her away from the married men at this shindig." Stella vanished into the crowd of dresses and suits.

Molly rolled her head back, hoping the crystal chandelier would possibly fall on her.

September laid a hand on her shoulder. "How did he know about the ball?"

Molly blinked several times. "I don't know."

"If he pulls anything, I'm going to kill him," September said, rolling her hand into a fist.

"Killing is serious business, ladies," a dark voice spoke. All three spun to see Tensley and Illya strolling over. Molly's heart pounded violently against her ribcage, remembering how his mouth had moved against her flesh.

He looked like heaven and hell—hair unkempt to the point of pure sexiness, stubble framing his jaw, and three-piece black and white suit cut to define his arms and shoulders.

Tensley surveyed Molly, not even bothering with a verbal address; his steeled look said it all: he wasn't happy to see her.

What the hell is his problem?

He still doesn't trust you, a voice whispered in her head.

"Why the hell are you here?" September asked harshly.

Tensley tensed under Molly's uncovered gaze. *Damn it.* She wanted his lips on her.

She needed to speak to him; to tell him how she really felt. That she wanted to try, to make their relationship work.

"Tensley," Illya interjected, touching his forearm. "C'mon."

Tensley stepped back, giving Molly a long, unreadable look. "Have a good night, *Molly*." Everything that came out of his mouth sounded like a threat.

Illya mouthed a genial *sorry* as they turned to go.

"Excuse me," Molly said, ruffled. "I need to help some people — seats, donations, you know," she stuttered, moving in the direction of the long buffet tables.

"That's fine, I'm gonna be by the bar!" September called after.

After socializing with some of the donators, she stood to the side, watching the lovely couples waltz. Why couldn't that be her?

"*Definitely* Tensley."

Molly jerked to see Tina and Stella beside her, scanning the room. "What about Tensley?"

"He's the hottest bachelor here. Of course, he's your boyfriend — off limits, but still not married yet." Tina bit her lip and winked. "God, he's gorgeous. So how big is he? Got any kinky tricks?"

"Molly's a virgin, Tina," Stella chided.

"Well, my advice is to sleep with him soon, or he's gonna dump your virgin ass," Tina said, sipping her drink with a matter-of-fact nod.

"Why does it bother you so much that I haven't had sex with someone?" Molly asked, giving both of the girls a hard look. Stella's smirk faltered and Tina frowned. "It's my choice, it's my body — I don't judge *your* choices, and I'd appreciate if you would show me the same courtesy. I want to wait for someone I actually *want* to have sex with."

Stella, for once, didn't seem to have a snarky comeback at the ready, and Tina started crying.

"God, she's such a drunk," Stella hissed, though her eyes were soft.

Molly turned to look away only to glimpse Tensley moving through the crowd.

The stuffy room spun and tilted, and her throat grew tight. She needed to talk to him, find out why he'd acted so off that morning, at least to understand his motives once and for all. She used her shoulders to maneuver through the crowds, spotting him. He was leaving though, and her heart skipped many beats and swelled to twice its size.

"Tensley!" she called and he turned his head.

She opened her mouth, but the glare he sent her froze her entire body.

His look alone made her stomach drop. She needed air.

chapter thirty-four

MOLLY TURNED AWAY from Tensley and moved down the hallway. Her vision blurred as she navigated through the hotel, past drunken partygoers and finally made it to the top of the Plaza's gold-bedecked staircase.

Someone snatched her wrist and she cried out, twisting her hand away. "Get off—"

"Molly, hey!"

It was Stella, not *the devil himself*. Molly fell against her friend's shoulder in a desperate embrace.

"What's wrong?" Stella cradled her like she'd done to Tina a short while earlier.

"I just need air. Tell September I left," Molly said, pushing away.

Stella looked genuinely concerned. "I'll go with you."

"No. You stay here. I'm okay." Molly forced a smile through the unwept tears.

"I'll come over as soon as this thing is done, and we can talk," Stella said as she combed a few golden curls from Molly's lashes. Molly hugged her quickly and then took off. She galloped down the stairs and collided with more distracted ball attendees.

Once outside, she shook her hands out.

Molly tripped over her dress, and in anger she threw off her shoes and decided to walk barefoot. The crescent moon hung above, half-hidden by dark clouds as the humid summer night swarmed her lungs.

"Molly!"

Molly turned. Illya jogged down the street toward her and slowed down, large-eyed, and let out a heavy sigh. "What's wrong?"

"Tensley's so hot and cold, I can't keep up," she said, waving it off. "One minute, we're fine, the next he's all distant and cold."

Illya stuck his hands into his jacket pockets. "It's because he's scared of you."

Molly cocked a brow. "Scared of me?"

He nodded. "Of what you're capable of making him feel."

Molly wrung her hands, wondering if she was that important to Tensley.

"We came tonight, because he wanted us to watch after you," he said, "But he's trying to distance himself."

She huffed out. "I wish he wouldn't do that. I wish he would just tell me how he's feeling."

"Communicating his feelings is one of his weaknesses, I know that for damn sure," Illya said, one corner of his mouth lifting.

One of the streetlamps flickered and died up ahead. Two more went out, until they were swathed in the night's inky blackness. Molly raised her head. *What the hell?* The street grew eerily quiet and Molly tried to swallow, but it seemed as if the inside of her mouth was covered in glue.

A howl bounced off the buildings.

Illya moved closer to her.

Then Molly saw them. The wolves paced back and forth, appearing and simultaneously vanishing into the shadows on one end of the street. An entire pack of familiars prowled farther back. They were about to be surrounded.

"Illya." She clenched his wrist. "Shit. This is not happening."

Illya focused on the moving figures and hissed lowly. "Run, now!"

Molly ran, legs thundering against the paved road away from the wolf pack.

The wolves howled and all the hairs on the back of her neck stood straight up. She led them into Central Park, hoping the few bushes and trees would buy them time.

"We need to get somewhere safe!" Illya yelled, jumping over a park bench.

Molly shook her head; Tensley was too busy sucking some woman's face at the Plaza. All they could do was run. "Come on." She ran under the bridges and toward a dark alley outside of the park. She ran into the alley, staying close to the wall to hide herself in the shadows.

Illya's scream stalled her, coming to an abrupt stop. She spun around to see Illya had collapsed on the gritty floor of the alley a few feet away with an arrow through his right shoulder.

"Illya, oh god!"

She stepped forward and his eyes aligned with hers, sharp and dark—for the first time since she met him, he looked like a demon.

The wolves lurked behind him, snarling at their meal. When one darted forward, Molly swung her arm and shoved the familiar back. It skidded across the dirt, dust clouding the air.

About five figures stood around them, unrecognizable in the shadows.

The wolves paced nearby, their growls ringing in Molly's eardrums. Her whole body tensed and she drew in a sharp breath. *No, oh god, no.*

"Molly," Illya cautioned as she stepped closer, voice quick and hard. "Go, run. *Now.*"

Her eyes watered. She went to speak, to protest but she saw the shadows dragging across the brick buildings. She stared at Illya. His own eyes were bloodshot and he attempted to stop his bottom lip from quivering in front of her. Her chest ached.

She fisted her shaking hands. "I can fight them."

Illya shook his head viciously and again, he looked like a rabid animal. "No, *no.* Go now, Molly."

She stepped toward him, gripping his forearm only for him to shove her. She stumbled, biting hard down on the inside of her cheek and tasted blood. She gawked at Illya's arched back, blood trickling down his gaunt muscles—his veins grew purple. "Illya," she cried out, breathlessly. "I can't leave you."

"I can't let them get you—Tensley wants you safe and I promised him I'd keep you that way. If they catch us both, no one will find us." He struggled to move his legs but barely any movement was made. *"Go!"* His voice grew hoarse and his accent grew stronger. She winced at the sound of his roar, his frame trembling with pain, with anger, with pure, utter fear. He hissed in his native tongue. His dark eyes held that fear incredibly tight.

Someone laughed. Molly spun to the dark alley behind her and took a step back.

"You should have ran, *Darling.*"

Molly squared her shoulders and glared at where the voice came from; she recognized the speaker's sadistic tone and could hardly form his name on her quivering lips. "Abaddon."

"I'm flattered you remember who I am." He emerged, tall and sturdy, fiery hair pulled back so tightly the strain around his hairline was evident. "You look ravishing tonight, Ms. Darling."

He took his time with each step, smoothing his tongue along his crooked teeth, and his eyes sought her left hand. He snorted softly. "Rings don't mean much to me."

Molly hid the engagement ring behind her back and frowned.

"Now, a mark *does*, and by the looks of it" — his eyes danced over her body as a feral smirk warped his mouth — "he hasn't left one."

No. No.

Terror climbed from her stomach to her throat, and she choked on air.

Abaddon leered at her exposed shoulders and the tops of her breasts with a bemused expression, and Molly wished more than anything that Tensley had marked her.

But she had one more ace.

Molly stepped closer, pinning Abaddon with her blessed eyes. He swayed and tensed, falling under their spell, but Illya cried out. She turned to find Illya had yanked the arrow from his shoulder and teetered on his unsteady feet. She glared back at Abaddon who refused to meet her gaze.

"Look at me!" she shouted, but the demon only cackled.

"Not happening. Now come here. *Eyes closed.*"

She glared. "No."

His smug expression stayed, though his large shoulders shifted at her disobedience. A snap of his fingers and chaos sprung forth. A familiar gripped Illya by his throat, a bone-chilling cry ringing out through the alley.

"Don't! Don't do that to him!" Molly said, rushing forward.

Abaddon put his hand out in front of himself and she stopped. "I wouldn't go near them. They don't just bark — they *bite*."

Illya thrashed his whole body back and forth and the familiar growled, nails puncturing the fragile skin until multiple streams of red ran down his neck.

Molly ran a hand through her hair in panic. "Stop! Please!"

Illya choked on a scream.

"You can either let your friend die, or you can come with me," Abaddon said, gesturing to Illya.

"Molly, don't go with him," Illya said in a small voice. Molly stared at him, battling herself.

Go with him, save Illya. Fight, risk both our lives. Her hands shook. *Damn it.* She didn't have a choice; she didn't have time to figure out how to save herself.

"Wasted too much time. Rip his heart out. We'd be doing Lord Fallen a favour—"

The familiar pressed his fingers into Illya's chest and a blood chilling scream left Illya's lungs.

"Stop! Fine! I'll go with you!" She couldn't do it, she couldn't watch them destroy Illya.

Abaddon's grin grew and he snapped his fingers again. The man released Illya and he stumbled forward on unsteady legs.

Illya rubbed his chest, the holes from the puncture wound bleeding through his dress shirt. "Molly, *don't.*"

Abaddon offered his hand, smirking. Molly walked forward, keeping her gaze down until the last minute when she grasped his hand, stared up at him, and quickly twisted his wrist until she heard it snap.

Instead of being weakened, however, Abaddon snarled and snatched her by the waist.

"I can walk by myself," she said sharply, shoving him. He stumbled back, unbalanced, but his features warped into something thoroughly infernal. She braced herself, preparing to fight the way the demon hunters had taught her.

"Foolish girl," he said. His voice morphed and seemed to detach from his human form. "You're not powerful enough to face me—not without the marking."

Her fists faltered, lowering, but she circled them tight again and glared. "I don't—I don't need him!"

I don't need anyone.

"Molly!" Illya called out.

Abaddon's smile was ruthless. "Sadly, you're mistaken."

He swung his long arm and she dodged, only to have him counter with his other hand and punch her in the cheekbone, throwing her off balance.

Abaddon swung her over his back and she shrieked, cursing and pounding against him. She dug her nails into his back and felt blood seep from the broken flesh.

It's not working. Relax, just relax and absorb his strength.

But she couldn't; her heart pounded violently. Abaddon walked forward, managing both tasks. At first he laughed, but then his anger grew and he reached up to punch her in the ribcage.

"Let her go!" Illya cried, a stream of profanities following in Molly's wake. The familiars kept him from reaching her, and Molly lifted her head to look behind just as a mysterious, shimmering portal seemed to open up in the air before them.

One more punch from Abaddon and darkness overwhelmed her.

chapter
thirty-five

TENSLEY MANEUVERED SKILLFULLY through the ballroom, scanning it for the small blonde. Even if he found *her*, he wasn't sure what he would say — not sorry; he wasn't sorry. Demons were never sorry for their natural actions.

But then why did his chest feel so goddamn heavy?

He wanted to keep himself in check, while his beast wanted to ravish her.

The live band was loud, along with the constant chattering of the Upper East Siders' nonsensical, materialistic conversations. A few women giggled and a busty woman even approached him, but with a glare and a good dose of aggressive pheromones she was soon scurrying away.

He shouldered some rich, loud-talking bastard out of his path, and his eyes landed on Stella and the other girl — the black-haired girl.

"Have you seen Molly?"

Stella's mouth hung open at first. Then she scowled

and appeared more demonic than the ones he'd actually grown up with. "You're going nowhere near my friend, *dick*. I don't know what you did to make Molly Darling — one of the nicest, most genuine people in New York — so upset, but you're not getting *any* fucking help from me."

He clenched his teeth and leaned in. "Where is she?"

Stella leaned in also, copying his stance and expression. "Go die."

He wanted to knock her into the wall, but he managed to hold on to his emotions for a bit longer. "If you don't tell me where she is, your life will consist of *maybe* five more breaths."

"I'm shaking in my Guccis."

"Oh, well *hello* hot man," the black-haired girl interjected, stumbling into Stella and then reaching out to touch Tensley's stomach.

"Shit, Tina." Stella pulled her away and let Tina rest her body against hers. Stella glowered at him again. "You better leave."

"Or what? You'll stab me with your Gucci stiletto?"

"Right between the eyes — or maybe in a *lower* domain," she snapped, eyes flickering down to his crotch. "Now fuck off. If you dare go near Molly again, I will rip you to shreds the Manhattan way." She bared her pearly whites and closed the gap between them.

Several ways to murder the little redhead at that moment flashed through his mind. "Molly's mine."

Stella's face flared crimson and she tightened her grip on her glass. "She doesn't belong to anyone, *Alpha*."

"Is this douche bothering you, Stella?" September appeared beside her, arm crossed.

"Oh don't worry. I had this covered."

Both girls glared him down.

Tensley had enough. "Where's Molly?"

September shrugged. "Nowhere you need to know."

Tensley unhinged his mouth to talk, but someone was shouting his name. His eyes darted to a disheveled Illya rushing through the crowd.

Illya gripped Tensley's shoulders, and he was shocked to see that his eyes were bloodshot and misty. "Tensley."

His throat tightened. "What?"

"Familiars showed up," Illya said. "We ran into the park and––and then they got us."

"You're bleeding!" Stella whisper-shrieked, clutching her own neck.

Illya shrugged it off. "It's nothing."

"It's not fucking nothing," Tensley snapped. He rolled up his jacket and tore a piece of his shirtsleeve off. He secured the material around Illya's neck, putting pressure on the wounds. "Where's Molly?"

Illya choked on his rapid breathing, eyes darting around. "He took her and I couldn't fucking do anything to stop him. I tried to tell her to run, but she was stubborn."

"Are you serious?" September glared at Illya.

Tensley gritted his teeth. "Who did?

"Abaddon––he took her," he said. "Molly went with him because he was going to rip my fucking heart out, and she tried to fight back––"

"What do you mean *Abaddon* took her? Who the hell is he?" Stella yelled. Tensley forgot the human girl was standing in their half-circle, clinging to every last word.

"She's gone?" September choked. "Oh god. We have to get her!"

"Fuck!" Tensley cursed, glancing at Illya. "I had two men on her tonight. What the fuck were they doing?"

He hadn't marked her.

And now Abaddon would do it; he would force himself on Molly, and once she was the duke's, Tensley couldn't do anything about it. Abaddon would rape her until she died, just like the dozens of other women over the centuries.

"I'll go with you to find her," Illya said, stepping forward.

"Me too," September said.

"No, you won't," Tensley shot back, vibrating with anger at himself.

"I want to help too," Stella said with a pout.

Tensley growled and turned to face them. "Illya and I will go down. You guys can wait at the house if you're that concerned."

"Sexist," September hissed, folding her arms.

Tensley sized her up, and she wasn't a weakling. She *had* stood up to him and that familiar who attacked her and Molly in the bar, or so Illya had told him. Plus, she loved Molly, which meant more than anything else at that point. "Fine, but don't get in my way."

September grinned smugly.

"What?" Stella threw her hands up and Tina giggled behind her. "Why does she get to go?"

"We still need someone to wait at the house to make sure the Darlings are fine," Illya explained, gently touching Stella's shoulder. "Do you think you can do that?"

Stella nodded, her frustrations quelled by Illya's attractiveness. "I can do that."

Tensley turned without speaking, and the others followed. When he went down to Babylon, he was taking Molly back up with him — no matter what.

He would rescue his fiancée from Duke Abaddon even if the Princes sentenced him to an agonizing death.

chapter thirty-six

MOLLY PEELED HER sore eyes open and scanned the dimly lit area. Sweat dribbled down her scorchingly hot limbs, and when she breathed in greedily, the thick, acrid air caused her to cough. The smell of smoky incense prickled her nose and she looked up. A series of white, long-stemmed candles stood nearby.

Molly squinted, straining to make out her surroundings. She appeared to be in a bedroom. She tried to move but her limbs were weighed down; they were *so heavy,* and her brain felt like it'd been anesthetized.

Molly looked down and saw that she was only wearing a white lacy bra and underwear. Her stomach plummeted.

She worked to sit up, leaning her back against the bed frame. The corners of the room were hooded in shadow, and she clutched at the silky sheets entwined around her legs. Molly studied the room, noting books and documents strewn across a desk, discarded bits of clothing piled on the floor. She rubbed at her face, disoriented; although a heat

R. SCARLETT

devoured her insides, her hands were icy cold.

"Glad to see you're up," a voice said.

Molly flinched and saw a large, solid form framing the doorway. It didn't surprise her to see Abaddon, red hair in complete disarray and a wine glass in hand. He swirled it and inhaled the bouquet, grinning at her.

She clung to the white sheets. "What are you going to do?"

Abaddon smirked, and his teeth were stained red so that he looked truly hellish. "With *you*?" He bowed his head and walked over, heeled boots clicking on the floor. "I'm going to mark you."

Her lips trembled and she tried to roll away from him to the other side of the bed, finally standing. Her legs shook under her weight and the room spun in circles.

"You can't just run away, *daemon*," Abaddon sneered.

Her nails dug into the mattress as she held herself up, shooting him an angry look. "What — what did you do to me?"

He placed the wine glass on his desk and shrugged. "Just a small dose of belladonna; causes lethargy. Nothing permanent. Might experience a cool sensation on the inside, but feels like your skin is burning."

She gaped. *He drugged me.*

"I'm going back home."

"To Mr. Knight?"

She stiffened.

"You think he won't force himself on you?" His gravelly words sounded distorted. "We're demons, Molly. We kill humans, we kill each other; we even kill the ones who love us. We're selfish creatures; nothing is good in us. We lost that many centuries ago."

She pulled the covers farther up to her neck. "When you fell?"

He nodded. "Tensley Knight is one of us. He's nothing different. If I don't have my way with you now, he will very shortly."

Her heart thundered in her throat. "That's not true."

"Don't tell me you've *fallen* for him. Oh, how sweet. How utterly *stupid*, to love someone who could never, ever truly return the affection you desire. His brother may have strayed, but your sweet Tensley won't. He's been trained as an emotionless soldier," he went on, strolling around the huge bed. "He's the monster you fear."

Their eyes aligned then, and she allowed her body to relax. His aggressive movements halted.

Her eyes...they'd maintained their power even with the belladonna.

She released a slow breath. "You're going to let me go now, or you're going to regret it, Abaddon."

He didn't frown or protest, only staring mindlessly back at her. She didn't blink, edging around him with the blanket clutched to her chest, their eyes still fixated on each other. The air was so hot, and tears streamed down her face from the strain. Her eyelids finally closed involuntarily. Abaddon gained control and roared, slamming his hefty hand against her ear and shoving her against the wall.

His breathing grew rapid, heavy, and low on the base of her neck. When she tried to turn her head he pressed it harder into the hard surface, avoiding her eyes.

"I like a bit of a challenge. It would be too easy if I hid your most valuable asset—those rare eyes." His fingers dug into her cheekbone, and she thrashed weakly.

She bared her teeth. "Don't *touch* me."

She didn't need to see his expression to sense the smirk there, to know what he would do next. He ripped the blanket away, exposing her. She pushed against him but he just held her down, grasping her thighs and lifting her around his waist.

"I can't mark you without touching." He chuckled, hurling her onto the bed. She scrambled away as soon as she landed, but Abaddon sat on top of her, turning her to look up at him. She hit him hard on the right side of his jaw with her fist and his cheek immediately swelled.

Relax. Relax, Molly.

Her powers only ever seemed to work when she was relaxed, but this was different—she was sluggish and feeble. She wanted her powers to work, she wanted strength, but she couldn't focus.

When he reacted with another snicker, she hit him until her hands were numb and red. He waved her fingers off like little flies, growling and holding her down when he'd had enough.

"Let me go!" she shrieked.

He reached up somewhere and pulled chains down from the bedpost, tying them in an intricate knot around her wrists and the bedframe. He yanked her arms up.

"Don't. *Don't.*"

Abaddon rose off the bed, removing his black dress shirt and pants. She desperately tried to catch his eyes with hers again, choking on her tears.

God. God. Oh god.

Abaddon grabbed a black scarf from his desk and tied it around her face. He grabbed a handful of her tangled locks and lifted her head up, pressing a cold metal object to her lips.

"Pain is a part of life, Molly."

He pricked her bottom lip with the knife, and she tasted blood. Her lungs ached, a scream quivering within them. As he moved across the bed again, she wiggled, attempting to get free.

At the ache in her wrist, an awful idea began in her head.

If I just...

He lifted her whole torso up, seeming to wrap her in some sort of silky material. "No, no, *no!*" She kicked wildly, hoping to land on a body part that might incapacitate him.

He breathed heavily, concentrating on tying up the corset he'd just fitted around her middle and tightening its strings. She gasped and gurgled, feeling her ribs shift and bend nearly to the point of breaking in the unnatural position.

"The more you panic, the tighter it gets," he warned, licking the blood off her lips.

"*Bastard,*" she hissed, wincing at his vile touch.

His hand rubbed her hip, sliding down to her pelvis. "I won't be gentle. It's not in my nature."

When she went to yell at him, the corset tightened and she shuddered, her torso pulsing in pain. "He'll come for me."

Even Molly knew it was a lie.

"He won't," he asserted, laughter in his voice. "You're

all bark and no bite, aren't you, honey?" He slid his hand along her neck, pushing her down. "I think I could grow some affection for you." His other hand pried her legs apart even as she struggled to keep them shut. He trailed kisses over her exposed skin, biting hard until she cried out.

Molly pushed her head farther into the pillow and felt something hard pressing into her scalp.

The hairpin!

She twisted her left wrist, ignoring the agony of the unnatural angle, and with one final *snap*, she freed her left hand.

"*Ow!*" She screamed and the corset cut her off. Abaddon didn't bother stopping, only egged on by her screams.

A horrifying thought crept into her fading mind.

Tensley isn't coming.

chapter
thirty-seven

TENSLEY GLOWERED FOR the fifth time at September following behind him. He stomped through a few dirty puddles and gazed at Abaddon's manor where it was partly hidden by evergreen trees. Babylon was a dark place. Only demons of the highest class lived there, and it was mostly so that they could carry out their duties to Fallen with ease.

"That portal seriously doesn't mix well with wine," September muttered, massaging her stomach.

Tensley casted her a dark look. "You can't speak a word about its location to anyone, got it?"

"I can't believe it's just sitting hidden at City Hall. I mean, it's abandoned, good place to have it, but really? Just a few fancy Latin words and bam, it's there!" September waved her hands. "It must get a lot of traffic."

"High class demons have the ability to produce a portal anywhere, while the rest of us use that one in Manhattan," Illya explained.

"Is there one in Brooklyn?"

"Shut up and focus," Tensley snapped. *Like babysitting a bunch of children.* "And stay here."

"Uh, no." September pulled on his black jacket and they challenged each other with glares. "We're coming in with you."

Tensley ran a hand down his face and shook his head. "Hell no. If you come along, I'll have to watch your ass too."

"I can watch my own ass," September said.

"She has a point, Tensley," Illya said, the only one not about to burst a blood vessel. "Abaddon could have tons of familiars lurking inside, and we might not be able to take them all out ourselves."

Tensley eyed him. "Fine. Illya, come. You stay here." The annoying brat whined and complained as the demons left. September yelled something offensive, but he didn't bother turning back.

The two approached the manor at godlike speed.

Tensley kicked the door open and found familiars already stationed and guarding the entrance.

"Well, good evening," he hissed, swinging a leg up to push the first one backward. Illya had snapped two of the others' necks already and cracked his knuckles as they scanned the entrance. The foyer was dark and gloomy, with granite floors in swirls of black and silver and old portraits on the walls. A grand staircase stood before them.

His adrenaline kicked in, something demons could easily summon, and he searched for the next round of familiars. They were dumb creatures, and didn't know a damn thing about stealth.

"Tensley," Illya said, and Tensley noticed the demonic glint in Illya's eyes. Illya rarely harnessed his supernatural abilities, because he didn't want to scare any nearby humans. Now, in Babylon, it didn't matter. "I'm just saying this as a precaution-, but if Abaddon has been with Molly, he'll be stronger than both of us. We have to think of a better plan."

He better not lay a fucking hand on her.

Tensley scowled. "I know, Illya. That's why I have this." He yanked a sword from one of the dead familiar's limp hands and grinned. "If I can kick your ass, I can kick his."

Illya went to challenge that, but doors across the hallway opened and in walked four more familiars. Tensley grasped one by the hair and sliced the sword straight through his chest. The man disintegrated into ashes, and Tensley moved on to the next one.

Someone grabbed his shoulder and swiftly threw him into a glass table, which shattered beneath him. He groaned, rolling over the shards. Tensley looked up into the face of a smug familiar with brown shaggy hair and a ridiculous goatee. The familiar smiled as he approached, and Tensley reached for his sword, realizing a second later that it was across the room.

Fuck.

No worries. He would use his bare hands if he had to. He'd rip the familiar's throat out—

The familiar paused, eyes wide and mouth going slack. Then he dropped to the floor.

September stood behind him with a bloodied sword in her hands. "Looks like you *did* need our help."

"I could have fucking killed him with my pinkie." Tensley rolled his eyes. "Illya, watch out for more familiars."

Illya nodded, exhaling deeply.

Tensley jogged over and picked up the sword. "And watch *her*."

September made a face.

Tensley stalked up the grand staircase into the poorly lit hallways, trying to listen for a sound from one of the rooms that might lead him in the right direction.

Then he heard her voice. Her soft, trembling voice. A door was slightly ajar and he ran to it, pushing it open with both hands. There was a bed. A massive bed and two bodies. Molly stirred underneath Abaddon, tossing her head back and forth. Abaddon kissed her neck roughly and collarbone and rubbed his hand around her thighs and pelvis. His back faced Tensley and he had spread her legs apart, lying in between them.

Tensley's skin boiled. A balcony looked out onto a violent night storm and woods that went on for miles. Abaddon chuckled when Molly let out a small whimper.

Tensley squared his jaw and raised his sword. He was trying his best to be quiet and not acting on impulse to murder the disgusting beast.

"You like it, don't you?" Abaddon muttered, laughing afterward. "You want me to hurt you. Don't lie now." Abaddon slapped her thigh hard and she bit back her cries of pain.

Candles glowed and flickered, and the air was smoky with incense. It didn't cloud his rage though.

"You want it rough now?" Abaddon's fat fingers wrapped around Molly's throat and squeezed.

Molly wheezed.

Tensley didn't care about being quiet anymore. He jolted forward, thrusting the sword--only to have Abaddon speed out of the way and stand by the balcony. The French doors blew in the wind and the rain thrashed into the room.

Abaddon huffed wildly and wiped his mouth.

"You forget the laws, Abaddon?" Tensley hoped to give him a chance to fess up. Even then, he would still gut him. "Fallen's seven laws, with number one being that if someone is engaged to another demon, *no one else* is to touch them."

Abaddon hummed, as if beginning to sing a melody. "I remember." His chin rose. "I just think Ms. Darling deserves a well-bred mate for her offspring—me. Not some young, weak, middle-class prick."

Tensley's hands shook and he rolled them into iron fists. "*I* will be her husband."

"You haven't even marked her yet. Turning you a bit soft? You shouldn't wear your weaknesses so openly, Tensley. Don't parents discipline their children on this anymore? You have to control it or she'll be the one controlling you. Tell me…is it father like son? Or brother like brother?" Abaddon laughed, glancing over at Molly. Her chest faintly fluttered and a cloth half concealed her eyes. A strange sensation began to throb in his chest. A corset hugged her torso so tightly, she looked smaller than usual.

Tensley's nostrils flared. *That damn bastard.*

He spun, marching full force towards the redhead beast. "If you so much as —"

An elbow jabbed at Tensley's face and he was thrown back, up against the wall. With the intense emotions clouding his judgment, he couldn't concentrate.

"I'm stronger than you, and a higher class," Abaddon said, thick fingers wrapped around Tensley's shaking throat.

Tensley thrashed his body once, trying to escape. His sword dropped to the ground. He squared his jaw.

Abaddon beamed. "You know what's perfect? When you die, no one will truly know what happened. Molly will have always been mine."

Tensley paused. It all made sense now. "You never told Fallen about her."

His eyes glowed with pride. "If I told him, he would have gone after her himself or denied my pursuit. She should've been *my* betrothed! I deserve her. Fallen thinks he knows how to rule, but if I gained the daemon, I could overthrow him. Make a better society for us." Abaddon leaned so close, he could make out the small hairs on his face.

Tensley's chest was full of fire and his hands were unclenching and clenching.

Only one thought raced through his mind.

He'd kill for her.

Tensley's forehead slammed against Abaddon's and he went stumbling back. Tensley kicked up his sword to his hand and gained his feet in a rush. Abaddon punched Tensley first across the cheek and then square on his mouth. Tensley tasted the raw blood and he spat, growling.

"Weak boy, she hasn't even been giving you strength," Abaddon commented, strolling around him like he was a king and Tensley a servant. "You don't want to hurt her or just not interested?"

"Shut up."

"Why haven't you?" Abaddon voice was harsh, almost angry that Tensley hadn't. "It's our right—we are beyond those humans, those daemons. We are the superior race. We have the right to anything we please."

"I'd stop talking. Might want to keep your energy." He breathed slowly.

Abaddon cracked his neck and worked his shoulders. "You have to control yourself. Or she'll be the one controlling you."

Tensley threw his entire body forward, a snarl leaving his lips. Abaddon dodged his attack and Tensley ended up sliding across the floor to the balcony. His sword was underneath Abaddon's foot, reflecting onto the ceiling.

Abaddon slyly smiled. "Give up; you're outmatched. She's—"

And then Abaddon froze, seizing up. Tensley furrowed his brow. Slowly, Abaddon shifted and revealed Molly, legs trembling as she stood.

"I bite," she choked, cradling her abnormal angled wrist.

Pure, raw panic plagued Tensley's chest as he jolted forward.

Abaddon spun and gripped her by her forearm. She flinched, but Abaddon yanked her forward and stabbed his sword deep into her abdomen. "You bitch."

Molly gasped, swaying on her feet and she collapsed in front of them, her hands frantically searching for something to grasp.

Tensley's heart seized and all he saw was bloody fucking red.

He sprinted, kicked his sword off the ground, into his grip and drove it deep into Abaddon's chest. A horrifying shriek left Abaddon's twitching lips.

"She's my fiancée," Tensley hissed, his breathing battling to take over Tensley tightened his grip on the sword in his hand and drove it deep through Abaddon. He made sure the angle was just below the ribcage, using so much force to shatter a bone in hopes of piercing organs. The bastard deserved to suffer. A horrifying shriek left Abaddon's twitching lips.

He jabbed it deeper, and Abaddon gasped. He gave a final twist before pulling the sword out and dropped him. Abaddon's limp body hit the floor with a loud thud. "Prick." Tensley heavily breathed out, running his bloody fingers through his dark, wet mane.

He spun.

Molly was a motionless heap on the marble floor, blood spreading across her middle and streaking down her legs.

Tensley raced over and collapsed next to her. He shook her limp figure. A corset hugged her torso so tightly that she looked even smaller than usual, and she wasn't breathing. The heavy weight in his chest throbbed violently as panic set in.

"*Molly.*" He patted her cheek, terrified to find it so cold. "Molly, don't."

Don't you fucking die on me.

He flipped her over and saw the threads skillfully woven back and forth on the corset. He ripped it apart, lace and threads fluttering to the ground. Her ribs expanded back to their natural shape.

"Molly?" He nudged her bruised, blood-splattered cheek with his knuckle, noting how his hands shook next to her still frame.

Too still.

Dipping his head, he pressed his lips to her bare shoulder blade. "I need you."

She gasped.

He abruptly sat up.

Molly gasped again, sucking air in greedily as Tensley rubbed her back, relieved. *If she died--*

A heart-wrenching sob tore him from his thoughts, and he lifted her up. Red marks and bruises lined her body, blood pulsing from a stab wound under her ribcage. Her bra was torn away, exposing her full, supple breasts. Big, pearly tears trickled down her face and over a cut, bleeding lip.

"It's okay. It's okay, Molly," Tensley said, emitting an influx of biochemicals to heal her worst lacerations immediately and prevent further blood loss. He kissed her body all over, shushing her with gentle whispers.

"I can't breathe, I can't breathe," she cried, her hand fumbling across his tensed stomach as he continued healing her. "Where is he, Tensley? Where is he?"

He stroked her hair. "He's dead, he can't hurt you anymore, okay?"

That didn't seem to help her. She gasped. "I can't breathe!"

"Yes, you can. You're all right." Guiding her palm to stay firmly on his chest, he rubbed over her dainty hand, trying to soothe her. "Breathe, Molly, follow me."

Beginning a slow, steady breath, she copied.

"That's good, there you go." He caressed her bare back, pressing their bodies together after he'd checked to ensure she wasn't wounded anywhere else.

Their breathing synced, and he hadn't ever felt that close to someone before in his life. It terrified him.

Tensley pulled off his shirt and began to wrap it around Molly. He fixed the shirt around her exposed body. "Did—" he swallowed thickly and tried to make sure his voice was even—"did he do anything to you?"

Molly shook her head weakly.

He took a deep breath, preparing to control his anger. "What happened?"

Molly wiped her tears away, smearing the dots of blood on her face. "He took me; I tried to fight back, but I couldn't control my strength. And then I woke up, and he was trying to..." Her eyes welled again. "He tied me up with—" She cradled her left wrist awkwardly below her breasts, face pained.

His fists curled. "*He* broke your wrist."

"*I* did. To get out of the cuffs."

He stared back at her face crumpling and before she could let the tears spill, he gently took her wrist and kissed it. "I'll heal it, don't worry, I got you."

He breathed in heavily and stroked the wrist, leaning over and dropping soft kisses onto the raw skin. He felt fresh skin begin to form, the bones mend back into place, and didn't move until they were fully healed as well.

"There. It's all over now," he whispered, tucking her snarled hair behind an ear.

She took a lengthy breath. "I want to see him."

Tensley's tender strokes stalled, and he stared at her. "Are you sure?" He couldn't understand why she would want to see him. Closure?

She blinked hard. "Yes."

He nodded and helped her stand, and she clung to his side as they walked back into Abaddon's bedroom.

Molly's gaze lingered on the dead body in front of them, her blessed eyes holding a fierce, animalistic fire. She kicked at Abaddon's side hard and Tensley stared at her disgruntled expression. Her eyes held a fierce fire. When she glanced up at Tensley her cheeks were rosy with exhaustion, and she felt along her bloodied lip with the tip of her tongue.

He so badly wanted to fix that lip.

"Tensley?"

He returned the look. "What?"

"Take me home."

He wrapped his arm underneath Molly's legs and lifted her up, cradling her as he marched out of Abaddon's hellish manor.

"You came back," she muttered into his neck. "You didn't leave me."

He wanted to shoot down any hopes for them. He wanted to tell her he was still a monster. But--he didn't have the heart to say anything. Instead, he walked in silence, listening to her breathing, her own heartbeat loud.

He'd tell her so later, even though he'd hate himself after.

He'd be the demon in a little while.

Now, he was her fiancé.

chapter
thirty-eight

TENSLEY SNARLED AS Illya dabbed more herbs onto the cuts he'd gotten in Abaddon's manor. His fingers gripped the unstable counter in his kitchen.

Damn holy herbs. Damn familiars throwing me into glass tables.

He was restless knowing that Molly was in the room down the hallway.

"Just hurry up," he groaned.

"Patience," Illya muttered. "You'll heal faster with these."

"My patience is about to kick your ass." He tensed as the herbs singed his skin, hissing through his teeth.

"Since when was patience able to do that?"

Tensley growled in his throat. When Illya was done, he stood up, twisting his head to see the bandages spread over his back. *Not bad.*

"You know we've just pissed them off even more, right?" Illya said, washing his hands in the kitchen sink.

Tensley gave him a hard look. "You might want to be

more specific. I piss a lot of bastards off," Tensley grumbled.

"The Hunters of Orion."

"They should learn their place," he spat. He grabbed a clean white T-shirt and pulled it over his head.

"They're going to put her on their blacklist," Illya said, turning off the water. "I've heard rumors about it underground."

Tensley yanked the shirt over his stomach. "Why just her? I did just as much damage."

"Probably because she's easily disposable—she broke their sacred oath."

Tensley ground his teeth together. He'd done just as much as Molly but now she was wanted.

"I'm gonna go check on her," he huffed, trying to replace his worry with annoyance.

He walked down the hallway, taking deep breaths. *Be cool.*

The door was slightly ajar as he approached and he found Molly newly changed into his clothes: an oversized T-shirt and baggy grey sweatpants that dwarfed her. She stood by the window, watching the outside world quietly.

She turned at his not-so-quiet footsteps. "Tensley, um, hi…"

He stuffed his hands into his pockets and leaned, trying to appear aloof and casual, distant. "I wanted to check on you. You shouldn't be up and moving yet." He nodded at her outfit. "See you found *my* clothes…"

She huffed. "Well, I didn't feel very comfortable in your bloodied dress shirt and lacy white underwear." Molly shivered, probably remembering Abaddon's disturbing choice of lingerie.

"Okay, well you're clean now, so lay back down," Tensley ordered, snatching a few pillows from the bay window and propping them behind her head. "You might feel all right now because your body's still in shock, but tomorrow will be an entirely different ballgame—a *painful* one." She sighed loudly but obliged, twisting her body into the covers.

He eyed the bed for a second, and then decided it'd be best to keep boundaries that night. He looked at a chair next to the bed and marched toward it. He relaxed against its leather upholstery, but he wasn't relaxed.

His heart burned, ate him alive, and all because of that damned gorgeous girl in the bed before him. She rested on her side, eying him softly. He ran a scarred finger across his bottom lip. "You should probably sleep."

She didn't respond for a good few minutes. He leaned closer, eyeing the large ring on her finger. When she did, her voice was hoarse and thick.

"Tensley?" His eyes left her hand and focused on her shaking lips. "You were never the monster. I realized after Abaddon took me that you're *not* like him at all. Demons aren't all the same. You were never the monster, Tensley," she said, her voice going quiet. "I am."

His chest grew lead-heavy. "No you're not. You're—"

"I saw her," Molly whispered, interrupting him.

Tensley narrowed his eyes. "Who?"

"Lex. The hunters had her."

"*What?*"

"I got her out, but then Cree came and I told her to run... You haven't seen her?"

He pinched his brow. *Fuck.* "No, I haven't."

"I'm sure she's fine. She's a tough girl."

He nodded; he'd have to look into that shortly — but for the time being, he only craved time with Molly.

Approval... It was something he had craved from his father, from his family, colleagues, even Evelyn, and he got it from Molly. Her hand grasped his and she pressed their linked hands under her cheek. Her eyes closed.

He forced himself not to pull back. As much as her tender affection terrified him, he wanted to be open to his emotions — but he couldn't, too risky. His fingers fanned through her blonde curls and she curled into his touch.

He would stay there until she woke up, however long that took.

Damn.

I'm fucked.

WHEN MOLLY WOKE, she heard birds singing. With sleep in her eyes, she rubbed them and yawned. Tensley's spare room was bright, streams of light seeping through the flapping curtains. The sore bones in her body rubbed together painfully as she shifted and cringed, screwing her eyes shut.

Ugh, it hurts.

Her head. Her ribs. Her chest.

She lifted the covers to look down at her legs, but her arms ached and she gave up with a heavy sigh. Tensley's healing had addressed her surface wounds, but it would take weeks to feel normal again.

"You slept most of the night." Her eyes swung to see Tensley still sitting comfortably in the faded leather armchair. His face was hard to read.

"Is everyone okay?"

He wrinkled his brow. "They were fine last night; nothing's changed. You, on the other hand, are probably going to be sore for a few days."

"Oh." Molly didn't know what else to say. She searched for something interesting, something thought-provoking, and came up short.

She sat covered in blankets and surrounded by massive pillows. None of that stuff had been there before; it was as if he'd bought the entirety of Bed Bath & Beyond to comfort her with. Tensley stared, making her uneasy. She went to sit up and groaned.

He stood up. "Don't move. You'll bruise yourself even more." He examined her through the blankets as if he had X-ray vision. "If that's possible."

"Are September and Illya still here?"

He waved a hand. "Illya is, somewhere. September was here but she left."

"Tensley," she said, shifting her torso. The pain shot up her legs, and she let out a whimper.

"God damn it, I told you not to move." Tensley pressed his hands to her shoulders, sending heat swirling in the depths of her stomach, and put another pillow behind her so she was propped up. Molly scrunched up her nose and bit her bottom lip, only to remember the cut on it.

Ow. Still very tender.

"Why does everything have to hurt?" she said in a weird half-cry, half-laugh.

"I can try and help you heal faster. Muscle injuries and bruises are a little more difficult than surface wounds, but with the right amount of...closeness...it might work." His voice was deep and husky.

When she peeked up at him, his chin was raised, eyes hooded and intense.

A faint blush caressed her cheeks. She'd love to be close to him.

Molly nodded and he took her mangled hand in his strong, large one. He caressed and kissed each knuckle, holding his lips there or dragging his tongue across the bluish bruises. To her surprise, after a few minutes the color had returned to normal and the pain subsided.

"It worked," she marveled, examining the flawless skin.

"Don't sound so surprised, ciccia. You can tell me how talented I am," he boasted, smiling lazily as he pulled the covers back. She didn't try to fight against her own smile.

"Why do you keep calling me 'ciccia'? What does it mean?"

Slowly, his eyes aligned with hers, and they were the softest she had ever seen them. No barrier, no annoyance—instead, tenderness that gripped her heart. "Sweetie."

"*Sweetie*?" She gawked at him. "You've been calling me *sweetie* this whole time?"

"At first, as a snide remark, but now..." He gave her a steady, warm look that completed the sentence as he continued pulling the blanket off.

Tensley pushed the fabric of the huge T-shirt up to her chest and frowned at her mottled skin. "He bruised you badly."

Molly held her breath, clenching a handful of covers. She grew uncomfortable as his eyes wandered over her exposed skin; she wanted him on her. "Yeah."

"That bastard," he said, glaring, the anger evident in his top lip.

"I gave him some bruises too," she said, softly but urgently. His eyes flickered up to hers, an amused grin spreading across his plump lips.

"That's my girl."

Her brows lifted. *His girl?*

He leaned over, placing his knees in between her legs, and tenderly pressed his lips to a few bruises on her abdomen.

Oh god, oh god.

Her body shook, heating up quickly. Moving his way up, he kissed each discolored spot and her stomach flexed. Her toes curled. She was enthralled, captured by his mouth, by his gentle fingertips caressing her scorched flesh. His lips nibbled at her damaged stomach and she could feel her ribs begin to heal. The herbs didn't compare to this type of healing—it was fast, strong, and overwhelming.

His mouth traced its way up to her chest and kissed the tops of her breasts. Once he reached her neck, she couldn't feel her toes.

He eyed her mouth. She could almost feel her cut expanding and her lips craving his—but he'd said no kissing on the lips. Her chest tightened at the loss of affection from him.

Tensley's eyes caught Molly's. She hadn't noticed how crazy his breathing was. His lips were pursed and full and swollen.

"It will heal," she concluded, out of breath. Their noses skimmed each other's.

Tensley looked between her hungry lips and her eyes. Leisurely, he lowered his head, eyes flickering back and forth.

"I want to be the person who takes away the pain." He breathed out. When his lips grazed hers, they were as soft as velvet.

Yes, please, yes.

Her heart stilled—and then all at once, thumped thunderously against her ribs. At first, his mouth only brushed against the cut. Her lower abdomen tingled at the touch. He stopped, slightly lifting his head, but not moving the rest of his body away. Again, his lips met hers and this time, she kissed back ever so gently.

He drew in her bottom lip and sucked, engulfing her in another overwhelming, breathtaking kiss. She wrapped her trembling arms around him, fingers combing through his hair. His chiseled stomach muscles pressed against hers, and he made a little noise in his throat, a hungry one, as she nibbled on his bottom lip. His hardness touched her thigh and she gasped as his lips reclaimed hers.

A knock came at the door. Molly paused for a second, but Tensley didn't stop.

Another knock, more urgent.

"We're busy!" he hollered before pressing a wicked kiss on her collarbone that left her moaning. Tensley sat up and leaned over to kiss her open mouth.

The door opened.

"Sorry to interrupt such an intimate moment," a dark voice said.

Tensley froze, his whole body stiffening. His eyes

bored into Molly's, and he tried to catch his breath, to regain his composure.

"Close your eyes," he whispered.

"Tensley—"

"*Close them.*"

He waited until she did and then she felt his body lift off hers. He pulled down her shirt and tossed the covers over her lower half, footsteps purposeful as he strode across the room.

Tensley's voice was cool and hard. "It would have been nice to know you were visiting."

An eerie silence filled the room, and she wasn't sure what was happening.

"Since you're the nineteenth battalion's leader and heir to the Scorpios, I need to keep a watchful eye on you. And since you've recently murdered my comrade, I thought I would visit you."

"Abaddon broke the law," Tensley stated harshly. "He abducted my fiancée."

Molly didn't want to move, afraid it would draw attention to herself, and even though she couldn't see anything, she could feel heavy eyes watching her.

"Hm. Pretty thing. Not very smart marrying a human female, though."

Chilling, dead silence again.

"I've been meaning to come see her for myself, actually."

She could sense someone looming over her rigid body. *Who the hell is that?*

"Your father isn't senseless, Mr. Knight. If anything, he's one of the more intelligent upper-middle-class demons I know. I can't see him approving of his heir being bestowed to a fragile human without reason." A cold hand touched Molly's hot cheek and she flinched. "Or are you going against your father's wishes? Are you in love with her?"

"No sir." The answer stung.

"Glad to hear it. I knew you were one of the smart ones. Loving humans is a wasteful thing," the intruder said, so softly that it didn't sound half as harsh. "But some have cravings for brittle things like her."

"Like Abaddon."

"He was a good friend of mine. I thought he had potential, but his weakness was gluttony. It's best to weaken the army than to have him serve me." The man's finger slid down to her lips. "Next time you want to kill one of my men though, run it past me. I don't like others going behind my back, Mr. Knight."

"Of course."

"Is she ill?"

Molly *definitely* wanted to throw up now; she was scared to the point of vomiting.

"She's just tired."

"You that busy with her? They can't keep up with our kind's needs." He chuckled. "Open your eyes." He grasped her jaw and squeezed it hard.

She froze, unsure of what to do. What did he want with her? She wanted to climb under the covers and pretend to be asleep, or dead.

"I said, *open your eyes.*" A fingernail sharp as a knife pierced underneath her chin and her eyes flashed open to see a man in his late twenties with long, luscious hair tangled into a bun. His light brown hair framed sharp, hollow features, and he looked slick and polished in his suit. He pulled his hand away and she saw that each finger was decorated with enormous rings of gold and jewels. He wouldn't stop staring, eyes as wide as plates and thin mouth parted. "She's...a daemon."

"She's also engaged. To me." Tensley's posture was straight and full of anger.

A wicked smirk appeared on the man's lips. "Finally, a daemon, and of an age to bear children." He was thinking aloud, and it scared her. "Just think of the power she could bring."

"You can leave now," Molly snapped. Her low, strong voice made both men stiffen.

Tensley's hands curled into fists and he shook his head at her. "My lord, I apologize —"

"And you haven't even marked her yet," the man said, licking his lips and studying every curve of Molly's body.

She wanted Tensley to do something, but he just stood there.

Molly glared. "How do you know that?"

"Because I'm a high-breed. We can tell if a human — or in this case, a daemon — is marked due to a pheromone that lets me know you're taken. And you, my dear..." The man paused, eyes lingering on her, avoiding her piercing gaze. "You are not marked."

Tensley snickered, nostrils flaring. He was pissed. "You'd be breaking your own rules. She's already engaged to me, has been since she was four."

The man rose, strolling to the door, but paused. "I don't know whether to call you clever or foolish. You hid her from everyone all these years. Then you didn't even have the balls to mark her." He shook his head and looked back at Tensley. "And you're the heir. You know, I could easily just chop off that lovely, dainty ring finger of hers."

Molly widened her eyes and clasped her hand, trembling.

"There's a three-hundred-year-old contract cementing us together. As I remember, you're very strict about contracts, aren't you?" Tensley said, fury barely masked in his demeanor.

The man laughed silently and snuck a look at Molly, his dark eyes raking over her form. She recoiled at his gaze. "It was nice meeting you, Ms. Darling. I hope to get to know you better very soon." He flashed his crooked teeth and she shot him a dark glower as he shut the door.

He knows my name? What?

Tensley paced, muttering to himself.

"Who was he?" Molly said, unable to steady her breathing.

"Fuck." He kicked at the chair in the corner, standing still for a while. Finally, he pressed his head to the wall and collapsed against it. "He can't do anything to you. It'd go against all of his rules." He pushed off and rubbed his forehead. "Fuck."

Molly curled the sheets up to her chest, heart beating fast.

"You shouldn't have responded to him! He could decapitate you before I could lift a fucking finger!" Tensley's face contorted in frustration, features darkening. His demon side was beginning to take over.

"Who? Tensley, who was *he?*"

Waves of rage and those oh-so-familiar aggressive pheromones filled the room, replacing any bit of tenderness that had remained.

"Tensley," Molly pressed.

He turned from her, muscles working under his shirt. "*Fallen.*"

An icy finger of dread dragged down her spine, and Tensley stalked out, not bothering to close the bedroom door behind him.

Fallen? As in the Crown Prince?

Oh shit.

chapter thirty-nine

MOLLY TIED THE robe tighter around her middle and edged toward his bedroom door. After his freak out, he let her be and stayed in his room. Now she wanted to see him. Her thoughts ate at her and she needed to say it out loud.

She tiptoed into the quiet living room to see him standing, facing his large window looking over the park. She couldn't stop roaming his muscular back and how his dress pants made his ass look so—

Focus, Molly. Focus.

She was sure he heard her from the floor boards creaking but she still edged closer and cleared her throat. He didn't move, he didn't even acknowledge her with a flinch. Her shaking hands smoothed down the white robe.

"What do you want, Molly?"

The suddenness of his solid, husky voice made her jump.

"You should mark me."

Those words stirred him from his grumpy mood and he turned to look at her. She fidgeted with the tie of the robe, looking through her lashes up at him.

His jaw tensed. "No."

Molly's hands dropped and she furrowed her brow. "Why not?"

He shook his head and moved past her to his bedroom. "It isn't the right time."

She glared and rushed after him, not caring how loud her footsteps were. "What do you mean it's not the right time? We need to get this over with, okay?"

"Drop it, Molly." He planted his hands onto his dresser and leaned forward.

Molly let her hands drop and sat down on the edge of the bed. He rejected her. Was it because he still didn't trust her? That he thought she would betray his trust?

He strolled forward and sat next to her.

She could see his white dress shirt in the corner of her eye. The three top buttons were undone, exposing his sharp collarbone.

Molly turned to face him; she was still bursting with desire, but it had been tainted by confusion and a touch of worry. He wouldn't look at her, his hands dropped loosely in the space between his legs.

His eyes were closed.

She hadn't noticed how straight the slope of his nose was, dusted with the faintest of freckles.

"I'm sorry, Tensley. I've done so many horrible things. I was wrong…" She paused, examining the way his lips parted slightly as his eyes opened. "About us. About you using me for energy. I know that's not true."

She gazed at him, at his slow movements to stand. He reached a hand out and she gasped at the jolt, even from the softest brush of their flesh.

"It's your blood," she explained, drawing back. If they kept touching, she might do something stupid, something desperate. "I can't stop...craving you."

That sentence alone scorched her skin, colored her cheeks with embarrassment.

Tensley smirked. "I lied."

She blinked back at him. "You lied? About what?"

"My blood does nothing of the sort." His eyes raked over her reddening skin. "But now that I know you naturally find me attractive, I can die happy." She gawked, bewildered.

All her feelings, her attraction to him, hadn't *been a product of his blood?*

"I said it out of curiosity, but it was selfish. *I* should be the one who's sorry." Tensley cleared his throat and tossed his tie on the bed. "And, um...I have to say...you look stunning right now."

"Stunning?"

He moved his body closer, muscles shifting deliciously under his shirt, leaving no space between them. "*Tempting,*" he added, frustration in his tone.

She wanted to take it away; she wanted him to relax with her. "Thank you — not just for the compliment, but for everything."

"No problem," he said, those dark eyes examining her flushed skin. He was so different to her now, so different from the night he'd rescued her at Stella's house only a few weeks before. "I can walk you home. It's getting late."

"Can I stay?" She moved closer, invading his space.

He licked his lips. "Molly, I—"

"Just for tonight." She chose her next words carefully. "I don't want to sleep alone."

He searched her expression, remaining silent. The pause was far too long and uncomfortable.

He doesn't want me to stay.

Finally, he nodded and walked around to the side of the bed, glancing at her every so often. He looked…suspicious.

She climbed under the sheets, still in her summer dress. She watched him shrug out of his shirt to join her under the sheets, keeping a great distance between them. Tensley sighed and stretched his arm to turn off the bedside lamp, his unspoken hesitance like a suffocating blanket, like a vine wrapping around Molly's heart.

Maybe he doesn't want me here. Maybe he wants someone else to be here.

"I can sleep in the spare bedroom, if you want me to," she muttered, voice far too soft.

He shifted around. "You just asked me to stay with you… Do—do you not want to stay?"

"No, no, I want to, but I don't want to force you."

His eyes traveled from her eyes down to her lips. "*Force* me?"

She hid her face in the pillow. "That's—that's not what I meant. I just don't want you to feel like you have to let me stay here. I'm fine."

"Maybe I want you to force me, Ms. Darling," he purred, causing her heartbeat to accelerate.

Her blush intensified as they looked at each other, and

she swallowed, instantly frozen with panic.

He sighed, stood up, and gripped a T-shirt out of his dresser.

No, no, no, no!

Molly scrambled to her feet, unbalanced. "Wait! Tensley, just...wait." She pressed her palms firmly against his hard chest, tossing the shirt away. "Sit."

She pushed him down on the bed and crawled on top, straddling him so they were face to face. He looked calm but his jaw was tight, his lightning-grey eyes taking in her every feature intently. Molly placed a hand on each one of his cheeks, his stubble tickling her palms, and kissed him.

She sucked in his bottom lip and felt powerful when she heard him moan into her open mouth. His hands grasped her hips as their tongues touched, the thin material of her dress barely separating them. Energy passed through her fingertips to his skin, and she dug her nails into his pecs. He groaned loudly as their movements became rougher, and she already noticed how her body felt more agile, strong.

"This is us exchanging power," he said as he exhaled and kissed her left dimple.

"Wow," she gasped. "We should have done this earlier." She smiled into his neck and giggled as he growled. Her hands gripped his belt, fumbling as she tried to undo it. She hummed into his open mouth. "I want to, Tensley. Mark me. *Please.*"

He stilled at her breathless voice. "Molly," he said, breaking the kiss. A single finger traced her cheek. "Let's not get ahead of ourselves."

She froze, so close to his features, to those dark grey eyes watching her wide ones.

He's not interested.

His fingertips brushed up into her hair, pulling it back so he could see her. "You've been through a lot the last few days. With Abaddon, with Cree, with *me*." His finger curved along her cheekbone.

Abaddon. Cree. Him.

If she thought about all of them, if she dwelled, she wouldn't be able to function. She needed to function, needed to keep moving.

"Tensley...I..."

"Shush." He stroked her cheek with two fingers. "I can't take advantage of you. I *won't* take advantage of you, ever again."

She stared unblinkingly at him. "Promise?"

His Adam's apple bobbed and he licked his bottom lip, hesitating an instant too long for her. "Promise."

Her chest tightened. He'd rejected her...

She stiffly got up and crawled to the spot she'd been laying in before, exhaling slowly and trying to hide her unsteadiness from his touch, from his words.

"Promise me, though, that you'll stay out of trouble until I mark you?" he asked, falling next to her on the mattress. His fingers rubbed against the side of her jaw, and she nodded and smiled shyly. "And when we do..." He paused, focusing on her mouth. "We can do it as much as you want, whenever, wherever." He nipped at her nose gently.

She playfully hit his chest and settled down beside him again, eyes darting to the dark lines of his tattoos as he stretched. She noticed a scorpion on his forearm, and her heart clenched. The demon she had killed in the woods had had the same one; were they connected somehow? "That tattoo? What does it mean?"

Tensley tensed and brought his arm forward. "It's the sign of Scorpios, the business I work for. Only the members who have proven their worth receive it; it's a sign of loyalty and oath. I'm the heir."

Her eyes widened. "The heir?"

He nodded curtly.

The covers rose and fell with every breath he took, and her fingers spread across her smooth lips. She ached for his kiss. "Tensley?"

He hummed in response.

"I think I still have a cut on my lip," she whispered.

A flash of pure wickedness flickered in his eyes. "Is that so?"

She hid her girlish smile behind the covers.

"Well, I guess it's my responsibility to take care of you."

He leaned forward and pecked her mouth once, twice, and then slowly drew her bottom lip between his own. "Better?" His husky voice created a delightful shiver and she nestled into his hard, massive frame of protection.

"Not quite," she murmured against his parted mouth.

His cool fingertips touched hers and caressed her ring finger, the one that held the vein of love.

TENSLEY RESTED HIS curled hands on his thighs. He eyed the darkness, listening to Molly's sweet murmurs behind him on the bed, her chest moving, evident of deep sleep. Even with her body beside him, his thoughts ran wild. He'd protect her. He wouldn't let her out of his sight.

Evelyn had left several voicemails and he debated whether to call her back. She'd heard through the grapevine that Lex had been captured by hunters, but was unsure if it was Cree or some other group; if that was true, he wanted those bastards dead.

He couldn't think straight, too many fucking thoughts—of Scorpios, of his family, of Evelyn, and most importantly, of Lex.

He still hadn't heard anything from Lex, and when he'd looked into possible travel information or sightings, he'd come up empty. His thumb rubbed along the side of his phone before he decided to call the person he dreaded speaking to the most in the world.

It rang three times before a hoarse voice answered. "Yes, brother?"

"I need you to find someone for me," Tensley said lowly, glancing over his shoulder to make sure Molly was still fast asleep. Her parted, thick lips drew heat to his length, and the outstretched hand that had a few minutes before laid on his chest made his heart throb.

"A deal gone sour?"

Tensley looked away, back into the shadows. "No. A girl named Lex Harvey who works for us. Been missing for over a month. No goodbye, nothing changed in her apartment. No sign she was even leaving for that long. I want you to track any leads. If you find her…" He paused, his throat growing dry. "I want all the motherfuckers, *every last one*, to be tortured, to their death."

Silence took over between them. "Every last one?"

"Every last one, Beau."

He hung up the phone.

Tensley took a shaky breath, steeled himself, and turned back toward the lovely threat in his bed. He took her dainty hand and placed it back on his bare chest. He wanted to feel her next to him. He wanted to know she was there.

His finger stroked the diamond ring representing their tie, their bond. The fear of his growing affection for Molly terrified him — more than Fallen, more than his father, and more than his past with Beau.

"You're going to destroy me, sweetheart," Tensley muttered. "Unless I destroy you first."

She was all claws
and venom.

body
of the
crime

r . s c a r l e t t

INNOCENCE WAS BLISS, and *hell*, Molly missed it. She tightened the delicate string of pearls around her neck and cursed her unsteady fingers. One two-hour-long party surrounded by a bunch of demons and she'd be back in her tiny bedroom studying for the upcoming term.

It couldn't come sooner.

Molly patted more foundation along the bruises dappling her collarbone, hoping Tensley wouldn't notice; she wasn't ready for the wrath *that* would bring. Why she had thought it was a good idea to search for Cree hours before meeting up with Tensley, she didn't know, but she knew it was stupid—especially since she had run into hunters who decided to jump her.

Her heart wouldn't stop pounding as she rinsed the remnants of foundation and clamminess from her hands. She needed to get a grip before—

"Molly?"

Molly jumped at the masculine voice and stepped out of the bathroom to find Tensley Knight, her demon fiancé, in the middle of the living room.

She eyed him in the middle of her apartment: six-plus-feet of perfectly controlled male power, clad in a black Armani suit and matching tie. Strong-boned, square-jawed, with gleaming dark hair and those penetrating eyes. Not the little boy from fifteen years ago. No. All man. All hers. *Sort of.*

"Typically people knock before entering."

Tensley's eyes scanned her slowly, *so slowly,* and she didn't miss the way a muscle in his jaw flickered.

She bit the inside of her cheek, praying he wouldn't

figure out she'd been breaking a hunter's arm an hour and a half ago.

Then he cleared his throat and any sign of interest was replaced with annoyance. "If I can just walk in here without a key, then we have a bigger fucking problem than I thought."

Molly sucked at her teeth. "Tensley, really, we'll get the lock fixed." *As soon as we have the extra cash.* "I'm fine."

He cursed under his breath and glanced away before drawing in a concentrated breath, composed as ever. "We'll discuss this later. Are you ready?"

Molly wiped her palms on her sides and nodded. He gave a curt nod for her to follow, jaw slicing the thick, stale air of her apartment like a sharpened blade.

You got this, Molly self-soothed, leading the way out of the dingy Lower East Side apartment she shared with September. *Meeting a bunch of your fiancé's coworkers is no big deal.*

Except that his coworkers were a band of powerful, bloodthirsty, *unpredictable* demons.

She repeated the notes Illya had given her a few days ago to herself:

Eric Rose, second-in-command. Sly, cunning. Doesn't like to discuss personal matters, only the demons' governmental system, the High Court, and of course their king, Fallen. Flattery and wit earn his respect.

He was the most important, but there were a few others Molly needed to be aware of. The party was for Edgar Daniels — *eighteen years old, an eager teen ready to join the Knight-helmed group of demons called Scorpios.* Molly had felt a distinct kinship with Edgar as Illya shared the details about him; she, too, had once been naïvely corralled into an extremist underground sect when Cree and his demon hunters came calling—and look where that had landed her.

A sleek black car idled on the side of the road outside Molly's apartment building, pumping white plumes of exhaust across the busy New York City street.

"C'mon." Tensley placed his large hand on the small of Molly's back as he opened the car door for her, and her skin vibrated beneath his touch. She scooted in, fully aware of the way her black lace dress rode higher up on her thighs as she did so. Tensley entered through the opposite door and signaled to take off with a firm flick of his wrist.

A heavy sigh left his lips once they had entered the stream of honking traffic, and he deftly straightened his tie.

Molly twisted the chain of her purse around her hand, reciting Illya's notes over and over in a near-silent mutter. *Eric Rose, flattery, no personal comments, he likes witty comments but don't overdo it, just act normal, totally normal, it's normal to go to a demon party, it's not like they could make me disappear without a trace —*

Tensley's calloused hand clamped over Molly's and she froze. When she stole a look at his face, he smirked. "Breathe." His vividly dark eyes traveled over her lace dress and up to her heated cheeks. He looked so dark against the bone-colored leather seat, so big next to her.

"You look far too tempting, darling," he nearly growled, smirk widening.

Molly instantly noticed how heat gathered between

her legs; they hadn't been this close for a while, and it was doing wild things to her senses.

He leaned in closer, one cool hand running up her spine to grip the nape of her neck. "You seem tense."

Her nails bit into the leather seat. "This feels like my death march."

Tensley's forehead creased, eyebrows dark and naturally perfect. "Going to the party does?"

Her chest tightened. "*Yes*. I've only been around you and Illya—not a large party of demons."

He rubbed a finger along her bare forearm in soothing circles. "I just need to make a quick appearance. My father requested you be there, but you don't need to talk to anyone. We haven't announced the engagement yet."

Yet.

"Is Fallen going to be there?" Molly squeaked, trembling under Tensley's roving finger. The hairs on her arm stood up, but Molly was sure it had more to do with possibly seeing the demon king again than her fiancé's caress.

"No, he's of too much importance to attend our work parties—not that we'd want him there anyway." Tensley snorted, leaning back against the leather seat so that it creaked under his sizeable frame. Molly eyed the demon, noting the dark circles on either side of his enviably straight nose, the frown lines tracking down his tanned cheeks. She wondered if he'd been struggling with insomnia as well.

She leaned back against him, tensing for the response she now expected: Tensley's retreat. It'd been a battle the last two weeks since Abaddon; if she got too close for

Tensley's liking, he'd move as far from her as possible.

Doesn't stop him from tormenting me with random fondling, Molly fumed. *Sadist.*

Molly shuddered at the memory of the high-class demon who had wanted her all to himself. They'd killed him—the image of life leaking from her psychotic redheaded captor was one she'd never forget—but he was still alive in her nightmares.

Molly had taken to sleeping in fifteen-minute intervals, oftentimes jolting awake drenched in a cold sweat, reaching frantically for some nonexistent weapon to protect herself with.

There was no finding comfort in Tensley, either; he still hadn't forgiven her after that stunt with Cree, and she understood why.

She just needed to earn back her fiancé's trust, figure out how to find Cree and get through the next few hours.

First things first.

Molly scooted away from Tensley in tiny movements, watching the blur of yellow cabs and flashing marquees whiz by.

"Are you angry with me?" he murmured after a brief pause.

Molly tilted her head back to answer, observing the way Tensley's lips now curved into a frown. "Not at all."

"Good." His calloused fingers traced her stiff jawline as he swiftly swung her legs over his.

Molly gasped. *This is what I want*—the closeness she had finally succumbed to desiring, her longing for a beast of a man who could break her in one breath.

Except they both knew, now, that she could break him

too. She could quite literally stab him in the back when he least expected it.

Trust me, Tensley, Molly tried to convey with her gaze as she toyed with his perfect white buttons. *I won't hurt you again.*

God, he smelled good. A hint of cologne, dark and masculine, and something else — the muskier fragrance of his sweat.

His hand ran up her leg like a whisper and met the rolled up fabric, dangerously close to revealing her. It moved farther up her leg, and when he teasingly squeezed the top of her thigh, she tightened her grip on his shirt. "Eager, dolcezza?"

It was when his fingers moved down the column of her throat and passed over her collarbone that she flinched.

Damn it.

His eyes narrowed before pressing the spot again, lightly, but still enough to make her cringe.

"You're bruised," he ground out.

She shooed his hand away. "I fell. An accident. I didn't tell you because I knew you would freak."

"That went well, didn't it, darling?"

"It's a bruise, it'll heal."

His features rearranged into a *decidedly* more erotic expression. "Can I heal it?"

"Uh—" She didn't have much time to protest before his mouth had descended onto her collarbone, each demon kiss equipped with biochemicals that could seal cuts and erase bruises, leaving only smooth, supple skin in their wake.

A throaty moan escaped as Molly curled her finger

into his back of packed muscles, endorphins pinging through her bloodstream as the heat between her legs grew.

God, just his touch and I'm on fire.

His teeth nipped at a tender spot and she cried out, lost in him entirely.

He lifted his head when he was done and she eyed him, pressing her fingers to the freshly healed skin that had been replaced by his own faded mark.

"You bit me." She hadn't meant for it to come out so breathless, so clearly interwoven with shock and arousal.

"And you liked it," he said with a flash of teeth.

Predator.

He was a predator.

And I'm his prey.

It was a reminder she didn't need, of the way those demons could decimate her body in a blink, erase her very existence —

"Stop worrying," Tensley said, brushing a few curls off her cheek. "They can't do anything to you — not without my permission."

She glared. "Oh, how noble of you."

He chuckled. "Just one night of obligations and we can go back to the way it was before."

Oh, joy. More small talk about nothing and awkward visits? Can't wait.

She turned to look at him, watching him rub at the dark circles beneath his stone-gray eyes with a huff.

How has he been getting strength? Has he been seeing other women? Molly wondered. *She* wanted to be the one to make him strong, not some random girl in a bar.

"Tensley, I —" Molly started, but the car rolled to a stop before she could complete her sentence.

"We're here," Tensley said, already out the door in a whir of black Armani silk.

acknowledgements

First and foremost, thank you to my friends and family so much for all the support and positivity. Especially to Breanne, Megan and Caley who were always there to listen to me ramble or rant on and on about this book. I love you all and appreciate everything you have done to support me.

Megan — you've read the book twice and were always ready to give me feedback on every single damn question I asked. Girl, you amazing.

Caley — you would sit through talking sessions of how plot point B didn't work or stood up for Molly when readers sassed her.

And Breanne, oh dear god, Breanne. This book should have your named stamped on the bottom of how many messages, emails, talks I badgered you with when an idea didn't flow or I wanted to squeal of how great a quote was. Seriously, I owe you for life. You were my backbone, the concrete spine I needed so thank you.

I don't think any of you girls will truly know how much your support means to me.

Thank you to all the beta readers so much for the feedback and the questions you answered. Seeing things from multiple perspectives made the book so much more.

Thank you to my editors Ashley Carlson, Megan Lally,

Ami Deason, and Claire Marie for pointing how problems and ways to improve every single piece of the book. Not to mention all the questions I sent your way.

Thank you to Lauren Perry at Perrywinkle Photography for the beautiful photo-shoot and Regina Wamba at MaelDesign and Photography for designing such a breathtaking full cover.

And thanks to all the indie authors and bloggers welcoming me to this amazing community of men and women hoping to reach readers to share their stories. I am truly blown away of how kind and open every single reader, author or blogger I've spoken with.

Lastly, thank you to all the readers who take a chance on a new indie author. It means the world to me and giving you a glimpse into Tensley and Molly's world is scary but so thrilling. I hope you loved them as much as I did!

Made in the USA
Middletown, DE
16 January 2021

31761003R00215